'A powerful coming of age story.'
Frolic Media

'Nuanced storytelling.'
Teen Vogue

'Asha Bromfield will take readers by storm in her
captivating debut about discovering yourself when
your world is out of control.'
Adam Silvera, bestselling author of
They Both Die at the End

'A great title . . . offer[s] a nuanced look at patriarchy,
wealth, and gender dynamics.'
School Library Journal (starred review)

'A promising writer . . . this is a must.'
Booklist (starred review)

'A sweeping debut.'
YA Books Central

'Searingly beautiful, heartfelt, and full of strength.
I could not put it down.'
Tiffany D. Jackson, bestselling author of *Grown*

'Accessible yet sumptuous.'
The Bulletin for the Center for Children's Books

'Stunningly written. An unflinching coming-of-age novel.'
Courtney Summers, *New York Times*

ABOUT THE AUTHOR

Asha Bromfield is an actress, singer, and writer of Afro-Jamaican descent. She is known for her role as Melody Jones, drummer of Josie and the Pussycats in CW's *Riverdale*. She also stars as Zadie Wells in Netflix's hit show, *Locke and Key*. Asha is a proud ambassador for the Dove Self-Esteem Project, and she currently lives in Toronto where she is pursuing a degree in Communications. In her spare time, she loves studying astrology, wearing crystals, burning sage, baking vegan desserts, and taking walks to the park with her dogs Luka and Kyra. *Hurricane Summer* is her debut novel.

ASHA BROMFIELD

HURRICANE SUMMER

faber

First published in the US in 2021 by Wednesday Books,
an imprint of St Martin's Publishing Group

First published in the UK in 2022
by Faber & Faber Limited
Bloomsbury House, 74–77 Great Russell Street
London, WC1B 3DA

faberchildrens.co.uk

Printed and bound by CPI Group (UK) Ltd, Croydon, CR0 4YY

Published by arrangement with Folio Literary Management LLC
through Rights People, London

The right of Asha Bromfield to be identified as author
of this work has been asserted in accordance with
Section 77 of the Copyrights, Designs and Patents Act 1988

A CIP record for this book
is available from the British Library

ISBN 978–0–571–37162–4

FSC
www.fsc.org
MIX
Paper from
responsible sources
FSC® C171272

2 4 6 8 10 9 7 5 3 1

For Little Asha,
And all the girls with holes in their hearts,
The size of their fathers.
You are worthy.
You are resilient.
You are love.
I poured my heart onto these pages,
With the prayer that it would give you the courage
To set yourself free.

Thank you, Mommy,
for teaching me that writers rule the world.
I discovered the magic of storytelling cuddled up in your arms.
Thank you for every book you ever read to me, and every
night you read them twice. Your love is my first home.
I believed in my magic because you did first.

Thank you, Ingrid Hart.
You are a divine light, shepherd, and a master coach.
You have taught me how to turn my pain into power,
and use it for great purpose.
Your love, guidance, and magic are woven
throughout my life, and these pages.

Thank you, Lori Mohamed.
You are a visionary and a true friend.
Your love has empowered me to be brave, and your
unwavering belief in me has given me strength
and deep courage. It never sounded
impossible to you.

And to my sweet girl Kyra,
Thank you for your boundless love.
May you soar with the angels until we meet again,
somewhere over the rainbow.

Hurricane Summer is my heart on pages.

I bled deeply to deliver it. I went into myself, over and over again, and opened wounds and memories, in an attempt to find healing. I poured all of me onto these pages, and just like the complexities of the human heart, this story encompasses an intensity of great love, pain, and heartbreak.

This book is my love letter to the island of Jamaica—the island where I spent many summers. Some of which birthed me, some of which destroyed me, but all of which, above all, shaped me. And just like love, this letter will be complicated. It might even break your heart, just like it did mine. But at its core, this letter is meant to take you on a deep exploration into the journey of what it looks like to move into womanhood. And while it will encompass a euphoria of joy and pleasure, this book will also journey through the devastation and very real dangers of becoming a woman.

Hurricane Summer is a story about the spiritual and sexual wounding that can happen when a girl moves out of her teenage years and into her womanhood—the sexual trauma, heartbreak, and sorrow that too often accompanies that transition. It will explore the deep resilience that girls are forced to acquire when their sexual nature is weaponized against them; when their pleasure is up for persecution. It is a story of how the world begins to disown you when you are forced to leave the innocence of girlhood behind, and the devastating depths that we will go to in order to be loved by others, particularly the ones we are told are supposed to love us the most.

My prayer is that you find healing within these pages, just like I did. I pray this story gives you the courage to confront your own storm, and once there, I pray it inspires you to find radical forgiveness for your parents, your experiences, and most important, for yourself.

But above all, I pray the hurricane leads you home.

PATOIS WORD BANK

A

Afta—After

Ah—To / Is / It's / At / Of / Are / On / In (Generally said before an action has taken place)

Ah fi him business—That's his business, not mine

Ah go—Are going / Going to

Ah go ah—Are going to

Ah lie you ah tell—You're lying

Ah me run tings round yesso—It's me who runs things around here

Ah nuh Canada yuh come from?—Don't you come from Canada?

Ah nuh di—Isn't that the

Ah nuh so me say—Isn't that what I said?

Ah so—That's how

Ah so him stay—That's how he is

Ah Tilla dis?—Is this Tilla?

All ah dem ah fi me—All of them are mine

Anotha—Another

Ansa—Answer

B

Backside—Buttocks. Used as a mild curse term to express surprise / No way!

Badda—Bother

Bammy—A Jamaican flatbread made from cassava flour

Batty—Butt / Bum

Bawn—Born

Bawn and raise—Born and raised

Betta—Better / Better be

Bod—Bad / Cool

Bod Bwoy—Bad boy

Bout—About

Bloodclot—Vulgar curse word meaning "blood cloth"

Bredren—Brother / Homie / Friend

Bright and outta order—You have some audacity / You're out of line

Bruk—Broke

Buddy—Penis

Bumba / Bumba rawtid—Mild curse word to describe shock or surprise / Holy Crap!

Bumbaclot—Damn / Fuck / Fucking

Bun and cheese—Classic Jamaican snack; spiced bun and Jamaican cheese

Bush—Bushes / Forest

Bwoy—Boy

C

Ca-ca / Ca-ca rawtid—Short for *cockfoot;* means "No way!" or "Wow!"

Catch up—Get involved with

Chat—Talk

Cha—A mild expression of impatience

Cockfoot—No way / Wow / Damn

Come follow me ah bush—Come follow me to the bushes

Come nuh—Come on

Cool nuh—Chill out / Relax

Coulda—Could / Could've

Cravin—Greedy

Crosses—Problems / Trouble

Cyan—Can't

D

Dat—That

Dat deh—That is

Dat mek—That makes

Daughta—Daughter

Degga degga—Mediocre

Deh—At / Are / Is

Deh inna—Is in

Deh so—Right there

Deh ya—Just here / Chilling

Dem nuh romp—They don't play

Dem ones deh—Those ones there

Den—Then

Dese—These

Desso—There

Di—The

Di man yuh ah talk—The man you are talking about

Did—Was / Were

Do—Doing

Dollas—Dollars

Drape her up—Grabbing her up / Handling her roughly

Dun know—You already know

Dunce—Stupid

Dutchee pot—A big pot used for cooking

E

Eediat—Idiot

Een?—Huh?

F

Facety—Rude

Fada—Father

Fass / Fasses—Nosy

Festival—A sweet fried Jamaican dumpling

Fi—For / To

Fi dead—To die

Fi true—For real

Fi him business—Is his business

Follow back ah me—Follow behind me

Follow me go ah shop—Come with me to the store

Fool him ah fool—He's a fool

Foreigna—Foreigner

G

Genklemon—Gentleman

Gi—Give

Gimme—Give me

Ginnal—Con artist / Crook

Go ah—Go to / Going to

Go long—Go along

God know—God knows / Swear to God

Good-good—Favorite

Guh—Go / Going / Going to

Guinep—Staple Jamaican fruit

Gunmon—Gunman / A man who owns a gun

Gwan—Going on / Go on / Goes on

Gyal—Girl

H

Haunted—Crazy / Possessed

Him deh—He is

Honn-ah—Honor

How yuh mean?—What do you mean?
How you do?—How are you?
How yuh pretty suh—How pretty you are
Hungry belly—Always hungry

I

Inna—In the (can also mean *nosy*)
Irie—Happy / Powerful description of anything good
It ah go wicked—It's going to be fun / sick
Iz—It's

J

Jus—Just
Jus ah come from road—Just coming from doing stuff outside

K

Know say—Know that

L

Lawd—Lord
Lawd ah mercy—Lord have mercy
Leff—Leave
Leh—Let
Leh we go—Let's go
Licks—Beats / Hit
Likkle—Little
Likkle more—See you later
Long time me nuh see uno—It's been a long time since I've seen you all

M

Mada—Mother
Mass / Massa—Master / Sir
Mass Tyson deh home?—Is Mass Tyson home?

Mawnin'—Morning

Me—I / I'm / My / Mine

Me ah go tek yuh pon nuff adventure—I'm going to take you on a lot of adventures

Me jus ah romp wit yuh—I'm just playing with you

Me know say—I knew that

Me tell uno ah lie she ah tell—I told you all she was telling a lie

Me tink you did—I thought you were

Me never know someone weh sleep so late—I've never met anyone who sleeps so late

Me nuh business—I don't care

Me nuh inna dat—I'm not into that / I'm not feeling that

Mek sure say—Make sure that

'Memba / Rememba—Remember

Mod—Crazy

Mod looking—Crazy-looking

Mon—Man

Mongrel—A dog of no definable type or breed

Mout—Mouth

Mussi—Must

Mussi mod—Must be crazy

N

Na more—No more / Anymore

Nah—Not / Won't

Neva—Never

Nine night—A traditional celebration for the deceased

No nuttin about you—Nothing good about you

No, sa—No, man / No, sir

Nuff—Enough / extra

Nuffi—Shouldn't

Nuh—Don't / Haven't

Nuh badda—Don't bother

Nuh business—Don't care
Nuh true—Isn't that true? / Right?
Nuttin—Nothing
Nuttin nuh go so—"Nothing goes like that" / That's not true
Nyam—Eat

O

Offa—Off of
Orda—Order
Out ah door—Outside

P

Pay him too much mind—Pay him too much attention
Pickney—Child / Children / Kid
Pon—On / At
Poppyshow—"Puppet Show" / Used to ridicule someone for being idiotic or foolish
Propa—Proper
Propa-ty—Property

R

Rawtid—Wow / Damn
Romp—Play around
Romp we ah romp—We're just playing around
Round yesso—Around here
Rude bwoy—A cool friend or to describe a tough guy, rebel, or criminal

S

Sa—Sir
Say—That
Sekkle—Settle
She did ah go look—She went to go see

Stocious—Well dressed, particular, or high class. Can sometimes mean stuck up.
Stop talk—No way / I don't believe you
Suh—So
Suh-um / Sumting—Something / Thing

T

Tan—Stay
Tanks—Thanks
Tek—Take
Tell you say—Told you that
Tink—Think
Tree—Three
Tree-qwatas—Three-quarters
True me did—Because I was
True yuh nuh—Because you're not

U

Unda—Under
Undastand—Understand
Uno—You guys / You all
Uno deh—You guys are

V

Vex—Mad / Upset

W

Walk good—Wishing good fortune on your travel / Get home safely
Wan—Want
Wata—Water
We ah go ah—We are going to
Weh—Who / That
Weh go a—Who goes to

Weh look so—That looks like that

Weh talk so—Who talks like that

Wha—What

Wha gwan—What's going on?

Wha'ppen?—What's happening? / What's up?

Wha mek?—What makes? / What do mean? / Why's that?

Wha name so?—What's named that? / What does that mean?

Wha uno ah deal wit?—What you guys up to?

Wha uno ah do?—What are you guys doing?

Wha we ah wait pon?—What are we waiting on?

Wha yuh tink?—What do you think?

Wit—With

Woulda—Would / Would've / Would just

Y

Ya—Your

Yah—You are

Yuhself—Yourself

Yawd / Yard—The country / Home / House

Yesso—Here

Yow!—Yo!

Yuh—You / Your / You're

Yuh nuh—You know / You don't

Yuh mod gyal?—Are you crazy, girl?

Yuh nuh need fi fraid—You don't need to be afraid

Yuh too ginnal—You're such a con artist / crook

Yuh zi me—You feel me

Z

Zeen—Cool / Sounds good

When it all goes quiet behind my eyes, I see everything that made me flying around in invisible pieces. I see that I'm a little piece in a big, big universe. And that makes things right.

—Hushpuppy

THE CALM

1

Mom says you get two birthdays.

The first one is the day you are born.

The second is the day you leave home and give birth to yourself.

I never understood what she meant by that, but standing in the middle of this bustling airport, I can't help but wonder if this is the day she was talking about. If it is, the tears in my eyes don't feel like anything to celebrate. Birthdays are not supposed to make you cry. Birthdays are not supposed to grow heavy lumps in the back of your throat that threaten to choke you on your words if you dare open your mouth.

Birthdays are not supposed to break your heart.

Be brave. Be brave.

I repeat it over and over again in my head as I squeeze my mom's hand a little tighter. My stomach drops, dreading the moment she'll inevitably let go. In the air, I can taste the sweet melancholy of joyous hellos and painful goodbyes that only the airport can bring. There is a buzzing to this place that feels like the center of heartbreak and joy. Its contradiction sends an unsettling shiver through my body. I feel like a child, embarrassed my emotions are giving me away.

Suck it up, I scold myself. *It's only two months.*

"We're here," Mom says into the phone. "They just checked in."

She's quiet as she listens, her ear pressed to the phone. "I packed some shirts for you. And there's a few bags of coffee in Mia's suitcase, so you'll be stocked up for work. Make sure you take them out. Mhm, everything's in there—uh-huh. Oh shoot." She lets go of my hand, turning her back to us. "I forgot to pack that deodorant you like. I'll send down a few packs this week—yeah, okay. And don't forget Mia's allergy medicine. It's in the side pock—I'm not saying you're going to forget, Tyson." Her voice goes hushed. "I'm just telling you where it is." She's quiet for a moment, listening. "Look, Tyson. Let's not do this now—call me when they land."

I bite down on my lip to stop it from quivering as she turns back around. My mother's eyes are so kind. They are a deep sea of brown that perfectly match her rich dark skin, and they stare back at me with a compassion only her heart could know. She smiles at me with longing in her eyes.

She knows this is not what I want.

"Did you remember to pack the gum?" she asks.

"Yes, Mom. You asked me that already."

"I'm just making sure. I don't want your ears to pop on the plane."

I feel guilty for the irritation in my tone. I know she's being helpful, but for some reason, it annoys me. Maybe it's because it's the first time my sister and I are flying alone. Maybe it's because I would rather be anywhere else than in the middle of a cold, busy airport at 8:00 a.m. on a Thursday morning. Or maybe it's because I don't want to spend the summer with my father.

Yet after months of protest, here I am.

"Are you sure you can't come with us?" my little sister, Mia, pleads desperately.

A sadness runs through our mother's eyes as she adjusts

her dark brown locks. "You know I have to work, baby. But your father is so excited to see you."

Mia sulks at the mention of our father.

I don't blame her.

Mom turns to me, cupping my face in her hands. "I love you more than words, Tilla." She kisses me so gently on my cheek that I barely feel it. "You're going to grow so much this summer." She can't hold back the tears that stream down her face.

And damn it, neither can I.

"I love you, too, Mom. So much," I reply, choking on that lump.

"It's only two months." She smiles, tucking a strand of my coily Afro behind my ears. "It's going to fly by."

"Two months without cell service." I muster a smile.

"I'm sure your thumbs could use the break." She laughs. "Come here." She pulls me in close, wrapping us both in a hug. "Take care of your sister, okay?" she whispers to me. "You're in charge."

"Of herself . . ." Mia rolls her eyes. Mom gives her a look. "She's barely eighteen. What does she know?" Mia mutters.

I ignore her. I'm too sad to argue with Mia right now. "I will, Mom," I reply.

Mom squeezes in one last hug before the inevitable. She lets us go, the warmth of her hug lingering on my brown skin. Suddenly, a crass voice comes over the speakers, pulling me out of our goodbye.

"Last call for all passengers boarding flight 416. Please make your way to Gate 8A."

I throw my backpack over my shoulder, and with one last look to our mother, we wave goodbye. "I love you!" she calls after us. In her eyes, I can see her heart breaking.

But there is no turning back.

The airport is big and daunting, and as we navigate through

it, I can't help but feel small. We head through security and approach our gate, where an attendant checks our boarding passes. When she flashes me a dry smile of approval, Mia and I head through the final doors and onto the plane.

It's completely packed when we get on board. I immediately feel claustrophobic as I look down at the plane tickets in my hand.

"Seat 15B," I tell Mia.

I can feel the eyes of the seated passengers burning into me, and I start to remember just how awkward walking to your seat on a plane can be. Mia and I continue down the cramped aisle as I search the luggage panels for our seat number.

Mia beats me to it.

"Right here!"

She plops down and slides to the window seat. I slide in next to her, relieved that we finally made it. Mia pulls out her Nintendo.

"Are you sure you want the window seat?" I ask.

"Duh," she replies distractedly. "Why wouldn't I?"

"Just making sure. I didn't know if you wanted to see everything . . . you know, when we're so high up."

"That's not gonna work, Tilla. I know what you're trying to do."

"I'm just checking. Swear." I buckle my seat belt, nudging her to do the same. Just then, a flight attendant walks over.

She leans over our seats, a tight grin on her face.

"Hello, ladies." Her perfume is way too strong. "I'm Lisa. If you need anything, don't hesitate to ask me. I may or may not have a secret stash of candy." She winks before taking off down the aisle.

"Candy?" Mia screws her face. "What am I, five?"

"She was being nice."

"She smells like car freshener."

I can't help but laugh. Mia always says what's on her mind, and I admire her for it. She's loud and rambunctious with warm reddish-brown eyes and thick dreadlocks that she insisted on when she was seven. Mom says she gets her carefree spirit from our dad. At only nine years old, she says whatever rolls off her tongue with little regard for the opinions of others, and I love that about her.

The irony is I resent that very same quality in my father.

Mia looks at me before popping in her earphones.

"Get up," she says.

"What?"

"I want the aisle seat."

I try to suppress my smile. "Oh. You changed your mind?"

"You're so annoying." She rolls her eyes, undoing her seat belt. I slide into her seat, just as another flight attendant comes over the PA, her thick accent muffled through the airplane speakers.

"*Ladiez and gentle-mon, welcome aboard flight 416 departing from Toronto to Kingston on this beautiful Thursday morning. We invite you to sit back, relax, and leave your worries behind you. From all of us here at Air Jamaica, it is our pleasure to have you on board.*"

The roar of the engine makes my palms clammy. I'm not sure what's more overwhelming—the pulsing vibration of the plane or my own heartbeat. The destination is inevitable:

We are en route to *Jamaica*.

A wave of anxiety rushes through me.

Breathe, Tilla.

I look over at Mia, who casually plays her Nintendo DS, and I'm reminded that she has little to be worried about. There is nothing at stake for her. She was too young to even remember. To *truly* understand.

Her heart is not on the line when it comes to our father.

Our father's name is Tyson, and he stands six foot two, with warm caramel skin and brown locks that fall down his back. He has gray eyes that look like an overcast sky and a smile that could light up the dark. He is a man of the land, and he spends half of the year going back and forth between Toronto and Jamaica, where he manages his cousin's trucking business.

But that is not the full story of his absence.

When I was a child, my father was the most fascinating person I knew. To my young heart, everything he did compelled me. During the summer when we were younger, he would look after us in the daytime while Mom went to work, and I recall using nap times as quiet opportunities to study him. On hot summer days, I would lie on the couch as my eyes tried to make sense of such a wonderful human being, who seemed to have transcended *human* being. I was fascinated by my father—he was the Rubik's cube I was determined to solve. I would watch in admiration as he sunbathed in the backyard, his Jamaican beaded chain the only thing to touch his chest. He was unaware of my peering little eyes, and I would fall asleep to the sight of his chest rise and fall under the rays of the setting sun. I experienced many sunsets this way, all of which confirmed that my father was pure, utter magic. The countless minutes, hours, and days we would spend together quickly became the same minutes, hours, and days that would shape who I was becoming. It seemed that I, by the grace of God, was a part of *him*. He was a ray of light that existed through some sort of magic, grace, and manhood. He was the hero in every storybook he had ever read me.

But all fairy tales must come to an end.

My father was born in the countryside of Jamaica, and although he moved to Canada in his twenties, his heart never left the island. Not like Mom. She moved to Canada when she was twelve years old and left all memory of her life in Kingston behind. But Dad could never let go. Although he started a family abroad, Jamaica was the one he longed for when he was with us. She was his first love. It didn't matter that together we had built a house.

We were not his home.

As the years passed by, his relationship with Mom grew strained. Every day in our house became a battlefield of screaming and anxiety, and the constant fighting caused him to lose any interest he had left in our family—in the picture we had worked so hard to perfect. Their relationship was chaotic, and Mia and I were no longer cute little girls but growing young women.

And he grew bored.

As soon as the world didn't fall at his feet, he was gone as quickly as he came. When the bills became too high or Mom became too much. When Canada got too cold or finding a regular job became too stressful. He would fly back to paradise, leaving us to mend the broken hearts he left behind. Every six months, he would come back like he'd never left, demanding to fit into the puzzle of our lives as if the pieces would still be the same. But they weren't. And neither were we.

We were changed with every goodbye.

The last time we saw him, the familiarity of anxious silence filled our house the way it did every Sunday afternoon. Silence on Sundays was the calm before every storm Mia and I were forced to witness. It was the prelude to the screaming, the yelling, the breaking things. The prelude to my mom telling him he was full of shit before slamming the door in his face. To him packing his bags and telling her to go fuck herself. Venomous words children should never hear their parents spew at each other. Words that cut deep and take away the little innocence you have left. Words that pierce through your heart and stay buried there forever.

Words that teach you heroes don't exist.

My nerves grow heavy as the seat belt light turns on, pulling me out of my thoughts.

Breathe, Tilla.

The plane picks up speed, pulling my attention back.

Faster, faster, *faster.*

I look out the window as we rip down the runway, my heart pummeling against my chest. I reach down and fiddle with the necklace my father gave me on my ninth birthday. A tiny, gold butterfly pendant that sits at the base of my neck.

"You're my butterfly, Tilla," he said when he gave it to me. *"You are soft, but you are powerful. Just like a butterfly."*

The memory makes me nauseous as I press my head back against the seat.

My father has been gone for 376 days.

And counting.

But he said he would be back. He said he and Mom would work it out.

How is he doing?

Has he missed us?

Is he happier without Mia and me around?

I am a vortex of mixed emotions. I dread the sight of him, but I ache to see him at the same time. I wish I could be like Mia. Innocent to his broken promises. Oblivious to the consequences of his absence. Too young to know the difference. I wish the thought of him didn't hold me down and fill me with rage. I wish I didn't love him so much my heart might explode. The plane engine roars louder.

Faster, faster, faster.

Breathe, Tilla.

And just as the plane lifts into the air, the inevitable truth drops to the pit of my stomach: Mom was right. You do get two birthdays.

Today is mine.

2

We touch down at 1:46 p.m. local time.

Warm air floods the plane as the doors open, and the sweet aroma of fruit wafts in the air. Passengers race to grab their bags as the thick accent comes over the PA once again:

"Ladiez and gentle-mon, welcome to Kingston, Jamaica. It iz a beautiful day here on the island, and we wish you nothing but irie on your travels. It has been our pleasure to have you on board. As always, thank you for flying Air Jamaica."

I gently shake Mia awake as Patois begins to pour out all around us. I grab our backpacks from the cabin, and we throw them over our shoulders before trudging off the plane.

As we make our way through the busy airport, we are surrounded by a sea of rich, dark skin. I feel courageous as we navigate through the brown and black bodies, and I can't help but wonder if the feeling of belonging is why Dad loves it so much here.

Once we clear at customs, we continue our trek through the massive airport. All around us, people smile and laugh, and there is a mellowness to their pace. Most of the women wear bright colors and intricate braids in their hair, Afros, or long locks down their backs. An array of sandals and flip-flops highlight all the bright painted toenails as Mia and I weave through the crowd.

"Stay close!" I yell, grabbing on to her hand. When we find the exit, I grow nervous knowing what awaits us on the other side. I look to Mia. "You have everything?"

She nods.

"Okay," I whisper to myself. "Let's do this."

With our suitcases lugging behind us, we spill out of the doors and into the hot sun. The heat immediately consumes me, and it is amplified by the chaos and noise that surrounds us. The streets are *packed*. Loud horns blare, and people yell back and forth in thick, heavy Patois accents. Men argue on the side of the road, their dialect harsh as they negotiate the rates for local shuttle buses. Along the roads, merchants sell colorful beaded jewelry and fruit so ripe that I can taste it in the air. Women wear beautiful head wraps and sell plantains and provisions, bartering back and forth with eager travelers. People spew out of overcrowded taxis, desperate to catch their flights as others hop in, desperate to get home. The sun pierces my skin as the humidity and gas fumes fill my lungs. The action is overwhelming, and I feel like a fish out of water. As we wait by the curb, there is no sight of our father.

"What if he forgot?" Mia asks.

"He wouldn't," I reply. "Mom just talked to him."

"What if he got the time mixed up?"

"He'll be here."

But the truth is, when it comes to our father, I can never be sure.

I fight with this idea as five minutes turn into ten, and ten into twenty.

The heat blazes, and sweat drips down my stomach.

I check my watch: forty-two minutes.

I pull my pink hoodie over my head to reveal a white tank

top, tying the hoodie around my waist to better manage the heat. Without my phone, I have no way of contacting him to see where he is.

But he said he'd be here.

He gave us his word.

Fifty-six minutes later, our father is nowhere to be found. My eyes frantically search the crowd as I ponder how much his word is truly worth. Time and time again, he has proven that the answer is not much. I turn to Mia, ready to tell her to head back inside. Worry graces her face for the first time since we left. Her carefree attitude fades as the concern of a nine-year-old takes over. I can't stand to see her like this, and I'll do whatever it takes to escape the feeling that is bubbling inside of me.

We'll take the first plane out.

"Mi, Dad's not coming. Let's go back insid—"

"Yow! Tilla!" A deep voice interrupts me mid-sentence. I whip my head around to find my father standing a few feet away with two freshly sliced pineapple drinks in hand.

"Daddy!" Mia screams. She drops her things on the curb and sprints toward him. My heart does somersaults.

One glimpse of my father and I am a child again.

He stands tall and radiant as ever in a baby-pink cotton button-up and white shorts. His smile is infectious, and the mere sight of him brings instant tears to my eyes. It is a joy that I have not felt for so long. A joy *I did not know* I hadn't felt for so long. His long brown dreadlocks fall down his back to meet his waist, framing his face like the mane of a lion. His bright gray eyes glimmer against his tanned complexion. His smile glistens, and my eyes are fixated on him as he beams in this hot sun. He is the manifestation of Jamaica in one man. A reflection of the paradise we now stand in. *How can I stay mad at him in a place like this?* He is the disposition of irie, and he glows as bright as the sun. I can't help it. I succumb to the spell of Jamaica as the fantasy of who my father is radiates in front of me. My heart instantly wraps around him, and I forget every time he has broken it.

Just like that, I fall victim to the love of my father.

Mia leaps into his arms, nearly knocking him over. I grab our things and sprint toward him, overcome with relief as all the emotions I felt begin to dissipate.

"Dad!" I yell.

"Tilla! Mi! Look at you!"

I lunge into his arms, surprising even myself. He smells like musky cologne, and he holds us in a tight embrace.

"I missed you sooooo much!" Tears of relief stream down Mia's face. "I thought you weren't coming! I thought you forgot." She squeezes him so tightly I don't think she'll ever let go. He takes his hand from me to wipe her eyes.

"I wouldn't miss it for the world." He smiles before turning to me. "Tilla, look at you! You've gotten so big! So grown up."

I force a tight-lipped smile to keep from crying tears of joy. Tears of the little girl who has needed her father.

Tears of the young woman who still does.

"I missed you, Dad." I smile. He pulls me close again and kisses me on my forehead. For a second, I imagine the warmth of this hug is exactly how Sunday mornings were supposed to feel in my home. "We . . . we were waiting for so long. I thought you forgot or mixed up the time. We were about to go back inside."

"Not me!" Mia brags. "I was going to wait. Tilla wanted to go back."

"You kidding?!" He laughs in disbelief. "I would never forget. I just got held up in traffic." I nod, barely listening to the words that come out of his mouth. The truth is it doesn't matter why he's late.

The truth is I've already forgiven him.

I am a roller coaster of inconsistent truths as my feelings for him turn from night to day in the span of seconds. My mouth wants to burst open—to let it all out. To say *everything* I've always wanted to. To tell him how much I've missed him, and how much he's missed out on in the past year of my life. I want to tell him about school, about home, and about Mom. About how he's ripped my heart in two. About how hard it's been trying to put it back together. I want to tell him how badly he's hurt me and beg him to never do it again. I want to cry tears of joy and confess the pain in my heart like a child in need of a Band-Aid. I want to tell him I hate him. I want to tell him I love him more than I could ever hate him. I want to curl up in his arms and be his little girl again.

But I hold back.

"Here." He hands us the drinks in his hands. "Fresh pineapple juice, straight from di source."

I take a sip and my taste buds spring to life. "Wow. This is amazing!" I beam. "It's so fresh."

"There's a lot more where that came from," he boasts as he grabs our bags. "This is all you?"

"Yeah, the biggest one's Tilla's," Mia says. "She packs like a madwoman."

Dad laughs. "You two both packed like you're looking to move out here." He loads our bags onto his back before gesturing to a man who stands beside a nearby car. "You remember your uncle Wayne?"

"No," Mia says for both of us.

Wayne smiles as he approaches us, dressed in brown khakis and a white marina undershirt. His eyes sparkle a rich dark brown.

"Diana's father. He's my ride," Dad continues. I nod as it all clicks. Diana is one of our cousins who I briefly remember playing with when we were younger. Uncle Wayne extends his hand for me to shake.

"Tilla. Mia. Long time me nuh see uno!" His accent is coated and thick. There's a relaxed, country pace to the way he speaks, and it makes him even harder to understand.

"Hi," Mia says, unsure of how to respond to his Jamaican lingo.

Uncle Wayne lets out a big laugh. "All right, me know say yuh just land. Lemme break it down fi yuh," he tries again. "How's it going?!"

"Good." I smile.

"I know you don't remember me." He chuckles, making his words clearer. "I've known you since you was a baby. Glad to have you back." He grabs our carry-ons, and he and Dad load up the nearby Honda Civic. "Hop in. But careful. Di seats are hot."

He isn't kidding. Mia and I slide in, and the leather seats are so hot that they burn to the touch. The car feels stuffy even with the air-conditioning, and the car air freshener on the dash is so strong that it makes me queasy. Regardless, it feels great to be in safe hands. Uncle Wayne slides into the driver's seat, and my dad hops into the front. They banter back and forth, their sharp Jamaican dialect rolling off their tongues with ease as they discuss the airport's lackluster infrastructure. I sip on my pineapple juice as I observe the distinct tempo of the airport. There is a rhythm to these people.

To *my* people.

I take a deep breath, finally relaxing. Here in the humidity of this car, the weight of the responsibility to get Mia and me from one place to another slowly melts off my shoulders.

We are in my dad's hands now.

We pull away from the airport and take off down the ramp. All around us, lush greenery decorates the freeway. Plants grow wild and full of life, intertwining around each other as if they're dancing just for us. Uncle Wayne keeps up with the aggressive pace of the other drivers, weaving in and out of lanes. After a few minutes, we exit the freeway and make our way into town. The paved roads become dirt ones as we drive past old shops, abandoned houses, and stores. Hibiscus flowers are everywhere, and their lush pinks and reds knit together over the zinc walls like crowns as we speed by.

The deeper we get into the city, the more people flood the streets—and the energy is *palpable*. I watch as a boy with dark, ethereal skin runs alongside his friends as they suck on frozen juice in tiny plastic bags. A small girl sits out front of her house as her mother braids her hair into an intricate design. As we make our way deeper into the town, the battered roads are lined with merchants selling fruit, coconut water, and fresh juices. Men and women sit alongside their artwork, oil canvases painted by hand. Rastas line the streets, locks swinging past their waists, just like my father's. A man plays steel drums as women carry gray grocery bags and baskets on their heads. Little boys in school shorts chase each other with water bottles, soaking their uniforms. There is laughter everywhere, and I can feel the heartbeat of the island all around me.

Uncle Wayne navigates through the busy roads like a pro, blaring his horn when necessary, which seems to be every five seconds. We pull up to a stoplight, and Dad rolls down the window.

"Yow! Rude bwoy!" he yells to a young boy who sells mangoes in the middle of the road. The boy, who couldn't be much older than Mia, whips around and runs over to the passenger side of the car.

"Wha gwan, sa?" he asks eagerly, lugging the big bag of mangoes over his shoulder.

"Wha yuh have?" Dad asks, his accent intentional and rougher, indicating that he has no time to barter.

"Julie mango."

"Gimme four." He hands the boy four crinkled hundred-dollar Jamaican bills.

The boy beams, digging into the bottom of his bag and pulling out the biggest ones he can find. "Tek five." He places them in a gray plastic bag before handing it to my father. He peers his head into the car and looks at me. "She look like she could do wit ah extra."

"Bless." Dad nods. The light turns green, and we pull off.

"What did he mean?" I ask as Dad fiddles with the bag.

"He meant you look *real* hungry." Dad laughs.

"Tilla's always hungry," Mia chimes in matter-of-factly.

"He can probably tell yuh come from foreign." Uncle Wayne laughs.

"Foreign?" I ask.

"It's slang. Anywhere that isn't here. People here call it *foreign*."

Dad pulls a mango out of the bag and turns to us. "You see this? This is a Julie mango. Only place you can get this is right here. Every other kind of mango—Guatemala, Trinidad, Guyana—is a lie."

"Real ting," Uncle Wayne chimes in. "None nuh even come close."

"Yuh zi me." Dad nods.

"When we was kids, school time dis woulda be yuh lunch."

"That's *if* you was lucky." Dad laughs.

"Or you could climb." Uncle Wayne chuckles.

Dad holds the mango out the window, skillfully using a bottle of water to wash it off before bringing it to his mouth and piercing it with his front teeth. He peels back the skin to reveal the rich yellow fruit, careful not to make a mess as he discards the skin out the window and offers the mango to Mia.

"Nuh badda mek a mess."

"I won't!" She throws her DS aside, snatching the mango from Dad's hands. He repeats the same process and hands one to me. As I bite into it, the sweetness explodes in my mouth. I look over to Mia, who's made the biggest mess as she devours hers. Mango seeps onto her chin, spilling from her mouth and onto the seat. She uses her fingers to wipe it up, creating an even bigger mess of juicy fingerprints before shoving her fingers back into her mouth.

"Gross," I mutter.

"It's sooooo juicy!" Mia says through a full mouth of mango hair.

"It sweet, nuh true?" Wayne asks, his thick country accent coating his words. Unsure of how to respond, we look to my dad, who grins wide.

"You two are gonna have to get used to the talkin' down here."

"Yeah, mon," Uncle Wayne chimes in. "Uno ah go haffi catch on real quick. We cyan water down di talkin' fi too long."

"It's the language of ya people," Dad says.

Mia shrugs, comprehending here and there. I understand most. Dad usually speaks Patois whenever he's around us at home, but considering he hasn't been home in a year, the lessons have been few and far between.

"Maybe if we spent more time with you," I say timidly. "You know, you could teach us more . . ."

Dad shifts. "You're right. I know we haven't had much time together for a bit."

"A year."

It slips out.

He pauses. "We'll have lots of time to make up for that this summer. You two are gonna leave here full-blown Jamaican girls. Accent and everyting."

"Woot! Woot!" Mia yells, sucking on her mango seed. Uncle Wayne and Dad laugh. I take a deep breath, easing up.

"Uno ah go chat like yuh come *straight* from yawd," Uncle Wayne says.

I peel back the rest of the skin on my mango before shoving my head out the window. We pass a man in a bright green mesh tank top riding a bike as he blasts music from a make-shift sound system that he carries on his shoulder. A smooth bass wafts through the air, its hypnotic rhythm drawing me in as I take in the words.

I and I ah Rasta children, I and I ah Rasta children
I and I come from Zion, I and I come from Zion

The warm breeze grazes my scalp, and sweet mango juice stains my mouth. I close my eyes, and I lose myself in the rhythm, the tight coils of my Afro blowing softly in the wind. As the car engine hums through the noisy city, I feel myself falling further and further into relaxation, the heaviness of the plane ride beginning to feel like a distant memory.

I awake a few hours later to find that we are still en route.

I look over to Mia, who's fast asleep, her DS still clenched tightly in the palm of her hand. Far out of the town and away from what feels like civilization, we are now driving through the mountains of Jamaica. Uncle Wayne navigates the danger-ously narrow edges, beeping his horn to let oncoming traffic know that he is rounding the bend. One wrong turn and we could go falling off the side. I distract myself by focusing on the lush greenery that swallows us into what feels like a hidden Jamaican jungle.

"Do you remember any of this?" my dad asks me.

I gaze out the window. "Not really."

"You woulda been too young to remember. Last time you come ah yawd you must've been five or six."

"Yawd?" I ask, confused after hearing the word for a second time.

He laughs. "Yard. The country. Where I grew up. We'll be staying here for a bit."

"Oh," I reply, slightly taken aback. "I thought we were staying in Kingston."

"We're staying here for a week or so first. You've got all summer to go to town." He turns back to look at me, his gray eyes bright. "Plus, this will be good for you. You'll have kids your own age to play with."

"I'm not a kid, Dad."

"You know what I mean, Tilla." His tone becomes slightly annoyed. "Just relax."

"I am," I say, defensive.

"Uno deh in for a real culture shock," Uncle Wayne interjects. "Yuh nuh deh ah foreign nuh more."

His words make me anxious as memories of spending time in the country begin to flood my mind. Mia wasn't born yet, but I remember visiting the remote part of the island where my dad grew up when I was just a kid. And although the memories are foggy, there's one person I could never forget:

My cousin Andre.

I haven't seen him in years, but the mere thought of him sends me into nostalgia. We would always play together when we were kids on my summer trips to the island. I remember him always being soft and curious, his energy matching mine when I felt shy among a family I barely knew. In more recent years, he would occasionally call the house to speak to my father. I would hear his quiet voice come through the phone, muffled by the distance and choppy connection.

"Mass Tyson deh home?" he would ask.

I always imagined him standing at a local shop as he whispered into the line. He would ask my father when he would be returning or what duties my father wanted him to fulfill around the house. I would usually hear his voice in passing, but growing up, I imagined him to be the long-lost brother I never had. And even though I know my imagination was only inspired by foggy childhood memories, the idea still comforts me. He is what I remember most about the country.

He was my friend.

We speed by tight corners and crevices until after a while the lush forestry becomes zinc fences and dirt roads. Soon, the bright blue sky turns gray, growing heavy with rain. In what seems like an instant, a light drizzle turns to a heavy, humid, and thunderous downpour.

"Welcome to di country." Uncle Wayne glances at us in the rearview mirror. "It soon start rain like dis every day. Hurricane season soon come."

The mention of hurricane season feels daunting. It's been Mom's biggest concern ever since Dad first had the idea to send us down here. I recall the arguments I would overhear late at night, when Mom thought Mia and I had gone off to bed. I would press my ear against her door as my father's voice came through Mom's speakerphone.

"*You're being ridiculous,*" he would say. "*Too Canadian for your own good.*"

"*Because I'm worried about the safety of my children?!*" she would snap. "*One of us has to give a fuck, Tyson! One of us has to be responsible.*"

"*Wha you ah talk bout?! All you do is coddle di pickney dem! They'll never know their strength, the way you shelter them from the world. They'll spend their whole life scared, just like you!*"

Thunder roars through the trees, snapping me out of the memory. I watch droplets of rain roll down the window as I consider my father's words. He wasn't wrong. My mom *has* spent most of her life afraid. Afraid to try new things, afraid to travel . . . Afraid he would leave her. The strange part is, they both grew up in Jamaica and had to deal with hurricanes every year.

But storms were never a big deal to my father.

"*You're too overprotective,*" he would say. "*Yuh ah go deprive di girls of a real connection to their roots.*"

They would go back and forth until the late hours of the night, until eventually he hung up or she gave in.

And now here we are.

The sky becomes dark, and the rain crashes down onto the windshield, waking Mia out of her slumber. I watch the water as it hits the ground, turning the hot dirt into thick mud. People rush out of the houses buried in the mountainsides, grabbing their laundry from the line.

We drive for a few more miles before taking a sharp right turn up a large hill. Our ride grows bumpy as we make our way over rocks cemented into the ground. I'm surprised this little Honda is able to make such an ambitious trek. Dad turns to me as if he can read my mind.

"Dis is a Jamaican car. It coulda handle anyting." His accent gets more apparent the deeper we get into the island. I stifle a grin. I don't have the heart to tell him that Hondas aren't made in Jamaica. He flashes a smile like an excited child, eager to get home and show off his new toys. *His foreign daughters.* I fight the smile that creeps onto my face as we continue through a narrow pathway in the forest, passing goats and cows that are tied to trees.

"Welcome back to Comfort Hall, Manchester," Dad beams. "Where me bawn and raise."

"Oh my God!" Mia says. "Look at all the animals!" I turn to look out her window. Lining the path is a wired fence where chickens run wild, and above our heads, tropical birds fly low. Despite the rain, mud, and poor infrastructure, it feels like we've arrived in some sort of a farmland jungle paradise.

Off in the distance, at the end of the path, appears a really big white house that looks as though it was built by hand. About ten people stand out back as younger kids jump up and down, awaiting what seems to be our arrival. They use spare shards of zinc to shield themselves from the heavy downpour.

"Uno ready?!" Dad yells over the sound of the thunderous rain.

"Yeah," I say anxiously.

We pull up to the back of the house, and Uncle Wayne brings the car to a stop. The eager eyes don't look away as nerves dance in my stomach.

Could they seriously be waiting on us?

"All right," Dad beams, opening his door to the heavy rainfall. "Come nuh!"

Before I even have a chance to respond, my door flies open, and I am met by a boy my age, staring down at me with bright brown eyes and a wide, crooked smile. He stands barefoot in the mud, drops of rain running down his soft brown face. He bats his wet lashes, holding a piece of zinc over his head.

"TILL-AH!" He exaggerates a nonexistent *h* at the end of my name. His smile grows so big I think his face might burst. "Wha gwan?!"

"Oh, uh . . . hey." I smile awkwardly, yelling over the sound of the rain as I rack my brain to remember who he is. He grabs my hand and pulls me out of the car, and in an instant, I am nestled under his jagged piece of zinc. Shielded from the massive downpour, he embraces me in the tightest hug.

"Yuh rememba me?!" he asks, his country accent thicker than my father's and Uncle Wayne's combined. He speaks rapidly and his words jumble together, making him nearly impossible to understand.

"Yeah . . . kind of," I lie.

"Ah lie!" he yells playfully, disbelief twinkling in his bright eyes. "Yuh nuh 'memba yuh big cousin?! Cockfoot!" He throws his head back and lets out a yelp of laughter.

I stifle an awkward smile, unsure of how the hell I'm going to get past this language barrier.

"Richie! Come grab a bag, nuh mon!" my dad calls out from the back of the car.

"Me ah come, Mass Tyson!" He turns back to me, mocking an over-pronounced American accent. "Well, I am your big cuzin. Call me RIH-CHEE." He winks.

"All right, Richie." I giggle.

"Come, gwan inside. Dem cyan wait fi see uno." He grabs my backpack from the car and ushers me toward the back door, where aunts, uncles, and cousins that I barely recognize await us with smiles as wide as his.

An aunt—who I vaguely remember to be named Adele—pulls me aggressively into her arms. "Me cyan believe say uno reach!" she beams. She wears a battered pink tank top with holes in it. When she releases me, another woman who I assume is also my aunt pats my back a little too hard. She speaks a clearer English.

"Tilla! Look pon you! You've gotten so big!" she yells over the sound of the rain. I grimace through the sting of her palm.

As everyone chatters around us, I meet eyes with a girl about my age. There is no mistaking that this is Uncle Wayne's daughter, Diana. She has rich tan brown skin and four long, thick braids that hang down her back. She has big brown eyes, and she gives me a closed-mouth smile as she sips from a juice box.

The adults crowd around us, and Mia just observes it all,

giving everyone a look that says, *Who the hell are you?* I search the unfamiliar faces for Andre—but no sight. Just then, Aunt Adele grabs me by the hand and leads us in through the back door and into a dimly lit, damp kitchen. Although the outside of the house is something to marvel at, the inside feels archaic.

"Dis is di kitchen." Aunt Adele beams.

Aged pots and pans are stacked on top of an old gas stove that sits in the corner. Built by hand, the counters and walls are made from cement and the floor from red clay. A small gas lamp lights the way, revealing barren cupboards.

We make our way through another door, stepping into what appears to be the living and main gathering space. It's much more updated than the kitchen, and natural light streams in from the open front door. Two long brown couches line the walls, and an old wooden TV set sits at the front of the room by the main door. Aunt Adele leads us out the front door to the most impressive part of the house:

The veranda.

As soon as I step out, it becomes clear that this is where they spend most of their time. The floors are checkered with red tiles that have been freshly shined, and at the front stand two giant white pillars with steps leading down into the yard. Chairs and plush benches line the patio that overlooks an *enormous* yard. There is nothing but greenery for miles, and at the end of the freshly cut grass are tall metal gates. The entire yard is surrounded by a forest that is blocked off by tall bush walls, adorned with hibiscus flowers. Trees spill over into the yard, revealing thick coconuts and succulent mangoes. The rain smells delightful as it hits all this vegetation, and birds sing sweet melodies, as if welcoming me to their home.

Out of the corner of my eye, I spot two older people shuffling over who I couldn't mistake if I tried: my grandparents. They use sticks to guide themselves over to the action. My grandma, Myrtle, beams a toothless grin and has silky gray hair that is hidden under a purple head wrap. My grandfather, Stanley, sports gray trousers, a matching button up, a red ball cap, and shoes that prove he was in the forest all day collecting fruit or chopping sugar cane. They hobble over to me with their arms wide open.

"Till-ah!" My grandma pulls me into a hug.

"Hi, Mama." She smells like sweet cornmeal porridge and freshly picked coffee beans all in one. When she finally lets go, my grandfather reaches out his hand for me to shake.

"Till-ah." He smiles brightly. "How you do?!"

"Hi, Papa. Good to see you."

"Uno want suh-um fi drink?" Aunt Adele asks.

My other aunt, who speaks better English—I'm still not sure of her name—clarifies. "She wants to know if you are thirsty. I can imagine it was a long trip."

"Oh, that would be great. Thanks."

"Adele does all the cooking around here," Dad calls. "Stay on her good side." Everyone chuckles as Aunt Adele heads inside. The attention focuses back onto us as Dad does a round of reintroductions. "You remember your aunt Herma?" he asks, gesturing to the one that speaks clearer English. "My big sister. She's the glue that holds this place together. The oldest out of all of us."

"Yeah," I lie. "I remember."

"I would barely recognize you if I saw you pon road," Aunt Herma says.

"Herma and Junior both make clothes. You go to them if you need anything made." Dad gestures to a man who stands next to a sewing machine on the veranda. He has green eyes and a buzz cut, and if it weren't for the few gray hairs that speckle my father's beard, the two of them could pass for twins.

"You two remember your uncle Junior, right?" Dad asks.

No.

I nod *yes*.

He's much skinnier than my father, and his build is quite frail. He couldn't be more than thirty-five, but the lines on his face are sunken.

"Wha gwan?" he nods, his face stoic.

"Hello, girls!" Another woman approaches us, gray hair lining her permed ponytail. "Nice to see you again." She shakes our hands firmly. "You prob-ly don remember me, but I am your aun-tie Shirley. Uncle Wayne iz my huz-ban." Her demeanor is strong, self-assured, and assertive. "We live in di pink house out back. Before you come up di path. Come by any time."

"Okay." I smile.

"You remember my daughta?" She waves Diana over. "Dee! Come here nuh girl." From the corner of the veranda, Diana walks over, still sipping on her juice box.

"Hi." She extends her hand as Aunt Shirley walks off to talk among the adults.

"Hey, Diana." I smile again.

"It's *Dee*-yanna. Mummy named me after di princess, but we pronounce it a likkle different. You remember me?" Diana asks. "I know it's been a while. You don't have to lie."

"Yuh tink dem could forget a gyal weh head so big?!" Richie interrupts. "Tell me who could forget a head weh look so. Nuh true, Tilla?"

"I remember you." I giggle. "We used to play together when we were kids."

"See, Richie? I'm unforgettable." She flips her braids, happy to be remembered. "She doesn't even know who you are."

Richie gives her the finger before calling out to two boys

standing nearby. "Uno come here nuh mon! Why yuh ah act so haunted?!"

The two boys stagger over, one around my age and the other around Mia's. As they get closer, I beam when I realize who it is.

Andre.

He's significantly darker in complexion than everyone else, and his big brown eyes sparkle beneath long, beautiful lashes. The last time we saw each other, we were children, but I could never forget that deep complexion and those twinkling eyes.

The younger one that stands beside Andre is a few shades lighter than my father and has the same green eyes that Uncle Junior has.

"I'm sure you cyan forget these two dry-foot boys," Richie clowns. "You rememba me likkle brothers? Andre and Kenny?" I light up at the mention of Andre's name.

"Yeah." I beam, hopeful that he remembers me. "Of course."

Andre gives me a shy nod, smiling to reveal dimples on either side of his mouth.

"Talk nuh, bwoy!" Richie instructs.

"Cool nuh, Richie!" Andre squirms. "Wha'ppen, Tilla?"

"Andre likes to act shy." Diana rolls her eyes. "In reality, he has the loudest mouth outta all of us. Blackest one, too."

I cringe as the words leave her mouth. *Did she just say what I thought she did?* I shake it off, convinced that it has to be some kind of Patois lingo I don't understand.

"You rememba Kenny?" Richie refocuses my attention. He points to the younger light-skin boy who sucks on his thumb even though he seems way too old to be doing so.

"Yeah." I nod.

"Lawd, Richie, looks like you ah di only one she forget." Diana laughs.

"Hush up yuh mout, Diana." Richie shoves her to the side. "So Till-ah, wha yuh bring we from foreign?"

"What?" I look at him confused, unsure of what it is he's asking.

"Tek yuh time nuh, Richie. Ah real foreign gyal dis, yuh know." Diana turns to me and begins talking in baby talk, "He-wants-to-know-if-you-brought-him-anything-from-foreign." She smiles, clearly feeling accomplished. "*Foreign* meaning Canada."

"Oh," I reply. "Yeah. Dad had us bring some shoes and clothes and stuff."

"Bumba!" Richie jumps up excitedly.

The boys tackle each other as they run for our suitcases. Diana turns to me. "The boys are idiots. They're not used to much." She rolls her eyes. "I'm the only civilized person around here."

I offer her an awkward smile.

"I'm serious," she continues. "It's because I go to school in town."

"Isn't town like four hours away?" I ask. "You go that far for school?"

"Well, unless I want to end up a beggar like these idiots, I have no choice. Town is where the educated people go. I board at an all-girls' school during the year."

"That's cool."

"It's pretty exclusive." she boasts.

"Where do the boys go?"

"You mean if they go at all? Comfort Hall Primary. Richie and Kenny are enrolled. Andre stays home and does work around the yard." There's a fake poshness to her that I can't help but find amusing. We take a seat on the ledge of the veranda, and she flips her braids behind her back. "Town people are much more civilized. Country is a poor man's land."

I nod, her bluntness making me uncomfortable.

"So, you all live in this house?"

"No, sa!" she replies, faux offended. "They do. I could never. I live in di house out back with my family, and it's much nicer than this one. Daddy just built it and finished the upgrades. White tile floors and everyting. You should come by sometime."

"That'd be cool."

She giggles. "Uno foreign gyal talk funny."

"What?" I struggle to understand her.

"I said, 'You foreign girls *talk funny*.'"

"What do you mean?"

"That'd be, like, so cool!" She mimics me in a cringeworthy Valley girl voice. "Me never meet anyone weh talk so." She throws her head back in an obnoxious cackle. I offer a weak smile, silently becoming self-conscious.

"Nuh worry yuhself." She smiles, picking up on my discomfort. "After a few weeks here, you'll be talking like us in no time at all."

After a while, the heavy rain lightens up, and Aunt Adele serves dinner. The aroma of stewed fish and rice fills the patio as she passes out fifteen plates, making sure no mouth goes unfed. When I take my first bite, I'm already tempted to ask for seconds. Everything is filled with so much flavor. Across the veranda, all that can be heard is the scraping of forks on plates as we sit in the dewy aftermath of the rain.

"Tilla!" Dad calls to me, mid-conversation with my aunts. "Yuh have di picture from when ya soccer team won di finals?"

I eye him quizzically. "Soccer team?"

"Yeah. When your team came first in the league!"

"From eighth grade?"

"Yeah, that one. Me wan show Herma."

"No, it's at home," I say, even though I know he already

knew that. I find it hilarious that he's bragging about my house-league soccer team from four years ago. Not only was I terrible, but my team won by default when the other team forfeited. I was beaming when I came home with a gold pendant around my neck, and Dad made me wear it to school for weeks. He said he wanted everyone to know I was a champion.

I wonder if he remembers that.

Everyone banters back and forth as the sun sets over the yard. A warmth comes over me as I listen in reverence to the laughter and the stories. I observe the glimmer in my father's eyes as he shows us off like brand-new toys and the sparkle in his smile as he brags about our accomplishments back home. This is a celebration, and we are the cause.

Finally.

They are celebrating us.

He is celebrating *us*.

And just like that, I forget all the birthdays he's ever missed.

3

As evening rolls in, everyone starts to get ready for bed.

Aunt Adele roasts a pot of cocoa as everyone gathers in the living room to watch the nightly news. The picture fades in and out from clear to static as Andre fiddles with the antenna, while Dad and Uncle Junior stay outside on the veranda discussing Jamaican politics. With no electronics or lampposts to light the sky, nighttime rolls in fast in the country. It's clear that it's going to be a summer of making my own fun.

Richie helps me lug the oversize suitcases to a room at the corner of the house. It has two entrances, with a side door that leads out to the veranda.

"Only foreign pickney coulda travel wit so much stuff," he says as he pulls the bag through the room door. "Me nuh have half as much clothes. Not even tree-qwatas."

"Pickney?" I ask. "What's that?"

Richie lets out a big laugh. "Jesus Christ!" he says through dramatic cackles. "Yuh haffi go learn how fi chat Patois if yuh wan keep up. Me ah nuh Rosetta stone."

He drops the bag in the corner before heading out to grab the other one. I enter as he exits, dragging the smaller bags into the plain white room. It's humble and small, but homey nonetheless. The bed is made up with fresh sheets, and over on the dresser sits an array of lotions and perfumes. In the corner of the room, a small white fan rotates back and forth. I dread the thought of a summer with no air-conditioning, but I wouldn't dare say it out loud. Richie brings the final bag into the room and places it in the corner with the other suitcases.

"Thanks," I say. "I really appreciate it."

"Anytime, foreigna," he replies. "Tomorrow yuh can set me up wit one of yuh white friend dem ah foreign," he assures me with such confidence that I can't resist laughing. "We'll talk about it inna di mawnin'."

"Right." I take a pillow from the bed and playfully toss it at his head. "Thanks again." He flashes another toothy grin before leaving the room.

Finally alone, I plop down onto the sheets and fall back onto the pillows. I notice the country has a distinct smell that I really like. The lush forest combined with the wet ground and burned firepits all come together to create a homey smell. Just then, the door swings open. I launch forward, sitting up to find Aunt Herma with extra pillows in hand.

"Oh, hey, Aunt Herma," I say, taken by surprise. "I was just—"

"What are you doing?"

"What—"

"Why is my pillow on the floor?"

"Oh, sorry. I meant to pick that up." I move to grab it, but she beats me to it.

"I won't have you disrespecting my things."

"I'm sorry. I honestly didn't mean—"

"And you shouldn't be on the bed in those clothes. You've been all over the place today. God only knows what nasty germs you've picked up and now you're rolling around in my sheets."

"Oh," I jump up. "Sorry about that. And the pillow. I just . . . got excited." I offer her a smile. She doesn't smile back. She places the pillows on the bed and abruptly begins to turn down the sheets.

"It's important to keep the place clean. Cleanliness is close to godliness. Your mother never taught you that?"

"She did . . . and I'm sorry. I didn't realize this was your room."

"Well, it is." She speaks with the Queen's English, but I can hear her Jamaican accent lingering. "You two will be sleeping in here for the next week."

"Wow . . . that's so nice of you. Thank you."

"Mhm."

"Where will you sleep?"

"In the living room. Which is unfortunate because I have a bad back."

I'm quiet, unsure of what to say. I can't tell if her bluntness is just her personality or if I should be taking it personally. Just then, Mia bursts into the room with a towel wrapped around her body.

"I'm all done! Your turn, Tilla." She jumps on the bed just as Aunt Herma finishes fluffing the last pillow. Aunt Herma makes a disapproving face.

"The water is freeeeeeezing!" Mia exclaims. "You're gonna die. And I couldn't get the showerhead to work."

"It doesn't," Aunt Herma interjects. "And there's no hot water here either," she says as she reorganizes the perfume bottles on the already perfectly organized dresser. "You're not in foreign anymore."

"But I could barely even stand in it!" Mia replies, her teeth chattering from the shower. "I almost froze to death!"

"Well, if the rest of us can make it work, I'm sure you can, too."

Before I can even process her words, there's a knock on the door.

"Come in!" Aunt Herma calls out.

The door opens, and my father peeks his head in, his locks dangling in the air. "How's it going in here?" he asks as he makes his way through the door.

"Good," Mia and I reply.

"Great." Aunt Herma smiles. "I was just preparing di room and letting them know some of di house rules. I'm sure they're used to something very different over in foreign."

"House rules?" Dad laughs. "Don't be too hard on them, Herma. They've come a long way. I want them to feel comfortable." He puts his hand on my shoulder. "Try not to give my princesses a hard time." He keeps his tone playful, but I can feel the energy in the room shift.

"Oh. Of course." Herma shifts awkwardly and looks around for something to do, as if embarrassed to not have a task being fulfilled. Her energy immediately switches around my father. Her overwhelming personality begins to shrink, and I fight the urge to roll my eyes. Mom would always say everyone treated Dad like a king in Jamaica. She said they still have "old-time thinking" here, where they believe the men are the most important and should be catered to. Even though Herma is the oldest and seemingly the highest in ranking of the house, around my father, she becomes the help.

"Let me know if you need anything, Mass Tyson." She smiles respectfully before exiting the room.

"Thanks again, Herma. I really appreciate it."

"Good night, girls." She musters another smile, closing the door behind her.

Dad sits down on the bed. "Are you two having fun?"

"Yeah," I reply, shaking off the interaction. "It's really beautiful here."

"Speak for yourself," says Mia. "It's so hot. And the shower sucks. It's too cold."

"Well, if it's so hot and the shower is too cold, then you should be perfect." Dad laughs.

Mia rolls her eyes. "That's not even funny, Dad."

Dad laughs. He looks at me and does a double take.

"Wait, ah nuh di necklace me give yuh?"

I look down at my butterfly pendant. "Yeah." I smile. "You gave it to me for my ninth birthday. You don't remember?"

"Ah lie." He laughs, clearly impressed that I still have it. "You've taken good care of it, Til. It almost looks brand new."

"I never take it off." I continue to smile as I fiddle with it. "Have you heard from Mom?" I ask.

"That's actually why I came in here. She called earlier. I thought you girls might want to talk to her before bed."

"Me first!" Mia lights up, grabbing the phone from Dad and putting it on speaker. Mom answers on the second ring.

"Hello?"

"Mommy!" Mia bounces around the room with the phone in hand.

"Mia!" Mom laughs. "Oh, sweetie, it's so good to hear your voice. Your dad told me you girls were getting settled in."

"We're in the country, Mom! And I just had a shower with no hot water. And there's cows and goats and chickens everywhere! Just randomly walking around."

"Sounds like you are definitely in the country." She laughs again. "Where's Tilla?"

"I'm right here, Mom," I call out. "I miss you!"

"I miss you both so much," she says. "How is everything? How's the weather?"

"I'm dyyying," Mia whines. "There's not even any AC. It's soooo hot."

"Has it rained since you landed? I've been watching the news, and it said—"

"Don't start, Marie," Dad interjects. "They just got here."

"I'm not starting anything. I just want to make sure they're comfortable."

"Your mother's become too Westernized." Dad looks to us, a trace of humor in his voice. "She forget hurricane ah regular ting round yesso."

"Hurricane?" Mia asks. "Ouuu, when?"

"More like a storm," Dad says casually. "And they come every year. But not until the end of summer."

"Cool!" Mia jumps up and down.

"Right?!" Dad laughs. "Your mom's overreacting."

"I'm not overreacting, Tyson." Mom's tone grows nervous. "The girls haven't experienced anything close to that before."

"Well, there's a first for everything," he says, annoyed. It's obvious they've had this conversation a million times. "Look, the girls are strong," he continues. "And they just got here. There's no need fi mek dem nervous when nuttin nah gwan." He turns to us. "Your mom seems to forget we used to run up and down in hurricane every summer. Nuh true, Mimi?" He calls Mom by the nickname they used to call her in Jamaica.

"I haven't forgotten." Her tone softens.

"You've been in Canada too long." Dad takes the phone from Mia. "The girls are fine. I promise. They have everything they need."

"All right, Tyson." She sighs. "Well, I know it's late, so I won't keep you girls. Call me if you need anything. I love you so much."

"Love you," Mia and I say in unison.

"Call you tomorrow," Dad says before hanging up.

"Is the hurricane scary, Dad?" Mia asks as she plops down on the bed.

"Nuttin yuh cyan handle." He pulls her into his arms, play-fully roughing up her locks. "Plus, you know how ya mother likes to worry. She's a town girl." Dad refers to Mom's more suburban Jamaican upbringing. Dad was raised in the countryside, while Mom grew up in Kingston. "Town people are afraid of everyting. Yuh lucky ya fada come from yawd," he jokes. "Sometimes your mother forgets where you get your strength from."

"And where's that?" I giggle.

"Yuh haffi ask?" He laughs, tossing a pillow at me. "You two are my daughters. Pure-hearted country gyal. Yuh built fi hurricane. Yuh coulda weather di storm inna yuh sleep."

I smile, his confidence relaxing me. I walk over to the window, peeking out through the shutters into the dark night. The land is so big and empty, and the moon is the only source of light.

"I still can't believe you grew up here, Dad."

"What's so hard to believe?"

"It's just so different from back home . . . so secluded. But there's so much going on at the same time."

"That's the country for you." He smiles proudly. "I'm happy you girls get to experience it. It builds character."

"Tilla could do with some of that," Mia chirps.

Dad laughs. "Well then, it's a good thing you two might end up staying here longer."

"What?!" I say. "I thought we were staying in town."

"You will. But right now, it makes more sense for you two to spend time here. There's more room to run up and down."

"I don't like running up and down," Mia sulks.

"Wait—you're not leaving us here, are you?" I ask, hesitant.

"No, no. Never. I'll be here during the week. Most trucking shipments come on the weekends, so we can all go up to Kingston then. We'll spend weekends in town." He gets up from the bed. "Plus, there's nothing for you two to do in Kingston during the week. At least here, you have kids your own age." He places a kiss on Mia's head before heading for the door. "It'll only be for three weeks or so."

"Dad." It slips out firmer than intended.

"Nuh worry yuhself, Tilla." He brushes me off as he reaches for the door handle. "You're going to have a lot of fun here. Give it time." He winks before closing the door behind him.

"At least we'll have a lot of friends here," Mia says as she heads to the counter to pick from the array of lotions. "Plus, we'll be with him every day. Who cares where we stay?"

I'm envious of her reaction. Mia is always quick to give him the benefit of the doubt. But she doesn't know our father the way I do.

She doesn't know the man who never keeps his word.

I leave the room and head down the hall to the small bathroom. Inside, it has bright yellow walls and a small cream sink with an old cement shower. I turn on the pipe, and as I'm about to hop in, I catch my reflection in the mirror. I haven't even been in Jamaica twelve hours and already my skin is dark, beautiful, and golden. I hop into the shower, and goose bumps flood my skin. It's so cold that it takes everything in me not to howl out in shock.

When I get back to the room, Mia is passed out on the bed. I tiptoe across the floor to my suitcase and take out my favorite set of pink satin pajamas. I pull them on as Mia stirs awake.

"You're gonna be hot in that," she mumbles.

"I thought you were sleeping."

"I am," she groans as I slip in next to her. I reach over to the nightstand and flick off the small lamp. The room instantly goes pitch-black. I blink a couple of times, hoping they'll adjust. They don't. With no light in the country, the blackness feels like something out of a horror movie. My awareness of my body suddenly feels disoriented and my heartbeat starts to race.

"Til?" Mia whispers. "It's so dark. I'm scared."

"I know," I reply. "Maybe the light from the moon will help."

I take the sheets off me, stumbling my way out of the bed, and into the abyss of blackness. I feel my way across the wall until my palms finally make contact with the jagged shutters. I shimmy them open to reveal the brightness of the moon. The light that streams onto the tiles is just enough to help me find my way back to the bed. I slide back in next to Mia, relieved to have my sense of awareness back.

"Maybe tomorrow Daddy can give us a night-light," Mia whispers.

"Yeah, maybe," I whisper back. But I won't hold my breath.

We lie in silence for a few moments as my eyes start to grow heavy.

"I'm happy you're here with me," Mia whispers.

"I'm happy, too, Mia."

The loud sound of crickets echoes through the black night as we doze off to sleep.

COCK-A-DOODLE-DOO!

I jolt out of the bed to the piercing sound of a rooster.

I look around, breathing heavily.

Where am I?

COCK-A-DOODLE-DO! it screams out again. I look to my right and find Mia sound asleep, and suddenly, it all floods back to me: Jamaica.

The countryside.

The crack of dawn.

COCK-A-DOODLE-DOO!

God help me.

The blaring call echoes through the room as I silently wonder how the hell I'm going to survive three weeks of this. I take a pillow and put it over my face to drown out the noise. After a few deep breaths, I slowly drift back to sleep.

I awake some hours later to the sound of chatter on the veranda. I look next to me, and there's no sight of Mia. I spill out of bed, groggy as my feet touch the warm tiled floor. I open the side door that leads to the veranda, and as I step outside, Richie's voice rings out.

"Bumba rawtid!" he calls out, shocked. "Canada! Now yuh jus ah wake?!"

"Be nice, Richie." Aunt Herma looks up from the sewing machine as she stitches together a blue fabric. "It's a foreign ting. Dem nuh have responsibility like we."

I flush with embarrassment. "Sorry . . . I guess I slept in. What time is it?"

"Time fi get a watch, gyal!" Richie laughs his head off as if he invented the joke.

Diana smacks him on his arm. "It's noon, Tilla," she says.

Shit. I can feel the judgment from everyone around me.

"Ah dat yuh wear go ah bed?" Richie says, observing my pink pajama set. "Cockfoot. You is a *real* princess fi true."

I cringe, turning to Aunt Herma. "Do you know where my dad is? And Mia?"

She looks at me over the brim of her glasses. "Mia's playing out back with Kenny. And your father went to Mandeville to get you girls some groceries. He'll be back."

"Oh. Okay."

"Gwan go brush ya teeth, my girl. Me can smell yuh mout from yesso," Richie clowns.

I head back inside, desperate to get out of this situation.

I walk down the hall to the bathroom, silently kicking myself for waking up so late. I close the door behind me and turn on the pipe, splashing my face with the cold water as I try to shake the embarrassment. I pull my Afro out of my face and up into a pineapple on top of my head, wrapping my fingers around a few strands until the coils bounce back to life. When I'm finished brushing my teeth, I make my way back down the hall. I open the room door to find Aunt Herma hastily making the bed as she mumbles to herself.

Shit.

"Sorry, Aunt Herma. I was just brushing my teeth. I was gonna do that—"

"But you didn't," she snaps.

I rush over to the bed. "I can finish up."

"I'm already done." She keeps her back to me as she fluffs the pillows. "I know in foreign, you may not spread your own bed, but here, we like to keep the place clean. You don't have any maid service around here. It's bad enough I have to give up my room. The least you could do is not turn it into a pigsty."

I stand in silence, stunned. There's no way not to take this personally. *Why is she being so mean?* She turns to me, reading my body language.

"Don't make a habit of it." She softens as she exits the room.

"Okay." I nod. I take a deep breath before changing out of my clothes and heading outside into the yard.

When I take a step into the grass, it feels like a warm embrace beneath my toes. I notice Andre sitting on a rock near the front gate, and I make my way over to him.

"Hey, Andre."

"Mawnin'. Yuh finally wake?" he asks innocently.

"Yeah. I guess I was more tired than I thought." I take a seat next to him on top of the big flat rock. Its smooth edges are warm beneath my legs.

"Me never know someone weh sleep so late."

"What time do you usually wake up?"

"Dawn. Soon as di roosta crows."

"That's crazy." I laugh. "Where's that rooster anyway?"

"Chicken coop out back. Me can show you if you want?"

"Sure." We get up and make our way through the yard. "This is so surreal," I say as I take in my surroundings. Forgotten memories of Andre and me chasing lizards flood back to me. "I remember playing here with you . . . when we were kids."

"Fi true?" He smiles.

"Yeah." I laugh. "We used to rescue lizards, right?"

"Mhm. Mass Tyson used to get vex when we would bring dem inna di house."

"Didn't you dare me to eat one or something?"

"Me still cyan believe yuh neva do it."

We both laugh. It's clear our connection hasn't been lost.

"So yuh nah go tell me about foreign?"

"What do you want to know?" I ask.

"Everyting. What's it like? Only place me ever go is yawd."

"Really?" I ask in disbelief. "You've never left the country-side?"

He shrugs. "Me go ah town one time when me did likkle."

"Wow," I say. "So only Diana goes to town regularly?"

"Only she can afford it. Uncle Wayne drive taxi so dem can afford fi send her go ah dat fancy boardin' school. Mummy nuh have job. She only mek wha Mass Tyson send down fi tek care ah Mama and Papa."

"Oh." I start to feel uncomfortable. My dad barely contributes at home, so the thought of him having someone else on a payroll makes me feel strange. "So you're the only one that doesn't go to school?"

"Yeah," he says casually. "Tell me about foreign, nuh?"

"Oh, sorry—it's nice. It gets really cold in the winter, though. Lots of snow." I smile as his eyes light up. "You'd like it, I bet."

"No, sa." He shakes his head. "Me nah go pon no airplane."

"It's not that bad." I giggle.

"Wha! When yuh up so high wit nuttin below you?!"

"It's not really like that. It's weird. You forget you're up there sometimes."

"Fi true?"

"Swear."

He smiles as he toys with the thought. "Well, maybe one day me come visit you ah . . . Wha it name again?"

"Canada." I smile.

"Kyan-ah-da," he repeats.

We walk through a gate at the side of the house, and the grass turns to dirt. The path is lined with rocks that burn my feet as we walk. Andre's brows furrow.

"Yuh neva bring yuh shoes?"

"I left them inside."

He nods, observing my feet.

"How many yuh have?"

"What?"

"Pair. How many pair ah shoes yuh have?"

"That I brought here?"

"No. Total."

"I don't know . . . I don't really count like that. Maybe seven . . . ten?"

"Bumba!" His face floods with shock. "Yuh have ten pair ah shoes fi true?"

I grow ashamed as I look down at his battered oversize sneakers. They're covered in dirt with holes on the sides, and they're so big that it's obvious that they were passed down. His big toe protrudes out the front.

"Richie was right! We took a bet. He say ten, and Diana say five. Me say six."

"Oh." I squirm.

"Ca-ca rawtid." He shakes his head in disbelief. "Me neva meet a rich girl before, yuh nuh!"

"I'm not rich."

"Someone could have ten pair ah shoes and nuh rich?!" he asks sarcastically.

"It's not like that in Canada. Most of my shoes are from Walmart."

"Wha name so?"

"It's like . . . a cheap store." I search for a better way to explain it. "In Canada, you can have shoes, but it doesn't really mean anything. I mean, we have privileges . . . but we're not rich. Not even close."

He shakes his head as if bored with me playing coy. "Lawd, Tilla. If you come from foreign, yuh rich. Period."

"That's not true," I say defensively. "My mom struggles with bills all the time."

"Dat nuh mean nuttin. Yuh have a suitcase full of clothes. Yuh prob-ly have a outfit fi everyday yuh deh here."

"Clothes don't mean anything, Andre."

He kisses his teeth. "They do when yuh nuh have none."

My heart sinks. I immediately feel guilty. He's right.

I remain silent, losing myself in my thoughts as we pass a firepit in the backyard. We pass Mia and Kenny, who stand by a handful of small kittens at the side of the house.

"Tilla! They're sooo cute!" Mia calls as she holds one in the air. Andre makes a face.

"Put it down before yuh catch suh-um!" Andre calls before turning back to me. "Only foreign pickney could touch puss."

"Puss?"

"Cat. We nuh touch dem tings."

"Why not?"

"'Cause dem dirty. Dem kinda favor rat."

I nod, taking in the cultural differences as I continue behind him down a forested path lined with coffee trees. Ripe beans surround us, and the aroma of the coffee mixed with burning wood is enough to send me into nostalgia. I have vivid memories of running down this path as a child. We pass a modernly designed but small pink house at one end of the path, which I assume to be Diana's. We cross over low barbwire fence, and as we go deeper, I start to see animals scattered in the forest all around me. Goats and cows peek out of tall bushes, tied to the trees as chickens run wild in their coop.

"All ah dem ah fi me," Andre says proudly. It's the biggest I've seen him smile since I got here. "Papa and I raise dem since dem did small."

"They're beautiful," I say, reaching my hand out to pet one of the cows. "We saw them when we were driving in. I didn't know they were yours."

He pulls a napkin from his pocket filled with seeds and hands it to me. "Here. You can feed di chickens if yuh want."

"Thanks," I say, taking the napkin from his hand. I throw the feed into the chicken coop, and they rush to gather at the edge of the gate. A giant rooster on the outside of the gate squabbles over to me as it flings its head back and forth.

"He name Mista Binky," Andre says.

"Mr. Binky?" I giggle. "How'd you come up with that?"

"Me nuh know, yuh nuh . . . it just come to me."

"So what happens when you're done raising them?"

"Papa and I sell dem to a man weh sell dem ah market ah Mandeville."

"Oh. That's kinda sad."

"Wha yuh mean?"

"I don't know . . . I guess just having to sell them . . . you know, to be killed. That must be hard for you."

Andre shrugs as if he's never considered it before. "Everyting have a place inna life. If me nuh kill dem, den me nuh eat. And if me nuh eat, den me dead. Den who ah go tek care ah dem?" I hand the tissue back to him, and he shoves it into his pocket. "Yuh cyan fight how God want tings fi go."

I nod as we step back over the wire fence. He reaches up to a low-hanging crab apple tree and pulls down two freshly minted apples. He hands one to me.

"Right from di source. God himself." His words echo my father's.

We walk back to the house, devouring our treats.

"So what else is there to do around here?" I ask as we come around to the front yard.

"Plenty. Me ah go tek yuh pon nuff adventure. And when hurricane come, tings ah go start get real excitin'."

"Exciting?" I ask, confused.

Before he can answer, Dad comes through the front gate with the omnipresent gray grocery bags in his hand. Andre rushes over to help him as I trail behind.

"Aftanoon, Mass Tyson!" Andre calls, bowing his head respectfully as if my father were the long-lost King of Manchester. I bite my lip to keep from laughing.

"Wha'ppen, Andre. Tek dese bags inside fi me. Put dem inna di kitchen."

"Yes, Mass Tyson." Andre grabs the grocery bags and scurries inside like a proud servant. Dad notices me and smiles wide.

"How's my girl doing?"

"Hey, Dad." I smile. "What does that mean, 'Mass Tyson'?"

He lets out an awkward laugh, clearly caught off guard. "Wha yuh mean?"

"The 'Mass' part. Why do they call you that?"

"It's short for *Massa*." He pauses. "It's a term from slavery that they never dropped around here. Old-time thinking. It means *master*."

"Oh."

"It's a sign of respect."

I cringe, almost wishing I hadn't asked.

"So, how are you liking it so far? Yuh first real day ah yawd."

"It's okay." I nod, my eyes falling on the veranda where Aunt Herma stitches at the sewing machine. "I don't know if everyone is too thrilled to have us here, though."

"Why would you say that?"

"I don't know . . . just a vibe."

"Well, your vibe is wrong, Tilla. It's just how they show their love. Country people—"

"Are like that. I know," I interrupt him. "There's also not that much to do here."

"What are you talking about? There's plenty of room to play."

"Dad, I'm not a kid."

"You're never too old to explore where you come from, Tilla. Remember that."

I sigh, knowing full well that I'm not going to win this one.

He shifts, changing the subject. "Anyway, I bought enough groceries for you and Mia for a few weeks. I even got that Lasco you like. Strawberry one."

"Why do we need our own groceries?"

He's quiet for a moment, looking out across the yard and at the house.

"Dad?"

He sighs. "I have to go into town tonight."

"Oh. When are we coming back?"

"Not *we*, Til. *Me*. I have to go handle some work stuff."

I feel my heart start to race. "When will you be back?"

"A few weeks."

"What?!"

"I have to take care of some business. It won't be for too long."

"Dad." I can feel the blood draining from my face. "We just got here. You said last night you were going to stay with us during the week. *You promised.*"

"Yes. But some things came up."

"So why can't we just come with you?"

"Don't be dramatic, Tilla. I have a lot to deal with right now."

"But, Dad—"

"You'll be *fine.* You're surrounded by family, and you have your cousins to keep you company. You won't even notice I'm not here."

"But that's not what it's about." My face starts to get hot as tears begin to well up. I rack my brain, running out of reasons to get him to understand. "We came to see *you*—"

"You always do this shit. Don't start with the crocodile tears. You're not about to embarrass me. Not here."

"I'm not—"

"Tilla, I said *stop,*" he says sharply. "I'll be gone for three weeks. You and Mia are here for *two months.* You have all summer to see me. And it's about time you take interest in getting to know your family. It's not always about what you want."

Sorrow fills my body.

My head spins a mile a minute as I try to process the backhanded words that leave his lips. The truth is it's never been about what I want, but every sentence that leaves my mouth digs me deeper into a hole that pushes my father farther and farther away from me. My mind races, desperately trying to find the right words that will take back the conversation. The right words that will get him to change his mind.

But I draw a blank.

All at once, it is Sunday morning all over again, but this time, it is me on the floor and not my mother. This time it is me searching for the right words that will make him stay. The right words to convince him that we are his *daughters* and he should *want* to stick around. That we are fun enough. Interesting enough. Good enough.

Why can't he see that?

The hot sun that beams down onto me feels suffocating as words and thoughts mix together in my head. I open my mouth to try one last time.

"But . . . Dad . . ." My voice cracks. "We traveled *miles* . . . across the world . . . to spend time with *you*."

"And you *will*," he says, annoyance seeping through his tone. He is visibly disgusted with me. Disgusted with my desperation. His words cut sharp, as if to say not to ask again. "In three weeks."

His gray eyes turn to ice as he walks away from me, making his way through the yard. I stand in the middle of the grass as I search for the words to make him turn around . . . but nothing leaves my mouth. The sight of his back is all too familiar, and it hits me that throughout my entire life, I've seen him go more than come. And just as I try to fight it, the tears pour down onto my skin like waves of hot lava confirming what I've always known to be true:

I am, and will always be, my father's second choice.

4

"Foreign gyal love sleep fi true."

I awake the next morning to Diana standing in the doorway. I rub my eyes as the sun streams in through the shutters, filling the room. The clock on the nightstand table next to me reads 9:00 a.m., and I realize I must have missed the rooster. Next to me, Mia lies sound asleep, her small frame folded in between the white cotton sheets.

"What?" I ask, groggy.

"*I said*, 'You love to sleep,' Canada. It must be a foreign ting or something." She shrugs as she ties her braids back into a ponytail. "Yuh wan follow me go ah shop?"

"Shop?"

"The store," she says in a matter-of-fact tone. "Mummy is sending me to run some errands. You can come if you like."

"For groceries?"

"Not really. You have to go to Mandeville for that, which is about an hour away. I'm just getting some snacks. Milk and bulla."

"Oh."

"It's just down di road. Thirty-minute walk there and back."

"Yeah, okay." I nod.

"Meet me out front," she says before closing the door behind her.

I stumble out of bed, careful not to wake Mia. As I change out of my clothes, a heavy energy lingers on my skin. It comes back to me in waves.

I am a vortex of fatigue and sadness.

I feel embarrassed at how I reacted to my father yesterday. I hate that he saw tears well in my eyes. I tried so hard to hold them back, but I couldn't fight the disappointment that shot through my body. That *consumed* me like I was a little girl all over again. I hate that he knows I need him. I wish his decision to abandon us over and over again made me angry and not sad, like some cowering child begging for her father's validation. I'm not some broken teenager who needs her daddy to put her back together again.

I'm not going to let his absence ruin my summer.

I head to the bathroom to get ready before making my way out to the patio to meet Diana. Aunt Herma kneels on the floor, shining it with a piece of coconut.

"Well, look who's up." She peers at me over the brim of her glasses.

"Good morning, Aunt Herma."

"You're up early. I had to fix my glasses to make sure I was seeing straight." I hold back the urge to roll my eyes. "How was your sleep?" she asks.

"Good. I haven't made the bed yet. Mia's still sleeping." I offer a strained smile as morning light fills the veranda. The house feels foreign without my dad here, and it starts to sink in just how far from home I really am.

"Good morning, Uncle Junior," I call across the patio. He ignores me, not looking up from his sewing machine as he works.

Diana walks over to me. "Don't even bother," she says under her breath. "He can be strange when he's in the zone. Yuh ready?"

"Yeah." I nod.

"Aunt Herma, we soon come," she calls as we make our way down the steps.

We cross the lush green yard and exit through the front gate, closing it behind us. Just past the gate is a rocky dirt road, and to the right is an old red house with bicycles out front and a clothesline that runs across the side of the house.

"That's Mass Crossley's house. He lives there with his wife and son. They have four big dutty mongrels. Sometimes they lay out front and block our gate."

"Mongrels?"

"Dogs. Ugly ones. Don't let them catch you walking home by yourself, either. They'll attack. Especially if they don't know you."

"For real? Like attack, attack?"

"Dead serious. Jamaican mongrel dem nuh romp."

"Nuh romp?"

"Am I going to have to translate everything for you?" She rolls her eyes. "It *means* they don't play around. If they start barking at you, don't run. Whatever you do."

I shudder at the thought as we continue down the hill. When we hit the bottom, the street is lined with small zinc houses and bushes. We walk for a while without seeing anyone, but after a few minutes, the roads become paved and lively, filled with people going to and fro. A few Rastafarians sit on the side of the street, engaged in a game of dominoes. Kids with no shoes run up and down the corrugated roads as women carry buckets of water on their heads. As we continue down the road, I feel the curious eyes glued to me.

"Round yesso, everyone know one anotha. So don't feel a

way if you catch people staring. They're either wondering who you are or know exactly who you are," Diana says.

"How would they know who I am?" I ask as more eyes look on.

"You're kidding, right?" Diana almost laughs. "Gyal, yuh come from *foreign*. Everyone knows Mass Tyson's daughters were coming to country. It's big news around here."

"*Really?*"

"Duh. It's not every day two foreign girls come to Comfort Hall. You might as well be a celebrity. These people don't know the difference."

I squirm at the thought as I try to avoid the gazing eyes. All the attention starts to make me uncomfortable. "You would think I'm Beyoncé or something." I smile awkwardly.

"Who?"

"The singer."

She shakes her head, clueless as to what I'm talking about.

"Wait—you've never heard of *Beyoncé*?"

"What does she sing?"

"You're kidding."

"What?" she asks, annoyed.

"It's just . . . pretty crazy that you don't know who she is, I guess."

"What's so crazy about that?" Irritation bathes her face. "She obviously can't be that popular if I've never heard of her."

"She's huge in America—"

"Well, she's not in Comfort Hall," she snaps back, clearly wanting to drop it. "I don't listen to that stuff. Secular music. I have a more cultured taste. Céline Dion. I doubt you would know about the stuff I listen to, anyway."

I bite my tongue, accepting her jab as I nod. Diana's annoyance reminds me how divided we are in class, and I immediately feel terrible for making her feel out of touch. I try to shift the subject.

"So, all these people know my dad?"

"Mhmm. Mass Tyson is a big deal around here. A lot of these people grew up with him. Some ah dem know him from him did small."

I nod again as I take in the sea of faces that probably know more about my father than I do. I feel slightly envious. My father operates in a whole other world that I know nothing about.

"Look, country is small. Real small," Diana continues. "Everyone knows everyone's business here. It's not easy to make it out of Manchester, and if you do . . . you don't usually come back. But Mass Tyson does, and he takes care of everyone. He looks out for us and brings gifts and stuff. He's like a father to a lot of these people."

Her words sting.

We pass a few women who sit on the steps of their houses, vigorously washing clothes in buckets by hand. A slender man with dark black skin and a missing eye sells chicken on the side of the road, aggressively bartering his prices with the people who pass by. He gives me a nod, indicating that he knows exactly who I am.

"Rodney," Diana says to me. "He's a likkle mod in his head, but he makes really good jerk chicken."

I smile back at him.

Farther down the road, a young boy with smooth black skin and no shoes stands in the middle of the street. His feet dirtied, he holds a bag of guinep that he tries to sell to people on their way to work. As we walk by, I slip him a hundred-dollar bill in exchange for a few pieces of the fruit. His eyes light up when he touches the crumpled paper, thanking me as he pockets the cash.

"Junior," Diana whispers as we walk past. "Him live ah roadside."

"He lives on the street?"

"Nuh badda feel sorry fi him. Him ah pure ginnal."

"Ginnal?"

"Con artist," she clarifies. "His guinep is way overpriced." She grabs a piece of the fruit from my hand and pops it into her mouth. "Di people in country tek care of him from time to time. He comes by di house sometimes for dinner."

"Wow. That's really sad."

"Still nuh mean he should be overchargin'." She kisses her teeth. Just then, a man in an old cream-colored Camry rolls down the road with a megaphone attached to the top of his car. He speaks into a microphone as his voice blares throughout the street.

"*Mawnin', Comfort Hall! Dasheen and provisions fi sale! Real guava jelly and hard dough bread! Come stock up fi hurricane season!*"

Diana rolls her eyes as he drives past us.

"Mark. Him ah eediat. Always ah sell suh-um and announce it to di world."

"Eediat?"

"*Idiot*. Him love di sound ah him own voice."

I nod as we continue down the road.

About ten minutes into the walk, we approach a sunken little blue house on the right side of the road. Despite its wear and chipped paint, its rich, bold color stands out from the rest of the houses scattered along the street. I spot an old woman sitting on the small deck, rocking back and forth in her chair as a young man hangs clothes on the laundry line in the yard.

"Miss Addie's house," Diana whispers to me as we get

closer. I notice her demeanor change. "She fasses in everyone's business."

"Fasses?"

"Nosy. As hell."

"Got it."

"Nuh badda make eye contact or she nah stop talk."

I nod, following instructions. "Who's the guy?" My eyes fixate on the young man and his toned, muscular frame as he moves gracefully in the blazing heat.

"Nobody important," she says dismissively.

I study him for a moment as he casually pins a wet T-shirt to the thin wire. I assume he's not much older than Diana and me. There's an air to him, a luminous energy. His warm brown skin glows a deep yellow under the rays of the hot sun. His light brown hair borders on blond, gleaming with golden specks, and I assume it's from time spent in the water. His eyes look up to reveal a rich and vibrant hazel. He works barefoot in a light blue shirt and red shorts. He notices us and peeks out through the clothesline, wiping sweat from his thick, furry brows with the back of his hand. A gentle smile creeps onto his face.

I keep my head down, trying to avoid his gaze as we draw closer. We pick up the pace, almost making it by without being spotted, when Miss Addie looks up from her Bible.

"Me know say yuh nah go pass by me yawd without say good mawnin', Miss Diana!" she calls down to us from the porch.

Diana stops dead in her tracks, mouthing the word *fuck*. She pivots back around. "Mawnin', Miss Addie! Me tink yuh did ah sleep."

"Stop lie, likkle girl! Yuh mout' soon drop off." She adjusts her glasses, squinting down at me. "Ah Mass Tyson pickney dat?" I freeze, surprised that she can make me out from so far away.

"Yeah." Diana bites her bottom lip to keep from laughing. She kicks the dirt beneath her feet as I stand awkwardly behind her.

"So bring her here nuh, gyal!"

"Jesus Christ," Diana mumbles under her breath. "Come." She takes my hand and pulls me down the path to the bottom of the steps. The guy looks on from the yard, curious and amused. We walk up the blue steps to where Miss Addie sits, Bible in hand.

"Long time me nuh see yuh round here, Diana. Yuh used fi come ah me yawd every day and now me cyan see yuh," Miss Addie says, making it clear that Diana used to spend a lot of time here. "Why yuh nuh come look fi me grandson since yuh come back from school?"

"Sorry, Miss Addie. I've been meaning to." She shifts awkwardly before gesturing to me. "I've just been busy with my cousin visitin'. This is Tilla."

"Good morning, Miss Addie," I say politely, my foreign accent giving me away. Miss Addie chuckles obnoxiously at my dialect.

"Mawnin', girl." She examines me up and down. "So you ah Mass Tyson daughta? Cockfoot." She purses her lips, smacking them together to reveal her missing teeth. "You is a real foreign gyal fi true. Which part yuh come from?"

"Canada."

"Lawwwd God!" She cackles, slapping her knee as she adjusts herself in the seat. Diana and I hold back a laugh. "Yuh meet me grandson yet?" She turns to the yard. "Hessan! Come here nuh, bwoy! Diana deh here!"

Hessan hangs the last shirt on the line before running across the yard and up the battered blue steps. Diana bites down on her lip, growing awkward as he approaches. Sweat gleams against his golden brown skin, and I can't help but marvel at his athletic build. He takes a handkerchief from the pocket of his shorts, dabbing his forehead before flashing Diana a gentle smile.

"Wha'ppen, Diana?" His voice is smooth and relaxed. "Long time no see."

"Hey." She blushes as she pulls on one of her braids. "It's been a while."

They hold eye contact for a moment. Hessan smiles.

"You're wearing your hair different now." He nods to her long braids. "I like it."

Diana smiles, flipping them behind her back. "Yeah. They make us wear it like this at school."

"It suits you." He smiles.

Miss Addie shakes her head. "Me nuh know why it tek her so long fi come round ah we yawd. She go school ah town and now she nuh know nobody."

"Nuttin nuh go so, Miss Addie," Diana reassures her. "I'll be in Wednesday prayer meetin' dis week."

"Hmp." Miss Addie adjusts in her chair, closing her Bible. "The Lord would hope so." She turns to Hessan. "Hessan, yuh meet Mass Tyson daughta yet?"

Hessan turns to me, and we lock eyes.

My body flutters.

"Wha yuh did say yuh name was, girl?" Miss Addie asks.

"Tilla." I smile.

Hessan stares at me, his hazel eyes twinkling with curiosity. "Nice fi meet you, Tilla. I'm Hessan." There's a depth and warmth to his tone.

He shakes my hand, his grip gentle but firm. He stares into my eyes as if he were reading every inch of me, before giving me a smile so charming that I can't help but melt. I try to fight the grin that takes over my face.

"It's nice to finally put a face to the name." He smiles. "I've heard a lot about you." I glance at Diana. She shrugs. "From yuh fada," Hessan corrects. "I manage his farm throughout di year."

"His farm?"

"Yeah. Up di road. Yuh neva know?" he asks, surprised.

I shake my head.

"He has a plot of land not too far from here," Hessan continues. "I tek care of it when he's in Kingston. Plant di crops fi him."

"Oh. I didn't . . . I didn't know that," I say. I feel myself start to burn up.

How could my dad not tell me he owns a farm?

"Iz all right. Yuh jus reach. I'm sure there's plenty fi learn." He offers me a reassuring smile. I nod, pushing the thought to the back of my mind. "That's a beautiful necklace." He examines the butterfly pendant that sits around my neck. I squirm uncomfortably as his eyes take me in.

"Oh. Thanks." A bead of sweat runs down my back. "My dad gave it to me."

I can feel Diana and Miss Addie staring at us, and between them, Hessan, and this heat, I think I might pass out.

"How long are you staying in Jamaica?"

"The whole summer." I blush. "Two mon—"

"A few weeks," Diana interrupts. "She won't be in country long."

"Rawtid!" Miss Addie calls out. "Mass Tyson ah keep yuh ah Jamaica fi di hurricane?!"

"I—I think so, yeah—"

"Cockfoot! Hurricane ah go bad dis year, gyal. Bad, bad, bad." She shakes her head and fear prickles through me. "We haffi pray to God if we nuh want fi dead. And speaking of di Lord—" She turns to Diana. "Should I expect you in church on Sunday, Miss Diana?" Her tone is riddled with judgment. "Long time me nuh see yuh face inna Sunday service."

"I told you, I was away at school, Miss Addie," Diana repeats. "I only got back last week."

"Me nuh hard of hearin', Diana." Miss Addie kisses her teeth. "Jus mek sure ya in attendance dis week. Di devil love a weak spirit. Especially a young girl like you." She turns her attention toward me. "And what about you, Till-ah? Will di Lord be a priority inna yuh life dis Sunday?"

"Uh . . . I think so." I look to Diana for confirmation. She avoids my gaze.

"Jesus is not something yuh tink bout, gyal. You either give ya life to Christ or to Satan."

"Oh, uh, yes. Definitely." I squirm.

"Wha yuh mean, 'definitely'? Which one is it?"

"Oh—Christ . . . I've given my life to Christ."

Hessan bites down on his lip to keep from laughing.

"Di Lord nuh appreciate half commitment." She furrows her brows, studying me through the tops of her glasses. "Would yuh be inna half relationship wit yuh boyfrien'?"

"No, ma'am."

"So why would yuh be inna half relationship wit God?"

"I wouldn't, ma'am."

"See?" She turns to Diana. "Me know Mass Tyson raise her wit some sense. Yuh could learn suh-um, Diana." She coughs into her hand, placing her Bible beside her. "So where uno ah head to dis mawnin'?"

"Shop." Diana offers a fake smile. "Mummy send me fi get milk and bread. We haffi go 'long now." She grabs my hand and pulls me down the steps.

"Nice to meet you!" I wave, locking eyes with Hessan one more time.

"Me betta see you pon Sunday, Miss Diana!" Miss Addie calls after us. "Me nuh wan haffi talk to yuh mada!"

"Mhm! Praise God!" Diana yells back dismissively before

pulling me down the path and back into the road. We quicken our pace until we are out of sight.

"I didn't know God was such a big deal around here." I giggle.

"Nuh badda say that too loud. Country people take church very serious. Miss Addie never misses a day. She go ah weekend *and* weekday service, plus she run Bible study."

"Wow." I laugh. "That's a lot of church. Do you usually go?"

"Do I usually *go*?!" She looks at me like I'm crazy. "Mummy is the pastor!"

"Wait . . . Aunt Shirley's the *pastor*?!"

"Mhm. We own the church." She looks at me. "What? You didn't know I was the pastor's daughter?" She boasts. "Not to brag, but it's a pretty big deal. The church runs the community, which means my family has a lot of power around here. It's why so many people know me."

"Wow." Suddenly her self-importance starts to make a lot more sense.

"Look, I know you're new here, so there's a lot yuh nuh understand as yet. But I'll break it down fi you: Andre and Richie and them may be my cousins, but we're not the same . . . *class*. They're country people. I'm more *town*." I nod, reluctant to point out that she lives five steps away from them. "Pretty much, I'm saying that hanging out with me has its privileges. Being the pastor's daughter puts me on a different level than everybody else."

She flips her braids. I can't tell if she's joking.

"How long has your mom been a pastor?"

"Since I was born. Daddy and Mass Tyson built the church years ago, and Mummy's been runnin' it ever since."

A pang of irritation runs through me. Yet another thing I didn't know about my own father.

"That's . . . really cool." I change the subject, trying to shake it off. "Well, Hessan seemed nice."

"Nice?"

"Yeah. Like . . . sweet, I guess."

She rolls her eyes, clearly growing irritated with me. "Hessan's not for you."

"What do you mean?"

"He's not *for you*. You're not his type."

"Oh. What's his type?"

She rolls her eyes. "Hessan's a Christian." She looks me up and down. "No offense, but have you ever even stepped *foot* in a church?"

"I mean, not often, but—"

"It's barely your third day, Tilla. Don't be so thirsty."

"I wasn't—"

"I said drop it, Canada."

Her sudden annoyance takes me by surprise. I let it go as we continue down the road. We walk another mile before approaching a shabby, yellow shop front made from old, decomposing wood. DEBBY'S COOKIE & CRACKER CONVENIENCE is scribbled on the door in faded chalk. Diana nods at an older gentleman who sits out front as we enter.

Inside, the tiny store is lined with candy, crackers, bread, bulla, buns, and other Jamaican goods. Bottles of Ting and Chubby are on display at the front. A brown-skinned lady sits behind the counter with one half of her hair braided and the other half undone. Diana walks straight up to the counter and places down her neatly folded bills.

"Mawnin', Miss Debby."

"Wha'ppen, Diana?" Debby obnoxiously smacks on a piece of gum.

"Lemme get a bun and cheese," Diana says before turning to me. I notice her accent is much more apparent when talking to people in the community. "Yuh wan one?"

I nod, drooling at the thought. Bun and Jamaican cheese is my favorite snack.

Diana turns back to Debby. "Make it two."

I walk back to the freezer and pull out a small red plastic bag of juice that reads SUCKSUCK. I grab coconut cookies for Mia and make my way back to the counter, where Miss Debby rings us up. I reach into my pocket and pull out a few of the crumbled bills my father gave me before he left.

"Here you go."

"I got it," Diana stops me. Her tone is prideful as she flips her braids behind her back.

"Oh, okay."

She reaches into her purse and pulls out crisp, freshly folded bills.

"Thank you." I smile. She nods, shrugging it off.

When we head back outside, the pavement is so hot I can feel it through my slippers. I pull out the bun and cheese and take a bite before swinging the gray grocery bag back and forth.

"Why do all the grocery bags look like this?"

"It's called a *scandal* bag," Diana says. "See how it's dark and you cyan see through it? They make it like that so nosy people cyan see what you buy ah shop. So dem cyan *scandalize* you and tell people your business—"

"Diana!" a voice calls out from behind us.

I swing around to see a tall, lanky, dark-skinned boy running toward us from down the road. He sports army-green shorts and a red fishnet tank top. Diana grabs my arm and spins me in the opposite direction, pulling me into a speed walk.

"Don't make eye contact," she says through clenched teeth.

"Who's that?" I ask.

"DIANA! Slow down nuh, girl!" he calls out again, sprinting down the pavement. Before Diana can pick up the pace, he pummels into her at full speed, almost knocking her over.

Laughing his head off, he picks her up and swings her around in the air.

"Dane! Cool nuh, mon!" she yells out, annoyed.

"Yuh neva hear me ah call to you?!"

"That's exactly why I was walking faster—"

"Tilla!" He puts her down and grabs me in his arms. He twirls me around before planting a giant kiss on my forehead.

"Hi." I laugh, confused as ever. "Nice to meet you."

"Meet me?! Yuh nuh 'memba ya big cousin?!"

"Cousin?"

Diana rolls her eyes. "Unfortunately."

"She nuh mean dat," he brushes her off.

"I do. Tilla, this is Dane."

Dane extends his hand for me to shake, a giant grin bursting on his face. "Neighborhood hustla, part-time gangsta, and full-time party." He bows.

"Jesus Chri—" Diana starts.

"Don't listen to Dee. She borin'. I'm surprised she nuh have you readin' books on di history of Comfort Hall."

Diana gives him the finger.

"I've been waiting so long to see me good-good cousin!" he continues. "Me tell everyone me have a rich cousin ah foreign." Just when I think his smile can't grow any wider, it does. "Are you coming to court? I'm running late."

"Court?" I ask Diana, who rolls her eyes for the millionth time.

"Dane thinks he's some sorta judicial official."

"A man thinks, therefore he is," he says with confidence as smooth as a fox. "Hurry up if yuh want fi get a good seat!" And with that, he sprints off down the road. We trail behind, curiosity forcing us to pick up the pace.

We drop off our items before heading to the forest out back, where court is being held. We follow the path deep into the woods until we reach a giant red dirt clearing, where children big and small have gathered from all over the country. Some wear battered clothes, some just dirty ones, and some go without shoes as they wait impatiently for the event to commence. Surrounded by the rich jungly forest, the majestic scene favors something out of a movie. Diana and I place ourselves at the back, standing on the bark of a giant fallen tree to get a better view. We wait for about twenty minutes before a deep voice cuts through the noise.

"Order inna di court!"

The bushes begin to shake. After a few seconds, Dane emerges with a long, red sheet tied around his neck trailing behind him like a cape. He uses a giant walking stick and is adorned with a crown made from broken sticks. Two boys carry the ends of the red fabric as he makes his way up to a giant boulder that sits at the front of the audience. The crowd hushes down to an excited whisper, restless as they await the show. Dane climbs on top of the rock and bangs down his walking stick. He eyes the crowd deadpan, the personality I saw earlier completely gone.

"Ladiez and genkle-mon! Order inna di court!"

The loud whispers die down.

"Tank you!" Dane clears his throat before using a highly dramatized English accent to address the audience again. "Ladiez and genkle-mon, we are gathered here today to stand tall in the face of injustice. A crime haz been committed today in Comfort Hall, but with di help of you, di jury, we shall decide dis man's fate."

The crowd hoots and hollers.

"May no lie go unmasked. May di truth always prevail . . . and may justice be served! Bring him fah-ward!"

Everyone erupts. Suddenly, two young boys ascend from the forest holding Kenny in their grip. Kenny squirms, biting his lip to stifle a giggle at the commotion. The boys place him at the bottom of the rock where Dane stands, before scurrying off to their places in the audience. Richie emerges from the crowd with a battered yellow tie around his neck and stands by his brother's side, organizing crumpled scrap papers in his hand. Dane looks down to Richie and Kenny. "Is dis your client?"

"Yes, Your Honn-ah," Richie says.

Dane nods, addressing the audience. "Will the prosecutor please approach di stage?" Everyone looks around, curious as to who it could be. After a few moments of whispers, a girl around my age with tan skin and short, permed hair emerges out of the audience. She walks confidently up to the stage, taking her place across from Kenny.

"Please state your name," Dane orders.

"Zory, Your Honor. Zory Fields."

Diana leans into me. "She's our half cousin." I look to her confused, unsure of how in the world someone could be a half cousin.

"And who will be representing you dis afternoon, Miss Fields?"

"I'll be representing myself," Zory replies confidently.

The audience gasps.

"Please address the jury, Miss Fields."

Zory takes a deep breath before taking a self-assured step toward the audience.

"Good aftanoon, jury." She speaks primly and properly, fighting her Patios accent in a similar way that Diana does.

"Good aftanoon!" the audience calls out.

"Around eleven o'clock dis mawnin', I was instructed by my father to watch di goats. I had just given them their mawnin' feedin' when I saw Kenny comin' down di road. He said he was on his way to shop fi get a Red Bull, but he know Miss Debby nah give it to him because everyone know she nuh sell Red

Bull to kids under fifteen. So he gave me five dollas and asked me to pick it up fi him. I agreed to do it—under one condition. I told Kenny to keep an eye pon di goat dem—"

"Pure lie she ah tell!" Kenny blurts out.

"Control your client, please!" Dane orders. Richie shoves Kenny, nodding his apologies to the judge.

"I live five minutes from shop. That's five minutes there and five minutes back. Dat mek ten minutes." A few of the younger kids do the math on their fingers, nodding in agreement. Zory continues, "When me come back, one of my goats was missin' . . . and Kenny was *nowhere* to be found."

The audience explodes in shock.

"Objection!" Richie screams. "Objection, Your Honn-Ah!"

"Order inna di court!" Dane yells. "Richie, please approach di jury."

Richie keeps his face stoic as he walks up to where Zory stood.

"Your Honn-ah, I first want to tek dis time out to thank you for givin' my client di opportunity to defend himself. Being a man of the law, me know dat you know di importance of a fair trial." A slight smirk creeps onto Dane's face before he gives Richie a nod of respect. I feel the bias of a boy's club creeping in. Richie continues, turning to Zory.

"Mizz Fields, how many goats yuh say yuh have?"

Zory turns to Dane. "Your Honn-ah, me and Richie are cousins. He knows how many blasted goats me have. He's just being annoyin'."

"Answer di question, Miss Fields," Dane instructs.

Zory sighs, rolling her eyes once more as she turns back to Richie. "Me have six goats. They're my father's."

"Six?" Richie asks again.

"Yes. Everyone here know me daddy have six goat."

"Interestin'. And when you arrived back from shop and saw one goat was missin', what did you do?"

"I was in shock."

"I can imagine," Richie offers with faux sympathy.

"I tied up di rest of di goat. Closed di open fence."

"Open or broken?"

"Nuh badda piss me off, Richie. I said open."

"Hmm." Richie taps his chin. "Di prosecution would like to present some new evidence." He gestures to a young girl in the audience, who makes her way to the stage, bringing forth a piece of wire. Richie takes it from her and holds it up for the jury to get a clear look. "Does this look familiar to you, Miss Fields?"

"No."

"Interestin'. You see, Miss Fields, when I took a trip to di crime scene, I noticed that your fence had been patched up. Like someone had put it back togetha. And I found dis at di scene of di crime."

"Kenny broke it when—"

"You said Kenny left it open. So dat couldn't make sense," Richie continues. "What *would* make sense is that your goat bruk out a di gate on *your* watch."

"Wha you ah talk bout—"

"What *would* mek sense is dat you was not keepin' a proper eye pon di goat because you was at di *shop*! Nuh true?! Where you saw Kenny and bought di Red Bull fi him!"

Zory is stunned.

"See?! Me tell uno ah lie she ah tell!" Kenny yells out.

"And so you tried to blame it on an innocent young boy who has to pass your house fi get home!" Richie continues, pointing his finger in her face. "Your Honn-ah! Me rest me *rawtid* case!" He throws his crumpled papers into the sky.

"All in favor of di prosecution, say aye!" Dane orders.

Diana grabs my hand, shooting it up to the sky.

"All in favor of the defense, say aye!"

The audience bursts into a thunderous eruption, shaking the forest. Birds shoot out of the trees as everyone celebrates Kenny's victory. Dane calls out over the madness.

"If the glove doesn't fit, you *must* acquit! The jury has spoken!"

A few kids hoist Kenny up into the air, and he crowd-surfs among a sea of brown hands. Among the rich deep green of the forest, the celebration feels magical, and I can't help but join in as Diana and I search the crowd for Zory. We find her standing in the middle of a dance circle, sipping on a melted bag juice.

"Zo!" Diana calls out.

Zory looks over to us and smiles widely. For someone who just got called a liar in front of so many people, she seems to be in great spirits.

"Wha'ppen, Dee?" she says as she makes her way over to us.

Her skin illuminates under the heat. She has big, dark eyes and a tomboy vibe, and she carries the same confidence she did onstage. "Can you believe di fuckery Dane ah gwan wit? Pure poppyshow him ah run." She kisses her teeth, but I can tell she's not actually upset. "Dis ah di last time me ah come ah court." Her eyes fall on me as if she's just noticed me. She looks me up and down as she sucks on her dripping bag juice. "Ah Tilla dis?"

"Yeah," Diana replies. "Tilla, meet Zory. Zo, meet Tilla."

"Hey." I smile. "I'm really sorry about your goat."

"Please." She rolls her eyes. "That damn goat is always es-capin'. Yuh really shoulda sorry fi di beatin' me ah go get later tonight."

I giggle as we make our way out of the forest and onto a busy back road.

"So how yuh like di country so far?" Zory asks.

"It's great. I'm starting to have a lot of fun." I smile. "It's so cool that you guys do stuff like that."

Diana and Zory stop dead in their tracks and burst out into laughter.

"What?" I feel awkward, tucking a coil into my Afro puff.

"Yuh was right!" Zory says through laughter to Diana. "She talk funny fi true!"

I smile uncomfortably as they spill over in obnoxious cackles.

"Lawd God!" Zory wipes tears from her eyes as if it were the funniest thing in the world. "I'm just playin', Tilla." She laughs. "Don't be so sensitive."

"I'm not," I say passively, eager to change the subject. "So how often does Dane run court?"

"Whenever his big head feels like it." Diana laughs.

"Mhm," Zory agrees, catching her breath. "Which might as well be every day. Country pickney always have some problem dem need fi sort out."

"It's all bullshit and politics," Diana says. "Dane's verdict is always biased."

"I wish we did stuff like that in Canada," I say.

"Wha yuh mean?" Diana asks.

"Just . . . make our own fun like that. Everyone's too busy on their phones and computers, I guess."

"Must be nice." Zory makes a face.

Diana hides a smirk, and I cringe, mentally making a note to not talk about the things we have back home.

"So which part uno ah come from?" Zory asks.

"Shop. And we stop round ah Miss Addie's house."

"Ah lie!" Zory laughs. "She meet church bwoy?"

Diana nods.

"Ah di first time yuh see him since yuh come back from school?"

"Yup."

"Me woulda love fi see di look pon him face." Zory laughs.

We walk for a few miles and approach a group of young men who hang out on the roadside next to a battered shop. They sit outside around a small table as they drink a pack of Red Stripe over a Ludi board game, passing a toke of weed back and forth.

Zory taps Diana and whispers under her breath, "Jahvan deh over desso."

"Who?" I ask.

"Shh!" both girls say.

We walk past the shop in silence until a deep voice calls out to us. "Yow! Dee! Zo!"

The girls stop and spin around on their heels, their demeanor nervous and giggly. A young man with beautiful smooth skin passes a spliff to his friend before walking over. He wears a loose army-green tank top, dark shades, and brown khakis, and he walks with an effortless cool. We meet him halfway in the road.

"Wha gwan?" he slurs as we approach. His voice is deep and raspy.

"Hey, Jahvan." Zory blushes.

"Wha uno ah deal wit?" he asks, looking at me over the top of his shades.

"Not much." Zory plays coy. "Jus ah come from road."

"Long time me nuh see you, Di. Hide you ah hide?"

Diana giggles. "Don't be silly, Jahvan. I was away at school. I'm back for the summer." Jahvan smiles, slowly looking her up and down for a moment. There's a bad-boy aura to him that intimidates me but intrigues me at the same time.

"Well, nuh badda get too busy fi me." He grazes her chin.

Diana flashes a toothy grin.

"Who's ya likkle friend?" He returns his attention to me.

"This is my cousin Tilla. She ah visit from foreign."

"Backside." Jahvan laughs. "Ah foreign gyal? Which part you come from?"

"Canada," I say politely.

"Kyan-ah-da. Bumbaclot." He looks me up and down as if he's the hunter and I'm his prey. I feel my body prickle with sweat under his razor-sharp gaze. He removes his glasses to reveal dominating brown eyes.

"Are all di girls dis beautiful in Kyan-ah-da?" he asks as he studies me. "Or just you?"

I blush, unsure of how to respond.

"You're a very pretty girl, Till-ah . . . Me want get to know yuh."

It's clear it's not a question. I squirm as the words my mother would always say come back to me: *Jamaican boys fall fast.*

"How long yuh ah stay inna country?"

"Just a few weeks."

"Bumba . . ." He bites his lower lip. He takes my hand from fiddling with my shirt and rubs his thumb across the back of my palm.

"Welcome to my district," he says, a mystery to his tone. "My name is Jahvan. I'm sure Dee and Zory can tell you say me run tings round yesso. If yuh need anyting, don' be afraid to ask . . . *Till-ah.*"

"Okay." I nod. "I won't."

He winks at me before dropping my hand. "I'll see you around, Kyan-ah-da." With one last commanding gaze, he slides on his shades and heads back to his boys. Before I can even process the interaction, Diana and Zory turn on their heels and continue walking. I jog to catch up with them.

"Who was that?" I ask.

"You shouldn't be so eager," Diana says sharply.

"What—"

"It's not a good look," Zory agrees.

They quicken their pace, making sure to stay a few steps in front of me.

"Does she plan fi sleep wit every bwoy pon di island?" Diana giggles, whispering under her breath. Anxiety stunts me as I hear the words fall from her mouth. They run ahead like two schoolgirls, and I fight the urge to run to catch up with them. *"Don't be so eager,"* they said. So I slow my pace. But I can't help but feel small in this moment, like I am silently begging for their approval. Like I was excited to feel wanted. Like I needed their company the way I needed my father's.

The idea repulses me.

I replay the events, trying to make sense of what just happened.

Did I do something wrong? Did I say something I shouldn't?

But the truth is I already know the answer:

I am a foreign gyal.

And they have no interest in being my friend.

5

I awake the next morning to noises of things bumping and slamming.

Before I have a chance to process what it could be, the room light flicks on, and Aunt Herma stands at the foot of the bed, humming an old tune.

"Aunt Herma?" I ask, lethargic.

She ignores me and continues to hum, drawing behind her a large, outdated mop and bucket. She walks over to the dresser and fiddles with an old radio, turning it up full blast. The jarring bravado of a morning show fills the room, and Mia begins to stir, awaking from her sleep.

"What's going on?" Mia asks groggily, pulling the covers up over her eyes.

Aunt Herma ignores her. She dips the mop into the bucket, wringing it out by hand before vigorously wiping the floor in figure eight patterns. The sleep starts to fade from me as the intention of what's going on becomes clearer. I look at the clock that sits on the nightstand table: 4:16 a.m.

"Aunt Herma?" I ask dryly.

She ignores me, pretending to be so engulfed in her own world that she doesn't notice she's woken us up. She sprays the dresser with a concoction in a bottle and begins to wipe.

"Aunt Herma!" I yell over the radio. My voice is strained and brimming with frustration. She finally looks at me, shocked that I've raised my voice.

"Did you say something?" she asks condescendingly.

"Yes. What's going on?"

She proceeds to mop, taking a moment before she answers my question. "I have a lot of cleaning to get done. My life doesn't just stop because you two are taking up space."

Her comment stings, but I bite my lip to remain passive.

There's no way in hell I'm imagining her contempt.

"Comfort Hall doesn't revolve around you two coming to town," she mumbles. "I don't know what kind of nasty habits uno gwan wit ah foreign, but here, I keep my space clean."

"But it's so early," Mia whines.

Aunt Herma says nothing and proceeds to move the dresser away from the wall. Then she takes out a rag and begins to meticulously wipe behind it.

"Aunt Herma . . . It's only 4:16 a.m.," I plead.

"No time like the present."

Venomous words rise up, but I swallow them.

"We're trying to sleep," I say, my heart racing fast.

She stops wiping and looks to me, holding my gaze. "And I'm trying to *clean*," she says sharply. "If you're not going to help, why don't you two princesses just put your head back on the pillow?"

She moves to the radio and turns it up louder than before. Then she proceeds to clean everything in her line of sight. I slam my head back down, fighting back tears of frustration as I use my pillow to drown out the noise.

Why does she hate us so much?

I search myself for the courage to stand up to her, but the thought only fills me with dread. Saying something will only further fuel her idea that I am an entitled, spoiled brat who doesn't deserve to be here.

So the words stay buried in me.

Two hours pass by as Aunt Herma repeatedly smacks the mop on the floor, running it aggressively along the tiles until the smell of bleach douses the room. When she grows tired of organizing and reorganizing, she turns off the radio and drags the bucket and mop into the hallway before slamming the door shut behind her. I look to the clock: 6:14 a.m. I take the pillow from atop my head and exhale.

Finally.

My eyes begin to flutter shut, eager to finally get back to sleep. My body starts to grow heavy with exhaustion, and I feel myself slipping back into my rest.

Cock-a-doodle-doo!

"Ughhhhh!" Mia groans as she buries herself deeper into the sheets. I shove my head into the pillow, trying not to lose my mind. The sleep has been completely wiped out of me. I throw the sheets off and sit up.

"Mi?"

"Mmm?"

"I'm going to the kitchen. Want anything?"

"Just sleep."

I yawn, sleepily dragging myself down the hall. I walk across the freshly shined floors and head into the kitchen, where Andre stands over the gas stove, boiling a pot of water.

"Hey, Andre."

"Mawnin', Miss Canada." He beams.

I cringe. "Can you not call me that?"

"Wha you mean? Ah nuh Canada yuh come from?"

I pause. "Sorry. Yeah, I just—" I immediately feel guilty for projecting my annoyance. "I don't know. You don't hear me calling you *Mr. Jamaica*, I guess."

He kisses his teeth, but he can't help but laugh. "Yuh know me jus ah romp wit yuh. Yuh want some coffee? It come straight from di tree out ah door."

"Sure." I let it go as he guides me out back. He roasts the beans in a pot on top of a firepit, and I let the sweet smell of burning wood and coffee fill my lungs.

"So you're the reason it always smells so good out here," I say.

"It smell nice, nuh true?"

The dawn of morning smells sweet as ever. The air is moist and dewy from the rainfall last night, and birds sing to each other as they fly over our heads. It becomes clear that nothing compares to the birth of a new day on a crisp Jamaican morning. I watch as Andre pours the boiling water into the pot and strains the beans with cloth, cooling the mixture before handing it to me.

"See it deh."

I take a sip of it, and it's divine. It instantly wakes me up. "It's incredible."

"Nuh must." He smiles.

"Nuh must?"

"It mean like, 'of course.'" He laughs. "So wha gwan wit you dis mawnin'? Yuh nuh usually up so early. Mista Binky ah terrorize yuh?"

"More like Aunt Herma." I roll my eyes as I take a seat next to him on an old milk crate. "She came in the room and started cleaning at four o'clock this morning. Singing and making a bunch of noise."

"Ah so Herma stay."

"So she's always like this?"

"It depends. She have her moments. But she nuh always so bad."

"Right," I say sarcastically. "It seems like she's been stuck in that house way too long. She's so miserable."

Andre laughs. "She never always used fi live here, yuh nuh. She's di oldest, so she was di first fi leave yawd."

"Herma moved out?" I ask, surprised. "To where?"

"Kingston. She used to work as a seamstress up a town. She was good, too. Had a whole heap of people lining up to have her mek dem clothes."

"Well, she couldn't have been that good if she had to move back," I mumble. I regret it instantly. "Sorry, I . . . I didn't mean it like that."

"Iz all right." He strains the rest of the pot. "It was actually Mass Tyson that cause her fi come back."

"My dad?"

"Yeah, mon. When Mass Tyson decide fi move go ah foreign, Aunt Herma had to move back to country fi tek care of Mama and Papa and mind di house."

"*Seriously?*"

"Yeah. Uncle Junior was di youngest at di time, so he couldn't do it. And Mummy couldn't manage everyting alone. So Mass Tyson ask Aunt Herma fi come back."

"Wait . . . so she moved *back* to the country so my dad could move to Canada?"

"Pretty much."

Guilt seeps over me. Suddenly, Herma's behavior starts to make sense.

"She neva really talk bout it," Andre continues. "Now she jus mek clothes fi people inna di community. School uniform and ting. But me know say it still badda her."

"I had no idea."

"Ah nuh your fault. Yuh weren't even born."

"I doubt she sees it that way."

I take another sip of the coffee and look out at the forestry to distract my thoughts. On each side of the house sit two enormous mountains covered in bushes from top to bottom.

"You ever go up there?"

Andre looks up from the fire, placing the pots on the ground beside him. "Bush?"

"Yeah. Up the mountains."

"All di time."

"Really? How do you even make it up there? It's so high, and it's all trees."

"You haffi use a machete. Chop yuh way through."

"Wow." I admire his confidence. "That seems so scary."

"Yuh cyan 'fraid ah where yuh come from."

"Oh, so *now* I come from Jamaica?" I tease him. "I thought I was 'Miss Canada.'"

"Yuh know wha me mean. Yuh may born ah foreign, but Jamaica yuh come from."

"You're so poetic." I laugh.

"Real ting. You should come wit us today. We ah go ah river."

"Who's 'we'?"

"Dane invited a whole heap ah we. Diana neva tell you?"

I shake my head and take another sip of my coffee.

"Maybe she forget." Andre shrugs. "A bunch of we ah go. We leave before noon."

"Okay. I'm in." I turn to head back inside. "I'll see you later."

A smirk grows on Andre's face. "Word of advice," he calls. "Yuh cyan say tings like 'see you later' and nuh except people fi call yuh Kyan-ah-da."

"What am I supposed to say?"

"Likkle more, mon."

"Likkle more, mon?"

"Lawd." Andre laughs. "We really haffi work pon yuh Patois."

I head back inside to brush my teeth and get ready for the day. I change into a yellow summer dress before making my way around to the front veranda. A thick mist sits over the grass as I make my way down the steps and into the front yard. The sky glows a warm pink as the sun rises over the land. Despite being wet, the grass warms the soles of my feet. I take a few steps out and head over to the rock that Andre and I sat on the other day.

"Tilla!" a voice calls out to me. I jump, turning my head to the side of the yard. There, passing by the bushed fence, is Hessan.

"Oh, hi," I say, taken off guard.

"Sorry. Me neva mean fi startle you."

"Oh, no—it's fine," I say as I stumble my way over. He carries a shovel and rake on his back, and he watches me with the same fascination as yesterday. He smiles as I get closer.

"Wha you ah do up so early?" he asks.

"Couldn't really sleep." I offer a faint smile. He nods, saying nothing—but his stare says it all. His eyes twinkle as he studies me for a second too long. I feel myself growing anxious.

"What?" I blush.

"Nothing . . . just—" He stops himself. "Yuh look good. In that dress. Wit di sunrise behind you and everyting. Kinda like a picture."

A smile shoots through my entire body. I turn to look at the sunrise in an attempt to hide it. "Oh. Thanks." I nod.

"You picked a good hour to be awake," he continues. "Mawnin's are di best time in country."

"I keep hearing that." I turn back to face him. "Are you usually up so early?"

"Yeah, me haffi look after di farm. Rain fall last night, so me haffi turn di soil."

"You do that every time it rains?"

"Yeah . . . and I'll be doing it a lot more with di storm comin' soon. Jamaica's supposed to get a lot of rain dis summer." He shifts, adjusting the shovel on his back. "I should probably get

going. But I'm glad I took di long way today. It waz really nice
fi see you, Tilla."

He studies me one final time, giving a gentle smile before
he turns to go. And then, as if by no doing of my own, a surge
of courage shoots through me.

"Wait," I call after him.

He spins back around, and we lock eyes.

"Can I come?"

A smile spreads across his face.

Five minutes later, we've ventured through a swarm of
bushes and onto a back road. Wild chickens nestle on the side
of it, and a few stray dogs wander aimlessly. I trail behind
Hessan as we make our way down a path that leads to a dirt
clearing. Soon, we reach a big field covered in crops and rich
vegetation.

"This is it," Hessan says proudly.

Rows of organized dirt span for miles. He steps out onto
the plot of land as I look around at all the greenery. As impressive as it is, a wave of annoyance passes through me.

How could my dad not mention this?

"We mainly plant provisions," Hessan says, snapping me
out of my thoughts. "But last year, Mass Tyson wanted to start
growin' moringa bush, so we do that as well."

"What do you do with all of it?"

"It's mainly fi up ah yawd. But he'll give yam and cassava to
di people inna di community who cyan afford it."

"He gives it away for *free*?"

"Fi di most part."

"Wow." I take it all in as I run my fingers along a fruitful
moringa tree. "And you've grown all this?"

"Pretty much. Mass Tyson nuh really come ah country
much, so him pay me fi manage it when him deh ah foreign."

"How long have you . . . worked for him?"

"About three years now."

His answer takes me by surprise. I watch in silence as he takes up his tools and rakes the soil back and forth. There's a distinct rhythm to his movements. I fall into a trance watching him guide each stroke with intention. His body is strong, and with every motion, his muscles grow even more pronounced.

"Yuh all right?" He glances at me, a knowing look on his face.

"Oh. Yeah, sorry." I blush. "I've just never really seen anyone plant crops before. Like that."

He smiles. "Mass Tyson neva teach you?"

"No. I didn't even know that he owned a farm. But I guess there's a lot I don't know . . . you know, about him."

"Well, you have di whole summa fi learn." Hessan smiles. "It's not too strange he never mentioned it." He gestures to the soil. "Farming is a regular ting round yesso. It's how we eat here in country. We live off di land fi di most part."

"Oh." I nod, feeling ignorant.

He pauses from raking before locking eyes with mine. His eyes are so kind, and they pierce through mine. "Your father's a great man, Tilla. A lot of folks would probably go hungry if it wasn't fi him. You should be proud."

I smile, eager to change the subject. "Did you always want to be a farmer?"

"Not always. When I was young, I neva knew what I wanted to do with my life. And when yuh poor, it's easy fi get caught up doin' stupid tings." He slowly rakes the soil. "My cousin was into di whole bad-bwoy lifestyle, and I got caught up hangin' round him. Caught up in foolishness. When my mom died, I realized I didn't want that for myself. I wanted my passion to be something different."

"When did you know that was farming?"

"Yuh ask a lot questions." He laughs.

"Oh," I blush. "Sorry, I—"

"I like it. Yuh have a curious mind. Yuh like to learn." I divert his gaze as he continues to rake. "I fell in love with it when I was around fifteen. I moved to Saint Ann's for a bit when I was younger, and when I moved back to country, I started to plant banana trees up ah Miss Addie yawd. I guess it just kinda stuck from there."

I listen intently as he bends down and begins to dig a small hole with his hands.

"There was something about working with di earth—feeling it—that connected me to someting bigger." He turns to me. "Come here," he says softly.

His request takes me by surprise. My heart starts to beat a little faster as I slowly make my way over to him. He gazes up at me as I bend down by his side.

"Let me show you someting." He moves his hands toward mine, placing them on top. A tingle runs through me as he guides our hands toward the dirt.

His touch feels so *warm*.

"Di only way fi understand di land is to experience it. *Feel it*. Become one with it." My entire body pulses as our eyes lock together. His hazel eyes glimmer.

"Do you want to feel it, Tilla?" he whispers.

I couldn't look away if I tried. I nod, and in a swift motion, he places my hands into the moist soil, softly rubbing them into the ground. He grips my palms, massaging them with a firm grip before locking his fingers into mine.

"Jamaican soil is full of all di nutrients you could imagine. It could grow anyting. Give *anyting* life." He softly grazes my hands, and my stomach ties into knots as he lets go. He begins to dig beside me as our fingers meet in the soil. His eyes search mine as the morning sun begins to take its place in the sky. I start to feel exposed, as if the daylight is revealing all of me, all at once. "How does it feel?" he asks, gesturing to the soil.

I'm locked into his gaze as my hands comb through the dirt. The answer is clear:

"Alive," I whisper.

He smiles, taking in my words.

"It's my favorite part about it. There's something so beautiful about watching something grow. From a seed into . . . a life. When I'm out here . . . I feel so connected, yuh nuh? A part of it all."

"Yeah," I say quietly. "I get that."

"Here." He reaches into his pocket and pulls out a handful of peculiar-looking seeds, before gently taking my hand and placing them inside my palm. "Moringa seeds. 'The tree of life,' dem call it."

I carefully place the seeds into the hole, and we begin to cover over it with the dirt, patting it down gently once we've finished. The dew of the morning has been replaced by the hot sun, and people start to walk along the roads behind us.

"I . . . I should probably get back," I say as I dust off my hands. "Before they start to wonder where I am."

He watches me intently as I stand up.

"Thank you . . . for showing me the farm."

"Of course." He smiles softly. "Anytime. Yuh ah go ah river dis afternoon?"

"Oh, yeah. Andre invited me earlier."

"I guess I'll see you later, then." He smiles. "Yuh sure yuh can get back okay?"

"Yeah. I should be good."

"All right." His eyes sparkle as he watches me. "Later, Tilla."

"See you." I try to fight back a giddy smile as I wave good-bye. With that, I turn around and make my way back up the road.

By the time I get in, most everyone is awake and busying around the house. With it still being early, no one seems to have noticed my absence. I head into the shower to get ready for the day, and around eleven o'clock, everyone meets outback to head down to the river.

Mia and I step out through the back doors to find Andre, Dane, Richie, Kenny, Diana, Zory, and a few other kids from the neighborhood saddled up and ready to go. Unlike Mia and me, who carry our clothes in backpacks, everyone else carries their clothes in their hands or tied to walking sticks. A few of the boys wrap their towels around their heads and shove their changes of clothes into their small pockets. I immediately look at my pink backpack and start to feel insecure. It's cheap, but it screams privilege. I look down at my sparkly flip-flops as some of the kids stand barefoot.

Shit.

"Princess!" Richie calls out. I want to crawl from my own skin. To them, it doesn't matter that it's from Walmart. It doesn't matter that that's all my mom could afford. When they look at Mia and me, all they see is money, privilege, new clothes, and shiny shoes.

"Ca-ca!" Richie laughs. "We just ah go ah river, Tilla. Yuh nuh need fi wear designer."

"It's not design—" I stop myself. There's no use. I make my way over to Andre, my defenses up. Dane turns and spots us as we move through the group of kids.

"Ladiez! Welcome, welcome!" he announces dramatically. I stifle a grin at his faux British accent. "I'm so happy you could join us on Dane's Manchester Excursionz. It's not every day we have two foreign girls joining us on di journey."

"So wha we ah wait pon?!" Andre asks impatiently.

"Patience is a virtue, Andre," Dane scolds. "We haffi go over some rules."

"Rules?" Zory rolls her eyes. "Me nuh inna dat—"

"LADIEZ AND GENKLE-MON!" he cuts her off. "Today, we have two very special guests joining us. They're foreigners, so we haffi mek sure say dem nuh drown." He turns to Mia and me. "This is no suburban swimming pool in the comfort of Kyan-ah-da. We are headed to the rough, rugged jungles of Jamaica! The harsh rapids of the unforgiving river."

Diana kisses her teeth. "You're so full a shit."

"Diana! Please do not challenge me in front of foreign company," Dane scolds. "These are mandatory safety precautions."

"It's okay, Dane," I interject, trying to divert the attention off us. "Mia and I know how to swim."

"Swim?!" Dane whips his head around. "Ha! Dis is not about whether yuh can *swim*. Di question is, can you *survive* the deadly waters of *Jamaica*?!"

My efforts backfire as all eyes fall on me.

"I'm a level-four swimmer," Mia chimes in.

"Bumba!" Richie lets out an obnoxious laugh. "Level four!"

Dane takes a step toward Mia. "Level four?" he asks, his voice becoming serious. "Yuh ever hear the story of Jimmy Lee?"

"No." Mia rolls her eyes.

"Hmm. He was a *foreigna*. Level four just like you. Him come fi di summer to visit him grandmada, Miss Delta. She lives right up desso." He points his long finger to the top of the giant, bushy mountain. The young kids in the group are silent, hanging on to his every word. "Well, one day, Jimmy Lee couldn't tek di Jamaican heat, so he went for a swim down ah river. He told Miss Delta he would be back before sundown . . . but he was *never to be seen again*. Some people say di river swallowed him alive. Others say shark tear off him leg—"

"A shark?" Mia raises her eyebrow. "In the river?"

"Yeah, mon. Bush mon find him body and roast him fi dinna. Ate him with breadfruit and a side ah fish—"

"Jesus Christ," Diana interrupts, her eyes rolling to the back of her head. "Dane, yuh too lie. Miss Delta nuh have no grandson."

"Diana!" Dane breaks character, frustrated. "Hush up nuh, mon! Cha. You are so hostile." He turns his attention back to us. "Now, everyone single file!" We form a straight line, following Dane's orders. "Stay close and follow back ah me!"

We make our way through the forest and down to the back road. I walk in front of Richie, who carries Mia on his back.

"Yow!" he calls to me. "How yuh gwan so boasie? Somebody can go ah river wit pink backpack?"

"Boasie?"

"Boasty. Stocious. Stuck up. Like yuh better den everyone else. Yuh come ah country wit all yuh nice tings and expect we nuffi say nuttin. Ah wear gold chain round ya neck. Just ah flaunt it inna we face."

I roll my eyes before running ahead, tucking my butterfly necklace into my shirt. There's no point trying to explain myself to Richie. I decide to take my chances and fall in line with Diana and Zory.

"Hey," I say, catching up to them.

"Canada. Wha'ppen?" Zory smiles. "We was just talkin' about wha happen when I got home yesterday. Mummy gave me licks fi every goat left over. Five licks in total."

"Licks?"

"Beats. Buss up me backside."

"I tried to tell her she got lucky." Diana smirks.

"Tell that to me batty. Me still cyan walk straight."

"I'm sorry, Zory. That sucks," I say. "Does everyone usually get beatings? Like, when you do something wrong?"

"Not really. Only di pickney dem get lick."

"And Andre." Diana giggles.

"Andre? Why?" I ask.

"Me nuh know." Diana shrugs. "Yuh haffi ask him. Why yuh tink, Zo?"

"'Cause Andre gwan stupid sometimes." Zory laughs. "Always deh out ah door ah go pon some kind of adventure. Out inna di sun ah get black till him ugly."

"Black till him ugly?" I ask. "What's that mean?"

"It means he's always getting darker." Diana laughs. "He's always outside getting up to some kind of trouble and getting darker by the minute. Getting *black* until he's ugly."

Shock floods my face. For a second I can't believe what I just heard. Their words make me so uncomfortable that I start to overheat. "Wait, what?" I blurt out. "How can you say that?"

"Chill out, Til," Zory says between laughter. "Romp we ah romp."

I feel a bead of sweat run down my back. *How can they say something so terrible? How can they just make fun of Andre's skin color like that?* I desperately want to stand up for him. But the truth is, I'm hesitant to say the wrong thing that would give them another reason to not like me. They laugh and speak fast in Patois, and this time, instead of trying to keep up, I tune out.

We continue trekking down abandoned roads, passing through seemingly deserted towns. We continue walking for two hours, but I don't dare say a word that would fuel their princess narrative. Soon, we approach a steep hill, and we all begin to pull our way up.

"WELCOME TO DI RIV-AH!" Dane announces dramatically as we reach the top. His chest is proud as he flings his arms wide to reveal the scene.

My heart nearly skips a beat.

Down at the bottom, surrounded by a lush green jungle, is the most *beautiful* waterfall I have ever laid eyes on. A grandiose current of fresh, crisp spring water cascades down mountains of rocks, pouring into the river to create its own private tropical paradise. The view is *majestic,* and sprawled throughout the stream are gorgeous hues of black and brown bodies. Joy rings through the air, and it's clear that if Jamaica is paradise, the river is the center of the magic.

The kids begin to run down the hill, stripping out of their clothes and plunging into the secluded oasis to escape the heat. Dane drops his walking stick and sprints toward the water as the rest of us follow. I claim a spot on top of a giant rock, placing my things next to Diana's and Zory's as we change into our swimsuits.

"Yow!" a deep voice calls out. I turn around to see Hessan and another guy jogging toward the group. Gorgeous as ever, he flashes a charming smile. "Sorry we late."

My stomach flutters as he greets the group. He smiles when he spots me.

"Tilla."

"Hey."

"Well, look who decide fi show up," Zory interjects. "I thought your big head wasn't coming."

"And miss di chance fi see *you*?" He laughs. "I'd be a foolish man."

Zory makes a face. Hessan looks to Diana.

"Miss Diana. Wha gwan?"

"Nuttin." She smiles, a coyness to her. "'Fraid of a likkle wata?"

"Neva."

"All right, all right," Dane interrupts the chatter. "Now, every foreigna gets a chaperone. Richie, you tek Mia. Hessan, you keep an eye pon Tilla."

"Cool." Hessan nods.

He looks at me, and I immediately look away, flustered. I feel myself grow nervous under his gaze. Everyone starts to disperse, and just as Hessan turns to go, Diana calls out to him.

"Hessan! Can you rub this on fi me?" She holds up a small bottle of sunscreen.

"Sure." He makes his way back over to us and takes the bottle from Diana's hands.

"Since when yuh start wear sunscreen?" Zory laughs.

"They wear it all the time in town." Diana smiles coyly. "I don't want to get burned."

"Where yuh want it?" Hessan asks.

She lifts her braids to reveal the bare back of her pink halter bikini. "Right there." She smiles. "Please. And mek sure yuh rub it in good."

I watch as he spreads the sunscreen across her back, massaging it in with his hands. I start to heat up as thoughts of this morning come back to me. I can't help but feel envious. Hessan glimpses up at me and smiles to himself.

Shit.

I look away, kicking myself. I try my best to act casually as I head down into the shallow part of the water.

"Stay close to your chaperones!" Dane calls out before doing a backflip into the deep end of the water. The sun scorches from above with not a cloud in the sky to protect us from its rays. I walk out into the water until I'm knee-deep, and my entire body cools down. I take a deep breath and plunge in headfirst, using my arms as wings to propel me deeper. The cool water engulfs me, and for a brief moment, everything goes silent. I can feel the beating pulse of the land. The vibration of the ripples in the water. I can feel everything that came together to create this moment.

To create *me*.

Running out of breath, I gasp for air as my head bursts through the surface.

"Tilla!" I hear a voice call out.

I whip my head around to find Andre calling to me from the rocks. Mia and Kenny collect stones at the shore next to him.

"Come nuh! Me wan show yuh something!" He gestures enthusiastically to the top of the waterfall. I smile, catching my breath as I swim over to where he stands. He extends his hand, hoisting me out of the water.

"Wait till yuh see dis!" His excitement makes it clear that it's not optional.

"Can we come?!" Mia calls.

"Dis ah nuh fi pickney!" he yells back before grabbing my hand and guiding me up the mountain of rocks. The hot stones burn the soles of my feet.

"Where are we going?" I grimace as I trail behind him.

"To di top of di waterfall! Get ready fi climb." And with that, he zips off farther up the rocks. "Andre!" I yell out as I trudge up the rocks behind him. I turn around to see how far I've come, and I'm surprised to see the brown bodies have turned to little specks below me—there's no turning back now. I continue up the side of the waterfall, tightly gripping the rocks to keep from falling. My heart is in my throat, but I'm careful not to look down. As I approach the top, the surface evens out and becomes a flat landing. I hoist myself up on top, and to my displeasure, the rocks have now become slippery. Andre grabs my hand, helping me stand up.

"Walk careful. Me nuh wan yuh fi drop."

"Andre, I swear to God—"

My adrenaline starts to pump, and a jolt of electricity rushes through my body. *I'm so high up.* I can't help the smile that bursts across my face.

"Concentrate. Watch ya step," Andre directs. He holds my hand, guiding me across the slippery rocks to a small, circular opening filled with water that sits at the top of the falls. He lets go of my hand and takes a step inside the pool of water before taking a seat in between two big rocks.

"Andre, are you fucking insane?!" It pours out of me in disbelief.

A deep sense of urgency and excitement rushes through me as I laugh in shock at the danger of what he's doing. He faces forward, turning his back to the thrashing waterfall that blasts him from behind. His entire face lights up as he clings to the rocks for dear life.

"It feel nice!" he screams before reaching his hand out for me to join him.

"No way in hell!" I yell, laughter stumbling out of my mouth. I grab a vine from a tree that hangs low beside me to steady myself. "Hell no!"

"Come nuh! How you ah go manage hurricane if yuh cyan manage a likkle wata?!"

"I'm not doing it, Andre!"

"Come nuh, Tilla!" He kisses his teeth.

"I can't!" I yell between rumbling laughter. I grin so wide my face hurts. Water from the rapid falls splashes into my eyes and mouth, blinding me every few seconds. I feel woozy. Drunk with adrenaline.

"I'm gunna turn around!" I yell out. "This was a mistake!"

"Nuttin nuh go so! God nuh mek mistake!"

A flare of goose bumps floods the surface of my skin.

"Do yuh trust me?!"

"No!"

"Do yuh trust yuhself?!"

Pure euphoria pumps through my veins. I look back at the slippery rocks we climbed up, anxiety speeding through me as I search for an ounce of courage. I take a deep breath, fear and laughter consuming me. I don't know what it is, but something tells me to walk toward him. I release the vine, carefully placing one foot in front of the other as I make my way over to Andre's extended hand. I can barely see my steps. My heart races, knowing that it would only take one wrong move to fall to my death.

Focus, Tilla.

Giving it all I have, I reach his hand and grab on to it for dear life. I steady my breathing before taking a seat beside him, perching my feet on a rock in front of me to keep from sliding. The water thrashes against my back, pushing me forward as I squeeze Andre's hand tighter. I look down to find Mia and Kenny hooting and hollering as they cheer us on. No one else notices that Andre and I could be inches away from our own deaths. I search the crowd for Hessan, and of all the eyes down there, his are the only other ones glued to me as he watches in amusement.

My chaperone.

I take a deep breath, soaking in the view. The green trees weave around the river like a sacred dance. Birds call to each other from across the water, singing sweet songs of irie that pierce through the sky. It is a magical jungle *wonderland*. Tears of joy instantly well up behind my eyes as I silently give thanks for the grace that I am witnessing. The nirvana that runs through me.

"Well? Wha yuh tink?"

"It's fucking stunning, Andre."

"It pretty, nuh true?!"

I laugh. "Gorgeous."

A permanent grin is plastered across his face. "Welcome to

Paradize." He exaggerates a nonexistent *z*, and I almost burst. My heart is *so* full.

This is where I come from.

I am born of these mountains and trees.

Of this calming water and sky.

"Yuh ready?" Andre asks.

"For what?"

"Fi jump."

"WHAT?!" I yell. My heart drops to my stomach. "Andre. Stop."

"How yuh expect fi get down?"

I look at him, speechless.

"Come nuh. Me do it all di time."

"Andre," I say between my teeth. "No fucking way."

"It's too slippery fi go down pon di rocks. We haffi jump."

I almost have an anxiety attack as my tears of adrenaline turn to dread.

"It's not deep enough!"

"Yuh tink me woulda kill yuh off when yuh come all di way from foreign? Come." He takes my hand. "Nuh badda tink bout it."

I stare down at the bottom of the waterfall, contemplating what feels like a decision between life or death. I watch as the water pours from above, crashing into itself like an eruption before dissipating into the calm stream.

Terror consumes me.

"Tilla," Andre interjects. "Me nah guh let nuttin happen to you. God know."

With that, he grabs my hand, and we stand up. My body shakes, and I think I might collapse before I even get a chance to jump. Andre smiles wide, and we walk to the edge of the fall as the water pushes us forward. Before I have a chance to look down, Andre squeezes my hand tighter. "Yuh can do it," he says, the innocence of a boy seeking adventure all over his face. A boy seeking the finest thrills that life has to offer. "One . . . two . . ."

Before I can object, we are flying off the rocks and through the sky.

I am a bird.

Soaring. Free. Whole.

My heart flies out of my chest, stopping for what feels like an eternity. I scream for my life as gravity takes over, and I plunge feetfirst into the clear water below.

I am submerged.

I kick my arms and legs around and squeeze my eyes tightly. I can't feel Andre anymore, and I fight to find the surface. After about five seconds too long, I find the sunlight, and I use all my might to burst through the water.

Before I can even process the magnitude of what just happened, Andre has come up for air, we have taken our first breaths, and we are laughing our heads off. Everyone looks on from around us, cheering us on and yelling our praises. They hoot and holler, clapping at the audacity of what we just did. Andre grabs me in the biggest hug as we bob up and down in hysterics.

"I can't believe I just did that!" I choke. "That was insane!"

"Me tell yuh me nah let nuttin happen to you!" He beams, squeezing me tighter. We fight to catch our breath before swimming to the shore.

"Ca-ca rawtid! Canada turn country gyal!" Zory calls from the other side.

Euphoria consumes me as tears of joy fill my eyes. They are impressed, and for once, it feels good. For once, I don't have to prove myself. I just jumped off the most dangerous cliff into the riverbed of Jamaica in a forest in the middle of nowhere.

What can they really say now?

I laugh, confidence shooting through my veins.

6

"Brownin'."

I laugh out loud by accident. I lie on my towel with my eyes closed as the warm sun dries me off. I open my eyes to lock them with Hessan's hazel ones as he stands over me.

"What does that mean?"

"Your brown skin."

"What about it?"

"It's so beautiful. It's the first thing I noticed about you."

My stomach ties into knots. "My skin?" I blush.

"The way the sun wraps around you." It rolls off his tongue so casually that I actually believe him. I squirm, biting down on my lip to stop from giving myself away. He takes a seat beside me.

"Everyone seems to have a nickname for me around here."

"It's a country ting. Everyone has an alias."

"Yeah, well, I seem to have quite a few." I smile. "What's yours?"

"I don't have one." He laughs, revealing that gentle smile. "Just Hessan."

"Liar."

"Real ting."

"So why don't I believe you?" I laugh, challenging him. I think I see him blush.

"All right, fine. Dem call me *red bwoy*."

"Red boy?"

"It's stupid. Dem call me red 'cause I'm light skin. Light-skin people burn in di sun. Turn red."

"You don't look red to me." I look away from him. "Your skin glows a warm . . . golden color. It's the first thing I noticed about you," I say boldly, borrowing his line.

He smiles and looks out to the river. "So, first time ah river and you ah jump waterfall? I didn't know you had it in you."

"Neither did I." I smile. "But in my defense, it was against my will."

"Something tells me they won't be calling you *foreigna* anymore."

I smile. I feel the adrenaline from earlier move through me.

"So, tell me, Tilla . . . How yuh liking Jamaica so far?"

"I like it. It's good."

"Good?"

"Yeah."

He looks at me, amused.

"What?" I ask.

"That's all?"

"Yeah. It's nice."

"Now me know say ah lie yuh ah tell." He laughs.

"Do you want my honest opinion or my rehearsed one?"

"Honest." He gazes at me. "Me always want di truth."

I think for a moment. "It's stunning. Majestic. It makes me feel beautiful. And alive."

"But?"

"But for some reason . . . I don't feel like the people quite match the island. They can be so . . . hard. Blunt. Judgmental. A little mean."

He nods.

"Sorry, I—"

"Don't be sorry." He locks eyes with mine. "I understand."

I pull at a coil in front of my face, tucking it behind my ear. "So I'm not crazy?"

"Not at all. Country people can be tough. But ah nuh dem fault . . . There's just a lot of old-time thinking. I think it's what makes the island so special."

"Richie's sarcasm?" I ask, faux perplexed. He blurts out an unexpected laugh, and it makes me feel really good. I smile to myself.

"No," he says. "Di contrast. Di people to di land. Jamaica is an island of survivors, yuh nuh. We came here by slavery, but our ancestors were rebels. Warriors. Revolutionaries." I contemplate his words, meeting his gaze as he continues, "Jamaicans were di slaves that freed themselves. They're born tough. They've had to be. We been through a lot."

I nod. "I never thought about it like that."

"Jamaica is paradise, Tilla," he continues. "But when you're stuck in paradise and it don't always feel like paradise inside ah ya heart . . . it can be hard. A lot of we are poor. Some ah we nuh know where our next meal ah go come from. And then yuh hear all dese amazin' tings about Jamaica havin' di best beaches and tourism." His eyes meet mine. "Tilla, dese pickney neva seen a beach inna dem life. They live in poverty."

A pang of guilt rushes through me.

"Dem nuh hate you, Tilla. Dem hate dat they'll never have di life you have. All a dese people here love you. When we heard you and Mia were comin' to country, it was all anyone could talk about fi weeks."

"Right," I say sarcastically.

"Real ting." He looks at me. "Dem never meet anyone who live so different from dem. But true dem nuh really feel worthy . . . dem nuh know how fi act around you."

"I guess sometimes it just feels . . . personal."

His eyes are gentle as he takes his hand and subtly brushes mine, locking our index fingers for a brief second. Goose bumps cover my skin before he lets go. His energy has a *hold on me*. It takes everything in me not to grab his hand and squeeze it back for a little while longer.

"Yuh soon find ya place, Tilla."

It sounds like a promise.

I look out to the water as Dane, Richie, and a few of the others start to soap up their rags, scrubbing their bodies before rinsing off under the falls.

"It's so cool that you can bathe here," I say.

"You can do everything here. Catch water, cook, clean. Fi a lot of di pickney dem, dis ah di only place dem can have a bath."

"Oh." I silently kick myself. "Sorry. I didn't know."

I feel self-conscious, ashamed for being so wide-eyed about their hygiene practices, as if it were *so cool* to not have a shower at home.

"You should never apologize for what you don't know."

"Sometimes I just feel so stupid." I watch as clumps of suds flow down the stream. "Like I'm marveling at a life I'll never fully understand."

"What's wrong with dat?" he asks, genuine. "And until yuh bathe in it, how would you know nuttin cleans you like river water?"

He stares into my eyes similar to the first day he met me— curious, kind, and filled with compassion. "Bathing in di river is a pretty regular ting. Especially after hurricane season. After it passes through . . ." He pauses, his jawline going tight. "After it passes through, there's no water. So we cyan really bathe ah we yawd."

"It's that bad?"

"Of course. Yuh neva experience a hurricane?"

I shake my head.

"Mass Tyson neva tell you?"

"He hasn't really said much about it. To us, at least."

"Tilla . . . Storm season usually mash up Jamaica. Some year, it nuh so bad, some year . . . Some year, it *destroy* di island."

An eerie feeling consumes me. "What about this year?"

"Only God know."

A chill runs down my spine as I process his words. Just as I feel my heart start to race, we lock eyes. My stomach flutters, and the fear begins to subside. He has a way of staring for a second too long, like he's trying to make sense of all of me, all at once.

I feel my body getting hot.

"Come wit me."

"Uh-uh." I smile. "No more surprises."

"No more watafalls. I promise." He stands up, and I do the same, following him down the side of the river and away from the group.

When we're out of sight, he takes my hand and holds it tightly. This time, he doesn't let go. My stomach does flip-flops as he guides me through the bushes and down the stream until we reach a more secluded part of the river. The air is quiet, and the laughter and screams from the other side begin to drown out. Across the water, a small waterfall pours delicately into the stream.

"I thought you said no more waterfalls," I say coyly.

"I meant no more *jumpin' watafalls*." He smiles. "I thought you would make an exception." He places his bag on a stone and takes out a rag and a white soap bar.

"So you lied?" I ask playfully.

"Only when it involves a beautiful foreign girl." He laughs. "Besides, I'm your chaperone. Yuh haffi do what I say."

Excitement explodes through my body.

He takes my hand again and guides me into the warm water

until we've reached the waterfall and we're waist deep. Small, colorful fish dance around us as they make their way downstream. Hessan swims out to the bottom of the delicate fall and sticks his rag and soap bar underneath the water.

"What are you doing?" I laugh.

He looks me in my eyes, studying me from afar as he lathers his rag.

"Come here," he says sweetly. He stares at me, not breaking eye contact for a second. My heart beats faster, growing heavy in my chest as I slowly make my way over to him. He studies me as I approach.

"You're so beautiful." His eyes twinkle underneath the sun. I'm speechless.

He uses his hand to pull me toward him. Our bodies are so close together that my breath stops in my throat. He takes the wet rag from under the waterfall and softly begins to wipe the corners of my face. The sound of the water melting into the stream takes over as birds sing faintly in the trees.

Breathe, Tilla.

Hessan's hazel eyes hold my gaze. I am in a trance, and I don't dare look away. His touch is so soft, but everything about his energy commands me. He gently grazes my cheek, but his touch is so intense that I feel him in the tips of my fingers.

My body is *pulsing* for him.

"What are you doing?" I whisper.

He glides the rag along my cheekbone.

"I want to show you how clean river water can get you."

Fuck.

My entire body vibrates, drawing me in closer. He takes his arm and wraps it around me, before pulling my entire body into his. Our bodies press together like magnets—my *chest* against his—and everything about him feels warm and safe. In a brief motion, he spins me around so that my back is to him, and I feel all of him pressed into me from behind. He soaps up the rag and begins gliding it against my skin. We stand under the waterfall as he gently moves the rag up and down my shoulders . . . and then my back . . . and then along my stomach. He gently traces the waist of my bathing suit bottom, and tingles shoot through my body as water from the falls speckles across the exposed parts of my skin. He's *bathing* me.

I nearly lose it.

My heartbeat quickens. Everything about Hessan is *so enticing*. I've never done something as bold as this.

I've never felt so wanted as I do right now.

He nuzzles his face into the side of my neck, gently moving my necklace before running his nose along the crevice. His hands glide down my body, and I shudder. I've never been touched like this before. *Felt* like this before. The boys back home were always shy and clumsy—but everything about Hessan's embrace feels *so* sensual.

So *right*.

I reach my hand out and wrap my fingers around his. He stays pressed into me from behind for a little while longer before spinning me back around. As we lock eyes, I nervously reach up to tuck a fallen coil back into my hair tie.

"Leave it," he says sweetly. "It's perfect."

His hazel eyes glisten as he pulls me deeper under the waterfall, rinsing the soap from my skin. Before he can finish washing me off, I put my hand on top of his.

"My turn," I whisper.

I'm surprised by my own courage. I gracefully take the rag and soap bar from his hands, rubbing them together until I create a lather. I take the rag up to his chest, gently running it along his collarbone. The suds pour down his skin and into the river.

"Turn around," I instruct.

I'm nervous that he might see right through me. That he might call my bluff and laugh at my faux confidence. But he doesn't. He listens without question, turning his back to me slowly. I bring the rag up to the base of his neck, firmly pressing down as a flare of goose bumps burst down his arm. I bite my lip to stop from smiling when I realize I've found his pleasure spot. He turns his head to look at me, a curious smile creeping up on his face.

"No peeking," I whisper.

He turns back around, and I glide the rag down to his lower back. He lets out a small laugh.

"Yah tickle me," he says, still facing forward.

"Shh." I giggle. I draw the rag to the other side, stopping when I notice an old scar. It looks deep, like a gash from something sharp, and I delicately run my fingers on top. He flinches. "Stop," he says suddenly, catching me by surprise. He whips around to face me.

"I'm sorry."

"Iz all right." He avoids my gaze, brushing off my apology. "I'm clean now, anyway."

"Oh. Okay."

My nerves turn into a wave of anxiety as he breaks away from me and begins to casually bathe himself.

I've clearly crossed a line.

I turn around, my mind racing a mile a minute, desperate for him to come back to me. But he doesn't.

He rinses off.

When he's finished, he wraps his soap bar in the rag and heads back over to me.

"Ready?" he asks casually.

I nod.

We swim back up to the shore and guide our way up the rocks. He takes a towel from his bag, pressing it against my shoulders before reaching back in to grab another one for himself.

"Hessan, I'm really sorry for doing that."

"It's fine. Nuh worry yuhself." He dries off, still avoiding my gaze.

"No. It's not. I should've asked you—"

"Iz all right, Tilla." He looks up, offering me that gentle smile. "Me already forget."

The scent of the soap bar lingers in the air between us. I search my brain for what to say next.

"Well?" he asks.

"What?"

He smiles at me with curiosity before responding. "How was your first bath in the river, country gyal?"

I blush. "It was amazing. It felt so good."

"I loved making you feel good." He stares at me.

"Thank you for . . . that. For everything."

"Don't thank me." He smiles. "River water looks good on you."

You look good on me, I think.

But I bite my tongue.

As evening sets in, the river starts to clear out, and we all begin to make our way home. We walk under the setting sun, exhausted from the long day, as we try to make it back before the dark of night that only Jamaica can bring. Dane guides us down the road, leading the group in a camp-like folk song. After a few miles, Hessan and most of the other kids say goodbye and head home.

Dane burns his walking stick with a match to light the path and guides the rest of us to the forest behind the house. When we reach the final path, he and Diana go on their way. I trail behind Andre, who walks next to his brothers, and as I watch them from behind, I can't help but notice the striking resemblance between Kenny and Richie. They're significantly lighter skinned than Andre, and there's a distinct confidence to their stride. It's almost as though they wear their complexion like a cloak of honor. I'm pulled out of my thoughts as Zory calls to me from behind.

"Tilla! Wait up!"

She quickens her pace, falling in line with me.

"Hey," I say. "How far are you from here?"

"Not too far. Me just live a likkle past yawd. Plus, me know a shortcut."

"You're brave." I smile. "It's so dark."

"Welcome to di country." She laughs. "Yuh have fun?"

"Are you kidding?" I laugh, too. "The waterfall was crazy. I've never done anything like that in my life. Nothing even close."

"Well, yuh did good, Canada. Yuh really surprised me."

"Thanks." I smile again. "I surprised myself."

We're quiet for a bit as the sound of our shoes scraping against the dirt fills the silence.

She breaks it.

"You disappeared for a while."

"Oh, yeah. I—"

"Where were you?" she asks, turning to look at me. "Diana and I were looking for you, and we couldn't find you. Yuh jus . . . vanished."

I search my brain, feeling caught. "I just swam upstream for a bit."

"Upstream?" She looks at me quizzically. "Fi forty minutes?"

"Yeah . . . Hessan was just showing me something."

"And what exactly was he *showing you*?" She raises an eyebrow. "I didn't know there was anything to see other than water."

I'm silent, unsure of how to respond. Her stare grows intense.

"Him tell yuh bout him and Diana, right?"

"Him and Diana? What do you mean?"

"Lawd, Canada. You're dumber than I thought." She rolls her eyes. "Him neva tell yuh about their arrangement?"

Confusion takes over. "What arrangement?"

"Diana and Hessan are *promised* to each other. Through di church."

I feel my entire body turn to stone.

"Their families have an arrangement. They're promised. *Betrothed*. He didn't tell you?" She laughs coldly, clearly enjoying this. "Strange. Yuh would think he would mention it in di forty minutes uno disappeared for."

"No, he . . ." I have no idea how to respond.

"Country is small, Tilla." Her tone goes cold, threatening. "Watch where yuh step. People talk." And with that, she takes off down the path toward her house.

I feel sick.

Promised? Through the church?

My mind races as my stomach drops.

How could he touch me like that?

Why would he say those things to me?

I trail behind the group as I try to calm myself down. Thoughts jumble together in my head, but before I even have a chance to process them, I notice a tall figure standing beside the back door as we approach the house. As we get closer, I realize that it's Uncle Junior. Alone in the night, he stands in a thick cloud of smoke, inhaling from a spliff. We slow our pace when he sees us. The group falls silent as we stop dead in our tracks in front of him.

"Evenin', Uncle Junior," Richie says respectfully, his tone formal.

"Evenin'," Andre and Kenny echo, nodding.

Uncle Junior blows a cloud of smoke in our direction. It instantly fills my lungs, and I hold my breath to stop myself from choking. He's quiet for a moment as he observes us, his green eyes piercing through the black of night.

"Wha uno ah do ah come in so late?" he asks, his tone hard and crass.

"We ah come from river," Kenny says mousily.

Uncle Junior stares at us, his expression cold and deadpan before taking another thick inhale of ganja. He looks me dead in my eye.

"Wha gyal pickney ah do ah road so late?"

"We all went to the river—"

"Dem did deh wit us," Andre interjects. "Me invite dem."

"Me did ah talk to yuh, bwoy?!" His eyes gloss over, ready to snap.

"No, sa." Andre looks down.

"Then shut up yuh *bloodclot* mout."

No one dares utter a word.

"Gwan inside," he demands.

The vibrato in his voice sends a chill down my spine. We waste no time and scurry to the back door. But just as Andre walks past, Uncle Junior grabs him by his face, draping him like a rag doll as Andre lets out a yelp. Richie, Kenny, and Mia rush inside, but I stand frozen. Junior squeezes Andre's jaw between his fingers as he brings his face to his, blowing a thick cloud of smoke into his eyes.

"Next time, watch ya fucking mout, bwoy," he spits. He squeezes down tighter, digging his fingernails into Andre's skin. Fear flashes through Andre's eyes like a deer in headlights, as Uncle Junior flings him onto the hard dirt. He scrambles to his feet, and we rush inside, stumbling over each other as we shut the door behind us.

"Are you okay?" I whisper to him.

His eyes water, but he says nothing, keeping a brave face.

We continue through the dark kitchen and up into the living room before heading to our rooms. Mia changes into her pajamas while I make my way down the hall to the bathroom. My head spins as I try to make sense of what just happened. Andre was the only one singled out.

He took the blow for all of us.

My mind circles back to what Diana and Zory said earlier.

Black till him ugly.

The mere thought fills me with disdain. I push it out of my mind as I turn on the tap. Just as I bend down to the sink, the door flies open, pushing me backward. I stumble, grabbing on to the sink's ledge to regain my balance. In front of me stands Aunt Herma—and she is *fuming.* Before I can even say a word, she shoves herself into the cramped bathroom and slams the door shut.

"Where di *fuck* have you been, gyal?!" Her eyes are filled with rage.

"We went to the riv—"

"Do you know what time ah night it is?!" She hovers over me. "What type of girl child walks the streets this late at night? Wha kinda *dutty business* is that?!"

"I—I didn't—"

"Yuh know what dem call gyal pickney who walk di streets so late at night?!"

My mouth opens but nothing comes out.

"Answer me!" she screams.

"I . . . I was with Andre . . . and Dane . . ."

Their names sound like whimpers leaving my mouth.

"Andre and Dane are *bwoy pickney*! What type ah *nasty gyal* business is that?! You have no *nuttin* about you. No *class.* You even have your likkle sister pon road with you. Gallivanting like some *slut*!"

I freeze.

I try to say something, but I can't. Heat shoots through my body, and that familiar lump rises to the back of my throat.

I cannot speak.

She pushes her face up in mine, so close I can feel her breath.

"What if something happened?! How would I explain it to Mass Tyson?! His likkle foreign princess come ah country and get raped off for gallivanting the streets like a *slut*!"

Everything goes muffled.

I hear nothing but that word.

"I . . . I'm sorry." Tears fall like shards of ice. I close my eyes. I pray that if I squeeze hard enough, I will wake up and realize this is all just a dream.

"Look at me when I talk to you!" she spits.

So I do.

And I am in fact awake.

She grabs my arm, and I yelp as she squeezes down tightly.

"Stop crying," she says disgustedly. "I don't know what shit you get away with back home, but you make a *sad mistake* if you think it's going to fly here." She releases my arm. "Spoiled brat." And with that, she turns to leave, slamming the door behind her.

My bare feet stand on the warm tiled floor.

In this moment, it is only me and the word she left behind. *Slut. Slut. Slut.*

It rings so loudly, it feels like my ears are on fire.

How could she say that to me? How could she spit that word at me with such force?

I stand in the middle of the bathroom, helpless, confused, and trapped. I feel ashamed. Disgusted with myself. I can't believe I put myself in this position. The way I threw myself at Hessan . . . I can't believe I gave Herma reason to justify what she believes to be true. And now I am questioning everything, including my own intentions.

Against my will, I am drinking her poison.

I start to sob. I am miles from home, in the middle of nowhere, on an island with no one to defend me. I try to calm myself down when suddenly there's a hard knock on the door. It's so forceful that it makes me jump. I hold my breath, silently praying it's not Aunt Herma coming back.

"Yes?" I say between sobs.

"Me need fi use di bathroom."

It's Uncle Junior.

"One second!" I call back, standing up from the floor. I blot my eyes before turning the door handle.

Uncle Junior stares down at me, hovering slightly too close.

"Wha yuh ah do in here so long?" The lines on his face are hard.

His eyes, empty.

"I'm sorry . . ." I try to get past him, but he moves his body to block the way.

I freeze.

"Yuh nuh hear me ah talk to you, gyal?" His gaze feels predatory.

I nod, unable to look him in the eye.

I can't go through this again.

"Wha yuh ah cry for?" he asks in the same disgusted tone as Aunt Herma.

"I fell at the river. I'm fine." I try to get past him again. He blocks me. Fear paralyzes my body. I want to scream. Yell for help. But I don't.

"Please," I whimper.

And as if on cue, he moves out of my way. I rush past him and run down the hall, back into my room. I shut the door behind me, pressing myself into it as the inevitable truth crashes over me like a ton of bricks:

There will be no fair trial.

They have decided that just by being from foreign, I am spoiled and spoon-fed. I am bad, and I need to be punished.

The princess will be put in her place.

I feel like a child all over again, reminded of all the days I waited for my father to pick me up from school. All the days he made excuses for why he was late. All the days we waited anyway. And once again, thousands of miles from home, nothing has changed.

I must wait for my father to save me.

I turn off the lights, crack the shutters, and crawl into bed next to Mia. I clutch my butterfly necklace and take a deep breath, closing my eyes tightly.

Breathe, Tilla, breathe.

But I can't.

I am not safe here.

7

"We do it every year."

I sit on the bed in Herma's room a few days later as Diana preps herself in the mirror. She applies a clear, sticky gloss to her lips, and I watch as she examines herself. "Sports Day is a big deal around here. The community puts it on so di pickney nuh die of boredom inna di summertime."

"The community, like the church?"

"Pretty much. But then Dane took it ova, and now it's di most exciting ting fi happen since hurricane."

The mere mention of the hurricane makes me anxious.

"What do you do there?"

"It's just a bunch of games. Cricket. Ludi. Football and such. Pickney come from all over."

"Who's all going?"

She reapplies another thick layer of gloss. "Why? You expectin' someone?"

"No, I—"

"Tilla." She laughs. "Yuh can tell me."

I take a deep breath, gathering my thoughts. "It's just that . . . the other day at the river, Zory mentioned about you and Hessan, and . . . I just wanted to say I was sorry. You know, if it seemed like anything was going on. I didn't know about your relationship. But there's nothing between him and me—"

"Of course there's not." She drops her lip gloss on the counter and turns around. "Why would I think that?" A look of confusion spreads across her face.

"I just thought, from what Zory said—"

"Hessan likes *me*. He's liked me forever. You think that would change just because *you* came to town?" She raises an eyebrow. "You haven't even been here two weeks."

"No—no, of course not—"

"So then why would I be *worried*?" She stares me down.

"I didn't mean it like that."

She shakes her head before turning back to the mirror. "No offense, Tilla, but you foreign girls really must think the world revolves around you. Not everyone is concerned with your every move. Or threatened by your holy presence. You're not Jesus." She smirks. "Don't be so obsessed with yourself."

I look away, unsure of how to respond.

"Besides, Hessan and I are going to di dance together. He already asked me."

"The dance?"

"Mhm. Youth concert. It's a big roadside party di church put on. We go together every year."

"Oh. That's cool." I feel nauseous. "When is it?"

"Next week." She flips her braids, turning around. "Anyway, I'm meeting Zory. See you at Sports Day." She pockets her lip gloss before heading through the door. I stay seated on the bed, stunned.

A few minutes later, I head out to the front yard, where all the kids are gathered to go. Kenny and Mia horse around, and I spot Andre standing by himself. I make my way over to him as the group trails out of the yard.

"Wha gwan, Tilla?" His face lights up when he sees me.

"Hey . . . you're in good spirits."

"Always." He trudges out of the yard with a giant walking stick in hand and an even bigger smile on his face. "Yuh ready fi Sports Day? It ah go wicked!"

"I'm not really that big into sports."

He kisses his teeth. "Stop talk. Everybody love sports. Yuh can play pon my team."

"Okay." I smile. He walks with pride, not missing a beat. I notice he hasn't said a word about what happened the other night. I decide to bring it up.

"So how are you feeling after the river?"

"Hmm?"

"The other night. When we got back from the river."

"Wha yuh mean?" I can hear the genuine confusion in his voice.

"I mean with Uncle Junior."

"Oh," he says as if just remembering. "Nuh worry bout him. Ah so him stay."

"So him stay?" I echo, confused. "So choking people is a regular thing for him?"

Andre shrugs, clearly growing annoyed with the topic. "Me nuh know, Tilla. Me nuh really pay him too much mind. Plus, a new day ah gwan." He gestures toward the sun.

"Andre," I say, hushed. "He grabbed your face and threw you to the ground—"

"Stop nuh, Tilla." He fans me off. "Wha him wan fi do ah fi him business."

I look at him as if he's crazy. He speaks as though what happened with Uncle Junior didn't involve him at all. As if the marks aren't still on his cheek.

"Besides," he continues, "why yuh wan fi tink bout dat day when today ah *Sports Day*?" He shakes his head. "Dat nuh mek nuh sense."

"Fine," I give in. It's clear he doesn't want to go any further. "Can I ask you something else, though?"

"Lawd God. What now?"

"I'm being serious, Andre. It's about Hessan."

"*Church bwoy?*" He looks at me, a knowing smile on his face.

"It's just, the other night, Zory said something to me . . . about him and Diana. That they have an arrangement . . . or something like that."

"Yuh neva know? Dem two love each other off since dem did small."

"Seriously? But it didn't . . . It didn't seem that way."

"It's a church ting." He shrugs. "Hessan's uncle is a big pastor up in Saint Ann's. And Miss Shirley ah di pastor ah Comfort Hall. Everyone just kinda assume dem pickney would eventually marry."

"*Marry?*"

"Yeah. Dem mek a promise before God two years ago."

I start to feel sick.

"Yuh all right?" He picks up on my discomfort.

"Yeah, I'm good."

But I'm the farthest thing from it.

We trail down a red dirt path for a couple of miles until, thirty minutes later, we arrive at a giant open field with a small cement school building tucked away to the side. The field is filled with dozens of kids running up and down, and at the center of the action stands Dane with a battered clipboard in hand as he goes back and forth with a shirtless little boy.

"Yuh know di rules, Delroy! No shoes, no shirt, no servi—"

"Dane!" Richie calls out.

Dane notices us and runs over. "Yow, yow! Uno ready fi di biggest, baddest, moddest Sports Day of ya life?!"

"Yuh say di same ting every year." Kenny rolls his eyes.

Mia snickers.

"Stop yuh noise, Kenny." He fans him off. "Tilla!" He notices me. He pulls me into a suffocating hug before letting go. "Do me a favor and fill dese up fi me?" He points to a pile of used, crumpled water bottles on the ground. "There's a pipe over by di school. Me need more hands."

"Yeah, sure." I collect the bottles in my arms before making my way across the field. The games are already in full swing as kids bounce around from different activities. A few girls participate in a handstand competition while some of the younger boys race each other back and forth. I walk up a small hill and onto the cement, where pieces of broken glass bottles litter the ground. When I round the corner, the plastic bottles nearly fall from my hands.

"Brownin'."

I stand frozen, unable to move, breathe, or think.

Hessan leans over a small rusting pipe, filling up bottles.

"Sorry." He smiles. "Me soon give yuh a heart attack."

"It's fine."

"Yuh need some help?" He makes his way over to me.

"Oh—no, I'm good," I lie as I fumble with the bottles in my arms. Just as they're about to fall, he catches them by wrapping his arms around mine. He smiles. "I cyan believe you carried all of these up yuhself." We lock eyes as he takes them from me. "Dane sent you to fill up?"

I nod.

"Yeah, me, too." He laughs. "Dat bwoy love fi hand out instructions."

I smile awkwardly.

"Here." He makes room for me at the pipe.

"Thanks." I reluctantly grab a bottle and make my way over,

leaning over the pipe and placing it under. The water couldn't trickle out any slower.

I feel him move closer.

"I was hoping I'd see you today." His voice goes quiet as he leans over my shoulder. "I missed you, and . . . I cyan stop thinking about di other day at di river."

I feel my body begin to betray me as I move from underneath him. The words leave my mouth before I have time to think.

"Why did you lie to me?"

Confusion spreads across his face.

"Lie? About wha?"

"About your . . . *arrangement,*" I whisper. "With Diana. You didn't tell me."

"Tilla—"

"Tell me the truth. Please."

He sighs. "Tilla. It's complicated."

"And you don't think *this* isn't?!" I whisper. "You're engaged to be *married,* Hessan."

"Look . . . I know it nuh fully mek sense. But there's more to it than that."

"Enlighten me," I say sarcastically.

He searches my eyes before taking a deep breath.

"Diana and I dated when we were younger, and we've been on and off. We're promised, yes . . . but we haven't been togetha for a while now. She broke up wit me before she left for school last year." He stares into my eyes, sharp and intense. "She told me she didn't want to be wit me before she went away. As far as I'm concerned, we're not together."

"So you're *promised* to her, but you're not dating her?"

He sighs. "We made a promise two years ago through di church. It was our families' idea. So yes, I have an obligation. But we're not together right now."

"So then why are you taking her to the dance?"

He goes quiet, caught off guard by my question. "We're both on youth committee." He looks away from me. "We go together every year. I made plans fi go wit her before we broke up . . ."

"Unbelievable." I shake my head, moving back to the pipe to fill up the next bottle.

"Tilla, you haffi understand that when you grow up in di church here . . . it's different. Country is *small*. My uncle . . . Diana's mom—*they're pastors*. And they both have expectations fi how tings should go. But Diana and I aren't together, and . . ." He pauses. "The feelings I have fi you. I cyan jus ignore dem. I cyan jus give dat up."

"You barely know me."

"But I *want* to. I want to know all of you, Tilla. If you'll give me di chance."

His eyes find mine, seeing right through me once again. "I know you feel it, too. Being around you is so *easy*. It feels so . . . natural. So *right*." His voice goes quiet. "Your smile . . . ever since I met you di first day, it's become my favorite ting. The way you ask questions, the way you seek knowledge . . . the way you seek *yuhself*." He brings his hand to my cheek and strokes it gently. "I want to know you, Tilla. I want to know *all of you*."

"Hessan." I try to fight the energy that buzzes between us. Our connection is strong—*visceral*. I shake my head, pulling away. "You should've told me. You shouldn't have *touched me* like that." I find his eyes. "I can't do that to Diana."

"Tilla—"

"We can be friends. But nothing more."

Disappointment covers his face.

"I'm really sorry," I whisper.

I gather the water bottles and make my way back down toward the field.

About twenty minutes later, a large crowd forms around Dane. I stand next to Diana and Zory, who go back and forth about the game rules. Across the crowd, Hessan settles in next to Richie and Andre. Diana notices him and instantly perks up. I shift my gaze, and just as I do, I spot Jahvan and a few of his boys across the field, making their way toward the group.

As if this day weren't awkward enough.

"Big mon!" Dane yells to him. "Yuh late!"

"Cool nuh!" Jahvan calls. "Game cyan start till me reach."

They settle in among everyone as Jahvan spots me and smiles.

"Pretty girl." He winks.

I flush as Dane speaks to the crowd.

"All right! Ladiez and gentle-mon, time fi get organized!" He holds up a soccer ball. "Di first game we ah go play is foot-ball—"

"Umm . . ." Mia shoots her hand up. "Isn't it called soccer?"

"Sekkle down, foreigna." He fans her off. "Now, we have two games and four teams." Dane points a finger into the crowd. "Team captains are Richie, Hessan, Andre, and Jahvan. One by one, I want yuh fi choose ya teams. Hessan gets first pick." The crowd parts as the boys make their way up to the front. They stand in a straight line, facing the crowd. Everyone goes so quiet you could hear a pin drop as Hessan scans the group. We lock eyes, and my heart sinks.

I could die in this very moment.

Please. Don't. Pick. Me.

I feel a bead of sweat trickle down my back. I look to Diana

and instantly regret it. Her eyes look from me to Hessan and
back again. The look on her face says it all.

"Hurry up nuh, Hessan," Dane calls. "Yuh ah hold up di
game."

Hessan opens his mouth to speak.

Fuck.

"Me ah play fi Hessan!" Diana interrupts. She walks over
to him and grabs his hand. "There's no way I'm playing for
Andre. And Richie's team neva win."

"Ah nuh so di game work, Diana." Dane holds up his hand.
"Let di mon decide."

Diana rolls her eyes. "I'm on your team, right?" she asks
Hessan.

He glances at me before answering.

"Uh, yeah. Diana."

"Lawd." Dane sighs. "Jahvan, yuh up next!"

"Kyan-ah-da," Jahvan says without hesitation. "Come play
fi me."

I freeze.

"Hol up, hol up!" Hessan calls out. "Tilla was my next pick."

"What?" I whisper. "No, I—"

"Dat ah nuh your decision, *red bwoy.* Yuh already choose."

"Who yuh ah talk to?!" Hessan challenges.

"Shut up yuh mout, Hessan." Jahvan dismisses him. He
locks eyes with me, razor sharp and focused. "Mek di gyal
decide."

I feel nauseous as all eyes fall on me.

"I—"

"Come nuh, foreigna!" Richie calls.

"Sorry, I—"

"Tilla deh pon my team!" Andre interjects. "We already
talk earlier. Nuh true, Tilla?"

"Oh. Yeah—"

"Den hurry up nuh!" Dane ushers me over. "All right, Richie, next pick."

I walk up to the front in a daze, my heart racing as the rest of the teams make their choices. I can feel Diana's eyes on me, but I keep my head low as I stand beside Andre. Once all the teams have been chosen, Dane resumes his position.

"All right! First match is team Andre verses team Hessan. Second match is team Jahvan verses team Richie. Uno get inna position!"

Excited cheers rip through the air as we take our positions on the field. I assume defense as Andre and Hessan position across from each other in the center of the field. Diana and Zory stand opposite on Hessan's team, while Kenny and Mia play on our team. Dane stands in the center of the captains, ball in hand.

"First team fi get two points iz di winna!"

Dane puts his fingers in his mouth and blows before dropping the ball in the center. Hessan immediately swoops around Andre and, with one swift kick, launches the ball down the field. The action is fast, but it doesn't take long before Kenny takes control, bringing the ball back up the field. He and Mia run side by side, passing the ball back and forth and dodging the sea of kids.

Boom!

Zory blasts the ball from beneath Mia's feet. Diana catches up to it and picks up speed, taking the ball down the field and heading right in my direction. We lock eyes just as the hoots and hollers from the sidelines grow louder.

"KNOCK HER DOWN!"

"FOREIGN GYAL FI DEAD!"

"SHOW HER WHO RUN TINGZ!"

My heart races.

"CHARGE HER, TILLA!" Andre screams from center field. "DON' MEK HER CROSS YUH!"

Following instructions, I run toward the ball at lightning speed as Diana charges toward me.

WHAM!

I fall to the ground with a thud as she speeds right by me. In a swift motion, she takes a giant kick, and the ball lands straight in the net. The sound of obnoxious cackles pours out from the sidelines as they celebrate Diana's victory. Andre jogs over to me.

"Yuh all right?!" he asks, offering a hand.

"Yeah. I'm good," I say, even though I'm not so sure.

"Dust it off." He pats me on the shoulder. "Game nuh done yet."

The sky starts to grow dark as we regroup in the center of the field. In an instant, the soft call of thunder rumbles above our heads, and rain begins to drizzle down. As Dane blows the whistle, Andre takes the ball down the field, focused and determined.

"Go deh, blackie!" I hear someone yell from the side.

He disregards it, staying focused as he skillfully makes his way past the other players. Just as Hessan tails him, Andre takes a shot at the net and scores. After a brief moment of celebration, everyone regroups as Dane blows the whistle.

BAM!

Hessan uses all his force to kick the ball down the field, but before he has a chance to catch up to it, I stop the ball in its tracks.

"Andre!" I call before launching the ball back up the field. Before it can reach him, another boy snatches it back.

"Tico!" The kid passes the ball to a tall, light-skinned boy, who stops the ball under his foot. "Yow! Andre!" Tico calls. Using full force, he purposely launches the ball directly at Andre's head.

WHAM!

The ball bounces off Andre's head, knocking him to the wet ground. The sidelines explode in laughter and jarring heckles.

"HANDICAP!"

"BLACKIE AH EEDIAT!"

"FOOL HIM AH FOOL!"

I race toward the ball as Tico and the other boy erupt in hysteria.

"Whoa, whoa! Wha yuh ah do?!" Hessan yells at Tico, visibly upset. But before Dane has a chance to blow his whistle, Andre springs up from the ground.

"Andre!" I yell, taking the ball up the field. He races toward me, and we rip through the rain, kicking the ball back and forth until he eventually takes the lead. Dirtied and wet, he runs at full force as Diana charges him from behind.

"Run, Andre! Run!" I scream as she catches up. Andre wastes no time. He fakes her out, and with a giant kick, he launches the ball into the net.

Everyone explodes.

"YEEEEES!" I yell.

"Team Andre tek di first match!" Dane calls, blowing his whistle. Lightning rips through the sky as our team thrusts Andre into the air. The sidelines rush the field with a mixture of excited and disappointed faces as Diana and Zory argue with Dane about the game rules. I run toward the school with Andre, Mia, and Kenny to seek shelter under the zinc roof.

"You did it!" I squeeze Andre tightly as we shield ourselves from the rain.

"Yuh eva have any doubt?!" he asks, his smile smug.

"You shoulda see dem face!" Kenny laughs.

"It was epic!" Mia laughs, too, as she bounces around. She's a burst of energy, and I can't help but join in the laughter. "Til, did you see when Kenny and I went back and forth?! None of them could even keep up!"

"I did." I beam. "You guys killed it, Mi."

Mia runs out into the rain and does a happy dance as Kenny follows. They are a ripple of laughter as they chase each other around, drenching themselves with their water bottles before rounding the corner to fill them back up. I sit down on a dry patch of cement, settling in next to Andre.

"Good game." I smile at the grass stains that cover him.

"Me try fi tell yuh. It nuh matter how many times dem kick yuh down. Long as yuh get back up." He extends his fist for me to pound. "Ah we run tings."

"Yuh dun know." I laugh as we bump fists. The downpour grows heavier, crashing into the zinc above us. "I'm sorry Sports Day got rained out, though," I say. "Does it usually rain so heavy?"

He contemplates my question. "Not so much," he replies. "It kinda strange—"

"Yow! Andre!" Hessan calls out, running toward us through the rain. "Yuh all right?!"

"Yeah mon, me straight," Andre says as Hessan approaches us.

"Yuh played wicked, mon. None ah we coulda touch yuh. Yuh footwork *bod*!"

"Respeck." Andre smiles as they dap each other. Hessan locks eyes with me, rainwater running down his skin.

"Yuh were great out there, too, Tilla. Strong."

I blush. Before I can respond, a chilling voice cries out.

"TILLA!"

My heart stops.

Mia.

I instantly leap up, running out into the rain.

"TILLA! HELP!" she calls out. The three of us race along the cement toward the pipe where they went to fill up their bottles. We round the corner to find Mia buckled over on the ground as Kenny leans down beside her.

"Tilla!" Mia cries out in pain.

"What happened?!" I race toward them.

"She fall down pon di glass!" Kenny yells through the rain. I bend down to find shards of glass piercing her hand. She hyperventilates as a pool of blood and rainwater mix in her palm, pouring onto the cement beside her.

"Oh my God." I assess her wounds. "How did this happen?!"

"She did ah run fi fill up her bokkle, and she trip and fall!" Kenny points to the broken glass bottles that I had noticed earlier.

"It—it—it's stuck in my hand," Mia sobs, unable to catch her breath. "It—it hurts, Tilla. It hurts so much."

I stare down at the pieces of glass that protrude from her hand. I feel helpless, unsure of what to do next as Andre uses his shirt to clear the remaining shards from around her.

"We have to take it out, Mi."

"No! Please—it—it hurts!" she cries. "Please. Don't. I can't . . ."

"Let me see it." Hessan parts us, bending down beside Mia. He carefully takes her hand in his, assessing the damage as he lifts her palm toward him. "It's not as deep as you think." He looks at Mia. "You're strong, Mia. I saw you pon dat field. Yuh can do this. Okay?"

Mia just sobs.

"Me ah go tek it out fi you, all right? But me need you fi tek a deep breath."

Mia nods.

Hessan wipes the tears from her eyes before gently lifting her palm. "Yuh ready?" he asks.

Mia sniffles, and I grab her other hand in mine.

"Just squeeze down on my hand, okay?" I say to her.

"Breathe in," Hessan instructs. Mia listens. "Breathe out."

And just as she does, he removes the small shards from her hand with his fingers. She winces, squeezing down hard on my hand. He repeats the process, and one by one, he carefully takes the shards out and drops them to the side. When he's finished, he examines her hand, ensuring no piece is left behind. Then, he reaches into his back pocket and pulls out a yellow handkerchief and gently wraps Mia's hand.

"You're all done," he says through the sound of the rain. "It nuh look too bod. Probably di shock was di worst part."

"Th-thank you." Mia's sobs begin to soften, and I pull her into a hug.

"Yuh all right, Mia?" Andre rubs her back to console her. Mia nods, quietly crying into my arms. "Nuh worry yuhself. Yuh is a soldier. Real country gyal."

"Yeah," Kenny agrees. They gather around her in a huddle. "Glass inna yuh hand is like a rite of passage. Nuh true, Hessan?"

"Yeah, mon," Hessan agrees matter-of-factly. "If you only knew di amount ah time glass catch up inna me foot bottom."

"Real ting!" Andre agrees. "One time, a nail go up inna me foot bottom when me did small. Me couldn't walk fi a month. It's a real country ting."

"Looks like ya one of us now." Hessan laughs.

A small smile creeps onto Mia's face as the boys' stories calm her down. She wipes the tears from her eyes as Kenny offers her some water.

"Thank you so much for that," I say to Hessan as a flurry of emotion floods me. "You were amazing. I wouldn't . . . I wouldn't have even known what to do."

His eyes sparkle as they search mine. "I'm here for you, Tilla."

The rain thrashes down onto us as our eyes stay locked for a moment. Drenched in rain with not a ray of sun in the sky,

Hessan's heart still shines so bright. Everything about him feels safe. Familiar.

Like I'm home again.

I fight everything inside me that lights on fire.

You're only here for a couple of weeks, I scold myself.

It.

Doesn't.

Make.

Sense.

But I'm only lying to myself.

"I should prob-ly head back," he whispers.

And with that, he stands up and heads back toward the field. I scold the butterflies that dance inside me as I watch him go. Thunder roars through the dark clouds as Andre turns to me, a concerned look on his face.

"Careful, Tilla." He keeps his voice low as lightning flashes through the sky.

"Mek sure yuh know wha yuh ah do."

8

"I'm so disappointed in you."

My father's deep voice comes through Aunt Herma's outdated flip phone.

"You were supposed to be keeping an eye on her. What if it had been worse?!"

"She's fine, Dad." I sit on the floor of the bathroom with the door locked. Nighttime has rolled in, so I keep my voice low. "It didn't cut that deep."

"That's not the *point*, Tilla. You're supposed to be more responsible than that. You shouldn't have even had Mia out there in the first place. Not with the weather so bad."

"Dad, it was Sports Day—"

"I'm not just talking about *today*, Tilla." His tone grows frustrated. "Herma says you've been gallivanting around the country. Coming in all hours of the night and dragging Mia behind you—"

"What you are talking about?!"

"I'm *talking* about the river. How come you didn't tell me you went out there?"

"Because . . ." I feel stunned. I had no idea that Aunt Herma told him about the other night. "Because it wasn't a big deal. It was a whole bunch of us, and—"

"Are you serious, Tilla?" Disbelief clouds his tone. "Do you know how dangerous the country is at night?! You're not *from here*. What don't you get?!"

"You're the one who told us to explore! To *run up and down—*"

"Not wit a pack of *bwoy pickney*!" His tone is jolting. My stomach drops. "It's like I can't leave you alone for *two seconds*." He pauses, frustrated. "Herma says you're wandering around di country wit all di bwoy dem."

"What?!"

"Don't raise your voice at me."

"But she's lying! It was a bunch of *kids*." Anger rises in my chest. "You're making a big deal out of nothing! It was days ago—"

"Me nuh business how many days ago it was! I won't have you wandering the streets at night. Do you understand me?"

I swallow hard.

"You are a *girl child*. I raised you betta den dat. Yuh cyan jus be walkin' di streets at nighttime." He pauses, his frustration getting the best of him. "Look, it's not up for discussion. Let today be a lesson. I won't have you wandering around the country like that."

I'm quiet, unfazed by his empty threats.

"You and Mia are going to come to town on Wednesday and stay until the weekend."

"What? Why?"

"Because I said so. I don't need you stressing Herma out down there. She's already doing me a big favor by looking after you girls."

His words are so comical, I hold back a laugh.

"So you're bringing us to town because you feel like we're a burden to the house?"

"Don't put words in my mouth."

"I didn't. Isn't that what you just said?"

"Nuh badda piss me off, Tilla." His anger gets the best of him. "Me not even gone fi a week and di tings me haffi hear from Herma—" He kisses his teeth. "Yuh need fi have some damn self-respect."

"I do!"

"Then cut di foolishness and stop actin' like a—"

My heart sinks to my stomach.

"What?" My voice is small as I grip the phone tighter. "Stop acting like a what?"

My hands tremble. I want to scream. To tell him that Herma's lying. Tell him the terrible things she said to me . . . the name she called me. But it's too late.

He already believes it.

"I'll come get you two on Wednesday." He clears his throat. "I gotta go."

The line goes dead.

Embarrassment floods my body as tears pour from my eyes. I quickly wipe them away. I am mortified. He's never said anything like that to me, and it makes me feel gross with myself. I'm furious at Aunt Herma for exaggerating the story. I can only imagine the lies she filled his head with—the vivid picture she painted of his privileged little princess.

Slut.

Slut.

Slut.

I feel so humiliated. So violated.

She knew everyone I was with, but still she lit my father's fury with a bald-faced lie.

I won't give her the satisfaction.

I won't give her the pleasure of knowing that she's upset me in any way.

I won't let her win this round.

I take a deep breath and make my way down the hall to return her phone. I stand in the doorframe of the living room as she dips a rag in soapy water, tending to Mia's hand.

"It stings," Mia whines.

"It's important to keep it clean." She wraps Mia's hand in gauze, securing it with a safety pin. "There. Now, go get ready for bed," Aunt Herma instructs.

Mia hops up from the couch and notices me, stopping to give me a hug. "Night, Tilla."

"Good night, Mi."

She makes her way past me to the bedroom as Aunt Herma settles into the couch. She sips a cup of cocoa tea and doesn't take her eyes off the static television as I approach her.

"Thanks," I say dryly as I pass the phone back.

"You shouldn't be thanking me." She puts the phone in her pocket, still refusing to look at me. "You really should be ashamed of yourself. Letting that happen to your sister on your watch."

"I didn't *let* anything happen to her," I say. "And she's fine."

"She's *fine* because I tended to it. If it were any worse, she would've needed stitches." She takes a sip of her tea. "Your behavior is so disgraceful. Your father must be so embarrassed."

Her words gut me.

I turn to go, uninterested in hearing any more.

"And don't forget you have church on Sunday. You've been running up and down the country with God knows who, and I'm sure you could use some of the Lord's forgiveness."

I stop dead in my tracks.

"God doesn't like promiscuous little girls, Tilla."

It takes everything in me not to give her some choice words. *Fuck you,* I want to scream. I want to tell her she is a *liar,* that she is jealous of a life that will never be hers. I want to tell her it is not my fault she had to come back to this place. That she never had the courage to leave again.

You're leaving Wednesday, I think.

I can't let her get to me before then.

So I bite my tongue.

9

"Pssst! Pssst! Wake up nuh, girl!"

I open my eyes the next morning to find Andre peering at me through the shutters. He pokes his fingers in between the cracks and launches a small pebble that hits the floor.

"Tilla! Wake up nuh!"

"What are you doing?!" I groan as I turn over. The clock reads 10:00 a.m., and I'm surprised Aunt Herma has let me sleep in today. Next to me, Mia lies asleep, her hand wrapped up in gauze.

"Come nuh, Tilla!" Andre calls. "Come follow me ah bush."

"For what?"

"Just come nuh, mon!" he calls back in annoyance. I yawn, pulling myself out of bed as I adjust to the harsh light that fills the room. As soon as I sit up, the events from yesterday rush back to me.

"How yuh move so slow?!"

"I'm coming," I moan. "At least let me get dressed."

"Hurry up! Meet me out back."

He disappears around the house, and I pull myself out of bed. As I change into a pair of worn overalls and a white T-shirt, my father's words from yesterday come back to me. I glance at myself in the mirror and when I catch sight of my butterfly necklace, I immediately start to feel uneasy. I don't want to be reminded of any of it, so I purposely hide it inside my shirt in an attempt to forget my father and his hurtful words. I brush my teeth before continuing out back to meet Andre.

"Lawd, yuh tek long," he says when he sees me. He stoops in the middle of the dirt clearing by the firepit, sharpening his machete with a piece of iron. "Mia still asleep?"

"Yeah. She knocked out last night after Aunt Herma bandaged her up."

"She lucky say it neva more serious." He looks at my neck. "Yuh nah wear yuh necklace? Me neva see yuh tek it off."

I shrug. "Didn't really feel like it today."

"Too bad. Me did kinda like it, still." He stands up, machete in hand. "Ready fi go ah bush?"

"Yeah." I shove my hands into my pocket. "Although you still haven't explained to me why we're going."

Andre kisses his teeth. "Yuh ask too much questions, yuh nuh, Tilla," he says, faux annoyance in his tone. "Yuh nuh always need a reason fi do tings. Sometimes yuh just wake up and feel it inna yuh spirit."

"And what exactly did you feel in your spirit today?"

"Di call of God."

"The call of God?" I ask, bemused.

"Yeah, mon. Me wake up dis mawnin' and God tell me fi go ah bush. So we ah go ah bush. Dat simple. Now, stop question God and follow di leader!" He grins, heading down the path. I fight a smile as I follow behind him. I feel the heavy energy of last night begin to dissipate as I push my father's empty threats to the back of my mind.

"Today, me ah go teach yuh how fi pick a orange." Andre beams, walking proudly with his machete in hand. "Di most important skill me want you fi tek home is how fi get yuh own food. You nuffi rely pon anotha man fi feed you. That's your responsibility."

I smile at his conviction. "We don't have orange trees where I live."

Shock covers his face as he turns around to face me. "Ah lie! Fi true?!"

"Yeah. It's too cold."

"Cockfoot! So uno nuh nyam orange ah foreign?"

"We do. We just buy it at the store."

"Bumba rawtid." He thinks for a moment, reconsidering his approach. "Well . . . at least you'll learn how fi climb a tree."

He leads us deeper into the forest before slowing his pace. He stops at a small clearing, scoping out the scene before deciding on the largest tree nestled in the corner. "Dat one." He points to it with pride.

"Are you crazy?" I ask. "You want me to climb *that*?!"

"Dat ah nuh nuttin. Stop actin' like a gyal pickney."

"Don't be sexist."

"Wha dat mean?"

"It means that you think I can't do something because I'm a girl."

Andre scoffs as he makes his way over to the tree. "Prove me wrong, den. And yuh cyan use so much big word and den complain when people call yuh 'Kyan-ah-da.' Country people nuh talk so."

I roll my eyes, ignoring him as I focus on the magnitude of the beautiful tree. Its dark green leaves illuminate under the sun, and giant oranges hang from its branches.

"Come nuh!" Andre sticks his machete into the ground and grips the bark. He hoists himself up, digging his feet into the jagged surface and begins to climb. He grabs on to a thick branch and pulls himself up on it with ease. Once there, he stands up and reaches for another branch above him. He pulls himself up again, hoisting onto it and taking a seat. I stare at him with my mouth agape.

"How the *hell* did you do that?"

"It's all inna yuh foot!" he calls down.

I grip the tree and use my feet to hoist me up, but I quickly stumble back down, hitting the ground with a thud.

"Ow! Shit," I mumble. My hands are dirtied and dented.

Andre laughs his head off.

"I don't have any upper-body strength," I whine.

"Di only upper-body strength yuh need is yuh mind!"

I roll my eyes. Andre swears he's Buddha.

I stand up and grip the tree once more, placing my feet firmly at the bottom.

"Stop doubtin' yuhself!" Andre calls down.

I take a deep breath and press my feet as hard as I can against the base of the tree. I grimace through the pain, using all my might to pull myself up.

"Yeah, mon!" Andre cheers me on. "Go deh, Kyan-ah-da!"

I hoist myself up to the first branch, using my feet for stability.

My body moves instinctively as I stand up, careful not to look down before reaching up to the branch above me where Andre sits. He helps me pull myself up, and I plop down next to him, beaming with pride.

"See?! Never so bad."

"This is nuts!" I laugh.

I look down below, and my stomach drops. Andre's machete looks like a small stick in the distance, and I can see the entire clearing. Andre grabs a big, juicy orange that hangs beside me and takes a small pocketknife from his shorts. I watch as he cuts into the skin of the orange, and a small burst of citrus sprinkles the air. He slices it with the pride of someone who has worked for their meal. *Climbed* for it.

"It's real juicy, so you haffi suck it."

He hands me my half before biting into his. I bite down, and the juice spills out into my mouth. It's *so* sweet.

"Me ah pick as many as me can before hurricane season start. Me only have a few weeks left."

"A few weeks?!"

"Seem so." He munches on his orange.

"Andre." I look at him, stunned. "The hurricane's coming in a few weeks?!"

He shrugs, his mouth full. "Hurricane ah regular ting round yesso, Tilla."

"When do we know how bad it's going to be?"

"Yuh jus haffi wait. One year when me did small, all di animals dead. Cow. Goat. Chicken. Everyting. Same year Hessan mada dead."

"Wait, what?" Shock floods my body. "Hessan's mother died?"

"Years ago. Di storm run her car offa di mountainside. She and Hessan."

"Oh my God."

Andre nods his head. "Him manage fi escape, but she never mek it out."

Memories of the scar on Hessan's lower back consume my mind as a wave of regret washes over me. I'm so angry at myself for putting my hand on something so personal to him. Something so painful. My heart feels heavy.

"So it go." Andre shrugs. "Nuff people dead from hurricane inna country. When it come, it nah tek no prisna. Uno nuh get hurricane ah foreign?"

"No?" I look at him quizzically. "It's Canada."

"Cockfoot! So uno never have hurricane ah foreign before?"

"Never."

"Ah lie! Seriously?" he asks, shocked.

"Yeah." I keep my tone gentle, careful not to judge. I have to remind myself that as wise as Andre is, he doesn't go to school. "Canada isn't tropical. We don't really get natural disasters."

"Lawd." He chomps down on his orange. "Me really need fi come ah foreign den. Every year hurricane come ah Jamaica and mash up di land."

His words chill me. Life-threatening hurricanes are an expectation here. A casualty. The idea baffles me, and it hits me that I've been privileged to not have to deal with such a deep level of devastation. I've never had to deal with the fear of losing my home.

Not in the way that they have.

We sit in silence for a while as we take in the majestic scene. It feels like it's just Andre and me in the entire forest, and that feels comforting. There is so much I want to ask him. So much I want to know. I turn to him.

"Can I ask you something?"

"Gwan nuh."

"Why do you call my dad *Mass Tyson*?"

"Wha yuh mean? Ah nuh suh him name?"

"No . . . I mean the *Mass* part."

"Short for *Massa*."

"Massa like *master*."

"So?"

"So . . . don't you think it's weird to call your *uncle* your *master*?"

"Sign of respect." He shrugs.

"I just don't get it. Respect for what? Every time he comes around, you guys all bow at his feet. You treat him like he's a king or something."

"He is."

I let out a laugh, almost choking on the orange. "No, he's not."

"How yuh mean?"

"My father is not a *king*, Andre."

"Yuh cyan say dat."

"Yes, I can."

"Stop talk," he says in disbelief. "You shouldn't say dem kinda tings, Tilla. Yuh word is yuh prayer."

"And what's that supposed to mean?"

"Dat God hear everyting yuh ah say. Every thought yuh have and word yuh speak—dat is ya prayer to God. Good or bad, him hear yuh. God nah sleep."

"Great. Then he knows what a shitty father I have," I snap back, annoyed. "And I wouldn't say it if it wasn't the truth."

Andre shakes his head. "Foreign pickney different fi true."

"Excuse me?"

"How yuh can say dat about ya own *fada*?"

"Andre, just because someone contributes to your creation does not automatically make them a good father. You don't get an award for starting a family and then abandoning them when shit gets hard and you stop giving a fuck."

Andre stops fiddling with the orange. My anger has stunned the both of us. I know that I'm coming across like the spoiled brat everyone makes me out to be, but I don't care.

I mean every word.

"You mustn't talk so," he says, his tone more serious than before.

"Whatever," I spit. "You have no idea what I've been through with him."

"Mass Tyson love yuh—"

"How can he love me when he doesn't even *like* me?"

"Him tell yuh dat?"

"He doesn't have to, Andre!" My voice is strained as

frustration gets the best of me. "I can *feel* it. The way he talks to me. The things he says—" My voice breaks as I recall our conversation last night. "He doesn't mind Mia, because she's still young. She doesn't remember all the ways he destroyed our home. But I do." A tear escapes down my cheek, and I quickly wipe it away. "I feel too much, and he hates me for it. I remember *too much*. The fights between him and my mom . . . the constant screaming . . . *the anxiety* that consumed all of us to live in a house like that. To wake up every Sunday morning to our own hurricane." I shake my head as the memories crawl all over my skin. "Mia doesn't remember all that. But I do. And every time he sees me, I remind him of all of it. So I stay quiet and try not to make him uncomfortable. I try not to say anything that will give him a reason to leave again. I try . . . I try not to love him *so much*." Tears stream down my face. I wipe them as quickly as they fall. "We don't make him happy. Not like you guys do. Not like *this* does." I gesture out at the land. "His heart has never been with us. It's always been on this island."

I feel desperate to be understood as Andre looks away from me. I silently beg for him to say something—*anything*—but he doesn't.

He just fiddles with his pocketknife.

"You're not going to say anything?" It comes out as bratty as it sounds.

Andre looks at me, his brown eyes focused in deep contemplation. "Me nuh know, Tilla. Me nuh really agree wit wha you ah say."

"What?" I look at him. "What do you mean, 'agree'?"

"Dat ah nuh di Mass Tyson me know." His eyes are remorseful. "Ever since we did small, Mass Tyson ah di only man fi tek care of us. When we need clothes, food, supplies . . . ah him buy it. When school time come, him ah di *only one* fi

mek sure Richie and Kenny have shoes and school uniform.
When we ah starve fi hungry, ah him mek sure we eat. Him
teach me how fi grow me own food. How fi tek care ah me animals. How fi climb tree. Everyting me know is 'cause of Mass
Tyson. So when yuh hear we call him *Massa,* iz a sign of respect. Him ah we hero. Di only fada we ever know. And when
yuh say dem tings . . . me just cyan agree wit yuh, Tilla."

His words gut me as I realize that my dad has been more of
a father to these kids than he's ever been to me or Mia.

"Yuh know how many pickney would *kill* fi have Mass
Tyson as dem fada?"

His question is genuine, but it makes me feel hollow. I
throw my orange peel down to the ground as I meet his gaze.

"Yeah," I whisper. "Me, too."

The weight of our conversation marinates as we sit in silence.
Resentment consumes me as I imagine my father parenting
these kids. Giving them the love that Mia and I deserved. Bitterness gets the best of me.

"What happened to your real dad?"

He grabs another orange from beside him and begins to
peel it with the knife. Juice runs down onto his green shorts.
He passes me the other half before licking his fingers.

"Me nuh have one," he says firmly. "Mummy say him dead
before me born."

"Oh . . . I'm sorry."

He fiddles with the knife, placing it back in his pocket.

"What about Richie and Kenny?" I ask. "You have different
dads, right?"

He scoffs.

"What?" I ask.

"Wha yuh wan know? Why dem so light and me so dark?"

"Andre, that's not what I meant."

"Ah nuh dat yuh wan know?" He looks at me. I squirm,

busted. "Everyone always ah ask why me so black and dem skin so nice."

His words stump me.

"Well, that's stupid. Your skin is beautiful . . ."

But the look in his eyes tells me it's the first time anyone has ever told him differently. I decide to drop it as we sit in silence for a little while longer, the vulnerability of our conversation sinking in. We look out above the trees, sitting in peace among the beauty of the clearing.

"Thank you for bringing me up here, Andre. This is magical."

"Yeah." He nods. "Sometimes me just want fi hear nuttin. Nuttin except God's voice. Down ah yawd dem always need me fi do sumting. Up here God nuh ask me fi do nuttin except eat di oranges." He smiles, reaching for another one.

I smile and do the same.

After about an hour, we climb back down carrying a handful of oranges. Andre walks with pride, excited to be bearing goods as we near the front veranda, where everyone does their daily activities. Diana combs a little girl's hair, and Aunt Herma sits around the sewing machine with Uncle Junior. Richie, Kenny, and Mia kick a ball back and forth in the yard, and Aunt Adele feeds Mama and Papa their meal. We approach the bottom steps as Aunt Herma calls out to us.

"Where uno ah come from? Bush?"

"Yes, Miss Herma," Andre says as he makes his way up the stairs. "Me teach Tilla how fi climb one tree." He lugs the heavy oranges in his shirt as I follow behind him. Just as he reaches for the top step, he misses and bucks his toe, falling flat on his face and landing with a heavy thud.

The oranges go flying.

Everywhere.

"Bumba!" Richie bursts out in laughter.

"What di fuck yuh ah do?!" Uncle Junior angrily storms over.

"Look how you drop di suh'um pon di floor!" Aunt Herma yells. "Get up nuh, bwoy!"

I stand frozen. Andre lies on the ground, bruised, silent, and humiliated. His pocketknife has ripped through his shorts, slicing his upper thigh. Blood runs out onto the veranda, and his eyes gloss over with tears.

Aunt Adele storms over. "Me nuh know how him gwan so." Disgust seeps through her tone. "Yuh slow, bwoy?! Get up!"

"Get up nuh, blackie!" Richie cackles obnoxiously. "Fool him ah fool yuh nuh!"

"Stop," I say forcefully. My heart races as I run to Andre's side.

"Me say fi get up!" Uncle Junior grabs him by the shirt, tossing him onto his back. "Fucking black bwoy. Yuh nuh hear me ah talk to yuh?!"

"Stop!" I scream. "He's hurt!" My eyes well up with tears. "Andre, are you okay?!" I beg for an answer as tears stream down his dark skin. The hot sun scorches down onto the veranda as his eyes gloss over with anger.

"Andre. Talk to me," I plead. "Please."

He flings his arm away from me. "Leff me alone nuh, mon!" he screams at me before storming inside.

I sit on the floor, paralyzed.

Everyone resumes what they were doing, and I look around in disgust. None of these people cares that Andre's blood stains the floor. Tears spill from my eyes as I look to Diana. I want so badly to yell at her, to tell her to say something. To stick up for Andre.

But I don't, and she doesn't.

And in this moment, I am forced to deal with the menacing

truth that lingers in the air. The difficult reality that no one here is willing to confront: If it were Richie, with his golden hue, or Kenny, with his green eyes, it would matter. But not Andre.

Not the boy with the midnight skin.

Because the way they treat Andre is a direct result of the racial bias that permeates the island. An island of black and brown bodies that are not exempt from their own internalized racism. Their own internalized *colorism*. Black and brown bodies that are not exempt from discriminating against their own, be he a few shades darker. Be he their own family ... their own *son*. The truth is that in the countryside of Jamaica, buried among the bushes, is the reality that being lighter-skinned offers your life inherent value. Being lighter-skinned offers you celebration and praise. It offers you homecoming, the same way it has offered it to my father time and time again.

And under this measure, there will be no celebration for dark boys.

There will be no celebration for Andre.

Because the dark reality of paradise is that there is little value for dark skin.

Everyone continues around me as if nothing happened. I head to my room, anger blasting through my veins. The truth is, there is nothing honorable about the cloak of perfection they adorn my father with. There is nothing righteous about the glimmer in their eyes when he enters a room. They would not worship my dad if his skin were the color of night. They love him for the soft locks that spill down his back, his light skin that tans caramel at its darkest, and his rare eyes that are so gray you can almost see through them.

The truth makes. Me. Livid.

The clouds grow stormy, and a few hours later, rain crashes down from the sky. I sit in the living room, curled up in a daze as I watch the water pour into the yard. When evening sets in, I walk through the house to Andre's room. I knock gently before peeking inside. He sits on his bed with a battered sketchbook in his lap.

"Hey. Can I come in?"

He looks up from his book, still visibly upset. "Come nuh."

I walk into the room, closing the door behind me. His room is tiny and cramped. The walls are dark green, and an old twin mattress with holes and no sheets sits on the floor. He keeps his head down as I approach him.

"How are you feeling?" I ask.

"Fine."

"Andre . . . how they spoke to you—"

"Iz all right."

"It's *not*. If my father ever heard them talk to you like that—"

"Just cool nuh, Tilla."

Tears fill his eyes, but he refocuses on his sketchbook. I take a deep breath, deciding not to push it as I wander farther into the room. I make my way over toward his dresser just as a blue baseball cap catches my eye. The material is battered, but I would recognize that cap anywhere.

"Was this my dad's?" I ask, picking it up. Andre looks up from his sketchbook and nods. Images of my dad wearing it over his locks come back to me.

"Him gimme last time uno come ah yawd."

"Wait . . ." I pause, racking my brain. "You mean when we were, like, six?"

He nods. "Yuh nuh 'memba?"

"I . . . I think so," I whisper as I try to recall.

"Mass Tyson tell we fi race go ah di gate. Fi see who could run di fastest. Him hat was di prize."

"And you came in first place." I laugh as the memory comes back to me. "I was so pissed."

"Yuh neva stop bawl. Me try fi give you di hat, but yuh hair was so big it kept fallin' off."

"I remember that!" We both smile at our childhood innocence. "Wow . . . I can't believe how long ago that was. I remember I hated my Afro back then."

He examines my hair for a moment. "Yuh neva want fi mek it straight?"

"What do you mean?"

"Like, perm it or suh'um. Sorta like Zory. Or braid it up like Diana."

"Are you kidding? I would've done anything for straight hair back then."

"So why yuh neva perm it?"

I walk toward the bed and take a seat beside him as the answer hits me.

"My dad."

"Mass Tyson?"

I nod as I meet his gaze. "We weren't allowed to straighten our hair. I used to hate it, how kinky and thick it was. How it grew upward and not down. I thought I looked like a boy." I pull on a coil. "I went to school with a bunch of white kids, and they'd always make fun of me for it. They'd call it ugly and try to put things in it. This one girl said it looked like a bird's nest, and soon everyone was calling me that." My chest feels heavy as the memories flood me. "Kids were really mean. I tried not to let it get to me, but it did. A lot. My mom said I could perm it if I really wanted, but my dad . . . he wouldn't let me."

"Wha mek?"

"He always said what was growing out of my head was exactly how God wanted it. He told me that all the time, and . . . I don't know. I guess eventually, I just started to believe him."

"So dat's why yuh always wear it so . . . *mod looking*?"

I laugh. "I guess I just think if God wanted me to have

straight hair or loose curls, he would've given it to me. So I figure I can spend my life trying to get my hair to do something it was never meant to do . . . or I can just love what I have."

The thought of my father encouraging me to embrace my Afro sends a feeling of longing through me. Even though I don't want to admit it, it's hard to disguise how he has shaped me.

I take a deep breath, fiddling with my butterfly necklace.

"I know what it's like, Andre. To be angry at how God made you . . ." His brown eyes are pained as they search mine. "But you are enough. More than enough. And God . . . he made you perfect."

He shakes his head, his eyes welling with tears. "Nuttin nuh go so." His lips grow tight as he focuses back on his sketch.

"What do you mean?"

"God neva want me fi look so."

"I thought you said God doesn't make mistakes?"

He stops drawing and goes quiet. I watch in silence as he contemplates my words. After a moment, he looks up at me through his long lashes. His dark brown eyes are sad.

"Dem hate me 'cause me skin dark."

"Andre—"

"*Ah di truth*, Tilla. How could anyone love me when me look so?!" A tear steams down his face. "All me want iz fi have God tek it back. Fi put me inna di same skin like me brotha dem. Jus give me a fair chance fi get di same love . . . di same *treatment*."

I feel my chest tighten as tears stream down his face and onto his sketchbook.

"When me did small . . . me used fi rub bleach pon me skin ah nighttime—"

"Oh my God. Andre . . ."

"*Every night* before me go ah bed." Despair fills his eyes. "Me would pray to God jus hopin' when me wake up me coulda look like Richie or Kenny . . . but it neva work. Nuttin me do *eva* work, Tilla. Dem *neva* ah go love me di same way."

"Good," I say firmly. "Because you don't need their love. You never needed it." My voice is small as my eyes search his. "You only need your own."

My words take us both by surprise. I reach over and wipe his cheek.

"Your skin is *beautiful,* Andre. *Regal.* You have to understand that. Your skin . . . it's what connects you to this land. To the sun . . . the earth . . . to *Jamaica*." I take his hand and squeeze it tightly. "Your skin is dark and *magical*. And every time you get darker, it's just proof that the sun is wrapping itself around you. Hugging you. *Tight.* Every ray of sun that darkens your skin is proof that you're soaking up *all* of God's light."

He diverts his gaze, wiping his eyes before focusing back on his sketch.

"We don't have to keep talking about it," I concede. "But I just wanted you to know—I *needed* you to know . . . your skin is dark because it was kissed by God himself."

We sit in silence for a moment as rain patters onto the zinc roof above us. I squeeze his hand a little tighter. He's quiet for a while, and I take it as my cue to leave. I place the cap on his bed, and just as I get up, I catch a glimpse of his sketchbook over his shoulder.

My heart stops dead in my chest.

There, on the battered page, is the most vivid, detailed drawing of a fully bloomed hibiscus flower. The drawing is so striking that it jumps off the page.

"Oh my God." I stare in amazement. "You *drew* that?"

He nods.

"Andre . . . that's *stunning*!" I gush.

He stops drawing for a second and looks up at me.

"Fi true?"

"Are you kidding me?!"

I take the sketchbook from his lap, completely mesmerized. Bright pinks and reds spring to life as green vines wrap around the base of it. "I had no idea you could draw like this." I flip through, and I can hardly believe my eyes. The pages are filled with stunning portraits of nature, animals, and people.

His eyes light up. "Yuh wan see some more?"

He reaches to the side of his bed and grabs an old brown box. He opens it, revealing more sketchbooks just like the one in my hand. He passes them to me, and I flip through them.

"No way." My amazement deepens at the brilliance of his artistry. "This is some of the most beautiful art I've ever seen, Andre. What does everyone else say?!"

"Nuttin. Me neva show anyone before you."

"What?!" My mouth is on the floor. "You're lying."

"Swear."

"Andre, you *have* to do something with these!"

"Dis ah nuh foreign, Tilla."

"It doesn't matter. I bet if we show my dad—"

He snatches the books from my hands. "Lawd, Tilla, me say fi drop it."

"But you're *really* good."

He shrugs me off.

"I really mean it. You're *talented*, Andre."

"Stop nuh, Tilla. Yuh nuh understand."

"What? What don't I understand? That you're a *brilliant* artist?!"

He stays quiet.

"Andre—"

"Lawd, Tilla! Yuh nuh know when fi stop?!" he screams, and it startles me. "Nobody cares me can draw stupid pictures! Dem nuh even send me go ah school!" He flings the sketchbook, and the colorful pages go flying. Everywhere. Tears of anger boil behind his eyes. "Ah nuh di same like foreign! Ah nuh . . . ah nuh di same," he weeps. "Not when yuh black like me and yuh come from country! Not everyone can have di tings weh you have, Tilla. Not everyone get a chance!"

"Andre—"

"Jus stop nuh, mon! Please, Tilla, jus leave it!"

He turns his back to me as tears stream down his face. His small body trembles, and I stand stunned, unsure of what to do next.

I feel like an idiot.

"Andre . . . I shouldn't . . . I shouldn't have said that."

I'm so angry at myself for making it worse. I sit down beside him and put my hand on his back. "Andre," I whisper. His entire body shakes as I wrap my arms around him. I search my brain for the right words . . . something to make it better.

But I can't fix this.

For me, this is a summer.

For him, this is his *life.*

I hold my sweet cousin in my arms, desperately searching for the right words to ease the pain. The dooming sound of thunder roars in the background, as the only words that seem to make sense stumble out of my mouth like a broken lullaby:

"I'm so sorry," I whisper.

10

"Are you having fun?"

I sit on the floor of the bathroom two days later as everyone prepares for bed. The sound of my mother's voice is soothing, even through the static signal.

"Not really." I sigh. "I feel homesick."

"Oh, Tilla." I can hear worry creep into her voice even at such a small admission. "I was so devastated when your father told me about Mia. I wanted to book the first flight down." Her voice becomes small—ashamed. "But I can't get the time off work."

"It's okay, Mom. You don't need to come down. Mia's fine."

"That's what your father said." She sighs. "But I just . . . I worry about you girls."

"I know," I whisper.

"Tilla," she says softly. "What else is going on? Is everything okay?"

"Yeah, Mom. Everything's fine, I just—" I feel my voice start to betray me. "I just miss you."

"Tilla, baby . . . I miss you so much, too. I know it can feel like a lot, but your father is so happy to have you girls down there. And as soon as things slow down for him at work, everything will start to feel different. You'll be able to spend more time with him."

We sit in silence as thunder rumbles through the night. I do my best to hide the fear in my voice.

"It's been raining so much in the country."

"Tilla . . ." I can hear her spirit breaking. I immediately feel bad for making her worry. "How bad has it been? You need to tell me these things."

"It's not bad," I try to backtrack. "There's just a lot of thunder. Every other day or so."

"That's not too unusual for this time of year." I can hear her nervously shifting on the other end. "I watch the news forecast every day. They don't expect it to be bad this year. But if anything changes, I need you to tell me. I need you to know you can come home."

"I know, Mom."

Everything in me wants to tell her what's been going on. To scream how badly they treat me, and how they treat Andre, and how all I want to do is come home. But the truth is, I know she can't afford to change our tickets. And I can't put that burden on her. Not from so far away.

"Give it time, baby. Things will get better. I promise."

I return the phone to Aunt Herma and head into the room, where Mia lies asleep. I slip into bed next to her as the sound of crickets pierces through the black night. My mind runs rogue until I drift asleep, the heaviness of the dark night slowly drowning out my thoughts.

I awake what feels like moments later to the sound of tapping on the shutters. I jolt out of my sleep, unsure if I had only imagined it. I look to the clock on the nightstand: 3:30 a.m. I rub my eyes, squinting to get a better look at the shutters. Moonlight streams in through the open cracks, but the night remains quiet.

No one is there.

I plop my head back down on the pillow. Just then, I hear the tapping again.

"Tilla," a voice whispers.

A gentle voice that I would know anywhere.

I slip out of bed, all fear leaving my body.

"Hessan?" I whisper.

I peer out the window and see his silhouette in the moonlight.

"Meet me at di side of di house."

He slips off into the night, and I stand perplexed. Careful not to wake Mia, I dig into my suitcase and pull out my pink hoodie. I slide it on and head through the door and out onto the veranda.

The moon is full and exceptionally bright. I tiptoe across the veranda, trying my best to stay calm as I walk out into the dead of night. My heart races as I cross the damp grass to the side of the house. As soon as I turn the corner, a tall figure stands waiting for me.

"Hi, beautiful," he says softly.

"What are you doing here?" I whisper.

"I wanted to come look fi you."

"You're crazy." I fight the smile that creeps up as I get closer. "It's almost 4:00 a.m."

"I know. But I was up. Yuh was on my mind."

"You're nuts." I can't help but laugh.

He takes my hand, gently pulling me in like he's done before. He wraps his arms around me, taking me in the deepest embrace. He smells like sweet Julie mangoes and burning wood, and against my better judgment, I melt into his arms. He holds me close, nuzzling his nose into my neck as he breathes me in. He stays like that for a quick second before letting go.

"Did I wake you?" he asks.

"No. I mean, yes . . . but it's fine." The dark of night makes me bold. "You're a nice surprise to wake up to."

"Yuh probably say dat to every bwoy who come look yuh ah nighttime."

"Just you." I smile.

His eyes light up under the moon.

"It's so good to see you, Tilla."

"You, too," I whisper. "Thank you again, you know—for everything you did for my sister the other day."

"Nuh badda mention it."

"But I want to." I meet his eyes. "It meant a lot. The way you took care of her."

He smiles. "How's she feelin'?"

"Better. I think her pride was bruised more than anything . . . Mia's used to being the strong one."

"It's clear where she gets her strength from."

"No way." I laugh.

"I'm serious." He smiles. "You're a lot stronger den yuh know."

"Is that so?" I ask playfully. "And how would you know that?"

"Yuh come all di way from foreign to a place where yuh barely know anyone. To a culture that you're not familiar wit. You're so far from home and yet still—yuh nuh 'fraid of any of it."

I blush. "I wouldn't exactly say that."

"All right. Well, yuh 'fraid, but yuh do it anyway. Which mek yuh brave."

His words hold weight. The moon beams down on us as the guilt of being alone with him starts to creep up. I take a deep breath, digging for courage despite the pull I feel toward him.

"Why did you come here?" I ask.

"Because I wanted to see you."

"No, I mean . . ." I pause. "You know what I mean."

He says nothing, but his eyes are so sincere that I get lost in them.

"Hessan . . . You can't be here. It's not fair to Diana."

"We're jus talkin'." He searches my eyes. "We nah do nuttin wrong. I jus . . . I jus want to talk to yuh. You're all I've been thinking about and . . ." He pauses. "I jus want to know how yuh doin'." He locks his fingers into mine, squeezing. "Please?"

I can't resist him. Everything about being in Hessan's presence feels *so familiar.*

I cave as he takes a step closer to me.

"How are you, Tilla?"

He asks as though he has been waiting to ask me for days.

"I'm all right."

"Talk di truth."

I exhale, surrendering.

"I'm still adjusting, I guess. Figuring everything out."

He softly grazes my fingers, and I shiver.

"Speak, Tilla." His voice is calm and soothing. "I'm always listenin'."

"It's just . . . My aunt and I. We're not getting along. And the girls here . . ." I search for the words but come up dry. "I don't know. Everyone here thinks I'm some spoiled princess. They all have an opinion on who they think I am, even my own dad."

I tremor as the thought of my father haunts me.

The word he almost called me.

"Yuh cyan mek dat get to yuh, Tilla," Hessan interrupts my thoughts. "Yuh cyan mek nobody define yuh. Whatever dem tink of you—your fada and di people here—whatever they're saying about you . . . you're none of those tings."

His words bring me peace. It's the first time anyone has told me differently.

"I guess I just don't really fit in with anyone. Except Andre. And the way I've seen them treat him . . . I don't know."

I pause. "I know you said I would find my place, but I guess I'm still looking for it."

"Maybe yuh ah look too hard."

"What?"

"Yuh nuh need dem fi make you feel like you belong." He gazes into my eyes. "Yuh come from foreign, yes, but Jamaica run inna yuh veins, Tilla. Yuh belong here just as much as anyone else." His words linger in the night air between us. "Plus, there's so much more to Jamaica than just country. You have so much more to experience." He gently tucks a coil behind my ear. "Negril, Ocho Rios, Kingston . . ."

"I'm going to Kingston on Wednesday, actually. To visit my dad."

"For real? When you ah come back?"

"Sometime next week, I think."

"Wow . . . so long? Me ah go miss you, still."

His words feel too honest, and I blush.

"You excited fi go ah town?"

"Kind of." I hesitate. "My dad and I, we're still . . . trying to make sense of our relationship." He watches me with a patient silence. "It's complicated."

He nods. "I get that. But we only get one set of parents. We haffi learn fi love them even with their shortcomings."

"I don't know if I believe that."

"What do you believe?"

"That parents should do right by their children." I meet his eyes.

"And what if dem nuh know how?"

"Then they shouldn't have children."

He smiles. "If only responsible people had pickney, then a lot of us wouldn't be here. Me included."

Shit.

"Hessan . . . I'm so sorry. I shouldn't have said that."

"Iz all right. I'm not offended." He laughs. "You spend a lot of time inna yuh head."

I bite my lip, feeling exposed. I adjust a coil that falls out of my hair tie.

"I can feel you thinking when I'm around you. Ah try fi mek sense of everyting. You start fi tug pon yuh hair." He smiles. I immediately drop my hands from my 'fro, a flustered smile creeping onto my face.

"How did you notice that?"

"I notice everything about you, Tilla."

He takes a step closer.

"I notice things about you, too."

"Oh, really? Like wha?"

"You lied to me the other day."

"Neva."

"Your nickname. You said you only had one . . . *church bwoy*," I put on my best Jamaican accent, and he bursts out laughing.

"Wow . . . that is di best thing I've heard all night," he says between laughter. "Me see yuh ah pick up di accent."

"Don't change the subject." I smile.

He rests his back against the fence. After a moment, his smile slightly fades. "Yeah . . . dem call me dat from time to time."

"Why didn't you mention it?"

"Me nuh know. It's kind of embarrassing."

"Isn't that the point of nicknames?" I giggle. "I'm assuming you go to church a lot?"

"Yeah, I started going a lot after my mada died."

My heart sinks. I feel terrible for making fun of him.

"Miss Addie sent me to live wit my uncle after my mom died, and that's when I became really involved wit church. I was fifteen when I moved back to country, but church sort of stuck with me. I go every Sunday."

"Hessan . . . I . . ."

"It's cool. You didn't know." He smiles. "Yuh all right?"

"Yeah," I whisper. But the truth is I'm not. The dead of night makes our time together feel raw and disclosed, and I feel like I should be honest about what I heard.

He beats me to it.

"Dem tell yuh bout her death, nuh true?"

Guilt covers my face.

"Iz all right, Tilla. Me know country people talk. Wha dem tell yuh?"

There's a vulnerability to his tone, and it sends a sadness through me. I'm hesitant, feeling as though by some degree I've violated his trust.

"That she passed . . . in the hurricane. And that you were with her when it happened."

He nods, slowly taking in the information. His eyes search the darkness for something that he cannot seem to find.

"You don't have to tell me about it."

"I want to."

He thinks for a while before speaking. "She never wanted to be a mother." He says it not to me but outward to the night. After a moment, he thoughtfully meets my gaze. "She was young when she got pregnant wit me. Real young. Bout sixteen . . . people always said she wasn't a good mother, but I never blamed her. She did young and . . . she never ready."

I nod, clinging to every word.

"She wasn't ready to give up being a teenager. Di drinking. Partying. Smoking. Everyting." He breaks eye contact with me and again looks out at the night. "Di tings dem used fi say bout her, Tilla . . . every man deh wit her . . . any man could *have* her. Me never want fi believe it. I was so young . . . But it was true. All of it. She did everyting dem say she did ah do . . . and I was so angry at her for it. Angry wit God."

I reach down and grab his hand. His grip is soft and warm, and our fingers immediately fall into place, wrapping around each other. He turns back to meet my gaze.

"Di night of di accident, she did ah go look some mon ah Kingston, and she decide fi tek me wit her. But we never leave out in time. We buck up inna di storm soon as we leave country. She hit a fallen tree and di car spun off a di mountainside."

My chest goes tight.

"There was blood everywhere. She asked me fi stay wit her, but . . . I jus couldn't stand to see her like dat. All I rememba was running to find help . . . but it was a hurricane. Di roads were empty." I give his hand a gentle squeeze, offering him the courage to continue. "Dem find me a couple of days later . . . but she was dead."

He looks away from me. But it is not sadness that he feels.

It is anger.

"I left her."

"Hessan . . ."

"It's true," he says sternly. "I left because I was angry. I was so angry at her for puttin' us in dat position. For takin' us out in di storm. For givin' herself away to all these *men*." He pauses. "I didn't know what to do, so I left."

"Hessan . . . you were so young."

"It nuh matter. I should've stayed." Regret fills his voice. "When I started goin to church, it was to ask for forgiveness." Tears start to well in his hazel eyes. He blinks them back. "Going to church was di only way I could make sense of her death. Di only way I could mek sense of why God took her and spared me."

I squeeze his hand. "I think it's beautiful . . . the fact that you go to church."

He meets my gaze, his eyes sad but nonjudgmental. "Do you believe in God?"

I think for a moment.

"Yeah, I do. At least I think I do. Not in a religious way, though. I don't go to church . . . but I've always felt really connected to something bigger than just . . . me. I think maybe that's why I think about things so much. I'm always trying to understand my connection to all of it, you know? Why things are happening . . ."

"Yuh know God is a feeling. Not a thought." He examines me for a moment. "Yuh haffi experience God. Not think about him."

"I never really thought about it like tha—" I start. "Wait. I mean . . . Never mind. You know what I mean." I laugh.

He laughs too, pulling us out of the heaviness of our conversation. "I love dat yuh have a curious mind. But yuh should try fi be inna di moment more. *Feel* God instead of thinking about what or who he is."

"I guess I just don't really know how to do that. My mind is always . . . going."

"I can show you how," he says softly as he moves to stand in front of me. In a swift motion, he carefully slides his fingers through my Afro, grazing my scalp. Goose bumps flood my body. He presses his thumbs firmly on my temples and rubs.

My body flutters.

"Right now," he whispers. "What do you feel right now?" He draws his hand out of my hair and glides his fingers down to my cheek. "What do you feel, Tilla?" he asks softly.

The dark sky starts to rumble. I can smell the rain before it even starts to fall. I take a deep breath, sinking deeper into his touch as I nuzzle my cheek into his hand. "I—"

"Don't think about it," he whispers.

So I don't.

And the answer rushes through me like a hurricane.

"*You.*"

We lock eyes, and his touch begins to feel intense.

"I feel you, too," he whispers. He moves his hand from my face and stares at my lips, as if searching them for the words he hopes that I'll say first.

But I'm speechless.

"The other day at the river . . . I wanted to do something," he says. "I should've done it but . . . I didn't know if you wanted it, too."

He presses our palms together and locks his fingers in mine, pulling me in closer. A jolt of electricity shoots through me. He traces his mouth up and down my jaw, and I can feel him resisting the urge to press into me. He gives my hand a gentle squeeze, and I can feel all of his energy radiate through his palms and into mine.

"Tilla," he whispers, breathing me in. "Watching you in the water . . . the way you moved through it." He moves his mouth to my neck. "The way your skin *glowed* . . . your body . . . your hair . . ." He moves his mouth to my temples. "Your *mind* . . ."

Rain starts to drizzle from the sky, delicately filling the space between us.

"Hessan . . ." I whisper, trying to fight the sensations that move through me.

But it sounds more like I'm pleading.

"You're so *beautiful*, Tilla." His lips graze my ear. "I want you so bad."

Everything is on fire. I'm desperate to feel every inch of him. His body is warm and strong, and I crave all of it, all at once.

"We can't," I whisper.

He belongs to Diana.

But I want *all* of him.

"Tilla," he whispers into my ear. "If you don't want this . . . please tell me now."

His breathing grows heavy, weighing me down. I am a million pounds, unable to move, breathe, or think.

"*Please, Tilla.* Please tell me if you want this . . ."

He draws his lips up and down my ear. A chill runs down the top of my head to the tips of my toes. I can feel the yearning in his tone. I can taste the desire on his tongue. My heartbeat quickens, and my breathing intensifies, and I feel every inch of me coming alive beneath him.

I feel the answer *so* clearly.

"Yes," I whisper. "Yes, Hessan . . . *I do.*"

He wastes no time.

He presses his lips into my neck, devouring every inch. He draws his lips across to my chest, pulling down the collar of my hoodie with his hand as his lips move in circles. Thunder roars through the night as he tastes the rainwater on my skin. I throw my head back as he runs his lips above my heart, drinking me in. He presses my back into the wall with his body before finding his way to my lips. When the fullness of his cover mine, he presses down firmly, and I let out a small moan. His lips are *so soft*, and they make me feel *so good.* He moves his tongue to the lobe of my ear, sucking down as he takes me in his mouth. Goose bumps cover my body, and I feel my heart start to race even harder.

"Tilla," he moans into my ear. It sounds so good rolling off his tongue. My body grows hotter, and I feel myself craving *all of him.* The rain grows intense as I lose myself in my own breath.

"Say my name again," I whisper.

He does.

He takes his hands to my waist and moves my hoodie up, gripping me firmly around my torso. We are soaked in rain. In pleasure. *In bliss.* I am raw and exposed as his fingers explore my skin, moving up my stomach as they brush against my breasts. I tingle with excitement. All at once, he takes them into his hands.

I nearly explode.

He kisses me intensely to stop me from making noise as he pushes my body deeper into the wall. I feel all of him through our clothes. He gently strokes my nipples as he pushes his waist into mine.

It feels so good it brings tears to my eyes.

Just as I'm at the height of every sensation, he takes his hands from under my hoodie. His kisses start to become softer. *Slower.* He peels his lips off mine, and we lock eyes. He separates a coil from my Afro and carefully wraps his finger around it.

"Every part of you is beautiful," he whispers. He kisses me again.

"Don't stop," I beg.

"I don't want to. But we can't stay out here too long. Di roosta soon crow." He smiles, kind and gentle like always. "I've never met anyone like you, Tilla."

I blush, suddenly nervous at how the moonlight reveals me. Nervous that he felt me in a way that no one ever has. Touched me in a way that I've never been touched.

"It's okay," he says as if reading my mind. "What just happened between us . . . that was your first time, right?" he asks compassionately.

I nod.

"I won't say a word . . . to anyone. This is between us." He kisses me softly on my forehead, and then my ear, and then my cheek. "You should head back. I'll wait here until you get inside."

"Thank you for coming to see me."

He smiles, placing one more gentle kiss on my forehead.

"Good night, Brownin'."

My head spins on a swivel as I rush off into the night. My

heart pumps faster than my feet as I make my way up the veranda steps, across the tiled floors, and back into the room. Careful not to make a sound, I close the shutters to erase any evidence of Hessan's visit before sliding back into bed.

I close my eyes and try to sleep, but the excitement of the night shoots through me like a jolt of lightning. Images of Hessan play vividly in my mind, and electricity rushes through my entire body, taking me to the height of my senses. I am a storm. I see every color like an explosion of fireworks. I feel every touch, and I hear every sound. I am consumed by pure adrenaline as the sound of rain crashes into the shutters. And then, all at once, a daunting question forces my eyes open:

What the *fuck* did I just do?

11

"Yuh mada ah suck di fun outta dis trip."

I struggle to hold the phone to my ear as I dig through my suitcase the next morning. Everyone is up bright and early for church, and the house is bustling as they run around in their Sunday best. The young girls wear fluffy white dresses and frilly socks, while the country boys have cleaned up head to toe in dress shirts and dress shoes. Even Aunt Herma wears a fancy yellow dress as she marches around getting everyone in order. My father's voice comes through the phone as I pace my room.

"She's being ridiculous. She ah call me phone every two seconds wit weather updates like she work fi di blasted news channel." He kisses his teeth. "Yuh tell her say yuh nah have fun?"

"No."

"Are you lying to me?"

"No."

"Because di last thing me need is di two ah uno stressin' about this. Hurricane nah go come fi weeks, and all di forecasters are sayin' it ah go be mild. Maybe just some heavy rains."

"I'm not worried about the storm, Dad." The lie easily floats off my tongue.

"Good." He's silent for a moment. "How's Mia?"

"She's fine."

"Wha bout Andre? Is he getting' his work done around di yawd?"

"Yes, Dad."

"Good. Tell him fi call me when him have a chance. Me need him fi start collect di zinc fi di windows fi when hurricane come." He clears his throat, and we both know what he wants to ask next. "How's everything else going?"

"Good."

"I'm serious, Tilla. Nuh badda mek me find out from Herma say yuh ah sneak round. Especially wit no bwoy pickney."

"Dad—"

"I'm not playin' wit you, Tilla. The last ting I need is people talkin' down desso."

His words stop me in my tracks.

"Jus nuh badda spread yuhself too . . . wide."

My cheeks start to burn up. I feel stunted.

My brain races as I struggle to make sense of his words.

"Me haffi go get some work done. Have a good time at church. Be good."

"Okay . . ." The word barely leaves my lips before the line goes dead. Dread takes over my entire body.

Nuh badda spread yuhself too wide.

I feel light-headed as I grip the dresser for balance. *Did he mean that literally? Or figuratively? Did he mean to say "thin"?* Humiliation plunges to the pit of my stomach as I try to decipher if it was simply a language barrier. *Maybe he just mixed up the saying?* My mind races as panic sets in. All of a sudden, I start to feel gross about last night. Gross in my own body. Shame crawls up the back of my spine.

He doesn't know. I try to calm myself back down. *You're being paranoid.*

I take a deep breath and place the phone down on the counter. I go back and forth in my mind, trying to decipher what he meant as I continue getting ready for church. I dig into my suitcase and pull out a long, white summer dress that I hope would be appropriate, and just as I begin to style my hair, there's a knock on the door.

"Come in!" I yell.

Zory and Diana enter the room dressed in their finest church attire. Diana sports a yellow floral dress, and her hair is pulled back by a bow. Zory wears a blue skirt and white dress top, and her shoulder-length hair is pressed and shiny.

"Yuh nuh ready yet?!" Diana asks.

They waltz into the room, making themselves comfortable as they plop down on the bed.

"Lawd, look pon her head!" Zory laughs, referring to my freshly washed Afro. "Yuh cyan wear it like dat go ah church." She flips her stiff permed hair as if it were something to marvel at.

"I can wear it any way I like," I say.

"Tell her, Tilla!" Diana laughs.

"Not in God's house," Zory says defensively. "Yuh look mod."

I ignore her, styling my hair into two buns. Diana eyes my suitcase. "Lawd, Tilla. All dat ah fi yuh clothes?"

I look over at my suitcase, sprawled open in the middle of the room. Clothes spill out of it and onto the floor.

"Yeah," I say self-consciously.

"Jesus Christ!" Zory says. "One gyal can have so much clothes?" She reaches over and grabs a red skirt from my suit-case. "This can fit you, Tilla? It look kinda small."

"Yes, it can fit me, Zory."

"Yuh sure?" She examines the skirt. "Yuh seem kinda big fi dis."

I bite my tongue.

"Over inna foreign—everyone have so much clothes like you?"

"I guess . . . People who are fortunate enough. Middle-class."

"Middle-class," Zory whispers to Diana, mimicking me.

They giggle, thinking that I didn't hear it.

Zory continues to rummage through the clothes. "Yuh like di colors, Dee?"

"Not really my style. The fabrics are too cheap."

I start to burn up.

"How do you know?"

"Hmm?" Diana looks up at me.

"The fabrics." I turn around. "How do you know that they're cheap? Do they sell better fabric in the country?"

Diana shifts. "Depends on where you shop," she says casually, sitting up a little straighter. "I don't buy off the rack. My clothes are handmade," she boasts.

I turn back to the mirror, ashamed my annoyance got the best of me.

"Well, you guys can take some stuff . . . if you like."

My offer hangs in the air for a second too long, and I hold my breath, praying I didn't offend them. Diana breaks the silence.

"Fi true?" She raises an eyebrow, skeptical.

"Yuh nuh haffi tell me twice." Zory digs into the suitcase.

"Calm down nuh, Zo," Diana scolds. "Stop act like yuh nuh used to nuttin. We see clothes like this all di time in town." Her tone is braggadocious.

I stare at my Walmart T-shirts. "Take whatever you want." I smile.

"This is cute." Zory holds up my favorite pink dress. "Wha yuh tink, Diana? Fi di dance?"

"It's all right," Diana says as Zory adds the dress to her pile.

"Me still nuh know wha me ah go wear. Hessan loves when I wear dresses, but I think I might go with a skirt."

"Maybe Tilla have suh'um yuh can wear."

"We're not the same size." Diana smirks, eyeing my body.

"True, but me haffi admit, she have style." Zory turns to me. "If I had this much clothes, I would open a shop."

"So, Tilla," Diana changes the subject. "Tell us about foreign. Yuh neva tell us much."

I search for the right thing to say. "It's okay. Not as beautiful as here."

"You have a boyfriend back home?"

I start to burn up all over again. Memories of last night rush back to me.

Hessan's fingers running along my stomach.

"No."

"Lie she ah tell," Zory says.

"I swear," I say nervously. "Maybe when I was younger, I had a play boyfriend or something. But I was, like, eight."

"Bumba!" Zory laughs. "Yuh have mon when yuh were *eight*?"

"No. I mean, like, as a joke . . . I've never had an actual boyfriend."

"I don't blame you," Diana interjects. "It's hard fi find a decent bwoy nowadays. That's why I was so happy when Hessan and I made our promise," she boasts. "Even when we break up, I already know who I'm going to marry. I'm sure you'll find that fi yuhself one day, Tilla."

I grow anxious as the thought of Hessan's hands cupping my breasts overwhelm me. I turn around. "Don't we have to go?" I grab my purse. "We don't want to be late."

"Foreigna's right," Diana says. "Plus, Hessan's savin' me a seat. I don't want to keep him waiting."

"As long as it's at di back." Zory smooths down her permed ends in the mirror.

"Yuh love fi sleep in church way too much." Diana laughs. They gather the clothes from my suitcase and head for the door. "We're going to go put these at my house, Tilla. We'll be back."

"Okay."

They make their way through the door, closing it behind them.

I feel all the blood drain from my body.

A few moments later, I head to the veranda, where everyone gathers to leave. As we head out through the gate, I fall in line with Andre.

"Hey."

"Mawnin'. Yuh ready fi church?" he asks me.

"I hope so," I say, grateful that he's not still upset with me.

"Ah yuh first time?" he asks.

"No, I've been before. But it's different here. Everyone is a lot more dressed up."

"First rule ah country—church and funeral are code fi fashion show."

"I can see that." I giggle as I look ahead to Aunt Adele's two-piece green ensemble, long white gloves, and kitten heels.

"Prepare yuhself, 'cause di service long to rawtid."

I smile as I debate what I want to say next. "I'm sorry about the other day, Andre. I didn't mean to be so insensitive."

"Iz all right."

"No, really. I want you to know I really mean that. It's just your drawings . . . I don't know anyone who can draw like that. I got excited."

He smiles. "Fi true?"

"I swear." I smile. "I was thinking . . . maybe one day in the future, you could come stay with me. In Canada."

"Lawd, Tilla—"

"I'll pay for it. Me and my mom or something. You could stay with us."

"Me cyan just get up and go ah foreign, Tilla. Yuh need visa and dem stuff fi travel pon plane."

"I know. And I would sort all that out for you."

He stays silent.

"There are so many art programs in my area. Summer camps and stuff. My mom signed Mia up for one a few years back. I'm going to talk to her about doing the same thing for you. You could go and come back. For the summer."

His face is stoic as he stares ahead.

"Look, you don't have to answer now. But just know that the offer's there. You always have a home in Canada. With me."

He ponders for a moment before speaking. "And yuh ah go pay fi it?"

"I'll save every dollar."

"I'll tink bout it." A smile creeps onto his face. "Under one condition."

"What's that?"

"Yuh haffi let me teach yuh how fi ride a donkey next."

I burst out laughing. "Deal."

We walk for a few more miles until we approach a small white church. Aunt Shirley unlocks the grille before opening the door to let everyone inside.

We walk up the steps and into the low-lit, wooden church. Mostly everything is made of wood and cement. Aunt Shirley takes her place at the front of the church while everyone socializes. I'm about to make my way to the front, when I spot Hessan and Miss Addie walk in. My heart catapults to my stomach as he takes a seat at the back. Miss Addie settles in with her church friends a few rows up, just as Diana and Zory make their way over and slide in beside Hessan. I continue toward the front, where Andre, Richie, and Dane sit in the first row. Just as I'm about to sit down, I hear Hessan call out to me.

"Tilla!"

Shit.

My entire body freezes as I turn around to lock eyes with him. He sits at the end of the row, and he gestures to an empty seat on the other side of him.

Diana and Zory watch my every move.

"Oh. Coming," I say anxiously as I make my way toward them. Hessan watches me like I'm Jesus himself walking down the aisle.

"Mawnin'," he says as I awkwardly approach the bench. I catch Diana roll her eyes.

"Hey, good morning," I say. I slide in next to him as the church begins to simmer down.

Zory whispers something to Diana, and they giggle. Anxiety consumes me, but I keep my gaze straight ahead as Aunt Shirley flips through the Bible.

"Good morning, everyone!" she says enthusiastically. "It iz a pleasure to see so many beautiful faces in church this morning. Please turn yuh pages to Psalm 23."

Everyone opens to the page without a second thought.

"Hessan," Diana whispers, leaning into him. "Help me find that?" She grazes his thigh with her hand.

Hessan takes the Bible from her and opens it to the page before handing it back. I tense up as her fingers linger on his lap.

"Thanks." She bats her eyes before turning her attention back to Zory.

I keep my eyes on my Bible, pretending not to notice as I awkwardly fumble through. When I eventually find the page, I rest my hand on the pew and continue to listen in as Aunt

Shirley preaches the word of the day. I'm following along with the sermon when all of a sudden, I feel Hessan's hand rest on top of mine.

My entire body goes to stone.

He cups my fingers, softly caressing them on the wooden bench. He keeps his eyes focused ahead as our hands stay low on the pew, nuzzled between the two of us. I glance at Diana out of the corner of my eye, but she doesn't notice a thing. She and Zory giggle as they whisper back and forth, completely oblivious. Hessan runs his fingers along the lines on my palm, and my heart races from my chest. He gently glides his fingers along the side of my thigh, moving them up and down the thin fabric of my dress—all as he sits right next to Diana.

I nearly die.

I keep my eyes straight ahead as goose bumps flare down my legs. All of the sensations from last night begin to flood me as he presses firmly into my skin. He traces circles up my thigh, his warm fingers exploring me as I relax into his touch.

I silently hope he wanders higher.

Aunt Shirley delivers the daily word with intensity and conviction, and just as I start to lose myself in Hessan's touch . . . something doesn't feel quite right. The stuffiness of the church starts to feel suffocating, and I turn to reach for a paper fan nuzzled beside me. But just as I reach for it, I spot Aunt Herma, who sits across the altar in her Sunday best. Her hat is low, and she grips her Bible so tightly that her knuckles turn white.

She is watching me.

12

"Yuh see what Miss Claudette wear go ah church?! Me almost drop down."

"But Jesus!" Diana spills over in laughter. "Somebody can wear purple fishnet stockings inna di house ah God?!"

"Yuh shoulda see Miss Shirley face!" Zory cackles.

I walk with Diana and Zory as we make our way back from church. I'm lost in my thoughts, unable to get Aunt Herma's gaze out of my mind. *How much did she see?* Terror consumes me as I recount Hessan's fingers crawling up the side of my thigh. And now, an even bigger question looms in the back of my mind:

Did she see us last night?

"You did see her, Tilla?" Zory asks.

"Huh?" I snap out of my thoughts.

"Miss Claudette. Di big fat one who sit ah back."

"Oh. No, I didn't."

"By the way, Tilla," Diana says, "We're havin' a sleepover tonight at my house. To celebrate your arrival to the country."

"Oh. I—" I rack my brain. "I don't know if I'm up for a sleepover tonight."

"We're celebrating *you*. Your attendance isn't optional." Diana rolls her eyes. "Plus Mummy has evenin' service, so we'll have the house to ourselves."

The thought alone makes me feel nauseous, but when I consider that a night at Diana's means a night away from Aunt Herma, it's clear that it's the lesser of two evils.

When we get back to the house, random churchgoers are scattered on the large veranda for Aunt Adele's Sunday lunch. I head back to the room and change out of my dress and into a T-shirt and shorts, careful to avoid Aunt Herma. By the time I head out onto the veranda, everyone has their plates of food in hand.

"Hey," I say as I settle in next to Andre. He chomps down on mackerel and dumplings. "Can I have a bite?"

"How yuh so cravin'?!" He playfully fans me off. "Gwan inna kitchen and tell Mummy fi dish yuh out a plate."

I make my way through the house. It feels oddly quiet with all the adults outside and the kids running in the yard. I head toward the closed kitchen door, stopping when I hear distinct muffles on the other side. I turn the knob and open it ever so slightly, stunned to find Uncle Junior hovering over Aunt Adele by the stove.

"Yuh nuh hear wha me say, gyal?!" he barks at her, moving closer.

Aunt Adele cowers, keeping her eyes on the pot.

"YUH DEAF?!" he screams.

I freeze.

"Me hear you," she whispers, keeping her eyes low.

"Next time yuh serve me from di bottom ah di fucking pot, me and you ah guh have problems. Yuh understand?"

She quivers under his frail but daunting frame.

"Open yuh fucking mout when me ah talk! Yuh hear wha me say?!"

She nods.

And that's all it takes for him to explode.

He flings the pot off the stove and grabs her by the neck, slamming her body into the wall. I nearly scream.

"Who yuh ah nod yuh head to? Een?! Fuckin' dutty gyal!"

Uncle Junior squeezes her neck with one hand and uses the other to pin her arm to the wall. She winces in pain. He takes her off the wall and slams her into it again. And then once more. The wind is knocked out of her. She lets out a terrified sob, tears pouring down her face as she tries to wiggle from beneath his grip.

"Me say yuh fi use yuh fuckin' mout when me ah talk! Yuh hear me?! Ah gwan like say yuh deaf! Answer when me ah talk to yuh!"

"All right! All right!" she sobs uncontrollably.

"If yuh tink say yuh ah go gwan wit dat blasted nasty attitude when yuh ah cook *my* food, yuh mek a sad mistake!" He pushes his face closer to hers. "Dutty stinkin' gyal. Yuh must nuh know who yuh ah romp wit." He takes his hand from her throat and moves it down to her leg, hiking up her housedress.

I can't watch for another second.

"STOP!" I scream out, busting the door wide open. Uncle Junior swings around, and Aunt Adele freezes like a deer in headlights.

What the fuck did I just do?

"Let go of her!" My voice is tender and coarse. I am unsure of what to say next. Unsure of what to do and who to call. "I said let go! Leave her alone!"

A wave of fury comes over Uncle Junior as he flings Adele to the ground. "Who di fuck yuh ah talk to, gyal?!" He takes a step toward me. "Yuh tink 'cause yuh come from foreign yuh can talk to me so?" His cold eyes drill into me.

"Leave her alone." My voice is small, but I do not cower. "Leave her alone or I'll tell my father."

Uncle Junior stares me down, and for a moment, we stay

just like that, unsure of who will give in first. I am shot with nerves as I tremble like a leaf.

Be brave, Tilla.

He walks toward me, and suddenly, we are face-to-face. Rage seeps from his skin, and in this moment, I swear that I am done for. His green eyes pierce through mine before he finally speaks.

"Mind yuh *fuckin'* business, foreigna," he spits before walking past me and out through the door. My heart falls to my stomach, and suddenly, my knees feel weak, ready to give out and collapse. I look to Aunt Adele, who lies on the floor.

"Are you okay?" my voice quivers.

She gets up, not meeting my gaze.

"Do you want me to call someone?"

"No!" she says abruptly. "Just leave it."

There is a space between us. An opportunity to help her.

But it is not what she wants.

"Okay," I whisper.

The kitchen is burning up from the midday heat. The air is suffocating as I take a deep breath, unsure of what to do with myself. For some reason, my feet stay planted. I watch as she starts to collect the food from the ground, throwing it in the trash. She keeps her demeanor laser focused as I quietly make my way over to her and begin to help. We scoop the food in silence as a tear falls down her cheek. She quickly wipes it away. I place my hand softly on her back, and she flinches, dropping the food in her hands as if finally realizing that I'm there.

"Does anyone know?"

She says nothing.

"I really think you should tell someone."

A glimmer of sadness flashes in her eyes. For a second, it feels as though she is about to break, but in the blink of an eye, she snaps herself out of it.

"No," she says firmly. She shakes my hand off her back and

focuses on the task at hand. "Women have duties to fulfill. *Responsibilities*. Yuh nuh know nuttin bout responsibilities inna foreign."

She stands up and places the pot back on the stove, getting back to work. I sit on the floor, stunned. Her words are not up for discussion.

I raise myself off the floor, feeling helpless. I stand in the middle of the kitchen, hoping that she'll turn around—that maybe she'll change her mind.

But she doesn't.

The truth is there is no reason for her to confide in me. In anyone. She is being abused by her brother in the mountainsides of Jamaica, and her secret will be buried somewhere deep in the tall grass and forested trees.

Living in the country, she is miles from justice.

Feeling defeated, I turn around to leave. There's so much I want to say, but instead, I walk toward the door, my heart heavier than when I came.

"Tilla."

The sound of her voice sends a jolt through my chest. It leaves her mouth commanding and forceful. I turn around.

She keeps her back to me, intentionally busy over the stove as she pours the mackerel from the can into the pot. The oil splatters, crackling as the fish hits the high heat. She places the empty tin on the counter.

"Don't say nuttin. To anyone. Yuh hear?"

She doesn't turn around, but the weight of her tone makes my skin crawl.

She is threatening me.

I nod, searching for my breath through the thick humidity of the hot kitchen.

"Of course," I whisper.

13

Later that night, I make my way down the dark forested path to Diana's pink house.

We gather around an old television set, watching the nightly news as we munch on cheese puffs. Despite the elaborate trimmings on the outside of Diana's newly built house, the inside is barren and feels barely lived in. With no couch, we sit in the dark on the cold tiled floor as the voice of the weather forecaster fills the room.

"*Meteorologists have confirmed that the tropical depression has strengthened into a storm that will now be designated as Tropical Storm Gustav. Gustav is expected to intensify as it approaches Haiti.*"

"Lawd. Wha typa name is Gustav?" Diana asks, screwing up her face. "Hurricane can name *Gustav*?"

"Gustav betta turn round and go back ah him yawd." Zory munches with her mouth open.

"How yuh mean?" Diana laughs. "Yuh wan hurricane fi mek a U-turn?"

"I'm just saying. Me coulda do without it this year."

"There's nowhere you can go to get away from it?" I ask. "Like town?"

"HA!" Zory lets out a loud cackle. "Hurricane hit *everybody,* gyal. It nuh business how much money yuh mek or which part yuh live. Town, country, gully, or roadside—it nuh matter. So brace yuhself."

An eerie chill runs through me.

"Stop frighten di gyal nuh, mon!" Diana scolds Zory. "Nuh worry, Tilla. Hurricane nuh last long. All storm must pass."

"And kill." Zory smirks. "Murder everyting in its *bumba-clot* path."

Diana smacks her on the arm.

"Wha?! Ah lie me ah tell?"

"You're going to be fine," Diana says to me.

"How do you even prepare for that?" I ask.

"Stock up on water. We usually lose it for a few months. And stock up on food. Matches and candles for light."

"Mhm. When di light dem go out? Cha." Zory looks me dead in my eyes. "Yuh coulda neva see darkness till yuh see country after hurricane."

Diana flicks off the television, and the room goes black. We gather our snacks and head down the hall into her bedroom. I examine the barren room, her peach walls freshly painted. Even though we're just down the path from the main house, the darkness of the country combined with the lack of furniture makes her house feel cold and slightly creepy. A single dim lamp lights the room as my eyes fall on a dresser lined with small plastic trophies.

"Are these all yours?" I approach the dresser.

"Yup. I have di record fi di most awards in school," Diana says proudly.

"Wow," I say. "It must be so fun going to boarding school."

"It's amazing," she responds a little too quickly. "Only di best of di best go school ah town."

Zory kisses her teeth. "Diana's only tellin' di good parts.

Town girls are obnoxious. Di whole school stink ah rich bitch."

"Me nah stress over no uptown gyal." Diana waves her off before turning to me. "They think they're better than us because they live in Kingston and we come from country. But me nuh business."

"Speak fi yuhself," Zory says. "You know how many fights me get in ah school? Me nah have no dry foot Kingstonian gyal talk down to me or Diana."

"Zo just loves to fight." Diana rolls her eyes. "Yuh just haffi look pon her wrong and she want fi lick yuh down."

"Shelly-Anne deserved it! Gyal have di nerve fi ask me which part me buy me shoes! Like she neva know." She kisses her teeth. "Facety."

I giggle, their camaraderie and closeness making me wish I could be a part of something special like that.

"By the way, Tilla," Diana says, "I need your help tomorrow to carry some bags from shop. Mummy's sellin' snacks at di dance, and me haffi go ah shop fi pick dem up. Zo has to watch di goats, and I cyan carry it all back by myself."

"Yeah, sure," I say. "What time?"

"Evenin' time. I'll come by di house."

"Why yuh nuh ask Hessan?" Zory smirks, eyeing her as she plops down onto the bed. "Wit him big, strong muscles."

"He said he has to run some errands outta town fi Miss Addie tomorrow. We'll prob-ly meet up afterwards."

"Backside!" Zory says, playful. "So uno back togetha?"

"Not just yet." Diana smiles coyly. "We're making it official at di dance."

My body tenses.

"Lawd." Zory shoves cheese puffs into her mouth. "That neva tek long."

"It neva does wit me and Hessan. We just . . . work, yuh nuh?" Diana says, an odd giddiness to her demeanor. "Yuh cyan deny what God has planned. We were made for each other."

"Why did you guys break up?" I ask, sheepish.

"She wanted fi marry rich." Zory chuckles. "Meet a Kingstonian bwoy."

"That's not true." Diana giggles, fanning her off. "I jus didn't want to limit my options when I went away to school. But I've always known Hessan is my soul mate." She blushes. "When yuh know, yuh know."

My body halts.

"Anyways, the dance is a *big* night for us. Always has been. We go together every year since we was twelve. And gettin' back together this year is only going to mek di night that much more special."

"That's exciting," I say. I feel sick with myself.

"I have butterflies jus thinkin' about it," she boasts, a wide grin on her face. "Mummy wants to start plannin' di wedding next year."

"Ugh, I cyan wait to be a bridesmaid," Zory says before turning to me. "Which reminds me, Tilla. What are the boys like back in foreign? Me need fi find my man. I'm thinking about gettin' my visa."

"Ha!" Diana laughs. "Don't listen to her, Tilla. Zory nuh have money fi no visa."

"How yuh know?!" Zory says, defensive. "Daddy's been payin' me fi watch di goats. I'll have enough by end of year."

Diana rolls her eyes.

"The boys are pretty normal." I shrug. "Nothing special."

"Me nuh believe dat. I've seen di movies where dem come ah ya yawd wit flowers or play music outside ah ya window." Zory giggles, the thought clearly entertaining her. "Me surprise yuh neva have a bwoy do dat fi you."

"I'm not," Diana interjects. "I could tell Tilla didn't have a man from day one."

"What do you mean?" I ask, confused.

"I could just tell you were single." She shrugs. "You *flirt a lot*."

"What?!" I smile. "That is so not true."

"Yeah, it is," Zory agrees.

"You flirt with everyone everywhere you go," Diana says matter-of-factly. "You were all over Hessan at Miss Addie's house that day."

"What?"

"Don't play coy, Tilla." She rolls her eyes. "Before you knew him and I were a thing. Me tink yuh did ah go fuck him right desso pon di porch. You even said you thought he wanted you the other day."

"That's not—"

"Yuh was basically sucking him off with your eyes at Sports Day."

My stomach drops.

"Diana—"

"Come on, Tilla. Admit it. You're *bwoy crazy*." She lets out a sharp laugh, and my entire body goes cold.

"You practically sprinted down di aisle when Hessan called yuh name today in church." Zory laughs. "You *love* mon."

"That's such a lie," I say through gritted teeth.

"But you think Hessan's cute, right?" Diana challenges.

"No, I—"

"Liar!" Zory jumps up, excited. "I can see it all ova her face."

"It's fine, Tilla. You can admit it. You wanted to fuck him di first day you met him. Right there on that porch."

"No, I didn't." My voice grows shaky.

"Dee, yuh cyan say 'fuck' twice pon a Sunday." Zory giggles.

"I'm kiddinggg." Diana laughs. "We're just playing with you,

Tilla. Relax." She throws a pillow at me. "Plus, foreign girls know all about girl code. Right? Them teach you that a foreign."

"I—"

"That's what they teach you," she challenges me. "Right?"

"Yeah . . . yeah, of course."

"See?" Diana flips her braids. She reaches into her pocket, whipping out a small red flip phone. "Foreign girls may be fast, but they're not dunce. Besides, Tilla's not exactly Hessan's . . . *type.*" She eyes my broad frame. "Hessan likes a more . . . *pure* woman. A Christian." She opens the phone, and the screen reads DIGICEL. She smiles as she reads a message that pops up.

"Jahvan's coming to look for us tonight."

"What?!"

"Yeah. I gave him Mummy's phone number." She gestures to the flip phone. "He's gonna text us when he's at the door." She points to the back door on her room that leads outside.

"Why is he coming here?"

"He wants to see you."

"Me?!" My stomach drops. "Why didn't you say anything?!"

"Didn't think it was a big deal." Diana shrugs. "Why do you think we're having a sleepover?" she asks casually.

"Diana, you said it was to celebrate me coming to the country."

"And the celebration includes a cute boy who wants to come look fi you." She looks at me as if I'm crazy. "I don't get the big deal?"

"The big deal is that she like someone else," Zory chimes in, shoving another handful of cheese puffs into her mouth.

"That's not true—"

"Then prove it," Diana challenges me.

Like clockwork, her phone buzzes on the bed. She grabs it, flipping it open.

"He's here," she says calmly. "At the back door."

I want to throw up.

"Are you going to let him in?" I ask.

"You mod?! He's not coming in here. Him want yuh fi meet him outside."

"Diana—"

"Relax, Tilla. He probably just wants to say hi." She gets up and makes her way over to the door, unlocking it. "Don't be so uptight."

"Gwan nuh, Tilla!" Zory says excitedly. "Tell us what he says!"

I sit on the bed, flabbergasted. "I—I don't even know him."

"Don't be dramatic." Diana rolls her eyes. "It's innocent. Come nuh!" She unlocks the dead bolt and puts her hand on the knob. Anxiety pummels my body as they usher me over to the door. Diana opens the door to the pitch-black night.

I can't see a thing.

"Don't worry," Diana says. "We'll be right here. Just knock lightly on the door when you want to come back in, and I'll open it. Here." She hands me the small flip phone. "Use this for light." I take the phone from her and step out into the blackness. Before I have a chance to protest, she shuts the door behind me, and I hear the lock turn.

Fuck.

The night is so dark that I can't see anything around me. I quickly flip the phone open and a small white light streams out.

"Jahvan?" I whisper.

Nothing. I start to feel spooked. I fiddle with my butterfly necklace to calm myself down.

"Jahvan?" I call again, this time a little bit louder. The only reply is the piercing sound of crickets. Just as I turn around to head back up the steps, I hear shuffling in the bushes and then footsteps. I jump, spinning back around to see Jahvan with a spliff in his hand.

"Hey, pretty girl."

"Jahvan."

"Wha'ppen?" he asks slyly. He takes an inhale of ganja before releasing a thick cloud of smoke into the black of night.

"Not much. I, uh, I was just about to head back inside. I thought maybe you weren't coming."

"And miss di chance fi see you?" He steps closer to me, and we stand face-to-face. "Neva." He smiles. The scent of his cologne fills my nostrils. He wears a red T-shirt, and a small gold chain sits around his neck. His brown eyes are intense.

"Diana said you wanted to see me?"

"Of course." He leans into me, his accent slurring and thick. My body automatically heats up. I can't help but feel flustered. "Why?" he asks softly. "Yuh never wan fi see me?"

"No, I—I do." I squirm. "What did you want to talk about?"

"Relax nuh, Till-ah." He smiles, revealing perfectly white teeth. "Me jus want get fi know yuh a likkle betta . . . Iz dat all right?"

I nod. "Yeah. Sure."

He smiles, holding up the spliff. "Yuh wan some?"

I shake my head.

"Wha'ppen?" He laughs. "Yuh 'fraid of a likkle ganja?"

"No . . . I've just never tried it before."

"Yuh ah hang round dem church people too long." He takes another inhale. "It'll help calm yuh nerves. And yuh cyan get dis anywhere else." He holds it out to me again. "Yuh sure yuh nuh wan some?"

"I'm okay. Smoking's not really my thing."

"Okay, Miss Kyan-ah-da." He steps closer. "Then what is yuh 'ting'?"

I shrug, unsure how to respond.

"Lemme guess. Yuh more of di church type?"

"Not really . . . I don't really go back home."

"Good. Dat mean yuh have a mind of yuh own." He takes

another inhale. "Me nuh inna di church ting at all. Me nuh want nobody fi tell me how God feel and wha him look like. I am God. No white man inna di sky ah go control my fate." He laughs. "Foolishness."

I fight back a smile. I have to admit, hearing a different perspective is refreshing.

"I thought everyone here went to church."

"I did when I waz small. But me learn fast dat all ah dem church people ah hypocrite. Clappin' yuh hand pon Sunday nuh mean nuttin if yuh ah sin pon Saturday. Nuh badda mek none ah dese church people fool yuh." He smiles mischievously. "Especially di church bwoy dem."

My chest tightens. "What?"

"Relax, Till-ah." He laughs. "Yuh nuh haffi pretend wit me. Me know all about church bwoy. Him used fi hang wit me bredren dem. Before him mada dead." He uses a lighter to relight his spliff before taking a pull. "Long as yuh know say every bod bwoy was once a good bwoy." He exhales, meeting my gaze. "And every good bwoy was once bod." His smile is sly as I try to decipher what he means. "Everyone have a past around here." He flicks his spliff into the bushes before taking my hand. "Jus know if yuh need anyting, yuh can talk to me . . . Till-ah."

"I appreciate that, but—" I gently wiggle my hand away. "It's not you, Jahvan. I just—" I search for the right words. "I just don't want to give anyone a reason to talk, I guess. More than they already are."

"People ah go talk, regardless . . . Yuh cyan worry bout dat." He leans into me. "Me jus ah try fi get to know yuh." He gently tugs on my T-shirt. "What's yuh favorite color?"

"What?"

"I'm serious." He laughs. "Me wan fi know."

"That's how you want to get to know me?"

"It's a start." He holds my gaze. His brown eyes are magnetic.

"Purple."

"Purple." He considers it. "I like dat. Mine is brown." He smiles before running his finger along my arm. His touch is soft and gentle. "People ah go say wha dem wan fi say. But they're all hypocrites. Yuh cyan let wha dem tink control yuh."

For a moment, his words comfort me. He studies me as he moves closer.

"Me like you, Till-ah." He hovers over me before taking his hand to my face. "Pretty likkle foreign girl," he whispers. He cups my chin, raising my eyes to meet his gaze. He moves his hand to the back of my neck, gripping it firmly as he slowly breathes me in.

All I can hear is the breath we exchange back and forth.

"Pretty likkle brown-skin girl," he slurs. He moves his hand from my neck to my face, and then slides it down my chest, intentionally grazing the tip of my nipple with his fingers before dropping his hand to meet mine again.

A rush of energy passes through me.

He moves closer to my lips. "Yuh like me?" he asks, his tone hushed.

I can feel his raw desire. He is hungry for me, and I can smell it on his breath.

"Yuh like me, nuh true, Till-ah?"

He's wrong.

But before I have a chance to resist, he presses his lips into mine, fully and firmly. His kiss is raw as he slowly swirls his tongue around in my mouth. For a second, I lose control of my own senses. He tastes like fruit and marijuana smoke as he presses my body against his, scooping me in his arms.

"Wait," I say, attempting to wiggle out of his grip.

But he doesn't. He only pulls me closer. He takes his hand and pulls my leg up to his waist, moving his hand to my thigh.

I place my hand on top of his to stop him from wandering inches away from the most private parts of me.

"Jahvan," I whisper as I push his hand back down my thigh. "I can't."

I turn my head away from him, but he just moves his lips to my neck and begins to run his tongue down the side. I peel my body from his, abruptly jumping back.

"I have to go," I say as I pull away from him.

He pulls me back in.

"We're having a good time," he slurs into my ear.

"I know . . . but . . . I have to go." I yank myself away from him, and he smiles.

"All right, all right," he says, his tone relaxed. "But me wan fi see you again." He stares at me, and a rush of grief passes through my entire body.

I almost buckle at the knees from devastation.

What have I done?

I back away from him, walking back up to the next step. I feel so dizzy I think I might fall over.

"Later, Kyan-ah-da," he calls as he slinks off into the night.

I follow the steps up, using the cell phone light to guide me. I search for my breath, but it is not there. I clutch the phone tightly to ground me. To bring me back into my body.

Breathe, Tilla.

I approach the door and knock lightly. I wait a few seconds. Nothing.

I knock again, this time a little harder. A few moments pass, and the door remains closed. I reach for the doorknob and try to turn it. It's locked.

I knock harder.

"Diana," I whisper.

No response. I look behind me into the black night. Jahvan

is nowhere in sight. The night is so dark that I can't see my own hands. I begin to lose awareness of my body. I know there is a forest beside the house, but I can't even make out one tree. I turn back to the door and knock again, this time even harder as the panic sets in.

"Diana! Can you let me i—"

The door swings open, and Diana stands in front of me. "Are you an idiot?! My mom just got home! Me tell you fi knock lightly."

"I'm sorry, I just . . . I thought you fell asleep or something."

"Obviously not. We saw you shoving your tongue down his throat."

Shit.

"Come. Get inside." She grabs my wrist a little too hard, pulling me into her room and shutting the door behind me.

A surge of relief washes over me, grateful to be back inside and out of the dead of night. Zory lies on the bed, flipping through a magazine with my nail polish sprawled out around her.

"Canada!" She laughs. "Is that how all foreign gyal greet di mon weh dem nuh like?" she asks sarcastically.

I plop down on the bed. My head feels woozy, and all I want to do is curl up beneath the covers.

Nuh badda spread yuhself too wide.

My father's words slither up my skin. I feel disgusting. Sick with myself.

"I don't even know what just happened," I whisper.

"Well, I do." Diana smiles. "And it looked like you enjoyed it."

"Tell us everything nuh!" Zory says excitedly.

So I do.

14

"Yuh nah get suh'um fi eat?"

I stand in line beside Andre the next morning as we wait to cash out our things at Miss Debby's shop. He holds a bag of cheese puffs, and I hold a pink bag juice.

"I'm okay," I muster.

The truth is I have no appetite. I am drowning in the irresponsibility of my decisions. Consumed by the guilt I have brought upon myself.

It's not a big deal, I try to convince myself.

But I know that is not true.

We pay for our things and make our way down the road. The country is lively today, and music blasts from a nearby house on the hill. Andre opens his bag of cheese puffs, stuffing a handful into his mouth.

"How yuh so quiet?"

"I'm not."

"Lie you ah tell." He kisses his teeth, and cheese puffs fly out of his mouth.

I look away, grossed out. "You can put one in your mouth at a time, you know."

"No, sa." He shoves another handful into his mouth. "Yuh nuh get di full flavor dat way. Uno nyam it wrong ah foreign."

I smile, biting off the tip of my bag juice. The sun beams down exceptionally hot, making this simple walk feel exhausting.

"It's so hot out today."

"So it go round dis time ah year. Country get real hot before hurricane come."

"Global warming?"

Andre looks at me. "Wha name so?"

"It's when the planet heats up. Because of pollution. Throws off the seasons."

"Pollution?"

"Fumes from cars and stuff. Agriculture."

"Wha me tell yuh bout usin' dem fancy foreign word?" he scolds through a mouthful of cheese puffs. I roll my eyes as we continue down the road. As we approach the little blue house, I feel myself start to panic.

He's out of town for the day.

I'm reminded of Diana's words, and I instantly relax, grateful I don't have to tell him about last night. Grateful he won't be able to read it all over my face.

"Tilla?" Andre whacks me over the head with his bag of cheese puffs. "Yuh nah answer me?"

"Huh?" I look at him, trying to keep my focus in two places at once.

"*Me say*, yuh tink me woulda have a chance wit a foreign girl? When me come ah Canada next summer?"

"Uh, yeah . . . I don't see why not—"

"Tilla!"

I halt. I whip my head around, and my entire body goes numb as I lock eyes with Hessan. He stands at the edge of his porch steps, his smile bright as ever as he makes his way toward us.

Fuck.

"Yuh just ah go walk by me yawd and nuh say nuttin to me?!" He smiles as he gets closer. "Wha'ppen, Andre?!"

"Jus ah come from shop," Andre says. "Wha yah deal wit? Besides Tilla." Andre laughs at his own joke. I want to kick him.

"Deh ya, still. Just ah wonda why Tilla ah pass by me yawd and nah say nuttin. Like me and her ah nuh friend."

"I didn't think you were home."

"So yuh neva come check?" He winks, his eyes glistening with intrigue. I blush.

Nothing has changed between the two of us.

Andre rolls his eyes before sucking back his Chubby. "We ah head back up ah yawd."

"Yuh can leave Tilla wit me?" he asks.

Andre shifts. "Me nuh know if that's a good idea." He turns to me. "Wha yuh want me fi tell Aunt Herma?"

"Just . . . tell her I went to my dad's farm for the day. I'll be back later on."

He studies me, doubtful. "Yuh *sure*?"

No.

"Yeah." I nod.

Andre shrugs, turning to Hessan. "Tek her den nuh. Me did wonder how me did ah go get rid of her big head."

"Woooow!" I laugh as he takes off down the road. And just like that, it is just Hessan and me. All my nerves subside. He takes my hand in his, commanding my focus.

"I want to take you out fi di afternoon. On a road trip."

"A *road trip*?!"

"It was a surprise." He smiles. "I was just on my way to come look fi you. I wanted to tek you out of town. Somewhere it can be . . . just us." He keeps his voice low. "We'll tek di country bus. If we leave now, we'll be back before sunset."

"Sunset?!" I say, stunned. "You're crazy. Where?"

"I cyan tell yuh." His hazel eyes light up. "I want fi be alone with you, Tilla. Somewhere far. Without havin' fi tink bout who ah watch."

"Hessan—"

"It's a long trek. But I *promise* it's worth it. Let me show you di beauty of Jamaica."

My stomach tightens.

Aunt Herma will have me dead.

"Yuh trust me?" he asks.

My heart screams the answer before I do.

"Yes."

He takes my hand, and we make our way back up the road.

We walk for about thirty minutes to an old dirt clearing before arriving at a bus stop. We wait a few minutes before the bus pulls up. It's not the traditional bus I would see in Canada but rather a completely packed van. Brown bodies spill out of the sides, their arms and heads sticking through the windows.

There's a covertness to Hessan as we wait for the bus to unload. He scans the crowd of people as he holds my hand, cautious not to draw attention. As the last person unloads, my entire body seizes.

Aunt Adele.

I immediately drop Hessan's hand, but it's too late. She spots me and stops in her tracks. We lock eyes, and all the blood drains from my face.

I think I might collapse under the midday sun.

Before I can even process the interaction, she looks away, hiking her purse onto her shoulder and continuing on into the crowd as if she didn't see us at all.

I feel dizzy.

Stunned.

What if she tells Aunt Herma? Or word gets back to Diana?

Anxiety paralyzes me. But just then, another possibility hits me:

Maybe if I didn't see anything in the kitchen, she didn't see anything now?

It's an idea that holds weight.

I glance over at Hessan, who hasn't noticed a thing. The driver gives us the signal to load on, and I take a deep breath. Leaving the interaction behind me, I shake it off, muster some courage, and make my way onto the bus.

The driver rips through the bumpy roads with reckless speed. We make countless stops, and with each one, Hessan tells me it is not our time to get off yet. I doze off a few hours, and when I wake up, we've arrived at what feels like the other side of the island. We pass a sign that reads WELCOME TO PORTLAND, and I look at Hessan quizzically.

"We soon reach." He smiles, kissing the back of my hand.

But I grow impatient with each passing second. I have no idea where I am, and the danger of what I'm doing begins to sink in.

But there's no turning back.

We continue through the rugged terrain, passing by wild, untouched greenery. All around us, bushes grow wild and unkept, and I'm blown away by how jungly the mountains in Portland are. As we make our way to the end of the town, a big sign reads PORT ANTONIO in chipped blue paint.

Soon, the bus comes to a park, and Hessan leads me off and out into the street. Swinging vines pour down all around us as we weave in and out of them. But the most extraordinary part is the large sea of blue water that sparkles at the end of the path. A rich, exuberant turquoise blue that glistens for *miles*. Hessan beams.

"Welcome to di Blue Lagoon."

I stare out at the water in awe. The sun radiates down, adding a rich glimmer to the vibrant blue. The water is literally *glowing*. He leads me through the bustling crowd of people and down toward the sandbank, where a string of long rafts crafted from bamboo are lined up. A bunch of people wait in line, anxious to pay their fare and get out into the water. Above all the action a giant sign reads: GLISTENING WATERS: LUMINOUS LAGOON.

"Dis was my favorite place fi come when me did likkle," Hessan says as we stand in line. "Nighttime di wata glow inna di dark when yuh touch it."

I feel like I'm in a trance as I take in my surroundings. The water glistens an iridescent color as if a million jewels were reflecting off the surface.

"Legend has it a sea creature live inna di water. But him sleep ah daytime."

"You believe that?" I smile.

"Of course," he says as we approach the front of the line. He pays our fare to the man in front of us. "People go missing ah lagoon nuff times. Nuh true, Rasta?!" He nods to the elderly man.

"All di time." The man nods, pocketing our money.

Hessan leads me down to the long rafts made from bamboo, and we climb on board. He picks up a large stick and begins to comb through the water. Soon, we are gliding past wooden tree houses and engulfed in coral. I sit back, basking in the bright yellow sun that rests over the mountaintops.

Hessan glances over at me. "Yuh look comfy."

"More than comfy." I beam. "This is incredible."

He smiles. "Yuh deserve fi experience di best of Jamaica, Tilla."

"And how do you know I haven't already?" I eye him playfully, and he smiles. I watch as he uses his toned muscles to skillfully guide us through the water. "You've done this before."

"Plenty a time. Me used fi come here wit my mada. It was her favorite place."

"I can see why she loved it so much." I dip my hand into the lagoon. "This is such a beautiful memory to share with her."

"Not so much." He shakes his head. "I was always 'fraid fi go out pon di wata. She used fi tell me she was gonna feed me to di monster."

"That's so mean." I giggle.

"Yeah . . . she wasn't really the comfortin' type of mada. More of a friend." There's a longing in his tone. "What about you? Yuh have good memories wit yuh fada?"

I think about it for a second. "Sort of. He used to take me on adventures. When I was younger, way before Mia was born."

"Adventures?"

"Yeah." I smile as I recall. "We would do some cool stuff. He used to take me down to the forest behind our house. We would watch fish in the stream or spend afternoons at the park." I get lost as the memories flood back to me. "I even re-member one time on our way home, we found a dead bird on our doorstep. Or at least I thought it was dead."

"Ah lie." He raises an eyebrow, his interest piqued.

"Yeah. I think it flew into our door or something. My dad wrapped it up and brought it inside. We kept it for weeks inside this big shoebox, and he took care of it. Every day. He nursed it until the bird came back to life."

"Seriously?"

"I swear." I laugh as the memory becomes vivid. "I'd never seen anything like it. I could've sworn the bird was dead but, my dad . . ." I pause. "My dad gave it life again. I used to think he had powers or something. I thought he was magic." I shrug as the memory falls from my skin. "I was six, so who knows. Maybe I'm just remembering it wrong."

"I think you're rememberin' it exactly as it happened."

"Maybe." I consider his words.

"When did he get you di necklace?" He gestures to my butterfly pendant.

"When I was nine." I place my hand on it. "For my birthday."

"Yuh always wear it?"

"I never take it off." I nod. "He used to always be around and stuff. I guess wearing it reminds me of that . . . who he used to be."

I tuck the necklace into my shirt. Hessan gazes at me, silent for a moment.

"I'm really sorry, Tilla."

"You don't have to be sorry."

"Yuh deserve a father dat wants to be there fi you."

His words send a sadness through me as I gaze out at the lagoon.

"My parents . . . they fight *a lot,* Hessan. I witnessed a lot of things growing up that I never should have." My breath becomes heavy as I meet his eyes. "It's strange, isn't it? How some of us never get the parents we want. Like, there's no do-overs . . . no second chance at it. Some people get these *amazing* parents. And all this love. And then the rest of us . . . the rest of us get the ones who leave."

"Maybe so . . . but I think we do get a second chance. When we choose di person we want fi be with." His words feel heavy against the stillness of the water. "Yuh can choose someone who will do right by you, Tilla. Someone that won't leave."

His words linger on my heart.

The intimacy between us begins to feel intense. Intoxicating. And I can't help but feel frightened by it. There are parts of Hessan that I can never quite have. Parts of him that are promised to someone else. I watch him with a longing in my eyes as he guides our raft to a secluded part of the lagoon. We settle into a small nook, hidden behind the bushes and vines as he puts down the stick and sits beside me.

"Will you be at di dance tomorrow?" he asks.

"I don't think so . . . I think I might sit this one out."

Disappointment covers his face. I silently hope he'll try to change my mind.

"I understand," he says. "I do."

But his hazel eyes are sad.

"Can I ask you something?" I ask. "About Diana."

"Yuh can ask me anyting."

"Why are you promised to her? If she's not what you want? It just . . . It doesn't make sense to me."

He sighs. "There's a lot of history between us, Tilla. It's hard to understand."

"You keep saying that. But I *want* to understand, Hessan." I search his eyes. "I need to. If *this* is ever going to feel right . . . I have to understand you."

I watch him go deep in thought as he contemplates my words.

"Please," I whisper.

He looks at the mountains. "When I was younger, I got caught up doin' a lot of bad tings, Tilla. I was runnin' wit my cousin and his crew, and . . . I was goin' down a bad path. Robbin'. Stealin'. Causin' trouble . . ." His eyes find mine. "When my mada died, I had to mek a decision for myself. About *who* I wanted to be . . . I knew I had to mek a change. And that's when I started gettin' close wit Diana . . ." He pauses. "When I moved back from livin' wit my uncle, tings between us got more serious."

"How serious?"

"As serious as yuh can be at fifteen . . . I guess, sorta like puppy love. I was still healin' from di death of my mada. And Diana . . . she was there fi me. But we were young, Tilla. Too young." He looks at me, his eyes sad. "We were foolin' around and doin' tings we shouldn't have been doin' . . . not at fifteen."

"Things like what?" I ask, although I'm fearful of the answer.

"She was my first, and I was hers, too." He sighs. "But we weren't using protection."

My heart beats faster as I brace myself for the words he says next.

"She got pregnant."

"*What?*"

He nods. "We didn't tell anyone. Only Miss Shirley and my uncle. Country would've turned upside down if anyone ever found out. Both pastor pickney havin' a baby." He shakes his head. "We were *kids*. We both weren't ready for that. So Miss Shirley sent her to Saint Ann's and my uncle . . . he took care of it. He paid for her abortion."

"Oh my God."

"After all dat, my uncle and Miss Shirley decided dat di two of us should be promised. Through di church. Dat we should mek a commitment to God and to each other after what we had done. To hide di shame of it, I guess."

"And you said *yes*?"

"After everyting we went through, it just seemed like the right decision."

"Hessan . . . I had no idea."

"It's not suh'um anyone knows, except us. If people found dat out . . ." His voice trails off, and he looks down at his hands. "Diana is a very prideful person. And havin' sex before marriage is a *big* deal . . . especially when yuh mother is di district pastor."

"So why didn't you stay together?"

"It was puppy love . . . we were too young for it to be real, Tilla. But we're still committed. We took a vow."

The weight of his confession covers me in guilt as Jahvan's words come back to me: *Every good bwoy was once bod.* I search Hessan's eyes.

"Why didn't . . . Why wouldn't you tell me this?"

"I couldn't. I promised Diana I would never say anything. To anyone."

I shake my head. "I can't do this to her, Hessan."

"Tilla." He takes my hand. "What happened between Diana and me was a long time ago. We were just kids. I'm not di same person I was."

"So then why go through with it?"

"Because I made a *promise.*" He searches my eyes as if needing me to understand. "I gave my word. To Diana, to my uncle, to Miss Shirley . . . to God." He looks out at the lagoon. "I went against my word, and I left my mother when she needed me most. I *cyan* do that to someone else. I have an obligation, Tilla."

He goes quiet for a moment, and in his silence, I hear the words he doesn't say:

He is trying to redeem himself for leaving his mother.

"Hessan," I say softly. "I understand. I do. But . . . all of this—what we're doing—it doesn't make any sense. I don't *live* here, Hessan. I'm only here for a few months—"

"I know that." He draws his hand up to my chin. "And I wish I had a better answer, but what I feel for you, Tilla . . . I cyan just turn it off."

"Hessan—"

"From di moment I met you, I've been prayin' to God. Askin' why he wanted our paths to cross . . ." He gently grips the back of my neck. Everything about his touch feels raw, bare. "I cyan give up dis opportunity to experience you, Tilla.

To *know* you. And even if it's only a month I get fi have wit you . . . I don't want to give you up like that."

I shake my head, wiggling from his grip.

"It's only going to make things harder," I whisper.

"Tilla," he says, gently turning my head back toward his.

My eyes flutter to find his, and I search his eyes in the same way that he has done mine time and time again. His hazel eyes are tender, and in this moment, I see him so clearly—his hopes, his dreams, and his fears all wrapped up in this island. I start to soften as the pink cotton candy skies cover us like a quilt, shielding us from our own sorrow. Giving us silent permission to be restored.

Silent permission to heal each other's broken hearts.

"Meeting you dis summer . . . it has been di best ting fi happen to me in a long time. And I *cyan* just give you up like that, Tilla. Not yet."

Everything inside me tells me *no*. Screams that this is a bad idea. But my heart yearns for him. His words only pull me closer. I am the match, he is the flame.

And my heart is on fire.

"Please say yes," he whispers.

There is agony on his tongue. He needs me, and he is pleading.

He brings his lips to mine, barely touching them as he glides his on top.

"*Please, Tilla.*"

I can't resist another second.

"Yes," I say softly.

And that's all it takes. He draws me in and presses his lips to mine. I resist at first, but then I melt. Into him and all over him. He grabs the back of my neck, not taking his lips off mine for a second. He kisses me over and over, soft and then hard, pulling away only to cover my cheeks and forehead with more kisses. We float atop the emerald water, hidden among the vines as his hands start to move down my back. He traces my skin with the tips of his fingers, and I start to heat up as they find their way under my white T-shirt. He wastes no time. He lifts up my shirt and moves my bra to the side, taking my breasts in his mouth. His lips are soft and full as he carefully kisses down on my nipples. My body shivers as my nipples grow hard. It feels *so good*.

"Hessan," I moan.

It escapes from my lips. I haven't felt anything this good before, and I lose myself in the warmth of his mouth. He kisses down again.

"Oh my God," I whisper. I can't believe the sensations that are flooding my body.

I move instinctively as my hands wander along the back of his head. He kisses down harder, and I moan.

"Shh," he whispers softly.

So I do.

I swallow my moans with every kiss he places onto me. He puts his hand over my mouth to stop me from making noise as he circles my nipples with his tongue. I lean back onto the raft as he slowly starts to make his way down my stomach. My body trembles as his lips glide down toward my navel.

"You taste so good, Tilla," he says through weighted breath. His tongue moves slowly, and I can feel the longing in his kiss. He knows I want him just as badly.

"Take off your shorts," he whispers.

I follow his instructions, unbuttoning my shorts as he slides them down my thighs. There are people around, but it doesn't faze him. Knowing that they can't see us makes him bold. We are nestled behind the bushes, miles away from where anyone knows our names.

And it only makes me want him more.

His fingers are gentle as he slides my underwear to the side. He presses down softly, rubbing his fingers in small circles as he caresses the most private part of me. It takes everything in me not to cry out. My body arches instinctively as I quiver beneath his touch. Pleasure erupts through every inch of me as I melt deeper into his hand. His touch is soft and warm, and I surrender to every single stroke as he caresses me.

Again.

And again.

And again.

Minutes turn to hours, and we stay just like that, tangled like the vines that sprout from the earth and wrap around each other like there is no other way. And as the evening sun sets over the mountains of Portland, I allow the water to wash away the worry that lingers on my own skin, stripping me clean of guilt, if only for now. I push all thoughts of Diana, Aunt Herma, and Jahvan to the bottom of the Blue Lagoon, where fears and monsters seem to belong.

Hessan is all I want.

And we are safe above the surface.

15

By the time we get back to Comfort Hall, it is pouring rain.

Evening has fallen, leaving the sky a mixture of burnt orange and deep gray hues. Night is only a few minutes away, and I can feel it creeping up on my skin. Hessan tries to shield me with his jacket, but it's no use. My mind is as heavy as the downpour as it drenches us from head to toe.

There is not a doubt in my mind that I will pay for my excursion today.

The rain beats down heavier than I've ever seen as we jog down the pavement. Off in the distance, the old cream Camry that I saw with Diana appears, rolling down the road toward us. The same man from before calls out through the empty streets.

"DI STORM SOON COME! DI STORM SOON COME! FOOD AND SUPPLIES FI SALE!" his voice blares through the megaphone on top of his car. He spots us as he continues down the deserted street. *"UNO GWAN INSIDE! STORM SOON COME!"*

A chill runs through me. Hessan grips my hand, and we sprint faster. When we finally reach the bottom of the hill, I am soaking wet and out of breath. Hessan refocuses my attention, softly kissing me goodbye. He can tell something is wrong, but he has no idea of the magnitude. He has no idea of how my heart beats out of my chest. He has no idea of what awaits me when I get inside.

Neither do I.

He brings me in for one final hug, engulfing me in his arms. I nuzzle my nose into the nook of his neck, and I'm reminded of how perfectly I fit there. It is warm and safe and far from any judgment or wrongdoing. I take one last inhale of him before he lets me go.

"I'll see you soon, Brownin'." He places a firm kiss on my lips, and I can taste the fresh rainwater that covers his skin. "Walk good."

And with that, he pulls away, sprinting back home as the sun leaves the sky.

I watch as he disappears down the wet concrete. I'm desperate to run after him and into the safety of his little blue house. But I know there is no running from it.

I know I must face Aunt Herma.

Country falls from evening to night in an instant. I begin to make my way up the hill, fear suddenly taking over my entire body. I feel weak . . . *ill* with anxiety. I have no idea what Herma will say to me, and my mind goes wild at the possibilities.

What if she's already called my father?

I shudder at thought. The lies she's probably spun in an attempt to push my father further away from me.

What if Aunt Adele told her about today?

No. She wouldn't. There would be too much at stake.

Maybe Herma hasn't noticed that I've been gone.

I silently scold myself for such a naive thought. She knows I am gone.

And she is waiting for me.

I trek up the hill past a line of clothespins and bushes. I've never walked this path alone, and doing it so late in the evening feels dreadful. Suddenly, the small island feels vacant and large. The only sound that echoes through the land is the rain, and I can hear every drop as it meets the ground.

There is not a soul in sight.

I try to quicken my stride as my father's warning of walking the country at night begins to creep up. But with every step, my flip-flops sink farther into the mud, making it nearly impossible to go faster. The silence of the yard is daunting, and it pours down so hard that I fight to see the path in front of me.

The island has never felt so empty.

As I approach the top of the hill, I hear a distinct ruffling sound that stops me dead in my tracks. I jump. *Is there someone there?* I scan the area and see nothing. Just bushes, dirt, and trees. I take a few more steps, pulling my heavy flip-flops out of the mud, but just as I proceed, I hear the sound again.

This time, it is louder.

Goose bumps spread to my entire body.

I am being watched.

I look to the old battered brown house that sits next door to our family gate.

Maybe there's someone in their yard.

The bushes begin to shake, and I nearly lose it.

I pick up the pace, tempted to take off my flip-flops and run. Just then, my entire body goes into shock: Out of the bushes appear three big, dirty mongrels. We spot each other at the exact same time.

"Dogs. Ugly ones."

Diana's words sound off like an alarm in my head.

I try to move, but I stand frozen. I feel time stop as we study each other, unsure of who will make the first move. The biggest one—a dirty brown one—looks to me with seething eyes. He begins to growl, snarling to reveal the sharpness of his rotting teeth. I am an intruder, and this is his turf.

His ears shoot up as their loud barks echo through the yard.

I nearly drop to my knees.

"If they start barking at you, don't run. Whatever you do," Diana's voice plays again.

Rain beats down on me, electrocuting my entire body with terror. I have only a second to decide my fate.

And in an instant, I am running for my life.

I use everything I have to sprint toward the gate as the dogs cut through their yard toward me. I am terrified. Paralyzed. But I will not stumble.

I have no choice.

I have to make it.

They chase me at full speed, barking viciously as they throw their hind legs into the air, kicking up mud as they race to keep up with me. I try to scream, but no sound leaves my mouth. There is no time.

FASTER, FASTER, FASTER.

I pump my arms and legs as fast as they will go as my sandals fly off into the air. I can see the gate . . . I just have to get closer.

RUN, TILLA.

The pungent smell of wet, dirty dog permeates the air as they zone in on me. Tears fly down my face as I rip through the rain at full speed.

FASTER, FASTER, FASTER.

I crash into the gate at full force, knocking face-first into the metal bars. A sharp pain shoots up my head, and blood falls from my nose, but there is no time to nurse my wounds. I yank the gate open and throw myself inside just as the dogs crash into the bars behind me. I let out a small yelp as they viciously try to rip the metal apart with their teeth. I fall onto my back as I hit the wet ground with a loud thud.

The wind is completely knocked out of me.

I lie still for a moment, my head woozy as the rain beats down onto my face. Each drop feels like a sharp pellet, stabbing me in the eyes. I grab on to the grass and push myself backward to get as far away from the dogs as possible.

"You're safe," I whisper to myself.

Tears fall from my eyes and onto the muddy ground. Relief begins to take over as the dogs eventually grow tired, offering a few final barks before turning to leave. I take a deep breath, uttering a silent prayer before standing up. I'm barefoot and covered head to toe in mud as blood drips onto my shirt. I let out a small laugh, grateful to be okay. The sound of my own voice sends me into a fit of giggles, and soon, a giant smile takes over my face.

I just outran mongrels.

Me.

Canada.

The foreign princess.

I can't stop laughing at the audacity of it all. I beat out stray Jamaican dogs. Three of them. I throw my head back in disbelief.

If only Richie could see me now.

I turn around and walk toward the house, navigating the darkness of the night. The giggles are short-lived when I notice pieces of bright fabric littering the yard. I move cautiously, and as I get closer, I notice more and more of them—about twenty-five pieces of colored fabric in total. I run over to a faded blue one that is covered in mud.

"What the . . . ?"

I reach down and pick it up. And then, all at once, shock stuns my entire body.

These are my clothes.

I barely have time to process. I run to the next article of clothing. And then the next. And then the next. Each one confirming what I know to be true: These are mine. All of them. Every. Single. Last. One.

How could they have gotten out here?

I pull each one from the ground, yanking them from beneath the swampy thick mud. My shirts, my pants, my shoes . . . even my underwear. Ruined. My head is on a swivel as I race through the yard collecting pieces.

How did this happen?

And then an inevitable knowing falls to the pit of my stomach.

And I am fuming.

I bolt up the stairs of the veranda, ready to release my wrath. I've had enough. This time, she's taken it way too far. With my arms full of dirty, wet clothes, I use all my might to swing open the front door. It flies open, smacking the wall with a thud.

Fuck. I immediately regret it.

Everyone looks up at me.

There in the living room sits Aunt Herma, Aunt Adele, Uncle Junior, and a handful of the neighborhood kids. Andre sits with Richie, and Mia and Kenny play with her DS in the corner. Everyone stares at me, and suddenly, my fury turns to embarrassment. I am a dirty, soaked, bloody, and shoeless hot mess.

Richie is the first to cackle.

"BUMBA RAWTID!" he calls out.

The kids explode into cackles.

"Leff her nuh!" Andre calls out over the laugher.

No one listens. Just then, Diana comes through the kitchen door, her hands filled with bags of heavy groceries. She stares directly at me.

Shit.

I. Completely. Forgot.

"Diana—"

"It's fine." She places the bags on the nearby table and unloads them. "I'm sure you had more important things to do today." She eyes me suspiciously. "Right?"

I don't even have the energy to lie. Right now, I am focused on my mission.

"Are you okay, Tilla?" Mia asks, concerned.

But I'm not. I am *so angry*. My eyes glue to Aunt Herma, who casually sips her tea, not taking her eyes off the television.

"Did you put my clothes outside?" My voice is shaky through the commotion.

She pretends not to hear me.

"Aunt Herma?"

Silence.

"Aunt Herma, I'm speaking to you!" My voice is filled with an urgent desperation.

The room goes silent, stunned that I've raised my voice. Aunt Herma takes her eyes off the television, turning her attention to me.

"Excuse me?"

"I asked you a question!" My voice cracks, filled with sorrow.

She casually brings her reading glasses to the tip of her nose. "And what question is that?"

"I asked if you put my clothes outside," I say between gritted teeth.

She looks down to my hands, pretending to just take notice of my wet clothes.

"Oh. Mhm. I was doing your laundry earlier. Since you seem to expect it to be done for you."

"I never asked you to do it—"

"Then how did you expect it to get done?" Her tone is cold as she stares at me, daring me to say another word. "Where were you today?"

"I . . ." I pause. My eyes fall on Aunt Adele, and I realize she didn't tell her. My breathing quickens. "I was at my dad's farm."

"For nine hours?" She eyes me.

"It's true," Andre interjects. "Me did deh wit her earlier. She was plantin' bush. Dat's why she so dirty."

Herma looks to Andre. Her lips go tight.

"If me find out say ah lie you ah tell—"

"I promise," Andre says, his voice small but sure. "On God, Miss Herma."

She turns her attention back to me. Her gaze is piercing.

"Uno foreign girls have some *nasty* habits. Letting your clothes pile up like that. It's disgusting. You should be thanking me. I washed them, and I put them out to dry."

"It's pouring rain." My voice is weak as I search for the words that will offer me vindication. "You *ruined* my clothes."

Aunt Herma smirks so subtly I almost think I imagined it.

"Well, maybe next time you'll get home in time to take them up."

And with that, she takes a sip of her tea and turns her attention back to the evening news. I am wet, cold, and pathetic as I stand at the door with my arms full of muddy clothes. Before I can find the courage to say anything else, Aunt Herma turns the television up to full blast.

The voice of a female reporter echoes throughout the room.

"*Hurricane Gustav's wind speed is currently over seventy-five miles an hour and only getting stronger. The government of Jamaica is urging everyone to begin making their plans for shelter. We are asking the people of Jamaica to use caution and prepare ahead of time. If you are watching this now, we are begging you*—do not wait."

All eyes are glued to the television as the forecaster continues. An eerie feeling fills the room as I silently accept defeat. There will be no winning tonight. I swallow hard. Just as the rain pummeled over me, right now the inevitable truth does as well:

This will be the first of many battles.

The storm has yet to begin.

BEFORE THE
STORM

16

"Me still nuh know wha me ah go wear tonight."

I sit on the steps out back the next afternoon as I scrub my clothes clean in a yellow bucket. I scour the fabric with a soapy bristle brush as Diana stands nearby, slurping on a half frozen Chubby. After a night of rain, the sun beams down exceptionally hot, beating into my skin as I use all my strength to remove the dirt from my clothes. The suds instantly turn black, and I silently curse Aunt Herma in my head. She should be doing this. She should pay for every last piece of clothing that she destroyed.

"Tilla? Yuh nah listen to me?"

"Pardon?" I look up to Diana, wiping the sweat from my forehead.

"I *said* I don't know what I'm wearing tonight. Wha you ah go wear?"

"To what?"

"Di dance, Tilla." She rolls her eyes. "Youth concert."

"Oh." I furrow my brow, returning my attention to the task at hand. "Sorry, Diana. I can't make it tonight."

"Wha yuh mean?! I promised Mummy we would sell di snacks fi her." She says it as though she asked me. "We're workin' di event."

"Since when?"

"Since you *ditched* me yesterday. Yuh know how far I had to walk wit all those bags?! Me haffi mek bout three trips."

"Don't you have plans with Hessan?" I look up at her.

"Duh. Tonight's the big night." She flips her braids. "But we're not meetin' up until nine o'clock. Money nuh mek itself, Tilla." She folds her arms, annoyed.

I submerge another shirt into the water, trying to hide my disdain.

"I appreciate you inviting me, but I don't really feel like going out. Plus, Mia and I leave pretty early tomorrow for town."

"Exactly. Yuh nuh wan see Jahvan before you leave?"

"No."

"Jesus, Tilla. Stop play hard fi get." She smirks. "Let's not forget that last time you saw him, your tongue was down his throat."

"I can't go, Diana. I'm sure you'll have fun without me."

"It's not about havin' *fun*. I need your *help*. What don't you get?" She glares at me. "Me nah spend me whole night ah sell sweetie and bag juice. I haffi meet up with Hessan."

The truth stings.

"Tonight is a big night for Hessan and me. Why would you not want to help my night go smoothly?"

"It's not that—"

"God forbid one night not be about di foreign princess."

"Diana—"

"Yuh rather stay ah yawd wit Aunt Herma?"

No.

"What time are you coming back?"

"Midnight. Hessan and I'll prob-ly get back together around nine and then dance fi a bit. Then we'll prob-ly go back to his place after."

I wring out the shirt in my hand, placing it beside me. The truth is that a night alone with Aunt Herma and Uncle Junior seems scarier than going to the dance. And I know I owe Diana for yesterday.

"All right. Fine."

"Perfect." Her smile catches me off guard. "Come round my yawd around five or so. Don't forget to dress up. But nuttin too fancy. And none of those cheap fabrics."

I roll my eyes, fighting the urge to throw the bucket at her head as she strolls back down the path to her house.

I finish up the rest of my clothes before dumping the bucket of muddy water in the bushes. I wring my clothes out one by one, attaching them to the clothesline. Just then, I feel someone come up behind me. I turn around to find Aunt Adele with a basket of clothes in hand.

"Oh. Afternoon, Aunt Adele."

She nods, making it clear this is not an invitation for conversation as she places down her basket. She focuses on her laundry, hanging her clothes one by one. I turn back to the line, feeling awkward as we stand side by side. I reach down into my bucket and grab one of my shirts. Just as I go to grab a clothespin from my stash, I realize I'm all out.

Shit.

I take the top and hang it over the line, feeling embarrassed to seem unprepared in front of her. I try not to show it as I move to grab another piece of damp clothing. Just as I turn around, she extends her arm to hand me one of her clothespins.

"Oh." I'm taken by surprise as I reach for it. "Thanks."

She hangs her final piece to the line before heading back inside, leaving me confused but hopeful at her kind gesture.

I head over to Diana's around five o'clock.

I feel apprehensive as I make my way down the dirt path. The girls wait out front of the house, and as I get closer, I notice

Zory wearing my pink tennis dress and white sneakers. I feel slightly envious, but I wouldn't dare say it out loud.

"Was that your first choice?" Diana calls, looking me up and down. She wears a collared dress shirt tucked into a red pleated skirt, and her long braids fall down her back. She looks unimpressed as she examines my knee-length green summer dress and brown sandals.

"Everything else was ruined in the mud."

"All right." She smirks. "I guess if that's the look you're going for."

I brush off her comment as we make our way down the path. The night slowly fades in, and the streets are bustling with activity. Country folk are out in full swing, and everyone is dressed to impress. All around me, I smell staple Jamaican soap, lotion, and hair gel, indicating that people are fresh and ready for the concert. The girls and I walk down the dimly lit road.

"Everyone's so dressed up," I say.

"Country people tek youth concert serious," Diana says. "It's their attempt fi get more pickney fi go ah church."

"Dem nuh know it's really just an excuse fi us to get drunk." Zory laughs.

They go back and forth with their usual banter, but I zone out. Hessan is foremost in my mind. The plans he has with Diana tonight. What he will say when he sees me.

"Tilla?" Diana says.

"Huh?" I snap out of my thoughts.

"I said, yuh nervous fi see Jahvan tonight?"

"Oh, no." I shake my head. "I'm good."

"Me tink Tilla jus happy fi be outta dat house," Zory chimes in.

"Mhm," Diana says. "Spend some time away from Aunt Herma. Puttin' your clothes in di yawd last night was a likkle extreme." She giggles.

Her words catch me by surprise. She hasn't said a word about Herma's treatment toward me since I've gotten here.

"She nuh like yuh since yuh come ah country?" Zory asks.

I nod. "Since the first day. She comes in the room almost every morning and cleans at four thirty on the dot. It's like she's trying to torture us for being in her room."

"Lawd, she wicked." Diana laughs. "Yuh cyan mek her get to you."

"Yeah, nuh badda stress yuhself," Zory says. "Most of di adults are just miserable."

"What about Uncle Junior?" I ask, hesitant. "Why is he like that?"

Diana kisses her teeth. "Nuh badda pay him nuh mind either. Junior's always been like that."

"He's just bitter about his life." Zory nods. "Ever since dem diagnose him wit blood cancer, him try fi mek everyone else's life just as miserable as his."

"*Blood cancer?!*"

"Mhm." Diana casually shrugs. "Mass Tyson neva tell you?"

"No."

"It's not a secret. Most people know. Him have cancer inna him blood."

"And poison inna him heart." Zory giggles.

Suddenly, it all makes sense. Uncle Junior's thin frame. The heavy cloud he storms around the house under. *What else hasn't my father told us?*

"Him soon drop dead," Diana says matter-of-factly. "But until then, we ah di one wit di real death sentence."

Her words are cold, but as I think back to the way that Uncle Junior handled Adele in the kitchen, all sympathy drains from my body. And as much as I want to confide in the girls about what happened in the kitchen, I can't.

I gave Aunt Adele my word.

"So wha time yuh meetin' Hessan, Dee?" Zory asks.

"Soon as di snacks sell off." Diana lights up. "He's savin' me a dance."

"Eh, eh!" Zory playfully nudges her. "Yuh nervous?"

"Fi wha?" Diana rolls her eyes. "Let's not forget it was *me* who broke up wit *him*." She giggles. "Plus, I have a feeling he's plannin' something special. He loves to surprise me." She turns to me as if I asked for clarification. "First year we went, he asked the steel drum band to play 'She's Royal' by Tarrus Riley and dedicated it to me. We danced onstage, and he asked me to be his girlfriend. Di rest was history."

"Got it." I nod.

I feel light-headed.

"She was so shy back then." Zory laughs. "You was runnin' from him di whole night."

"We were just young." Diana giggles. "Him used fi chase me down every year until I finally said yes." She flips her braids. "It's always been a big night for us."

I cringe, making a mental note to leave the dance early.

Breathe, Tilla. Breathe.

But my nerves only worsen the closer we get.

When we arrive at the party, the festivities are in full swing. Night has fallen, and parked cars line the dirt road, their headlights lighting up the night. People are dressed to impress as they make their way down the hill to the roadside party. A sign made from an old white sheet hangs above the stage and reads CHURCH OF GOD OF PROPHECY ANNUAL YOUTH CONCERT DANCE. A few older women serve soup on the roadside, and others hand out flyers for the night's program. Up on the stage, a few young children dressed in church attire sing songs while the adults play tambourines behind them.

I stick close to Diana and Zory as we navigate our way

through the bustling group of people. I grow tense, praying we don't run into Hessan. As we walk down the road, I can feel the peering eyes of the older men who lean on their cars and watch us as we walk by.

"Yow! Diana!" an older gentleman calls out. "Come here nuh, girl!"

"I'm workin', Binky!" Diana kisses her teeth before whispering to us, "Binky love call me name, yuh nuh. Like him nuh have wife and pickney. Cha." She rolls her eyes as we disperse into the party.

"Uno want soup?" Zory asks.

"Get me one, nuh. I'm starving," Diana says.

"Tilla, yuh want one?" Zory asks me. "Sista Bernadette mek a good corn soup. Come like she put her foot in it."

"Ew." Diana makes a face. "That's nasty, Zo."

"Sure." I nod.

"And nuh badda tek too long!" Diana calls after her. "Mummy ah wait pon us, and yuh know how she miserable already."

Zory heads over to the side of the road where Sister Bernadette and a few other church ladies pass out Styrofoam cups of soup. Diana and I wait in the grass as groups of people head toward the stage. A male artist performs an upbeat worship song as everyone claps along, their voices echoing through the night.

"This is really cool," I say to Diana. "I didn't think it would be like this."

"This is nothing. You should see di parties dem keep ah town," she boasts. "All di girls I go to school wit have money, so every minute, dem ah keep sweet sixteen. They even have big Jamaican artists come perform."

"Wow." I smile. "That's so fun. You're so lucky you get to go to school there."

"Lucky?" She looks at me. "What do you mean *lucky*?"

"Oh—no, not like that, I just mean—"

"It's not *luck*, Tilla." Her brows furrow, and her brown eyes turn cold. "Luck has nothing to do with it. I'm *smart*. Smarter den all ah dem."

"I didn't say you weren't—"

"Just because I come from country doesn't make me some *lucky bush gyal*. Rich gyal like you aren't the only ones who deserve a good education."

"Diana. I didn't mean it like that."

"Yes, you did. And you're *wrong*." Her eyes drill into me. "I work hard for everything I have, and I *deserve* to be there. Yuh have no idea what it even means fi work hard. Fi deserve *anything* inna yuh life. So nuh badda come talk to me about *luck*."

Her words are seething, and I can feel her daring me to question them.

"Okay," I concede. "You're right. I'm sorry."

She turns away from me, looking out toward the stage.

"It's fine," she says coldly.

But it's not. I'm so angry at myself for saying the wrong thing, and I make a mental note to keep my mouth shut for the rest of the evening. Just then, Zory approaches with three cups in hand. I quietly take mine from her, and we continue down the road.

We make our way to a small makeshift table where Miss Shirley has set up the snacks. A big sign overhead reads SNACK SHOP: CHUBBY AND CHEESE PUFF painted onto a piece of wood. A handful of kids and teenagers form a line, eager to get their snacks. I'm jolted when I notice a few of the kids wearing my clothes. A couple girls wear my T-shirts, and I notice a boy wearing my black hoodie. I realize that the clothes I gave to Diana and Zory have made their rounds. I look away, pretending not to notice.

"Come, come nuh, girls! Hurry up," Miss Shirley says. "Uno late."

"We were hungry, Mummy." Diana rolls her eyes. "We had to stop and get food."

"I told you six o'clock, Diana. Money nuh mek itself."

Her words echo Diana's as she hastens our pace, handing us battered church aprons to tie around our waists. "Diana, you tek di orders. Zory, yuh can handle di chips. A hundred dollas each. Tilla, you're responsible fi di drinks. Fifty dollas each. All di money goes in dis box." She points to a metal tin. "Me haffi go back up ah yawd fi get some change. Me soon come back."

With that, she heads back through the party, and Diana begins to take orders.

"Mek me get a Chubby and a . . . and a . . . and a bag a chips," a small girl in a pink dress stutters to Diana.

"Wha kinda Chubby?"

"Yuh have . . . yuh have orange?"

"One hundred fifty dollas." The girl hands Diana the money, and Diana slides fifty dollars in the tin and fifty in her pocket. She turns to me and Zory. "One chip and one Chubby," she says, before handing Zory the remaining fifty. I pretend I don't notice, doing exactly as I'm told. I sift through a red cooler on the ground and pass her the orange Chubby just as Zory pockets the bill.

Mind your business, Tilla.

About fifty kids move through the line, and the girls continue the same routine. I reach down into the cooler just as Mia and Kenny come through the line.

"Whatcha got?" Mia slaps a crinkly bill on the table. "We're thirsty."

"And hungry," Kenny chimes in.

"Chubby and cheese puff." Diana rolls her eyes. "Read di sign."

"Are they expired?" Mia eyes her.

"Uno bright," Diana says before pocketing the cash, placing fifty dollars in the tin.

"Mind me tell Miss Shirley, Diana," Kenny threatens. "Yuh too ginnal."

"It's called *commission*, Kenny. If you went to school, you would know that."

I place two Chubbys and chip bags on the counter.

"Don't stay out too late, Mi," I say. "We leave in the morning."

They grab their snacks before heading back into the crowd. Andre steps up next, wearing a brown dress shirt and oversize dress pants that were clearly passed down from our grandfather.

"Wha'ppen, Dee? Wha yuh have?"

"Are all ah uno that dunce?" Diana asks. "Read di blasted sign."

"Pass me a Chubby." He looks to me and smiles. "Wha gwan, Tilla? Me like yuh dress."

"Oh, thanks." I smile.

"Isn't it cute?" Diana chimes in. "It hides her wide shoulders."

"Cool nuh, Diana." Andre kisses his teeth. "Why yuh haffi say dem tings?"

"It's a compliment." Diana smirks. "Everyone gwan so sensitive."

"She's just being honest." Zory giggles.

"It's fine," I say, although her words sting. "I'm not offended."

"Diana nuh have no manners. Nuh pay her no mind." He takes his Chubby and heads back into the party. I'm desperate to leave with him, but I stop myself.

I only have one more hour to go.

I'm pulled out of my thoughts as a woman takes the stage to introduce a new act.

"Good evenin', ladies and gentlemon! Welcome to the ninth-annual Church of God of Prophecy Youth Concert! We are honored to have uno here wit we today. We have plenty performances in store fi uno dis evenin'. Please welcome up next Sista Pearl and Sista Brown singing a duet of 'God's Holy Mercy.'"

A few people clap as two women make their way up to the stage, dressed in their finest church clothes and accessories.

"Lawd gawd," Diana says to Zory. "Dem ah guh give Pearl di mic *again*?"

"Dem neva learn from last year? Ca-ca rawtid." Zory laughs as the ladies' dry, tired voices come over the mic. They belt out an old gospel tune as a few people start to boo. The women wail in unison as they try to keep the tempo of the karaoke track. Eventually, the crowd can't take it. People start to throw empty Styrofoam cups.

"Tek dem offa di stage!" I hear someone yell out.

"Run dem!"

Everyone explodes into laughter. If there's one thing about Jamaicans, they're not shy to let you know when they don't like something. Soon, the lady hosting the festivities runs up to the small stage, grabbing the mic.

"All right, all right!" she cries, trying to calm the antsy crowd. "Let's have some respeck for our performers dis evenin'. It takes a lot to come up here onstage. Tank you, Sista Pearl and Sista Brown, for that beautiful rendition of 'God's Holy Mercy.'"

"Blasphemy!" someone yells out.

Diana and Zory continue to snicker as they sell the remaining snacks.

"One grape Chubby," Diana calls to me.

"I think we're all out," I say as I sift through the final flavors.

"What else uno have?" I hear a deep voice ask.

I freeze.

"What exactly are you looking for?" Zory giggles.

"Anyting chocolate."

"We don't sell chocolate."

I raise up from the cooler and turn around to lock eyes with Jahvan.

He smiles. "Yuh sure?" He stares at me.

"Yes, Jahvan," Diana interjects. "We're sure. No chocolate for sale."

"Too bad."

"Is there anyting else we can help yuh wit?"

"Me wan talk to yuh friend." He gestures to me.

"Oh, I . . ." I search my brain for an excuse. "I'm working, sorry."

"It's fine, Tilla. We're not dunce." Diana rolls her eyes. "We can do di rest."

"Yeah, Tilla. Go talk to di mon," Zory agrees. "Yuh tink we cyan handle sellin' a likkle juice?"

I look from Diana to Zory and back again, unsure of what to say.

"Gwan nuh," Diana ushers me. "Just nuh badda tek all night. I'm meetin' up wit Hessan at nine, and me need yuh fi help clean up."

"Okay," I mutter.

Jahvan watches me as I untie my apron and make my way around the counter. I follow him through the crowd and off to the side of the party. We approach a tree, and he rests on it as people dance to the music around us. Before I even have a moment to think, he pulls me into him.

"Kyan-ah-da," he slurs as he breathes me in. He holds a Guinness in his left hand, and I can smell it all over him. "Me neva know yuh did ah come tonight."

"Yeah . . ." I shift, stepping back. "I decided last minute."

"Yuh look beautiful." He tugs on the hem of my dress. "Green look good pon yuh."

"Thanks . . . Did you just get here?" I attempt to make small talk.

"I was jus leavin'." He grazes my chin. "I'm headin' up to yuh yawd fi see Junior."

"*Uncle Junior?*"

"Yeah. I sell to him."

I look at him quizzically.

He laughs. "Ganja."

"Oh."

"Yuh wan walk up wit me?" He takes my hand. "Get to know each other a likkle more."

"I can't." I pull it away. "I have to finish helping at the booth."

"Come nuh, Till-ah." He pulls me in again. "Dem already tell yuh say dem nuh need yuh." He draws his finger up my arm, tracing circles on my skin. I start to feel woozy.

"Jahvan—" I pull away from him. "I'm sorry. I—I have to use the bathroom. I'll be back." I instinctively break away from his hold and make my way back through the crowd, kicking myself for leading him on the first time.

I walk for a few minutes, searching for the bathroom when I spot a porta-potty off to the side. As I make my way toward it, the musical act finishes, and the host takes the stage again.

"All right, everyone, give it up for Peta-Gaye! What a voice!" She's praising a young girl with long pigtails who takes a bow. "Next up, we have Mr. Castile and the steel drum band!"

A couple of middle-aged men with steel drums take the stage. Everyone begins to dance as a melodic rhythm fills the streets. The sharp sound of steel is electric, and it instantly lights up the night. I spot Dane in the center of the grass, moving and shaking along to the music as a crowd begins to form around him. He pops and locks, exploding into a series of dance moves as everyone goes wild, cheering him on. I can't help but smile as I begin to lose myself to the music.

"God is good! God is good!" the lead singer belts outs. "God is good to me, how could I let him down?" His voice fills the roads

as the catchy rendition of the song brings everyone to their feet.
People sing along, praising and worshipping God as they move
in sync to the music. Everyone is caught up in the magnetic energy of Dane's performance, and soon the crowd gets bigger and
bigger. The energy feels explosive. I laugh and dance along with
everyone else when suddenly someone grabs my hand from behind and spins me around. My dress twirls in the air, and a rumble of laughter escapes from my lips. I regain my balance and
almost lose it again when I lock eyes with Hessan.

"Brownin'."

His entire face lights up as all the breath leaves my body.

It. Is. *Fireworks.*

In one swift motion, he pulls me into him and wraps his
arms around me. My green dress clings to him like a magnet.

"I thought you weren't coming?!" His face is full of surprise.

"I changed my mind." I smile.

"I'm so happy to see you." He beams, almost speechless.
"You look *so* good. In that dress, with your necklace . . ." He
touches my butterfly pendant before whispering into my ear.
"Come."

He takes my hand and leads me toward the side of the
porta-potty, so we're out of sight from the crowd. He spins me
around again before dipping me.

"Hessan!" I laugh. I come back up and we lock eyes.

"I cyan believe you came." His gaze is magnetic. "Did yuh
come here wit Andre?"

"No. Diana and Zory. We're selling snacks." I gesture to the
porta-potty. "I'm on a bathroom break."

He laughs. "And to tink dem say foreign gyal nuh work hard."

I burst into laughter. He watches me, amused as he pulls
me in closer. I can tell he's had a bit to drink. He is intoxicated.

But so am I.

He puts his hand to my chin just as a few people walk by the stall.

"Not here." I move his hand.

He traces my body with his eyes. "I want you, Tilla," he whispers. "Bad."

I want him, too. There's no denying it. As the sound of steel drums rips through the air, the energy between us only intensifies. I burn up under his gaze as he takes his hand to my Afro, gently tugging on a coil.

"Dance with me at least," he whispers.

He moves his hands down to my hips and draws me into him. I collapse into his embrace as the familiarity of his touch relaxes every inch of my body. I wrap my arms around his neck, and he grinds into me, swaying me this way and that to the rhythm of the music. He spins and dips me, and soon, we are dancing in a world of our own. It is hypnotic.

We are under a *trance.*

I move in time with him as we dance along to the beating of the steel drums. He twirls me and pulls me in closer, and soon, my back is pressed into his front as he wraps his arms around me from behind. He pushes his whole body into mine, and I feel him grow hard as our hips sway to the music. I want to cry out for him. Everything drowns out as he breathes into my neck, raw and *hungry.* My entire body tingles as he pushes his hips into me, and I push back. Music explodes from my lips. As he twirls and dips me, I forget that I am damaged. I forget that I am the girl whose father has deserted her in the abandoned hills of Jamaica's countryside. In Hessan's arms, I have permission to forget that at my core, I am a rage of sorrow. I have permission to forget the words Diana drilled into me mere hours ago, and I forget the way Aunt Herma made me crawl from my own skin. In this moment, I don't have to face the truth that my father isn't here to save me. I don't have to face the truth that he doesn't care.

Because in the arms of Hessan, I am reminded that someone else does.

The booth.

It crashes over me as the song comes to an end.

I'm supposed to be helping clean up.

Hessan spins me around to face him. "Yuh all right?" he slurs.

"No, I—" I can't think straight. My head is on a swivel. The night is humid and hot as drizzling rain starts to fall from the sky. "What time is it?" I ask.

But I don't hear his reply.

The rain begins to pour as each droplet stings my skin.

Slut.

Slut.

Slut.

My father's voice

Echoes all around me

Crushing me

Consuming me.

Don't. Spread. Yuhself. Too. Wide.

I can't breathe. The steel pans fade out, and the announcer takes the stage. "Give a round of applause for Mr. Castile and the steel drum band!"

The crowd erupts in thunderous applause.

"I'm sorry, Hessan I . . . I have to get back." The words leave my lips in a whisper as I search his hazel eyes. I back away, tripping over my own two feet as I turn to take off into the crowd.

I don't get far.

Because there stands Diana, witnessing the entire thing.

17

We leave for town early the next morning.

Uncle Wayne comes to drive Mia and me to Kingston. We trek through dirt roads until they become paved ones as old Garnett Silk tunes play over the radio. The smell of car freshener makes me queasy as images of last night play over and over again in my head like my worst nightmare. I replay every detail, praying that the events might change.

They don't.

The look on Diana's face. The horror that consumed me. The image of her back as she turned to walk back through the crowd. *How could I have been so stupid? So careless?* My mind runs a mile a minute, consumed by every problem that sits on my shoulders. How I'm going to face Diana again. Aunt Herma and her spiteful ways. Aunt Adele's abuse at the hands of Uncle Junior . . . And seeing my father again and having to fake a smile.

The thought alone makes me sick.

I feel like a zombie—hollow, tormented, and deprived of rest. Soon, the lack of sleep catches up to me, and I drift off in the car. When I wake up a few hours later, we've arrived in Kingston. A complete contrast to the country, it's filled with modern architecture, and I can immediately sense the shift in class. The roads here are paved and smooth, compared to the roads in the country that were rugged and unkept. Instead of lush forests, we are surrounded by suburban-looking houses and palm trees, and the pace is much less relaxed.

We weave through a neighborhood, passing large, pristine houses that are blocked off by gates. All the lawns are beautifully landscaped with large pillars at the ends of the driveways. We pull up to the gate of a decent-size house.

"Uno reach," Uncle Wayne says. He parks the car in front of the gate and hops out to ring the buzzer. After a few seconds, the gate slides open and my father stands at the front door.

He stands effortlessly cool, locks hanging down his back as he waves us out of the car. Uncle Wayne parks, and we hop out.

"Wha'ppen, girls!" he calls out. He walks toward the car wearing a loose white button-up, blue shorts, and white sandals. Mia runs toward him and launches into his arms. He spins her around with a giant smile on his face. "Wha gwan, Mi?"

"I missed you, Daddy!"

"I missed you, too, princess." He flips his locks behind his head as they fall forward. "Yow, Wayne! Tanks fi droppin' dem off." He hands Uncle Wayne folded bills.

"Yeah, mon. Likkle more!" Uncle Wayne says before hopping back into the car to make the long trek back to the country. Dad shuts the gate behind him before turning to me.

"Tilla. Yuh too big fi give yuh fada a hug?" His smile is warm, as if he's completely forgotten our phone call from last week. He walks over to me with his arms extended, and I feel myself begin to warm up.

I can't help it.

"Hey, Dad." I give him a quick hug.

"I missed you girls." He lets me go and pulls Mia into his arms. "How's your hand doin'?"

"Better," Mia says as Dad examines the wound. "I don't have to wrap it up anymore. It's just scrapes."

"Well, I'm glad you're feeling better." He places a kiss on her palm. "Come, I want to show you girls inside." We walk toward the house, and he uses a key to unlock the grille.

"Whose house is this?" Mia asks as we step inside.

"It's where I stay while I'm here." He smiles. Inside, the house is humid from the heat and smells like fresh furniture. It has white walls and is simple in its furnishing. As he shows us around, it reminds me of the nicer houses back home. It's got two bedrooms, two washrooms, two separate living areas, an office, a kitchen, and a basement that has a walkout entrance. We make our way through the kitchen, and I'm surprised at all the modern fixtures. The place is beautiful.

"This is di kitchen. Yuh can have anything in di fridge and cupboards. And di living room is over desso." He points to a room across the hall. "Di TV works, so you can watch that in di daytime when I'm not here."

"Fiiiinally," Mia says. "A real TV and not a cardboard box."

"Who else lives here?" I ask, hoping he'll answer the question this time.

"It's your uncle Andrew's summer house," he says. "I spend most of my time here when I work."

"Who's Uncle Andrew?" Mia asks. I wonder the same thing.

"My cousin. He lives in Florida."

We walk through the main hall, and he shows us to our room, a quaint space with light green walls and a connecting bathroom.

"This is where you girls will sleep," he says, putting our bags down in the corner. The room is beautiful, and a part of me wishes we could stay here all summer. We unpack our things before he leads us out to the backyard. When I step outside, I'm in awe. The backyard is a plush, tropical wonderland captured within three walls of bush fences. Rich pink hibiscus flowers bloom all throughout, and a large water fountain sits in the middle of the yard as butterflies dance around. It's enchanting.

"Nice, right?!" Dad calls over to me.

"Are you kidding me?" I laugh. "Dad, this is stunning."

"Til! Come look at these baby lizards!" Mia calls to me from beside the fountain. My toes sink into the fresh-cut grass as I head over to where they sit.

"The grass is filled with them!" Mia says excitedly.

"No way." I jump, examining where I place my feet.

"You've become a real bush gyal." Dad laughs, playfully ruffling Mia's locks. "Especially this hair. Yuh definitely need a touch-up."

"Dad!" Mia smacks his hand away. I examine his freshly twisted locks.

"Who did yours?" I ask.

"A friend of mine owns a braid shop. As a matter of fact, I should take you two tomorrow. What you think, Mi?"

"Fine. But just not tight. I hate when they do it tight."

The next morning, we head to the salon.

We drive for about half an hour until we reach a dark red building with a sign that reads PAULA'S BRAID SHOP. When we enter, the salon is filled with people of all ages getting their hair washed, braided, and locked. A beautiful woman, who I assume to be in her early thirties, stands at the front desk, with long, single braids falling down her back. She notices us and steps from behind the counter, a big smile spread on her face.

"Tyson!" She embraces my dad.

"Wha gwan, Paula?" He smiles.

She lets him go and looks to Mia and me. "Oh my God. Are dese yuh daughtas?"

"Yeah, mon. Tilla, Mia, meet Paula. Best hair braider in Kingston."

She laughs, fanning him off. "Yuh fada's just being nice,"

she says humbly. There's a sweetness to her. Her accent is thick, and there's a warm poeticalness to the way she speaks. "It is so lovely to meet you both."

"It's nice to meet you, too." I smile.

"I feel like I know you already. Yuh fada's always talkin' bout you girls." She smiles warmly before heading to the counter and flipping open her appointment book. A small boy waddles over to the counter with his finger in his mouth. "Braxton! Come here!" Paula moves from behind the counter and scoops him up into her arms. "This is my little boy, Braxton," she says to Mia and me. He has caramel skin and big, bright eyes that light up the room.

"Oh my gosh! He's soooo cute," Mia says. "How old are you?"

"Fibe," he says with his fingers in his mouth. We all laugh.

"Braxton!" Dad beams, taking his hand. "You ah get big pon me, bwoy!"

"He's growing like crazy." Paula smiles. "So what are you girls looking to get done?" She puts Braxton down, and he wanders off into the store.

"Dis likkle ragamuffin needs her locks twisted." Dad puts his hand on Mia's head.

"I like it like this," Mia whines. Her locks frizz at the roots, her beautiful coils matting together. "I'm free-forming."

"Ahh. You're a real Rasta pickney, like yuh fada." Paula giggles. "How about we just touch it up a likkle?"

"Fine. But not too much."

"Deal." She smiles. "And what about you, pretty girl?" She looks at me. "What did you want to get done?"

I look at her hair, admiring her long braids. She adorns them with beads and string, and they frame her round brown face perfectly.

"I love your braids," I say.

"You're too sweet." She examines my Afro. "How about I give you rope twists? I tink dat would look gorgeous on you."

"That's perfect."

"How long yuh ah go need?" Dad says. "I was thinking of taking them to the beach later."

"Really?!" Mia beams. "I've never been to the beach here before!"

"You two ah go love it." Paula smiles. "It shouldn't tek more than three hours. Which beach yuh ah tek dem to?"

"I was thinking Hellshire."

"Ouu, mek sure you tek dem to Papa's fried fish." She winks at me. "Yuh cyan go ah Hellshire and nuh try it."

"Yuh should come," he offers. "Bring Braxton."

"For real?" Paula asks, taken aback.

"Yeah. I'm sure Braxton would love some fresh air."

"Done. I've been cravin' Papa's fish all week."

"Cool." Dad gives Mia a kiss on her forehead as he turns to go. "You girls be good."

A few moments later, Paula washes both of our hair before handing Mia over to another employee. She sits me down in her chair and begins to blow-dry my hair, before parting it into small sections and twisting in the coarse extensions.

"So how are you liking the island?" she asks. "Yuh fada tells me you and Mia have been spending time in the country."

"It's beautiful. I mean, it takes some getting used to, but it's nice." I smile politely.

She lets out a small giggle. "You don't have to tell me wha you think I want to hear," she says. "I grew up inna country. I know how dem stay. As soon as I turned eighteen, I was out of there. To dis day, I cyan stand dead silence at nighttime."

"Right?! It's so creepy."

She laughs. "Di only ting yuh can hear is crickets. And wake up by a rooster at *dawn*? No, sa!"

"I almost died the first night." I laugh.

She smiles. "How are di people treating you?"

"They're okay. There's a lot going on in that house, I guess."

"Trust me, I know all about dat. I grew up with all my aunts and uncles under di same roof. It takes its toll."

"Yeah," I say as she looks at me in the mirror. "It can be really hard."

She nods, clearly understanding what I'm trying to say. "It's just jealousy, Tilla. They look at you . . . yuh fada . . . you live a life that they never will. But if they want to treat you bad for being who you are, let that be their own bad mind ways. God nah sleep." She smiles. "I know it's hard to see now, but country builds character. You just have to figure out how you want it fi serve you." She speaks with the confidence of someone who's lived it, and it brings me comfort. "Summer is going to fly by. Don't overthink it. Tek wha yuh need, and leave wha yuh don't."

I smile, grateful for her advice.

"Thank you, Paula. Seriously. I appreciate that."

"Nuh mention it," she says, waving me off. "Us Jamaican girls haffi stick together." She winks at me, and I can't help but laugh. I'm seldom referred to as that, but the idea makes me feel really good.

Two hours later, she finishes my hair, and long rope twists fall down my back. I stare in the mirror, flipping them from side to side, in awe of her craftsmanship. I look like I come straight from the islands, and it makes me feel *beautiful*.

As if for once, I belong.

Around two o'clock, Dad comes back to get us, and we make our way to Hellshire Beach. We drive down the busy highway as Dad bumps old reggae tunes.

"Oh my God, I *love* this record!" Paula beams as a Gregory Isaacs tune plays over the radio. She turns the radio up and throws her hands up, dancing in her seat as she sings along. "You remember this one, Tyson?!" She laughs, throwing her head back to the rhythm.

Dad laughs, joining in on the chorus melody. "Night Nu-uurse, only you alone can quench dis ya thirst." His voice fills the car as we exit the highway.

When we pull up to the beach, the roads are lined with horses, goats, merchants, and musicians. Dad parks the car, and we head down toward the water. Mia and I hold Braxton's hands as Paula and my dad lead the way.

The beach is packed, lined with colorful bustling restaurants. The energy feels extremely festive as people scatter all about, enjoying the beautiful day. Dad picks out the perfect spot and spreads out a large blanket for us as Paula unpacks. Mia strips down to her bathing suit, sprinting toward the water, and I do the same, following behind her.

All around me, brown bodies swim freely. I submerge myself in the ocean as I take in mouthfuls of salt water, spitting it back out as it hits my face. I turn onto my back, floating atop the waves as the sun radiates down onto me, deepening my tan.

There's something so transformative about the waters of Jamaica.

I feel myself reborn every time I enter them. Here in the ocean, the troubles of the country feel like a distant memory. Aunt Herma, Uncle Junior, and the dance all become a hazy afterthought. I am miles away from my problems, if only for now.

Mia and I play in the water for a little while longer, and after about an hour, we all head over to Papa's Electric Fish for lunch. Dad reserves a table, and we sit on wooden chairs on the outside patio overlooking the beach. The sweet smell of fried festival food fills the air, and my stomach rumbles the moment we sit down. The restaurant is shabby, made from battered wood and a dried grass roof, but the inside is filled with character. A slim woman with glowing dark skin approaches the table to take our order.

"Aftanoon," she says, not a care in the world.

"Aftanoon," my dad replies. "Leh we get five snapper fish, four festival, and one bammy." She writes down our order on a small scratch pad and walks off to tell the chef.

"Mummy, can I go back inna di wata?" Braxton asks Paula.

"After lunch, baby." Paula smiles. "You can swim wit di girls."

"That would be cool," I say, looking to Braxton. "If you wear your life jacket, we can take you to the deep end where the big kids swim." Braxton lights up, clapping his hands as Paula lays out napkins.

"Uno enjoy di water?" Dad asks.

"I loved it." I smile.

"It's too salty," Mia whines. "It almost gave me high blood pressure."

"What do you know about high blood pressure?" Dad laughs.

"A lot." Mia shrugs. "But at least it's better than river water."

"What do you mean?" I ask Mia. "The river water is so clean."

"Nuh-uh. Everyone bathes in it. I'm not tryna swim in all that." Mia makes a face, and Paula laughs.

"I feel you on that one, Mia," she agrees.

"How are you two getting on in the country, anyway?" Dad asks.

"I love it!" Mia lights up. "I wish we could stay there forever."

I look to Paula, who offers me a discreet, knowing smile.

"See?!" Dad says to Paula. "Wha me tell you? Everyone love country."

"Speaking of the country, Dad," I start, "have you ever seen Andre draw?"

"Andre can draw?" He looks at me quizzically.

"Yeah. And he's *really* good," I say. "He showed me his books, and I've never seen anyone draw the way he does. His sketches are so . . . full of life."

"Wow, that's nice," he says casually.

Just as I open my mouth to convince him further, the server returns with a basket of food. She places the steaming assortment of fish and festival in front of us.

"Ew, Daddy!" Mia yells. "It looks like it's still alive!"

The server gives Mia a screw face before walking away.

"It nah go bite." Dad hushes Mia. He reaches for the basket, placing a piece of fried fish on our plates. "All right, girls. Now, pay close attention. Me ah go show you how fi eat snapper fish."

"They've never had snapper before?" Paula asks before breaking her fish apart and handing a small piece to Braxton.

"Nuh matter. If dem neva have it ah Jamaica, it nuh count." He turns his focus to Mia and me as he begins to dissect it. "Now, be very careful when eating this. The bones can be very sneaky. That's why you haffi have it wit festival, bammy, or dumplin'. To stop you from choke."

"Mhm." Paula nods, munching down on her bammy. "If you swallow a bone, it stays inna ya system fi seven years."

"Folktale." Dad playfully kisses his teeth.

"It's true!" Paula giggles like a schoolgirl as she fans him off, and all of a sudden, I start to feel uncomfortable.

"Tek yuh fork like this, and cut it down the side," Dad continues. "Then open it like a sandwich and take out di bone."

"Can you do mine?!" Mia asks eagerly.

"Here, pass." Dad takes the fish back from her plate.

"Me, too!" Braxton squeals out.

"Dad?" I say, trying to get his attention.

"Hmm?"

"Andre."

"What about him?" he asks distractedly as he dissects Mia's fish.

"His drawings. It's some of the best artwork I've ever seen."

"I wanna see them," Mia whines.

"They're incredible, Mi. He can literally draw anything." I

turn back to my dad. "Maybe you could check them out some-time."

"That would be nice," he says dismissively.

"I feel like he could really do something with them. Sell them or something. There's got to be a way for people to find out about his talent. Maybe you could help him—"

"Tilla." Dad looks up from the fish. "Stop."

"What?"

"Just leave it. I don't want you getting Andre's hopes up. Things are different when you come from yawd."

"So? That doesn't mean he shouldn't have dreams."

"It's not the same, Tilla. People don't just leave yawd and become the next Picasso. These kids don't have the same lux-uries that you do."

"You did it," I say defensively. "You came from the country, and you've done so much for yourself."

"It's not the same. I wasn't doodling on paper and trying to sell it."

"He's not *doodling on paper*, Dad." My cheeks start to burn. "Andre's *talented*. He just needs someone to give him an op-portunity. To believe in him." I look down at my plate. "I'm going to ask Mom if he can stay with us next summer. So he can do an art program at the community center—"

"Don't you dare go involving your mother in this, Tilla. I said to drop it."

"But, Dad—"

"Tilla," Paula interjects. "Yuh fada is right. It's unfortunate, but there's not as many opportunities in the arts for kids who come from country."

"But you said it yourself. You left when you were eighteen."

"That's true, but I also had a well-to-do father who lived in town and afforded me that opportunity. Most people who come from country don't ever leave. They can't just afford fi just pack up and go town. Dem nuh even know where their next meal is coming from. Andre's not special just because he can draw."

"He's an *artist*—"

"He's *poor*, Tilla. You have certain privileges that these kids don't."

I start to fume.

Who the hell does she think she is?

"Just because *you* got out and didn't help anyone doesn't mean I shouldn't." It leaves my mouth before I can stop it.

"Watch yuh mouth." Dad's voice is threatening.

"It's fine, Tyson," Paula says.

I ignore her, turning my attention to my father.

"We can *help him*, Dad," I plead. "He can come visit us for the summer in Canada. I already know Mom would say yes—"

"*Tilla.*" He slams his fist against the wooden table. "I said to *drop it.* It's hard enough as it is for kids born in the country. I don't need you filling Andre's head with pipe dreams when he should be focused on his duties around the house."

I start to shake. I can't believe the words coming out of his mouth.

"Sounds like bullshit," I mumble under my breath.

"What'd you say?" He drops his fork.

"I said it sounds like an excuse." I look him directly in the eye, ready to go to battle for Andre and his future. "A weak one."

"All right, everyone." Paula tries to de-escalate the situation. "Let's just enjoy this meal. Your father knows what's best."

"What are you talking about?!" I yell. "You don't even know Andre! You're not even family!"

"*Tilla!*" my father screams. The bass in his voice stuns me, and people in the restaurant look on. "Me say fi watch yuh mout! Me nuh know where yuh get dis blasted attitude from, but me nah go warn you again."

His gray eyes dare me to say another word. But I'm boiling.

Who the *hell* does Paula think she is, telling me how to interact with my own father? As if I haven't only known her for a few hours. I slump down into my seat, my entire appetite lost as I look away from them in disgust.

I stay silent for the rest of the meal, avoiding Paula and my dad at all costs. After lunch, I escape to the water with Mia and Braxton, desperate to stay far away from my dad. Mia talks aimlessly as I tune in and out, my mind still focused on Andre. His drawings that will never see the light of day. The way my dad dismissed him as if he didn't matter. As if *my* voice doesn't matter.

My anger only grows.

"Tilla!" Mia splashes me with water as she treads through the current. "Bet I can hold my breath longer than you can, big head!" she says.

"My lungs are bigger than yours, dummy," I mumble.

"Watch me," she says as her head dips in and out of the water. "Count!"

She takes a deep breath and plugs her nose as she dunks her head under the water. She hovers just below the surface, squeezing her eyes and nose tight as Braxton and I watch. I hold Braxton's hand as he bobs around in his life jacket.

"One . . . two . . . three . . . ," I start counting as I glance out at the water.

And then I spot them, directly in my line of sight.

My heart stops.

My dad and Paula are embraced in a kiss.

They float near the shore as Paula drapes one arm around his neck. She throws her head back and laughs as he pulls her closer . . . and closer . . . and—

"Daddy says I shouldn't put my head underwata," Braxton says, breaking me out of my daze. I turn to look at him. The sun streams down onto his caramel skin, and I realize his eyes are lighter than I'd noticed.

"What?"

"He says that's how you drown—"

"Time!" Mia squeals. She pops up in front of me, her head surfacing above the water, blocking my line of vision. "How long was that?!" she asks.

But I can't hear her.

Everything becomes muffled.

"Tilla!" Mia calls to me.

I can't breathe.

"Were you not counting?! You were supposed to time me, you idiot!" Mia splashes me with water. I finally break eye contact with Braxton.

"What? Oh—sorry . . . I . . ."

But I can't find the words.

There are none.

I squeeze my eyes tight as if that might erase the memory, as if my eyes have possibly deceived me. But no matter how hard I squeeze them, Braxton's words play over and over again like the beginning of a nightmare. I feel dizzy.

Why are his eyes so light?

"You suck at losing," Mia says. She takes Braxton's hands, and they start to swim away. I open my mouth to call out, but just as I do, a giant wave crashes into me, taking me under all at once. Salt water pours into my nose and my mouth. I am suffocating, but I barely feel it.

I barely feel anything at all.

The wave passes and I resurface, but this time, I am not okay. This time, a different wave crashes into me, its raging current consuming me, drowning every inch of my soul.

He is the father.

18

"How was your day?"

My mother's soft voice comes through the phone. We're back at the guesthouse, and I sit on the warm floor of the bathroom.

"Good." I hold my breath, praying that she can't tell I'm lying.

"Your dad said you guys went to the beach today. Did you have fun?"

I think I might throw up.

"Yeah, we did."

"That's really good to hear. I'm so glad you two are in town. It's so much harder to get in contact with you when you're in the country. Whenever I call, Herma says you're not home."

"Really? When did you call?"

"Every day. Sometimes twice. I think we just keep missing each other."

"Yeah," I lie. Aunt Herma hasn't told me about one missed call.

"So . . . has your father told you the good news?!"

"About what?"

"The hurricane." I can hear her smile through the phone. "I've been tracking it all week. It just made landfall in Haiti, but it's been slowing down. Lost a lot of its strength. They're saying it's going to fizzle out before it can hit Jamaica."

"Wow . . . That's really great news."

"Isn't it amazing?!" She laughs. "I couldn't believe it when I heard. I've been calling your father all day, but I couldn't get ahold of him."

I'm silent, careful not to say the wrong thing.

"Til? You okay?"

"Yeah. I'm fine," I lie. I pray she doesn't press any further. Anxiety fills my chest as I go back and forth in my mind on whether or not I should tell her what I saw today. "Mom?"

"Yeah, baby?"

I open my mouth. My chest weighs heavy, but the words are stuck. If I tell her what I know, my family will be torn apart. There will be custody battles and separate homes. There will be no fixing it this time.

I close my mouth. I can't be the one to bring her so much pain. I can't be the one to hurt Mia. I love them too, *too* much.

"I just wanted to say that I love you. A lot. And . . . I can't wait to come home."

"Oh, Til, I love you so much more. Call me anytime, okay?"

"Okay."

"Can I talk to Mi? I'm sure she's dying to tell me all about the beach."

"One second."

I stand up, and my entire body feels heavy. It is weighed down by the secret that now lives inside me. The secret I decided to keep.

The secret that is now mine, too.

I hand Mia the phone before heading to the backyard. I take a seat by the waterfall as my thoughts consume me. After all these years, it is finally clear: My father is not interested in being a family with us. All his yearly trips to Jamaica were not for work. They were for his family. His *real* family. A family that gave him a simplicity that Mia, Mom, and I never could.

A family that allowed him to be free.

They bring him light, and we bring him dark. They are his sun, and we are his night. They are the ones that he looks forward to when he wakes up, and we are the ones that he dreads to be alone with at night.

They are his paradise.

And we are his problem.

I will never be enough for my father, and now there is a hole in my heart the size of him that I cannot fill up.

It only grows bigger and bigger.

Swallowing me whole.

Ripping me apart.

Eating me alive.

What do I do with the despair that swims inside me, drowning me with every single breath? How do I escape the sorrow that strangles me? The expectations that suffocate me? I am a fatherless child. I am worse. I am a child whose father does not want her. A child whose father throws her away.

Again.

And again.

And again.

I fiddle with my butterfly necklace as a heavy pain sets fire to my chest. Tears well in my eyes, but this time, I will let them fall. They pour from my face like the ocean I have been so afraid to drown in. I surrender to every single tide.

I have wanted my father's love for too long.

But now, I am weary. Now, I am done.

It's a strange pursuit—chasing the love of your father. When the first man who was supposed to want you, doesn't. You eventually stop running.

You eventually grow tired.

19

I awake the next morning with a mission in my heart.

My body is buzzing, and there is a stale taste in my mouth.
My stomach feels hollow, and I am sick with disgust. But
this morning I am clear.

This morning I know what I must do.

I get up out of the bed and head into the kitchen. As I approach, I can hear Mia's laughter spilling from the walls. My
body tenses. When I enter, I find Mia and my father sitting at
the breakfast table around a box of Froot Loops and milk.

"Hey, sleepyhead," Dad calls as he pours Mia a bowl. "You're
up late today."

"Yeah, it's almost noon," Mia says matter-of-factly.

"I know. I was tired," I say, taking a seat next to Mia.

"You two had a full day yesterday." He heads to the cupboard, grabbing a bowl and placing it in front of me. "I got your
favorite cereal."

I eye the box in front of me.

"I hate Froot Loops," I say.

"Wha?! Since when?!" he asks. "Yuh love Froot Loops. For
as long as I can remember."

"You mean when I was nine?" I ask dryly. "I don't eat sugary
cereal."

Mia rolls her eyes. "Well, I do. You're missing out," she says as she munches down on a spoonful.

I get up from the table and sift through the cupboards, searching for something else to eat.

"Someone's in a mood," Mia says. I pull a loaf of bread from the cupboard. I look to the top of the fridge and notice an array of colorful kids' cereals.

I want to scream.

"Why do you have so many kids' cereals here?" I turn to him, my temperature rising.

"I knew you two were coming. I thought that's what you liked."

I can't take another lie.

"Mia, can I talk to Dad for a sec? Alone."

"But I'm eating my breakfast!" Mia whines. "It's gonna get soggy!" She shoves another spoonful into her mouth.

"Bring it with you to the living room," I say. "You can watch TV."

"There's only the news channel. And all they ever talk about is that stupid hurricane."

"Mia," I say sternly.

Dad looks to me quizzically.

"Wha yuh want fi talk about?"

I look to Mia. "Please. Just bring it with you."

Mia sulks, rolling her eyes as she carries the bowl out of the kitchen and into the living room.

Dad looks to me, confused. "What's—"

"He's your kid, isn't he?"

The words fall right off my tongue. I stare into his eyes as if I were staring down the barrel of a gun, ready to die for what I know to be true. "And this is your house."

"Wha you ah talk bout?" he asks blankly, his Jamaican accent growing thicker.

"Braxton," I say. "And Paula. They are your family. They are why you're here."

"Tilla." He looks away from me, disgusted with my accusation. "What are you saying to me right now?"

"I'm saying that they are *yours*. Your family. I am saying to tell the truth. This is your home. With them." His gray eyes pierce into me, daring me to say another word.

"Tell the truth, Dad." My voice shakes. "For once, just tell the truth. That's why you leave us all the time. That's why you're here."

"Wha di fuck yuh ah talk bout?" he spits. His voice stays low, but his words cut deep.

"I want you to tell the truth." Tears begin to well in my eyes.

He walks over to me. "Did your mother put you up to this shit?"

"No!"

"Don't lie to me, Tilla!" he says, raising his voice.

"I'm not! Dad, I saw you with my own eyes! I saw you and Paula in the water yesterday! I . . . I saw everything!" I stumble over my words as the memory of them flood my brain. "You and Braxton . . . the way you looked at him. You held her and . . ." The tears start to pour, and I hate myself for it. "You made us *play* with him! How could you do that?! How could you *lie* to us?!" I sob. "I *saw*, Dad! And I'm not stupid. I know . . . I know what's going on." I wipe my face with the back of my hand, angry that I've betrayed myself. I was supposed to be strong. "You are his *father*!" I scream.

"Wha di fuck you ah talk bout?!" he yells. "You always do this! Create shit when it's not there!"

"Dad, I SAW YOU!"

"LOWER YUH FUCKIN VOICE!"

"JUST TELL THE TRUTH!" I cry. "Tell the truth for once! He's your kid—"

"*SO WHAT?!*" he screams. "He's mine, and so what?! You need to mind yuh fuckin' business! Yuh gwan just like your mother—"

"Don't talk about my mom!" I sob. Tears spill all over me like a storm. "You have no right to talk about my mom!"

"SHUT THE FUCK UP!" His rage splatters onto the walls, stunting me. "YUH LUCKY ME NUH TELL YUH MADA DI SHIT YOU'VE BEEN UP TO! HERMA CALL ME EVERY WEEK AND TELL ME DI TINGS YUH AH DO! AH RUN UP AND DOWN DI COUNTRY LIKE SOME KINDA *SLUT*!"

My body. Goes. Cold.

"HOW DARE YOU!" I scream.

"TILLA, STOP!" Mia runs into the kitchen.

But I can't.

My entire body shakes.

"HOW DARE YOU SAY THAT TO ME?! ALL YOU CARE ABOUT IS YOUR STUPID FUCKING MISTRESS!"

"WATCH YUH FUCKIN' MOUT!" He slaps the box of Froot Loops off the counter. Colorful cereal goes flying everywhere as he raises his hand to strike me.

"DAD!" Mia's voice rings out.

It's the last thing I hear.

He stops his hand midway in the air, lowering it back down as the shock of what he was about to do sits in the silence between us. All I feel is the crumbling of my own chest. The tears no longer flow.

Just like the lagoon, we are still.

I meet the rage of my father's gaze, staring him straight in the eye.

My voice is a whimper.

"We may have the same blood, but as God is my witness, you are *not* my father."

I march past him and Mia and back into my room.

I shut the door behind me and sink onto the bed. I feel weak and depleted, like I have nothing left to give. All around me, the room buzzes as I fall deeper into the nothingness. I have faced the wrath of my father.

And I am empty.

I awake from a nap four hours later to Mia entering the room. I look out the window to a gray sky. Rain cascades down the window, and lightning flashes. My head feels heavy, and the events of yesterday and today begin to blur together, but the feeling they have left me with is still very much present.

I am heavy.

I am sorrow.

I watch Mia as she walks into the room, her head hanging low. She wipes the tears that stream down her face as she bends down beside our luggage.

"Mia, what's wrong?" I ask.

She ignores me. She weeps in silence as she pushes clothes deep into her bag.

"Mi?"

"It's all your fault!" She breaks. "I told you to stop!"

"What are you talking about?"

Confusion takes over as my dad walks up to the room door.

"Pack your things," he says to me. His voice is calm, but firm.

There will be no changing his mind.

"You're going back to the country."

HURRICANE

20

Uncle Wayne comes to drive Mia and me back to the country the next morning. We leave town just after dawn, and by noon, any trace of us having been there is gone.

We make the long trek through the monstrous mountains of Jamaica just as we have done twice before. Mia weeps silently as she presses her head against the window. She's been mad at me before, but this time, it feels different. This time, I know I have really hurt her. But that isn't the only worry that consumes me. I am leaving one battlefield to enter another, and there is nowhere to hide.

It is time to face Diana.

We arrive into Manchester a little after noon. This time, no one awaits us at the back door. There is no celebration. No joyous hellos or praise. All that awaits are Andre's stray chickens that walk aimlessly in circles around the dirt yard. Mia and I grab our bags and lug them back through the house. I hold my breath, praying I don't run into Diana as I make the agonizing walk to Aunt Herma's room. I take a deep breath when I approach the door, grateful to be in the clear.

When we enter the room, it looks like a brand-new place. It's been cleaned top to bottom, with fresh sheets and pillows. The white tile floors are gleaming, and the entire place smells like floor polish. I scoff. I know Aunt Herma couldn't wait to erase any memory of us. I throw my stuff down in the corner and plop onto the bed. Just then, there's a quick knock on the door, and Aunt Herma enters. I instantly sit up straighter. She looks over her reading glasses with the same disapproving look that always covers her face when she sees us.

"You girls don't say hi when you walk in?" Her tone is chastising.

"We didn't see anyone. We came through the back," I say.

"Hm. We were on the veranda." She looks down at our suitcases. "I see your father has shipped you back early. He get tired of uno already?"

I say nothing. I don't have the energy. Not after yesterday.

"Hopefully you picked up a few things in the short time you were there. Like manners and responsibility." She looks at me directly. "Did you have fun, Mia?"

"Yeah," she whispers.

"Good. Now, I'm sure you two noticed that I cleaned this room from top to bottom. I expect it to stay this way. It was disgusting when you left. I found socks under the bed, and the sheets hadn't been changed in a few days. God only knows what your mother has been teaching you ah foreign." She wipes her hand on her apron as if she were trying to get the dirt off her hands from just being in our presence. "Adele made food if uno hungry," she says before shutting the door behind her.

I sigh, slumping onto the bed. I look to Mia, who hasn't said a word to me the entire day.

"Mia . . . I'm sorry for what happened yesterday."

She ignores me as she loads her clothes back into the drawers. I take a deep exhale, trying again. "I know you wanted to spend time with Dad. I'm really sorry I screwed it up."

"It's fine," she whispers flatly.

"It's not. Please, Mi, just tell me how much you hate me or

something. I don't like you being mad at me. I can't stand you not talking to me."

"Obviously, I don't hate you." She rolls her eyes. "You're so annoying, Tilla. You always find a way to make everything about you."

"That's not true."

"It is! This whole trip you've just been pushing Dad away and . . . and . . . you're not the only one who doesn't get to spend any time with him!" Tears start to fall down her soft brown cheeks. "You never care about what I want."

"Yes, I do."

"No, you don't! You knew Dad was going to get upset, but you yelled at him anyway. You know he gets overwhelmed easily and—" Her small voice cracks. "He would send us away. Or leave. Like he always does." She breaks, heaving in and out. I rush to her side. "Daddy just wanted things simple, and . . . I just wanted to spend time with him for once," she sobs. "Just because you're not having fun in Jamaica doesn't mean I'm not. I love everyone here, and I'm having so much fun. For once, there's no arguing, and we get to spend time with Daddy. And then you went and messed it all up."

"Mia, *I'm sorry*. I didn't want to—"

"It's not always about what you want, Tilla! Don't you get that?! You're not the only one here!" she cries. "He's not just *your* dad. And this isn't just *your* family. It's mine, too."

And then it hits me. It's the first time I've ever taken into consideration the differences of our experiences. The innocence behind Mia's summer. The joy she must feel by simply being in the presence of our father's family. Just being with these people is enough for her. Spending weekends with our dad is enough for her.

In fact, it's all she has.

"I'm so, so sorry, Mia," I whisper. "I'm really sorry that I screwed that up for you. You're right about everything. I've been so selfish."

I feel riddled with guilt for confronting my father. The truth is it doesn't matter what secret I am protecting her from. Mia loves it here, and they love her, and it is not my place to take that from her. For the first time, I see clearly the different perspectives the world has about girls and young women. The way we are treated, and the way we experience the same summer. Mia is good, and I am bad.

Mia is innocent, and I am soiled.

Our experiences are severed at the line between girlhood and adulthood.

I cup her small face in my hands and stare into her copper-brown eyes. I see sadness all through them, and I wonder if her eyes have always seemed so sad and I just never noticed. A tear falls down her puffy face, and I wipe it with my thumb.

"I love you so much, Mia. I don't know what I would do without you. And I'm so sorry I made Daddy mad," I say gently. "I'm so sorry I've made it uncomfortable for you here. Can you forgive me?"

She heaves in and out, rubbing her eyes. "Duh." She smacks my hand away, pulling away from me. "It's not like I have a choice."

I smile. This is the sassy Mia that I know and love.

"Thank you," I whisper.

I help her unpack her things, and an hour later, she heads outside to play with Kenny. I head to the bathroom, and when I get inside, I am disgusted with my reflection. The long twists that cascade down my back. I look just like Paula, and it makes me sick. I'm resentful that I looked at her with such awe. Such applause. I run to Herma's sewing machine and return to the bathroom with a pair of scissors. I cut every last extension out of my hair until any trace of Paula is gone. When I'm finished, I take a deep breath and head out the front yard with only one destination in mind:

Hessan.

I head through the gate and trek down the hill to the main road, and I don't stop until I approach the little blue house.

What if he's not home?

I'm on pins and needles as I head down the path toward the front door. I see Miss Addie on the porch, rocking back and forth in her chair with her Bible in hand. She sits in her usual position, sipping on a cold glass of water.

"Tilla?" I hear a voice call from the side of the house. I turn to see Hessan emerge from behind the trees. He beams under the midday sun, his eyes twinkling like usual and his smile wider than ever.

He is *beautiful.*

"What are you doing here?" He laughs. "Me tink you did gone ah town."

"I came back early," I say softly. The words barely fall from my lips.

He stares at me as if he's unsure that it's really me standing in front of him. He walks closer, wiping off his hands on a handkerchief in his pocket.

"How long are yuh back for?"

"A while. My dad sent us back early."

"You came to look for me by yourself?" he asks, impressed. "I was just doing some work out back for Miss Addie. You know hurricane is coming this week?"

"*What?* I just talked to my mom. She said it was slowing down—"

"That's what everyone thought . . . But it nuh look so anymore. It ah go hit Jamaica at full speed. Everyone's gearing up. It ah go be worse than they thought." He reaches for my hand, squeezing it tightly. Worry graces his face as a jolt of terror flashes through me.

"I thought . . . I thought for sure it wasn't supposed to be that bad."

"We all did. I've been nailing down zinc all day." My thoughts trail as he stares into my eyes. "Is everyting all right? You seem . . . sad."

He knows me better than anyone I've ever loved. I open my mouth to respond, but I don't need to. He knows the answer.

"Come," he says. "Let's go talk somewhere."

He leads me past the house and down into the backyard. We begin to descend a hill filled with trees, and at the end is a small clearing where a beautiful ravine runs through. I sit down on a flat stone as Hessan walks over to a guinep tree. He breaks off a generous branch and brings it over, taking a seat beside me.

"Yuh ever have guinep before?" he asks.

I grab a piece and crack it open, sucking the fruit out of the skin.

"Never mind." He smiles, impressed.

"What? Yuh nuh tink foreign gyal know how fi nyam guinep?"

"Wow." He laughs before cracking open his own. "You know, every time you come around me, yuh Patois seem fi get better. I must be rubbing off on you."

"Maybe so." I smile as he cracks open another one.

"So how was town? I missed you."

"I missed you, too." I ponder his question, thinking of how to answer. I take the guinep seed from my mouth and toss it into the ravine.

"My dad is cheating on my mom."

"Wha?" Hessan looks at me, stunned. "Wha you mean? How yuh know?"

"I saw him." My voice goes hollow. I look out at the ravine. The water spills delicately down the rocks as a small orange butterfly follows down the stream. I take a deep breath as I let the next part of the story sink in. "He has a child." The words roll off my tongue without meaning. Devoid of emotion. I meet Hessan's gaze as he processes the news.

"What did you see?" he asks.

"I saw him with another woman. Paula. And her child. Their child. In front of me and . . . and he admitted it to me." The old familiar lump forms in the back of my throat. "I have a brother." Saying the words out loud for the first time to someone makes me realize their severity. I bite down on my lip to stop it from quaking. "I confronted him about it, and he got mad . . . and then he sent us back here."

"Tilla." He takes my hand, shaking his head. "I'm so sorry. Yuh nuh deserve that."

"I do."

"No, Tilla. You don't."

"*I do.*" The tears start to spill. "I've known for a really long time that my father . . . he doesn't want us, Hessan. But I kept holding on. I wanted to be wrong about it, but I wasn't . . . and I feel so stupid. I feel so stupid that I cared so much about coming here. I feel stupid that the moment I saw him I forgot *everything.* The birthdays. The promises . . . *He never wanted us.*" I wipe the tears from my face. "I can't fix this, Hessan."

"Ah nuh your job fi do that." He moves closer to me. "Those are his wrongs that he will have to right. You are not the mistakes of yuh fada."

"But . . . *I lied,*" I cry. "I lied to my mom, and now I'm just as bad as he is. I can't . . ." I can't handle it anymore. I lose it as the pain of it all begins to sink in. "I can't do this!" I cry. "I feel so . . . broken."

"You are a warrior, Tilla. *Yuh cyan break*," he says softly as he rubs my back. "You are not di worst of yuh fada. You are all di best parts."

"He doesn't have any," I say resentfully.

"That's not true. I'm looking at it right now." He raises my chin to meet his gaze. "You are half yuh mada and half yuh fada. They came together to create *you*. Your only job is to take di best parts of dem. Leave di parts you don't want behind and create *Tilla*." I look away from him and out onto the ravine, reluctant to accept his words. "Sometimes parents cyan be what we want. Sometimes they don't know how."

"That sounds like an excuse," I spit.

He takes up the guinep and cracks it open, handing me the fruit inside. I put it in my mouth and suck down hard, hoping the sweetness will pacify the bitterness I feel inside.

"I want you to do suh'um fi me." His eyes are soft, compassionate. "Close yuh eyes."

I'm skeptical before following orders.

"Breathe," he says gently.

I do.

"I want you fi imagine yuh fada di same way me last see my mada. Covered in blood. So beat up you cyan even see him face."

"Hessan . . ."

"Jus trust me."

I grimace, but I follow instructions. I start to envision my father lying helplessly in that car. Bloodied. Bruised. I barely recognize him.

"You see him?" Hessan asks.

"Yes."

"What does he look like?"

"Bad. Hurt . . . helpless."

"And how do you feel?"

I pause for a moment. "I feel . . . sad." My eyes start to well. "I don't know . . . I feel . . . terrible. I feel really bad for him."

"Okay. Now, what if I told you dat is what your fada looks like on di inside?"

I try to make sense of his words.

"What if I told you that is *exactly* what your fada looks like, without di bruises?" I open my eyes and meet his gaze. "You might not see it, Tilla, but he is hurtin' just like you. He has a lot of wounds within himself."

I feel stumped as bitterness arises.

"So you want me to feel sorry for my dad that he's having an affair?"

"No. I want you fi understand dat hurt people, *hurt people*. No two ways about it."

I take the guinep seed from my mouth and throw it into the ravine. I'm not ready to forgive. Not even close. My father has caused too much pain. Too much *chaos*. But as Hessan's words land on me, it hits me all at once:

So have I.

My father was right. I am just like him.

In fact, I have become what has hurt me the most.

I am the other woman.

My chest tightens as his words consume me.

LIKE

SOME

KIND

OF

SLUT.

"Stop." I feel sick with myself as I wiggle away from Hessan's touch. "I can't . . . I can't do this." I feel my entire body seize. "What makes me any better than Paula? *Than him?!*" I shake my head. "He made a commitment to our family just like you made a commitment to Diana . . . to the *church*. And I helped you break it. I'm a hypocrite."

"Tilla—"

"It's true, and you know it. The secrets . . . the sneaking around. I'm only causing more pain. I've done so much damage. To Diana . . . to Mia. To *everyone*."

"Stop, Tilla," he says firmly. "Yuh cyan put that on yourself." He grabs my hand. "This is *my* mess, not yours. And I shouldn't have dragged you into it." He looks me in my eyes, deep and intense. "Ever since di dance, I've been reflectin' on everything." He takes a deep breath. "My whole life, I've been trying to redeem myself for leaving my mother. I thought if I kept my promise to Diana, that somehow it would mek up fi it. I thought God would forgive me if I stayed this time . . . when someone needed me." His eyes water as he searches for the words. "But what happened wit my mother . . . I *cyan* mek that right, Tilla. I have . . . I have to let it go." He searches my eyes. "I haffi break tings off wit Diana."

"Hessan." My stomach drops. "No. There's no way—"

"I cyan continue fi wear a mask, Tilla. Pretendin' to feel somethin' when I don't. Being with you—*knowing you*—has shown me what I want to feel. How I want to love. Di typa man I want to be."

"It wouldn't make any sense."

"I *know* what we have is temporary, Tilla. But I have to do this for myself. I *cyan* live my life for Diana, or my uncle, or di church . . . or even for my mada."

I'm speechless, unsure of what to say next.

"I'm so sorry for everyting I put yuh through dis summer . . . but I need you fi know you are not like yuh fada. Or his *mistress*. Not even close." He shakes his head, disgusted by the thought. "You are so far from any of that, Tilla. And I want to prove that to you . . . I need to follow my heart." He stares into my eyes, and I feel the vulnerability of his spirit as it radiates through him. He brings my hand to his mouth, placing a gentle kiss on the base of my palm. "You are so special to me," he says. "Your mind . . . it's so beautiful. And I care about you so deeply."

It becomes quiet all around us. All I can hear is the gentle stream of the water and the beating of my own heart.

"*Tilla,*" he whispers.

He says my name so poetically, it sends a shiver down my spine. The bass in his voice is so sweet, and it flows off his tongue as effortlessly as the butterfly that flowed down the stream. It dawns on me that in one summer, Hessan's tender rhythm has become my favorite song. He is the gentle irie that has soothed me this whole time. And as he holds my heart in his hands, I realize that there is no one else. I have fallen, so deeply, for the church boy from the little blue house. I have found, so clearly, a home in this foreign land. He breathes me in as he caresses my brown skin, his eyes gentle.

"I'm so in love with you," he whispers.

I feel time stop.

And in this moment, I know.

I know what I should say.

I should tell him not to throw it all away.

To reconsider.

But I can't. And I don't.

Because I love him, too.

So I press his soft lips into mine and let him bathe me once more.

21

That evening, everyone in the house huddles around the old television set in the living room.

I haven't seen Diana yet, and I'm on edge as I tuck myself into the crevice of the couch. An eerie feeling lingers in the air as the reporter's voice echoes through the house. Even the kids quiet down to pay attention to what is being said.

"We are being told that the island of Jamaica has declared a state of emergency. The effects of Hurricane Gustav are expected to be devastating, with the hurricane regaining full strength. Island officials are asking everyone to stock up on food and rations, as Jamaica is expected to lose water and all power sources."

"You cyan tek dem too serious," Andre breaks the silence. "Dem say di same ting every year. We just haffi mek sure we stock up pon wata."

But for the first time, I can sense fear in his voice. A lone candle burns in the corner as a haunting feeling permeates the air. No one dares to take their eyes off the staticky black-and-white picture.

"We are asking everyone to take shelter. Gustav is expected

to leave catastrophic damage as it reaches Category 5 strength. I repeat, Jamaica is under a state of emergency."

"I'm getting you girls out of there."

I sit on the warm tiles of the bathroom floor later that night, listening as my mother battles her frustration. "I can't believe your father sent you guys back to the country . . . He always does shit like this. I swear to God he doesn't think sometimes. *Fuck.*" Her frustration only mounts. "I'm getting you out of there if it's the last thing I do, Tilla. I swear to God."

I can hear her fingers slamming against the computer keys.

"This fucking thing keeps freezing—"

TAP. TAP. TAP.

"For fuck's sake," she mumbles to herself. "I seriously can't believe him. He knew there was a possibility the storm could still hit. He's so goddamn irresponsible sometimes—"

The line briefly chips out.

"Oh, shoot—That's him now. Hold on, Tilla. I'll call you back."

The line goes dead.

I head down the dimly lit hall and into the room.

"Fiiiinally," Mia says as she makes her way past me. "You take forever." She wraps a towel around her body and continues down the hall. I slip into my pajamas and hop into bed, eager to sleep off the eeriness of the day. Just as I reach to turn off the lamp, Herma's Bible on the nightstand table catches my eye. HOLY BIBLE shines in metallic gold letters. I notice an old, faded black-and-white picture poking out of the pages.

I can't help it.

Curiosity gets the best of me.

I pick it up, cracking it open to the page of the photo.

The image makes my jaw drop.

It is a picture of a young Herma holding hands with a handsome young man. A tight-lipped smile spreads across her face, her brown eyes bright. The lines on her face are softer, and her gray hair is nonexistent as thick brown braids fall down her back. The look on her face is foreign, taking me by surprise: She is happy.

Just as I'm about to put it back, I notice a handwritten note on the back that bleeds through the image in black ink.

Mind your business, Tilla.

But I don't.

My hands tremble as I turn the picture and read the faded cursive.

My love,
I'm wearing the jacket you made for me. You have a
way with fabrics like no other, Herma. England would
have loved to see your artistry, but you are an honorable
woman to stay behind. Your brother should be very
grateful for your sacrifice. All that you have given up—

"Are you finished with my phone?" Herma's voice cuts through the heavy sound of the beating rain. She stands at the door, sheets in hand.

I slam the book shut.

But it's too late.

"Is that my Bible?!" Dread spreads across her face as she marches toward me.

"Oh, yeah. Sorry, I was just—"

"Give me that!" She snatches the Bible from my hands. "Are you an idiot?!" She wipes the Bible with her dress. "You got your nasty fingerprints all over it!"

"I'm sorry. I was just looking for a scripture—"

"There's no scripture in the world that could clean the filth on your blasted hands!" She throws down the sheets. "I don't need you soiling my things. Do you understand me?!" She doesn't wait for a response. She marches out of the room, slamming the door shut.

I'm awoken by the sound of thunder the next morning.

It pours rain as lightning cascades through the sky. The room is dark from the heavy clouds, and this is the first overcast morning I've experienced since we got here.

The first real sign of the hurricane.

I lie awake in bed, trying to doze back to sleep, when I hear a voice call to me through the shutters.

"Brownin'."

My body halts.

"Meet me out back."

Hessan.

I shoot up out of the bed, anxious as I look toward the window. *No one is there.* My heart races. *Why would Hessan come and visit me here?* My chest clenches at the thought of what Aunt Herma will say if she sees him waiting for me. Or *Diana.* I throw off the covers and jump out of bed, careful not to wake Mia. I throw on an old dress and walk briskly through the house, careful to avoid Aunt Herma and Aunt Adele as I head out the back door.

I step out onto the wet dirt, and rain drizzles down onto my skin. Stray cats seek shelter under an abandoned piece of zinc, and Andre's chickens squawk in their coop. I walk down the muddy path with my head on a swivel, searching the yard for

Hessan. I see no sign of him. I continue deeper into the forest, but all I see are Andre's goats and cows tied to the trees. Just as I turn to go back, I hear a voice call out.

"Brownin'."

I turn to my right, and in the middle of the bushes with a spliff in his hand is Jahvan.

"Wha?" he says. "Yuh nuh know me no more?"

A wave of disappointment crashes over me.

"Come here, nuh," he says softly.

I stand frozen as I wipe the rain from my face.

"I came to talk."

He watches me as I contemplate my next move. I have to tell him that I'm not interested in him. I have to tell him what happened between us at Diana's didn't mean anything. I have to tell him it will never happen again.

It is now or never.

I slowly make my way over as he throws his spliff into the bushes. He stares down at me with his sparkling brown eyes, and I feel myself grow intimidated. The familiar scent of cologne and weed fill my lungs as he takes my hand and draws me closer.

"I missed you, Kyan-ah-da."

"Hey," I say softly. "What's up?"

"Yuh wan go fi a walk?"

I don't. But I'm nervous that Aunt Herma will see us so close to the house.

"Sure," I say.

He leads me deeper into the forest.

The rain begins to pour down even heavier, and I use my hand to wipe the droplets from my face. He guides me into a clearing, and we stop at an orange tree. He leans against it and pulls me in front of him.

"What's up?" I ask again.

"Relax, Till-ah. I jus came to see how yuh doin." He gives my shoulder a gentle squeeze. "Yuh nuh haffi be so tense every time me come round. Me nah go hurt yuh."

"I know."

He smiles.

"Yuh ready fi di hurricane?" he asks. "Ah yuh first time?"

"Yeah. I don't really know what to expect."

"You'll be all right." He gently wipes the rain from my cheek. "Me nah go let nuttin happen to yuh." The rain grows heavier. He opens his jacket and pulls me into it, shielding us from the fierce downpour. I take a breath.

I have to tell him.

"Jahvan . . . I think you're really great, but—"

"But?" He hovers over me. My body grows hot, but I resist. "But I'm not interested in . . . this. Anymore."

"Wha you mean?"

"Us," I say firmly. "I just want to be friends."

I can hear my own heartbeat. His expression stays the same, and I start to wonder if he heard me. He places his hands on my arms, gently rubbing up and down. His touch is soft and warm.

"Till-ah . . ."

There's a longing to his tone. He glides his hands up my arms to my neck, placing his fingers there softly. His touch is *enticing,* and despite my better judgment, it's enough for my feet to stay planted.

"I cyan jus be yuh friend, Till-ah," he whispers into my ear. He moves his hand from my neck, and without warning, he kisses down passionately. Goose bumps instantly flood my skin as he grazes my nipples with the tips of his fingers. "Me nuh wan be yuh friend," he whispers again. He moves his hand down my body to the hem of my dress, sliding his hands underneath the thin material.

"Jahvan, I can't—"

He kisses my neck and then moves to my lips. He presses down full and firm, and the taste of ganja awakens every single one of my senses.

"Jahvan," I whisper.

His hands trace against my wet skin, grabbing down firmly onto my breasts as my senses forsake me. The warm rain beats down even harder as he massages me in his hands.

"Jahvan," I try to say again. He doesn't listen.

He continues to swirl his tongue in my mouth. Taking me in. All of me.

"Jahvan." I resist. My blood runs cold.

He ignores me.

He continues to devour me.

"Stop." My head is woozy.

The rain blinds my vision. "Jahvan," I say again, this time loud and firm. "Stop."

I try to pull away, but he pulls me in even closer. His touch becomes forceful, and I start to cringe. He places one hand on my back and moves the other one down to my waist. He turns my body and presses me against the tree, pushing all of his weight into me. My face slams into the bark, and I feel its sharp edges scrape my cheek.

"Relax nuh, mon," he whispers into my ear. "All summer yuh ah lead me on, and now yuh wan fi act shy." He pushes harder against me, and I can feel him erect.

"Please," I beg. Tears start to well in my eyes. *"Please, stop."*

But he doesn't.

"Jahvan!" I use all my might to push him off me, but he does not budge.

He is too strong.

Too aggressive.

Too forceful.

"Stop!" I say between gritted teeth as he continues to suck on my neck. "Just—please . . ." I burst into sobs.

"Just relax nuh!" he says through frustrated moans. "Yuh always ah give me a hard time." He shoves his hand into the seam of my underwear and begins to pull them down. I use all my strength to wiggle from beneath his body, but I am pinned between him and the tree. He uses one hand to push my face deeper into the bark and the other to drag my underwear off. Everything goes dark as the sky wails out in thunder. It explodes through the clouds as the rain crashes down onto my body. Sorrow clenches my chest until I have become the storm.

Until I am disaster.

"Me say fi relax nuh, gyal," he whispers into my ear.

So I do.

And all the breath leaves my body.

He wiggles his fingers in between my legs, and I wince out in pain.

His fingers are inside of me.

Slut. Slut. SLUT.

Blood drains from my body as he digs his fingers in and out.

Over

And over

And over again.

I can't breathe.

I am no longer in my own body.

I wait until he is finished, and then finally, he eases off me. He pulls his hand from between my legs, and blood drips down his fingers. *My blood.* He looks to his fingers, impressed with himself.

"You *cyan* tell me say dat neva feel good," he says.

I hold on to the tree to keep from collapsing.

Women have duties to fulfill. Responsibilities.

I heave in and out as Aunt Adele's words rage in my mind.
I feel woozy.

"I have to go," I whisper.

I pull up my underwear and do the only thing I know how:
Run.

I run through the downpour and down the muddy path, and
I don't stop running until I am on the floor of the bathroom.
I collapse onto the warm white tiles, locking the door behind
me. I pull my panties off.

They are stained with my own blood.

I move robotically as I turn on the pipe. Cold water blasts
down, and I hold my underwear underneath it. I scrub and
scrub until the water turns red . . . but no matter how hard I
scrub, the stain still remains. I take a rag from the counter and
try to wipe away the horror of what just happened from between my legs. It makes no difference. My hands are stained.

There is a knock at the door, and I freeze.

"Don't come in!" I say through tears. My voice is shaky, and
it betrays me.

"It's just me."

Diana.

My stomach sinks. *What is she doing here?* My mind races
a mile a minute as she continues to knock. *I haven't seen her
since the dance.*

"I'm using it!" I call, trying to swallow the lump in my throat.

"Come nuh, let me in!" She knocks harder.

"Please—" My voice breaks. "I'm busy, Diana."

"Tilla, open di door. I know something's wrong." Her voice
goes quiet, concerned. "I was on my way over to di house, and
I saw you running back."

Shit.

I start to panic. I drain the water from the sink and wipe

my eyes. In a daze, I reluctantly unlock the door. Diana slides in, closing the door behind her.

"Wha gwan wit you?" she asks as she crams herself into the small space. "Is everything okay—" She stops mid-sentence when she notices the sink.

"Oh my God." She stares at the blood, and her eyes go wide in shock. Confusion spreads across her face as she searches for the words. "Tilla . . . *what happened*?" she asks frantically. And that's all it takes. I break. My entire body shakes as I fall into her arms and let it all pour out of me.

Sorrow streams from my lips.

"Talk to me, Tilla. What happened?! Why is there blood?"

I have no idea.

"It's gonna be okay," she whispers. "Don't cry, Tilla . . . it's gonna be okay."

But she is wrong.

It will not be okay.

The massive downpour beats against the zinc roof as tears pour from my eyes and onto Diana's chest. Thunder rumbles throughout the house, echoing the agony of my broken heart. I can feel it in the air, and I couldn't stop it if I tried.

The storm is coming.

22

"There are no planes leaving the island."

My mother's tormented voice comes through the phone. For a moment, I swear I can smell her sweet pheromones through the call. The calming smell of hemp and coconut oil that has always been woven into her locks. I picture the small shells she adorns her hair with knocking against each other and making music as she walks. Her deep brown skin glistening from too much shea butter after a shower. My mother has always been sweet music to me. A magician who could whip up any cure for ailments from herbs and teas when I am sick. A sorceress who could pacify me with concoctions of sage and castor oil to alleviate any aches and pains. She is the calming grace that soothes me when I am weak. But this time, I must soothe her.

"Please don't worry about us, Mom." My eyes water, but I keep my voice strong. I sit in my usual spot on the bathroom floor as she sniffles into the phone.

"All the flights are full. I've been calling the airlines all morning. They won't even let any planes fly into the island. I . . . I tried *everything,* Tilla."

Her heart shatters as she speaks.

"I can't believe I was so *stupid.* I had no idea, Tilla . . . I thought for sure it wouldn't be worse than Category 3. I would have never sent you girls down there," she whimpers. "If anything happens to you or Mia . . . I'll never forgive myself."

I have no heart to tell her the worst has already come.

"It's okay, Mom. Really. Mia and I are fine."

I nearly choke on my own lie.

"I should've just listened to myself, I . . . I shouldn't have sent you two down there. Not alone." I'm quiet as she sniffles. "They're expecting catastrophic damage, Tilla. Jamaica hasn't seen a Category 5 storm in years."

"Nothing's going to happen, Mom," I whisper. "Please don't cry."

"I'm sorry, I just . . . I thought it was turning around."

"Yeah," I whisper, wiping the tear that rolls down my cheek. "We all did."

I spend the next four days in my room.

The winds have gotten worse, and with all the rain flooding the yard, we have to stay inside. The days are gloomy and long, and Mia and the neighborhood kids spend their time running around the house.

We haven't seen sun in days.

I bury myself in books, desperate not to feel anything at all. Desperate not to feel the bile in my throat when I think of Jahvan. I feel angry with my body, as if it has somehow betrayed me. As if I have somehow betrayed myself.

I feel foreign in my own skin.

As if my body is no longer my own.

As if it never was.

I am at war with myself. *Was Jahvan right? Had I been leading him on this whole time? Did I bring this on myself?* The thoughts cripple me. I am weak and depleted, and I cannot find the courage to bring myself to get up. The gloominess of the weather gives me good reason, so no one comes to check on me.

I sleep to pass the time.

By the time Thursday afternoon comes around, the downpour is treacherous. The winds are so loud, it becomes hard not to jump at the sound of them. I'm in the middle of reading a book when there's a knock on my door.

"Come in," I call out.

The door handle wiggles and opens to reveal Andre.

Concern bathes his face. "Yuh nah come outta yuh room?"

"I'm just reading."

"Yuh frightened 'cause ah di hurricane, nuh true?"

"No, Andre. I'm fine."

"Yuh can tell me, yuh know." He smirks, genuinely convinced that I'm scared.

"You think I'm hiding from the hurricane?"

"Yes," he says matter-of-factly. "But nuh worry yuhself. Hurricane nah come till weekend. Yuh nuh need fi 'fraid." His innocence brings a small smile to my face. "Yuh wan help me bake cake?"

"No. I'm okay."

"Come nuh!" He grabs my hand, dragging me out of the bed.

"Andre, I really don't feel like baking a cake."

"Well, yuh nuh have a choice. Me nuh know wha yuh ah sulk fa, but yuh ah go help me mek dis cake."

I give in as he drags me from the sheets. I follow him through the living room and into the kitchen. It's only midday, but the house is dark with no natural light to stream through. The living room is packed with kids as Mama and Papa sit on the couch and watch the news. The sound of the reporter's voice is daunting.

"Gustav has ripped through the west end of Cuba, devastating thousands of homes and killing a dozen civilians. Forecasters

are expecting it to upgrade to a Category 5 storm by this time tomorrow evening."

We leave the living room, stepping down into the kitchen. I lean against the fridge as Andre takes out the ingredients and places them on the counter.

"Me learn fi bake from watchin' Mummy." He smiles. "But she always run me out 'cause bwoy pickney nuffi be inna di kitchen."

"That's silly," I say. "A boy can be in the kitchen if he wants."

"Nuttin nuh go so ah country." He shakes his head. "Sometimes me would hide under di sink fi watch her. Dat's how me learn." He opens a box of cake mix and dumps it into a bowl. There's a childish spirit to him that brings me comfort. His need for nothing and joy for everything. I watch as he takes a bottle of oil and pours it into the mixture.

"You don't measure?" I ask.

"No, sa. Me just guess."

I pick up the box and flip it around. "It says a half cup right here."

"Me nuh know how fi read that."

"The numbers? I can show you. Do you have a measuring cup?"

"Ah nuh di numbers me ah talk," he musters. "Di words."

I look down at the box and then back at Andre in confusion.

"You can't read?" I try to keep my voice gentle.

He shrugs.

"They didn't teach you in school? When you were younger?"

"Me neva go ah school."

"Ever?!"

"Mummy cyan afford fi send all three ah we to school. True Kenny ah di brightest and Richie ah di oldest and me ah di duncest . . . dem mek me stay home and look after di animals dem."

"Andre . . ."

"Me nuh mind." He shrugs it off. He mixes the batter until it's smooth. "Me ah go have me own plot ah land, just like Mass Tyson." He keeps his focus on the cake. I look out the open door at the rain, deciding not to push it.

"Over inna foreign, dem really care bout art and drawing and ting?"

"Yeah." I nod. "Especially if you're good."

"And people really mek money offa dem tings fi true?"

"Yeah. I mean, I imagine it takes time. But people do it."

He considers the idea, excited. "So wha dem teach yuh inna dat program? Di one yuh did ah tell me bout?"

"I guess they would teach you the basics. Like how to sketch. Sculpting, maybe. Or even how to paint—"

"Paint?!" His eyes light up. "Ah lie! Me neva paint before, yuh nuh." He smiles, considering the idea as he pours the batter into a baking pan. "If I had di money, I would travel di world and draw everyting I see . . ."

I smile. "What about your animals?"

"Me prob-ly haffi hire someone. Di same way Mass Tyson hire people fi look afta tings round yesso. Or maybe I'll go back and forth."

He speaks as though saying his dreams out loud for the first time. I watch him get lost in his imagination as he takes the pan and places it into the rusting oven. He pulls out the burner and lights it with a match.

"So wha'ppen wit you?" he asks after a moment. "Yuh nuh come outta yuh room fi a whole week. Me know suh'um ah gwan."

I hold my breath, staring out the door as the ground floods. "I'm fine."

"Me know say ah lie you ah tell. Suh'um happen wit Zory and Dee? Dem two gyal love fi cause trouble."

"No," I say, envious of the time that that was my only problem. I think of the way Diana held me in the bathroom last week, and tears form in my eyes. She was so kind to me, despite everything. Despite how I betrayed her.

Andre looks at me. "Talk to me, nuh. And how yuh get dat scape pon yuh cheek?"

Shit. My body goes cold as I rack my brain for an excuse.

"I accidentally scratched myself," I lie. "And I'm fine, Andre. I just miss home, that's all."

He nods as if he understands. "Me figure say ah dat. But nuh worry yuhself. Once hurricane done, we ah go start have fun again."

I offer him a weak smile.

We clean up the kitchen while we wait for the cake to bake. Andre tells me stories of his animals and how he got each one, including a cow he traded for moringa bush. I listen as he gushes over which animals are the most well behaved and which ones give him the hardest time. It's the perfect distraction from the chaos brewing inside me.

Thirty minutes later, we take the perfectly brown cake out of the oven. Vanilla and cocoa fill the air, in juxtaposition to the weather and warming my heart. We take a bite, and it's so fluffy. Andre divides it up like a proud chef.

"Me ah go bring dese to di livin' room. Yuh wan bring a piece go ah Diana?"

My stomach turns at the idea. But I know I cannot cower. Despite all the pain I've caused her . . . Diana was there for me. At the very least, I owe her a conversation. So, I take a slice of the hot cake and wrap it in foil. As Andre heads into the living room, I throw on an oversize jacket and head out into the rain.

The day is dark and gloomy as I sprint down the path

toward Diana's house. I'm reminded that the last time I traveled this path, I was running away from my own assault. I rip through the rain, pushing the memory to the back of my mind as I approach Diana's pink house and knock on the door. I wait a few moments, but there's no answer. I try knocking again. Nothing. Just as I turn to go, the door flies open. Diana stands in the doorframe, her long hair pulled back.

She looks behind me as if expecting to see someone else.

"Hey." I smile.

"What's up?" she asks dryly.

"Nothing really, I just . . . I hadn't seen you in a few days." She stares at me, her expression blank. I shield myself from the downpour, trying my best to read her. "I was wondering if maybe we could talk?"

She crosses her arms. "I'm good."

I squirm as we stand in silence for a few seconds. "Look, Diana . . . I know things between us haven't been the best. I know I've hurt you and . . . and I owe you so much." I search for the words. "But I just . . . I wanted to say thank you. For everything you did for me the other day. And I was really hoping we could have a conversation . . . about all of it."

She lets out a small laugh. "My God. Cut the crap, Tilla."

"What—"

"What is it this time? Yuh want me fi follow you down a shop fi go see Jahvan? Or tek you down to Hessan's so you can suck him off behind another bathroom stall?"

"*What?*" I feel my face getting hot. "Diana . . . I—I came here to bring you a piece of cake. I was coming over to say thank you—"

"Keep it. I don't eat *shit* from dogs. Especially foreign ones."

Her words floor me. My heart starts to race.

"Yuh couldn't satisfy wit one man, yuh haffi go fi his cousin." She laughs. "Disgustin'. If you wan fi go spread ya legs fi Hessan, that's your business. But I'm done playin' ya likkle games. Leave me outta ya nasty foreign-gyal shit."

"Wait—what?" My mind races as I try to make sense of her words. "His *cousin*?"

"Hessan and Jahvan are *cousins,* you idiot! What did you want to do? Fuck di whole family? Or di whole ah Comfort Hall?!"

My heart drops to the pit of my stomach.

Cousins?

Hessan's words come back to me, and suddenly, it all starts to make sense. The bad-boy crew he used to hang out with . . . the tension between him and Jahvan at Sports Day . . .

"I didn't . . . I didn't know," I whisper. Confusion takes over as everything jumbles together in my head. "Why did you help me, then? The other day? In the bathroom—"

"You're really dumber than I thought." She laughs. "You really think someone like Jahvan would actually want *you*? You really think him want fi deh wit some nasty foreign gyal who would fuck anything weh come her way?"

"Diana—"

"Shut up," she says firmly. "I'm so sick of your whiny foreign-gyal act! Don't you get it?! HE DOESN'T WANT YOU, TILLA! Ah me send him to yuh!"

My body goes. To. Stone. "*What?*"

"You heard me." Her eyes fill with ice. "I sent him over there. Foreign gyal like you need fi know ya fuckin' place." The rain consumes me, and in an instant, everything goes blurry. But she doesn't stop. "Yuh really thought you could come here and try fi tek *my man*?! You're so *fucking* selfish! You have EVERYTHING, and yet you still want what's mine!" she yells. "I had to teach you a lesson, and I would do it again."

"I . . ." But I don't know what to say. My voice is caught in my own throat. I cannot process the words that are coming out of her mouth. "*It was because of you?*"

"Oh, shut up, Tilla." Her eyes fill with disgust. "I'm not falling for your innocent likkle act anymore. You *cyan* hide. I see you for exactly who you are." She steps into my face. "You're nothing but a spoiled bitch. Daddy's *dutty* likkle princess."

Her words bore through my skin.

I am speechless.

Enraged.

"You fucking bitch," I say, acrimony dripping from my tongue.

"Ha!" She laughs. "Like that means anything coming from you. You're a *WHORE*, Tilla! Everyone knows it! You would fuck any man who comes your way. Jahvan. Hessan. Probably even Andre wit di amount of time uno spend alone in those bushes." She kisses her teeth. "You foreign girls are *disgusting*."

I've had it.

I take the piece of cake and whip it straight at her face. She jumps back, but it's too late. The hot foil strikes her, smacking her dead in the face.

She is stunned, and so am I.

And then she erupts.

"YUH MUST BE FUCKIN' MOD!" She lunges at me, and we both fall to the ground, tackling each other in the rain and mud. She wraps her hands around my throat and uses her elbows to pin me down. I fight to get from under her, reaching my hand up and grabbing her hair. I slam her into the mud and drive my fist into her face.

I. Will. Not. Lose.

The rain pummels down, and rage fills my body as we strike each other back and forth. We slip and slide in the filthy mud, blow for blow, but I don't care. I will not stop.

This is for all the moments she made me feel like shit.

I straddle her on the ground. She grabs my hair from behind and tries to pull me backward, but I stay on top of her.

I take my fist and slam it into her face.

Again.

And again.

And again.

She bites down into my arm and flings me to the side, knocking me straight in my ribs. There is blood, but I can't tell if it's hers or mine. I kick and scream and do whatever I have to until I can plant my feet and stand up. I grab her arm and drag her straight through the mud as she punches my legs.

"LET GO OF ME!" she screams.

But I don't stop.

This is my vindication.

I throw her facedown to the ground, holding her in the mud as she wiggles beneath my grip. She scratches and claws before wailing and kicking. She grabs me by my hair and yanks.

"LET ME GO, YOU FUCKIN' NASTY *BITCH*!" she screams, piercing my skin with her nails. I finally let go, and like clockwork, Aunt Herma and Aunt Adele come running down the path.

"STOP!" Aunt Adele screams. "STOP!"

"GET OFFA HER!" Aunt Herma yells. "GET UP! GET UP!" Aunt Adele grabs Diana by the wrist and pulls her to her feet. Aunt Herma grabs me by my jacket and wrestles me backward.

"UNO AH EEDIAT?!" Herma screams. "WHAT THE HELL IS GOING ON HERE?!"

"THIS DUTTY BITCH!" Diana yells. "SHE THROW CAKE INNA ME FACE!"

"SHE CALLED ME A WHORE!" Tears of fury pour down my face.

"AND I'LL SAY IT AGAIN, YOU NASTY BITCH!" she screams, her voice hoarse and strained. "With ya fuckin' bloody panty. Everyone know say you a slut! Everyone!!"

My heart sinks.

"That's not true!" I cry out. Her words cut deep, and I feel so defenseless. *How can she say that about me?* I heave in and out, and suddenly I feel dizzy, like everything is spinning. Like I might fall right over. The warm rain blasts down hard, blurring my vision. I have no concept of time. Just anger. And pain.

And it is oozing out of me.

"SHE'S A NASTY SLUT!" she cries to Adele.

"STOP SAYING THAT!" I scream. But it sounds more like I am pleading.

Begging.

"TILLA! Get your ass back inna di house!" Aunt Herma yells, pulling me back by my jacket collar. I stumble over my feet.

"I didn't even do anything!" I plead. I lock eyes with Aunt Adele, silently begging for her to come to my rescue. "Aunt Adele?!"

"SHUT UP NUH, GYAL!" Aunt Herma screams at me. "Stop call to Adele! You've been runnin' around here acting like a *slut*! Adele saw you with her own eyes!"

I feel time stop.

Aunt Adele . . . How could she? I've kept her secret. I've offered her nothing but support. I look into her eyes, begging for her to see me—to *help* me—but her face has turned to stone.

She wants nothing to do with me either.

The three women glare at me with hatred in their eyes, and what is happening could not be clearer. I have come to Jamaica and discovered all their secrets. I have seen things, read things, and done things that I shouldn't. I have uprooted all their pain.

And they hate me for it.

"From the moment you got here, I could tell you were too comfortable! You have the nerve to sleep in my bed and go complain to Diana about what time I clean it?! Flauntin' around here in all your fancy clothes! Bringing crosses to di country! You think we don't know about you?!" Herma yells. "How much trouble you've brought to our home?! Diana told us *everything*!

Sneaking around with Hessan! Convincing him fi break a promise he made to *God*!"

Shock floods my face.

I am mortified.

Diana. Told. Them. Everything.

"That's . . . that's not true." I choke over my words.

"Diana told us how you invited Jahvan to come see you at her house!" Herma grabs me by my arm. She squeezes down so hard I let out a yelp. "Fucking eediat gyal. You're running up and down the country wit a *gunman,* and you think we wouldn't find out?! Havin' sex in bushes!"

"Gunman?! What . . . what are you talking about?!"

Images of Jahvan fill my mind. Him sitting on the side of the road with his boys. His bad boy attitude . . . but a *gunman*?

"We didn't . . ." My voice shakes, fragile and weak. "I never had sex," I cry, desperate for them to believe me.

"Yuh expect we fi believe dat?!" Adele yells. "Yuh have boyfriend since yuh was eight! God knows how many men you been wit!"

It all crashes down on me at once. My breathing grows so heavy I can't keep up with it. I look to Diana. How could she sell me out like that? How could she tell them all those terrible things about me? How could she make up such *lies*?

I feel empty. Depleted. I have nothing left to give.

"How could you?!" I sob to Diana. In this moment, it feels she is all I have left. I am *pleading* with her to make this right. She is the only one that can.

"You're a nasty whore," Diana says calmly, looking me straight in the eye. "And now the whole of Comfort Hall knows the truth about you."

"Get your ass in the house!" Herma yells at me, flinging me down the path like an unwanted dog. She moves toward me, grabbing my arm again. "I SAID GO!"

"STOP!" I hear a voice call out.

Andre.

He sprints down the path through the monstrous downpour.

"STOP DRAPE HER UP!" he screams. He grabs my arm, ripping me out of Herma's grasp. "UNO LEAVE HER ALONE!"

"ANDRE, GET BACK INNA DI HOUSE!" Adele yells.

"NO, MUMMY! THIS ISN'T RIGHT!" His voice is raw, coarse. I am dizzy, hollow. "STOP IT RIGHT NOW, OR ME AH GO TELL MASS TYSON WHA UNO AH DO!"

"SHUT UP YUH MOUT, ANDRE!!" Herma screams. "MIND YUH BLASTED BUSINESS!"

"ME SAY FI LEAVE DI GYAL *ALONE!*" He uses all his might to shove Herma from beside me as lightning crashes through the sky. But that doesn't stop her. She launches to strike me just as Andre blocks her blow.

"RUN BACK AH YAWD, TILLA!" Andre screams.

His voice is the last thing I hear.

I stumble over my feet, but I don't fall. I want to explode. I want to disappear out of my skin. Wake up in Canada and realize this is all one big nightmare. But it's not.

Diana is responsible.

She has been feeding them information this entire time. They have been forming an alliance against me since the beginning. It all makes sense. Herma's hatred for me. Aunt Adele's disdain. I am outnumbered. I am on an island, in the middle of nowhere, and I am so far from home. No one is coming to save me.

I wipe the tears from my eyes, but I do not feel sorrow.

I feel rage.

I hate these people, but they will not break me.

So I run. I run fast, and I run hard.

I run to the only place that makes sense.

23

The rain crashes down from the sky as I sprint across the hot pavement.

I can feel the heat of the road penetrating through the soles of my shoes as I try to shield myself from the downpour with a banana leaf. It's no use. The wind sweeps through the island faster than I've ever seen wind go in my life. It smacks through trees and rattles the zinc roofing on houses, throwing around everything in its way.

I am scared, but I don't stop.

I run harder than ever before, pushing every bone in my body to take me faster. Blinded by the falling rain, I race against the wind, and I don't let up until I arrive at the only place I can feel safe in the middle of this disaster:

The little blue house.

I stand at the bottom of the path and stare down at the small house. Flat pieces of wood fly from the roof and out onto the yard. The grass that surrounds it is flooded with pools of murky water that reaches my shins. Muddy and exhausted, I discard the banana leaf and run down the path and up the steps, crossing the small porch. I pant heavily as I make my way up to the small wooden door. It takes everything in me to not allow the fear to paralyze me. I look down at my clothes, and I realize that I'm showing up unannounced, dirty, and uninvited.

This is a mistake, I think.

I stare out at the yard, weighing my options until I realize I truly have none. I turn back to the door. I take a deep breath, pushing the insecurities that creep up to the pit of my stomach, where they turn into an explosion of nerves.

I close my eyes and knock.

Just as I'm about to turn around, the door handle starts to wiggle. It yanks opens, and Miss Addie's small frame stands in front of me. She furrows her brow when she sees me, staring at my dirtied clothes in disbelief. "Wha di rawtid—Wha yuh doing here, girl? Yuh nuh see hurricane ah come? And wha'ppen to yuh clothes?! How you so dirty?!"

"I'm sorry, Miss Addie. I came . . . I came to see Hessan. Is he home?"

She looks me up and down, assessing the audacity of my request. "Me say *yuh mod gyal*?! Yuh nuh see rain ah fall?! Yuh want we both fi blow away?"

"I know . . . I—I'm sorry, Miss Addie. I just . . . I need to talk to Hessan. Please."

She stares at me for a moment before crossing her arms. "Him nuh want fi chat to you."

"What?" I ask, confused, as I try to make sense of her words. "Why?"

"Stop try fi ruin di bwoy life." Her eyes go cold. "Go back ah ya yawd, gyal," she says crabbily before moving to shut the door. Desperate, I put my hand on it to stop it from shutting.

"Wait!" I plead. "Please. Miss Addie—"

"Me say fi go ah ya yawd, gyal! Yuh nuh see hurricane ah come?!" she instructs harshly, scolding me like a child. I move my hand from the door just as Hessan approaches from behind her.

"Iz all right, Miss Addie," he says softly. "Gwan go lie down." Miss Addie looks me up and down before kissing her teeth and walking back into the house. I stare at Hessan, confusion taking over as he moves toward me on the porch. My brain races, wondering what he could have told her about me. He avoids my gaze, closing the door behind him.

"What is she talking about?" I ask him.

He doesn't answer but finally meets my gaze, deadpan. His face is creased and he's visibly angry. I search his eyes for something that might give me an indication of what is wrong, but this time, his eyes do not search mine in return.

Something is not right.

"Hessan?" I ask, confused. Leaves fly from the trees, and the strong wind blows over Miss Addie's plants that line the porch. The ceramic pots smash, shattering as soil seeps onto the ground.

Hessan doesn't flinch.

"Hessan. Talk to me," I urge. I search his eyes for the answers, but I come up blank. They are not the compassionate, gentle eyes that I know.

I don't recognize these eyes.

"Wha yuh want, Tilla?" he asks dryly.

"I . . . I came to see you. I needed to see you. I . . . I didn't know where else to go." My voice is desperate. I sound like a child, and I hate myself for it. "Diana and I got into a fight. My aunts . . . my aunts took her side and . . ." My voice trails as he looks away from me and out into the yard. His face tenses. "Hessan?" I ask. "Is everything okay?"

"I don't think you should be here, Tilla. You should go home."

"What?" The word jumps out of my mouth, and I feel my knees begin to buckle. I couldn't have heard him correctly. "I don't have anywhere to go. I . . . I can't go back right now."

He turns his head to meet my gaze, his eyes cold as ice. "Why'd you come here?"

"To see you. I needed someone to talk to."

"Why you nuh go look fi Jahvan, den?" His name spits out like venom, seeping into every inch of my body until I am poisoned.

Oh. My. God.

My stomach drops.

"What are you talking about?"

He shakes his head in disbelief. His face is stone cold, and he drills into me. "So yuh just ah go lie to me face?" he asks. "I went to look fi Diana. Fi break tings off . . . and she told me everyting about you and Jahvan . . ." His voice trails as he looks away from me in disgust, like he can't stand the sight of me. His voice starts to shake. "How could you . . ." His eyes water. But at a moment's notice, his sadness turns to rage. "God, Tilla," he says between clenched teeth. "How could you do this? I was going to risk everyting fi *you*. How could you . . . how could you embarrass me like that? I haffi hear from Diana dat you ah see someone else. . . . that you let a next man *have you*."

I am mortified.

"What . . . what did she tell you?!" I sob. He looks at me with a mixture of disgust and pity, but he doesn't answer me. The wind roars, blowing through the yard and knocking over the clotheslines. "Hessan, I . . . I'm not seeing him. I . . ." I struggle to find the words. I'm desperate to put together the right sentence to get him to understand. But the inescapable truth smashes into me, shaking me to the core:

I have lost his trust.

The damage is done.

"I jus cyan believe this." His voice grows louder, threatening to break. "Yuh know how me did feel about you, and yuh go give yuhself to *anotha mon*. And Jahvan of all people?!" Tears boil up, and he slams his fist into the wooden rail. "Yuh knew about everyting wit my mada. I told you *everyting*! You knew how it would make me feel. You knew it would *kill* me, Tilla. You let anotha mon *inside* of you—"

"That's not true!" I plead. Sobs pour out of me, and all I want is for him to look at me . . . to see me. To remember that I am the Tilla that he loves.

The Tilla that loves him too.

"You expect me to wan deh wit you after you go give yuhself to *someone else*? My *cousin*, Tilla?!"

His eyes are empty. Flat. Stone.

"I . . ." My entire body trembles. "I didn't know—"

"And dat mek it right?!"

"No! Hessan—"

"Do you know what they're *saying* about you?!"

His words pierce through my heart, and I feel it break in real time. I have become his mother. The woman who embarrassed him in front of the entire community. The woman they whispered about.

SLUT. SLUT. SLUT.

"I cyan believe yuh would embarrass me like that." His voice breaks.

Anxiety clutches my chest.

I pray that my tears will speak for me.

They don't.

"Hessan," I whisper, silently begging him to look at me. "You . . . you just have to believe me. It wasn't like that."

"Then what was it like, Tilla?"

The truth is I don't know.

He stares at me, his expression blank. His eyes no longer dance when they see mine. The gentle compassion behind them is gone, and in this moment, I know that forgiveness is not an option. I have cut him too deeply. I know that look anywhere.

The look you give when someone has ripped your heart out of your chest with their bare hands.

It is the look I have given my father.

I rack my brain for the right words to make this all go away . . . but I have nothing left. I am depleted. The tears that pour from my eyes hit the ground at the same speed as the rain. I swallow, but my throat is so dry it feels like a thousand tiny knives stabbing at my vocal cords.

Say something, my mind screams. *Say something, Tilla.*

But I can't.

So I don't.

Hessan stares at me as if I were a stranger. For the first time since we've met, there is no recollection in his hazel eyes. The look is all too familiar. A look that tells me that he is finally seeing what everyone else has seen all along:

Foreigna.

Something foreign.

Something that does not belong.

He looks away from me for what feels like the last time, and in the subtlety of this very moment, I feel our hearts break at the same time.

His cracks, and mine shatters.

"I *cyan* do dis no more, Tilla," he says dryly. The disappointment in his voice nearly knocks me over. I grab on to the porch ledge. "Go home. Hurricane ah come."

He doesn't know it's already passed through me.

I bite down hard on my lip to stop it from quaking, but this time, I can taste my own blood. Hessan's face goes blank for the final time. I cannot read him. He turns away from me and walks inside, uninterested in giving me one more look. He slams the door shut behind him.

I hear the lock turn.

"Hessan, please!" The words finally stumble out of me.

But it's too late.

He does not return.

I turn to run, but I have no direction. And in one swift motion, the razor wind pushes me to my knees. I fall onto the cold, wet wood as the piercing rain rips through my chest. It slices into me like shards of glass, and I wince in pain. I fight to catch my breath, but the aggressive winds deny me. It forces itself into my mouth, attacking my lungs from the inside out. Here, on bended knees, I have been abandoned by Hessan in the storm. And just like that, I am my own natural disaster, shattering into a thousand tiny pieces on the stairs of the little blue house.

Surrender, Tilla, I hear a voice say.

The hurricane is here.

24

We lose water and power the next day.

I spend the day huddled in bed as everyone makes final prepa-
rations for the hurricane. Our only news source is the tiny radio
that statics throughout the living room, and even that chips in
and out. I get out of bed only to peek through the shutters as
Andre and Richie board up the house with pieces of zinc. Dad
is on his way back to the country today, and I am crippled with
terror at what my aunts will tell him when he arrives.

The house is buzzing with activity, and a few neighborhood kids from the shantytown take shelter in the living room.
Kenny and the boys help to bring in all the furniture from the
patio while Mia and the rest of the kids collect candles and
draw buckets of river water and place them in the bathrooms.

I toss and turn in bed, empty.

I decide I will spend my days right here in this position until it's time for Mia and me to go home. I will not leave this
bed. I decide this is the only way to survive.

I spend the day falling in and out of a deep sleep. Around
three o'clock, there's a knock on the door. I poke my head out
of the mangled sheets. "Come in," I say groggily.

The door cracks open, and Kenny sticks his head in.

"Mass Tyson deh pon di phone fi you."

Hesitant, I reach out and take the phone from his hand. He heads back through the door, and I brace myself, ready to hear my father's scolding voice on the other end of the line. I put the phone to my ear, and he immediately knows I'm there.

"Tilla," he says. His voice is neutral, and I let out a small sigh of relief. "How's everything going?"

"Fine."

"How's Mia?"

"Good . . . she's helping Aunt Herma."

"That's good. It's getting really bad out, so make sure you guys are stocked up."

"Okay."

"So listen . . . I talked to your mother this morning. She wants you girls home next week."

"What?"

"Your flights are already booked. She wants you home as soon as planes can leave the island."

"Really?" My stomach turns, but I can't tell if it's with excitement or fear. "When are we leaving?"

"Monday."

I'm silent as I process this.

"You have everything you need for the storm?" He changes the subject.

"Yes."

"Okay. Did you eat?"

No.

"Yes."

"Good. Yuh have candles?"

I start to grow weary of all his questions. "Are you on your way?"

"That's why I'm calling." He pauses, letting out a heavy sigh. "I'm not going to be able to make it down in time."

"*What?!* I thought you were on your way!"

"I know. I thought I could make it down before the storm got too bad. I left out this morning, but I had to turn around. They closed down all the freeways, and driving on those mountainsides won't be safe."

My heart sinks.

"But . . . you promised you'd be back in time." My voice starts to quiver. "You *promised* you'd be here. What if something happens?!"

"I'm so sorry, Tilla." Remorse fills his voice. "I tried. I really tried."

I'm speechless.

"I know this isn't easy. But I need you to be brave, do you hear me?" he asks. "I need you to remember what you're made of."

"But, Dad—"

"You are my daughta, Tilla. Remember what I told you. Where you get your strength from." He's silent for a moment before continuing, "Yuh have my blood running through your veins, yuh understand? Jamaica runs *through you*."

"But I need you," I whisper.

"I'm so sorry, Tilla." Static begins to cut through the phone. "I need you to be brave. Yuh can weather *any* storm, yuh hear me?"

I nod as a tear runs down my cheek.

"Nothing is going to happen." His voice is calm but firm. "The storm won't last more than twenty-four hours." The static starts to take over. "I'll be there as soon as it dies down to bring you back to town." Suddenly, I hear a voice in the background. My body goes to stone. It is the voice of a woman. "Hold on, Til," he says before covering the receiver. He says something inaudible before coming back to the phone. "Mek sure you're stocked up. I'll call when—" His voice chips in and out.

"Hello?"

"Yeah . . . signal is . . . bad—"

"Dad?"

"I'll call . . . from the landline."

The phone goes dead.

I wait fifteen minutes, but it doesn't ring again.

Thunder rumbles throughout the house, and goose bumps cover my body. I feel sick with myself, disgusted at my own desperation. I feel stupid for believing that he was ever on his way. That he ever had any intention of saving us from this storm. I toss the phone to the side and lie back down. Just then, Mia walks through the door. She spots me and smiles.

"Hey, Tilla," she says as she wanders into the room. "Do you have any spare T-shirts? Kenny and I are corking the windows and doors so water doesn't come in."

"I don't think so," I say somberly. She reaches into the drawer and pulls out a few of her bedtime T-shirts. She wraps them into a ball before turning around to face me.

"Is everything okay?" she asks.

"Yeah, Mi. I'm good."

"Okay . . ." She walks toward me and takes a seat on the bed. "I also just wanted to check up on you. You've been spending a lot of time in the room and . . . I was a little worried, I guess."

Her sunset eyes make me sad. Everything about Mia is so innocent.

"I've been hearing some things around the house and . . . I just wanted you to know that I don't believe it. What they're saying about you. Not for a second."

"Mia—"

"I don't know the whole story, but I know you, so it doesn't matter what happened. I know you didn't do anything wrong."

My heart flutters as she wraps her small arms around me.

"I love you, Mia," I whisper.

"Love you more," she says. And with that, she rises from the bed and makes her way out of the room.

Tears spill down my eyes as I lie back down. I fall asleep a couple of minutes later, and when I wake up, the room has become dark. I look at the clock: 6:41 p.m. A lone candle burns on the dresser, and glowy shadows fill the room. The eerie vibe prompts me to get out of bed. I head into the living room just as Andre comes through the front door. Drenched from the rain, he spots me and smiles.

"Tilla! Come lend me a hand nuh mon. Me need help fi tie down di cow dem."

"Oh, I . . . I was just headed to find food—"

"Me nah ask yuh, yuh nuh."

I sigh, giving in. I head back to the room for a jacket and follow him out through the kitchen. He opens the back door, and we are met by the monstrosity of the falling rain. Lightning flashes through the sky, and thunder shakes the trees. I take a deep breath to brace myself, but as soon as I step out, my foot is sucked shin deep by the mud. I lose my balance and nearly fall forward, but Andre catches me just in time.

"Careful!" he calls, pulling me out. The thunder is so loud that his words are almost inaudible. The rain smashes down as we make our way through to the forest. It pours down so heavily, all I can see is Andre's blue jacket that leads the way a few steps ahead of me. We approach the clearing where his animals reside, and Andre opens the gate. His cows and goats are helpless as they moan loudly, desperate to escape the intensity of the rain. Andre pulls out a long, woven rope from the inside of his jacket. He starts to wrap it around his biggest cow before tossing me the other end.

"Tie dis to di tree fi me!" he instructs.

I can barely see a thing. As I step farther into the bushes, the water nearly reaches my knees. I follow orders, taking the other end and wrapping it around the trunk of the tree before double knotting the ends. We do the same routine for the goats until all the animals are firmly secured to the base of the trees, and we cover the chicken coop with a tarp, zinc, and stones to protect it from being knocked over.

WHAM!

I duck just as a giant piece of wood crashes into the coop, missing us by a few inches. I stumble backward, falling into the flooded mud.

"CAREFUL!" Andre screams as he rushes over to hoist me back up. Lightning rips through the sky as we run out of the forest and back to the house. "Hurry up!" he yells as the wind continues to pick up speed.

We sprint through the rain, the mud sucking us deeper with each stride as I pull myself forward. Andre reaches the back door, and I race to catch up, a few feet behind.

WHAM!

The sound is so loud that I trip over my own feet, falling forward and flat onto my face. A stinging sensation rips through my skin as I fight to catch my breath.

"TILLA!" Andre yells.

I wipe the mud from my eyes and turn my head back to see that a giant palm tree has fallen at my feet. Uprooted by the wind, it has smashed into the earth. A second later and it would have killed me. Andre lunges toward me.

"COME!" he yells. "GET UP!"

The only thing I can see is his hand as he extends it toward me. I grab on to it for dear life. The wind pushes against him, threatening to knock him over, but we prevail as we reach the door. We thrust ourselves inside just as the strongest beam of lightning flashes through the sky. The entire forest lights up. We use all our might to shut the door, but the wind pushes back with intense force.

"PUSH HARDER!" Andre screams. We use everything we have left. We push and push until the door finally slams shut.

Andre bolts it closed and then runs to grab a propane tank. He slides the tank over, and we secure the door shut, dropping down to the floor. The sound of roaring thunder shakes the house as we struggle to catch our breaths. I place my hand on my chest to calm my beating heart, and my entire body seizes.

My necklace.

"Yuh all right?!" Andre pants.

"No, I . . ." I scan my neck with my hand. "No. No . . . Andre, my necklace." Tears fill my eyes, and my voice grows shaky. "It's gone."

"It mussi fall off outside?"

"I don't know." My voice is small. The truth is, I can't remember the last time I've even seen it. Tears pour down my cheeks. I'm *so* exhausted. Goose bumps race up my spine through the thin material of my raincoat as I take in the severity of everything that just happened. *I almost died.* I could have been buried underneath that tree, another casualty in the way of nature's course. And now, the one thing that has meant so much to me is *gone.* I swallow hard, that old familiar lump burning the back of my throat.

The storm is here.

And for the first time, I am scared of what else it will take with it.

Later that evening, everyone curls up in the living room around the small radio. I'm aching to call my mom, but the phone lines are down. I sit huddled in the corner with Andre, avoiding any eye contact with my aunts, who sit in the couch on the other side of the room. There is a rawness in the air. A lingering feeling that tells you at any moment you could be face-to-face with death. Foreign objects smack against the house, and eerie moans permeate the room.

We are in the middle of a hurricane.

A shiver runs through me. No one says a word, the only sound the static of the radio that echoes throughout the thin walls. A deep, husky voice hauntingly comes through the speakers.

"The Hope River Bridge has collapsed, and the rescue force is looking into casualties. Gustav has inundated the city of Kingston and is now ravaging through the island as it picks up speed to the countryside. We are asking everyone to take shelter—"

WHAM!

Something pummels into the veranda. Everyone jumps as Uncle Junior gets up to check out the situation. Richie gets up from the couch, where he sits with Kenny and Mia, and makes his way over to me and Andre.

"Uno 'fraid?" he whispers.

"Never," Andre says. "Me nah guh dead from no rain and breeze."

WHAM!

Another large object smacks against the window, this time cracking the glass where Uncle Junior stands. We all jump, frightened as Junior stumbles backward. Richie runs back to his seat.

"Move from di window, Junior!" Aunt Herma yells, her voice shaky.

The strong winds shake the house, and seconds begin to feel like hours. We are on pins and needles, unsure of what the coming moments will hold. The kids lie on the floor under a pile of blankets, shaking as they clutch on to each other. It hits me that the materials used to build the house might not be strong enough to outlast the storm if it gets any more intense.

Aunt Herma disrupts the eerie silence. "Come. Everyone time fi bed," she directs. "No point staying awake with the storm."

Mia and Kenny tuck their pillows close to each other and gather into the safe haven of pillows and sheets with the other kids.

"Bow your heads," Aunt Herma tells them.

The kids follow instructions, holding hands with one another.

"Dear Father who art in heaven," Aunt Herma begins. "We ask you to anoint us with your love tonight, Father God. Bless us with your love and protection, and keep us safe from this storm. We know that even in the midst of disaster, this is your will, God. Help us to guide and protect each other as we weather your storm tonight, Father God. In Jesus' name, amen."

"Amen," everyone responds.

I keep my mouth shut. It blows my mind that she calls herself a Christian.

Aunt Herma blows out the candles that surround the living room, leaving one burning on the sewing machine. The glow is dim, casting a shadow around the room. She turns down the radio, and the husky voice becomes background noise.

"We are begging you not to leave your homes," it statics. *"It is too late to evacuate. Emergency responders will not get to you on the roads."*

I lay my head back down on the pillow. I am scared, but I am even more resentful. I am angry that my father made us come here this summer to leave us again. He has no idea what he's put me through. The pain I have experienced without him. The fear I am enduring because of him. And in the final analysis, it was all for nothing. Even in the midst of disaster, when it matters most, he has chosen something else. *Someone else.* I feel myself burning up. I am angry at this storm. I am angry at my father. But more than anything, I am angry at myself.

"Yuh all right?" Andre plops his head down next to mine. He turns on a small, dim flashlight and tucks it behind his pillow.

"Yeah," I respond flatly.

"Lie."

"I'm fine, Andre."

"So why yuh face look so? Yuh 'fraid?"

"No. Just thinking."

"Bout wha?"

"Why do you always ask so many questions?" I snap, annoyed.

"Stop pretend like yuh nuh love chat." He kisses his teeth. "Talk nuh."

I'm silent for a moment as I consider. "I'm thinking about God's will."

"Wha yuh mean?"

"Herma's prayer. She said this storm was God's will."

"Yeah."

"Well, I don't agree." I scoff. "This storm isn't his will. And if it is, that's not a God I want to know."

"You cyan say dat." His tone gets more serious. "Yuh cyan question God's will."

"Just did." I roll my eyes.

"Wha make you tink God nuh want dis?"

"We're supposed to be God's children, Andre. Why would he want us to suffer? Unless the whole thing is bullshit and there's no God at all. Just a man in the sky pouring water on us right now to torture us."

"So yuh tink God only want us fi experience di good stuff in life?"

"I don't know what God wants," I say dryly. "I thought I did. Not anymore."

"Me know wha him want, mon. Him tell me all di time."

"And what exactly is that?" I say sarcastically.

He thinks for a moment.

"To feel," he whispers. "Him want us to feel everything. Di good and bad stuff."

I grow angry at his ignorance. Andre has no idea what that even means. He has no clue what I've had to go through this summer. My father's betrayal. Diana's and Herma's attacks. Jahvan's fingers digging into my flesh.

I want no part of a God who wanted me to experience that.

"You don't know what you're talking about," I say bitterly.

"Maybe not." He contemplates for a moment. "But nuttin God have happen to us is 'bad' . . . sometimes we just get confused."

"Confused? What are you even talking about?"

"Yuh cyan know light without dark, Tilla. Just 'cause di storm is scary nuh mean say it meant fi harm you."

"It killed Hessan's mom."

"Yeah." He shrugs. "Hurricane kill nuff people. But just 'cause we nuh like fi experience pain nuh mean say God did ah try fi hurt us. Sometimes he just want us fi grow. Me nah go pretend fi undastand all of God's will, but me nah go question it either. It's not for us to understand. We just haffi trust."

"Trust?" I say sarcastically. "In what? Destruction?"

Andre nods. "Trust dat God love us and that what we go through is meant fi serve us . . . and if it cyan serve us, it can at least change us. Make us betta people. Stronger people. Yuh cyan 'fraid of a likkle rain and breeze."

I'm quiet for a moment as I stare at the ceiling.

"There's a sayin' weh go . . . 'When we lose God, a nuh God who is lost.'"

"What's that supposed to mean?"

He shrugs. "We tink we lose God. But we're di ones who are lost. Not him. He's always wit us. It's up to us to find our way back."

His words send me into myself. And all I feel is lost. All I feel is anger about the atrocities that have taken place. About these people. How they've soiled me with sex and buried me in shame. How they've stripped me of myself and made me forget the way my name flows off my own tongue. I have nothing left. I can't imagine a God that would have me experience so much destruction. So much pain. Unless I deserved it.

And the scariest thought is, maybe I do.

"Wha'ppen, Tilla?" Andre whispers. He turns to look at me, wiping the tear that rolls down my cheek. He takes my hand under the covers.

"It's just . . . everything that happened . . . everything they said about me . . ." I turn to meet Andre's brown eyes. "What if they're right, Andre?"

His eyes search mine, clear and firm.

"They're not."

"How do you know that?" I sniffle. "They all said the same thing. What if it's true? I'm just a slut. I'm easy . . ."

"Stop it, Tilla." He squeezes my hand tight. "Don't let dem mek yuh forget."

"Forget what?"

"Who you are."

His words stun me.

"Only God know di heart weh ah beat from yuh chest. Yuh understand?" he whispers. "Yuh haffi decide who you are before di world does. Don't mek nobody decide fi yuh. Only you decide dat. You and God."

I nod. We sit in silence for a while as we listen to the rain.

"I want yuh to come wit us tomorrow."

"Come with you where?" I look at him as if he's crazy. "There's a storm outside."

"Dane ah organize a mission."

"A mission?"

"Yeah. Fi go running inna di hurricane."

"Are you nuts?!" I whisper-yell. "Andre, you guys can't go out there."

"Cool nuh!" he whispers, trying to quiet me back down.

"No way. You guys are insane."

"Ah nuh so bad. We just ah go pon an adventure. Dane do it every year." A wide grin spreads across Andre's face as he stares at the ceiling. "You should come."

I let out a small laugh of disbelief. "No way."

"We nah go too far. Just round di yard and up di road and come back. Di eyewall of di storm nah go hit till evenin', so we have time before it get too bad."

"Andre, I—" But my mind spins as I think about the possibilities. His proposal fills me with adrenaline, and a small smile creeps onto my face.

"Me nah guh let nuttin happen to you, mon," he reassures me. "Me ever steer yuh wrong?"

"Who's going?" I ask.

"All di boys."

I start to become drunk with excitement. I can't help but feel enticed.

At this point, I have little to lose.

"I'm in," I say.

"Me know already," Andre says, cocky. "Yuh tink me did ah go leave you behind?"

"No." I giggle. "I didn't."

"Good." He snuggles into the sheets, turning off the dim flashlight that rests behind his pillow.

The haunting sound of the wind screeches loudly as I fight to keep my eyes open. I surrender to the fear that consumes me, and sleep begins to take over in its place, weighing down my eyelids like bags of sand.

"Get some sleep." Andre lets out one final yawn before turning onto his side.

"We leave at dawn."

25

The night is long, and the morning comes agonizingly slow.

I toss and turn, waking every time a foreign object smacks into the house. When I awake, the rain still beats down as heavily as before, but the wind has slowed, and the house no longer shakes. Water drips down beside me from the roof, and I can tell it's morning from the gray dewy overcast that fills the room. I open my eyes to find Richie and two other boys creeping over bodies as they make their way to the front door. Andre taps me, and I immediately sit up, following behind him as we tiptoe our way over to the boys. We move quietly, careful not to wake any of the adults or other kids. God only knows what Herma would do to us. But this time, I'm not going to let Herma hold me back. The worst is over.

I owe her nothing.

Richie puts his hand on the door handle, slowly turning it until we hear a click. Adrenaline shoots up through my body, and I bite my bottom lip to stop from laughing. Somehow, my inhibitions have been lost.

Just as Richie starts to open the door, a small voice stops us dead in our tracks.

"Til?"

I freeze. We whip around to see Mia sit up as she rubs her eyes. "Where are you guys going?"

"Shhh!" We all hush her in unison.

"What?!"

"Mia!" I put my finger on my mouth, fearful that the plan might be ruined in the blink of an eye.

"Where are you going?"

Aunt Adele stirs in her sleep.

"Outside, Mi. Go back to bed."

"But I want to come," she whines.

"Shh!" Richie turns back to the door, growing impatient.

"Mia," I say firmly but quietly. "Go back to bed."

"Where are you going?!" she sulks.

"Jesus Christ." Richie throws his hands up.

"Running. We're going running in the storm," I whisper. The words feel odd coming from my mouth, and a numbness fills my body.

Mia screws up her face. "You guys are nuts," she says before plopping back onto the pillow. Before I can contemplate whether or not she's right, Richie pushes the door open, not wasting a second more. We step out onto the veranda and close the door shut behind us.

My heart catapults into my stomach.

The yard and the veranda have been destroyed. Torn limbs and fallen trees cover the property. As we move from the shelter of the veranda, the rain immediately drenches us, beating down hard into our skin like little tiny stones. All at once, we are met with a strong gust of wind, and there is no time to think.

There is only time to *run*.

We race through the flooded grass, around to the back, where Dane and a few other country boys stand waiting for us. His eyes come alive when we round the bend.

"FOREIGNA!" His tone is filled with joy as he runs over to me, scooping me up and twirling me in the same way he did when we first met. I scream out in excitement, throwing my head back as I fly through the storm like a bird.

"WELCOME TO DI HURRICANE!" he yells.

Laughter pours out of me, and everyone hoots and hollers as he places me back down. We are a ripple of hysteria, dancing in the mud until we are covered from head to toe in red dirt. It feels *so good* to bask in the madness. The audacity of it all.

Adrenaline rushes through my entire body, and my heart dances in tune with the sound of laughter. The droplets hit me with force, each one stinging my skin and pushing me further into an aliveness that I have never felt before. I close my eyes tightly, and my laughter grows into hysterics. I open my mouth to the sky and allow the sweet rain to fall into it, coating the back of my throat. The ferocity of the downpour cascades into me with intense pressure, and although I almost choke, I keep my mouth open.

I want to taste every single drop.

The air smells piercingly sweet, like ripe mango and coconut have been blown around the island and busted open by the wind.

"TILLA!" I hear a voice call out.

I open my eyes to see Andre a few feet in front of me.

"YUH NAH COME?!" he calls to me through the rain. I realize then that the group has taken off down the path into the forest. I sprint toward him, but just as I approach, he takes off farther down the path. With each stride, my legs grow farther and farther apart, but it seems no matter how hard I run, the wind keeps me at a distance. Through the vicious downpour of the rain, the boys have become little blurs of brown hues that look like mere specks in my vision.

The group swings a right at the bottom of the forest, running out onto the back road. I follow behind them for about a mile as we dodge fallen objects and giant banana leaves. Uprooted palm trees have fallen everywhere, and fruit and zinc litter the streets. My heart pumps faster than it ever has, and the smell of fresh rain fills the air as we begin to sprint up a dirt hill. I can taste blood in my lungs, but I don't care. There is a vigor to my spirit that fuels me, sending me ripping up the steep hill.

When we finally reach the peak, we collapse onto the ground in rumbling hysterics, desperate for air to reach our lungs. We pant in and out, gripping each other to regain our balance. Dane is the first to spring to his feet, a giant grin on his face as he walks to the edge of the steep hill to marvel at the view.

"UNO COME NUH!" he calls over to us.

I grab on to Andre, who extends his hand to me, and we make our way over to the ledge. Gripping on to each other for stability, we reach where Dane stands, and I am breathless:

The view is *heart-stopping.*

At the bottom of the high hill is a cascading stream of forestry. Rich in vibrant hues and deep greens, the trees perfectly frame the small houses that occupy the countryside of the island. The wind rips through the town below in real time as objects fly around in the storm. Bright pink, blue, and yellow houses stunningly contrast with the sea of greenery as foreign objects dance in circles as if in a sacred ritual. The dance is majestic, and as we look down at it with peering eyes, it feels like we are watching God destroy his most beautiful work of art. We watch as the rain pummels the land, tearing apart houses and sheds and wiping out what has been so perfectly crafted. Objects crash into one another, and there is an evolution to their madness as they shift and alter, displacing themselves to destroy each other. I watch in awe with a feeling that rings abundantly clear: We are standing in the midst of the destruction of paradise.

And it is *beautiful.*

Everything on the island is alive. Everything is interrupted by the raging winds. It is all affected. The hurricane tears through the town as we grip on to each other, and it becomes clear that everything must be changed.

Even us.

When a hurricane finally forms, you feel it in the depth of your bones. It is the feeling that tells you nothing will ever be the same.

That nothing *can* ever be the same.

A strange sensation begins to take over. I am excited but sad. I am overcome by an eerie feeling of joyous hellos and painful goodbyes, just like at the airport the first day I left home. On a mountain peak in the rural ends of Jamaica, we are standing in our own oxymoron. I can feel everyone's entrancement as we mourn the death of the island but celebrate its rebirth at the same time. We celebrate the way that the island is coming alive in a way like never before for its own destruction. We watch in reverence as it is being forced to destroy itself, to re-create itself again.

And then, I hear a wail that nearly brings me to my knees. It is Dane.

Yelling at the top of his lungs.

"AHHHHHH!" He stands with his chest proud as his voice rips through the island. Like a king reclaiming his throne. And then Richie follows, and then Andre, and then the rest of the boys, young and old, who stand with us.

"AHHHHHHHHHHH!" they scream, exploding on top of the hill, yelling out to the winds, to the Gods, to the land. They yell from the pits of their stomachs to the tops of their hearts. From the tips of their fingers to the tops of their chests.

And it's contagious.

As if by no doing of my own, I open my mouth and finally let it out.

I am electrified as my own voice almost brings me to my knees.

As if the depths of all that I am is finally seeing the light of day.

"AHHHHHHHHHHH!" I scream. It rips out of me. Chilling. Full-bodied. *Whole.* Tears pour from my eyes as my voice rumbles in sync with theirs. In this moment, we are one, and this is our tribal song. We are the children of Jamaica, and we are screaming out in agony, in pain, in love, and in joy. We are screaming in tune with our ancestors and anyone who has ever called this land home.

And just like that, it all clicks.

I am screaming out to finally hear my own voice.

My summer. My time here. My broken heart that shattered like the storm to which I am bearing witness. My heart is being forced, just like this island, to change. And in this moment of melancholy and excitement, I finally understand exactly what Andre meant.

There is beauty in destruction.

I watch in awe as the island crumbles, tearing itself apart for no other reason other than that is what it must do. I watch as the island bows to the request of Mother Nature. To her strong winds and roaring rains. It doesn't object to disaster. It flows with chaos. Breaking itself, on its own, it welcomes its own destruction with a palpable rhythm:

The rhythm of life.

I stand hand in hand with the boys of this land, drenched head to toe in the tears of Jamaica as the winds howl out in pain. It calls out to us, drowning us in its inevitable sorrow. In its inevitable *rebirth.*

I peer over at Andre and Dane, whose eyes well with tears that do not fall. They grin wide with pride, beaming as they look on in amazement at the masterpiece that is taking place in front of them. They are open to what comes next. Their disposition of sadness and joy is a paradox that I finally understand. I squeeze Andre's hand a little tighter as he looks at me with tears in his eyes.

"Welcome to Jamaica." He beams.

And for the first time since I've been here, I have truly arrived.

As I hold tight the people who have, in one summer, become sort of like family—the people who call this place home—I can't help but feel that they are the true heart of this island. The beating pulse that keeps it alive. And even as their home is being ripped apart, they are resilient. They are beating strong. The heart of Jamaica has not been broken and can never *be* broken. Because here it stands, hand in hand, ready to pick up the pieces.

Ready, always ready, to find their way back home.

And in this very moment, as I watch paradise gracefully succumb to its own death, I succumb to my own as well.

I have never felt so alive.

THE
AFTERMATH

26

We sneak back inside before anyone has a chance to wake up.

We peel out of our clothes and change into dry T-shirts before crawling back into bed. Complete euphoria takes over as I lie back down on the living room floor, listening calmly to the sound of the storm. I can't believe that merely minutes ago, I was *in* it . . . that I was *of* it. As I inhale and exhale, my breaths feel lighter—like the bricks on my chest have turned into feathers. I can feel the sorrow that has been living inside me begin to subside, wiped clean as the storm passes through the island and passes through me. Andre lies down, his face plastered with a permanent grin that proves to be contagious.

"You had fun, nuh true?"

"I'm still shaking." I beam.

He cuddles up next to me, pulling the sheets up to his chin. "Tilla versus di hurricane." He laughs. "Yuh ah go have plenty story fi tell when you go back ah foreign."

"Yeah," I whisper. Tears start to well in my eyes as I remember that in a few days, I will have to say goodbye. "I'm going to miss you so much, Andre."

"Me ah go miss you too, Kyan-ah-da."

"No, really." I struggle to find the words. "You . . . you were the best part of my summer."

He shrugs off my affection. "Me soon come visit you ah foreign. You can show me around di shoppin' malls. Me neva go ah one before."

A tear rolls down my cheek, and I wipe it away before he can see. "Oh, I'll take you to *all* the shopping malls." I laugh. "That's a promise."

"Jus mek sure yuh have a friend yuh can hook me up wit. A white girl if yuh know any. Me neva see one inna real life."

I giggle at the seriousness of his request. "I got you, cousin."

We go quiet as the sound of rain pummeling into zinc fills the room. Andre stirs, pressing his head into my shoulder.

"Me neva have a best friend before you, yuh nuh."

My heart flutters.

"Me either," I whisper softly.

He nuzzles his head into my shoulder like the missing piece of a puzzle as we doze off to the sound of the morning hurricane.

I feel God watching over us as we sleep.

The storm lasts all day and night and carries over into the next morning. By day three, the worst of the hurricane has passed, and just as night turns to day, the sun eventually shines again, lighting up the island as if nothing happened. But I step outside to find that is the furthest thing from true.

It is catastrophic.

The island is a complete disaster. The entire front of the patio has been uprooted and dismantled. One of the pillars that holds up the roof has been ripped in two, and wood from its foundation is scattered all across the grass. The yard and the veranda are littered with fallen trees and garbage, and battered fruit decorates the demolished ground. Dead birds lie still in the grass, shot down from the sky by the winds. The trees are bare, and zinc and wood scatter the yard as if an explosion had taken place. The beautiful perfection that once stared back at me is gone.

Paradise has been destroyed.

The sky shines brightly as if it has no recollection of the damage. No recollection of the destruction the hurricane has caused for so many people. I feel helpless. The truth is I'll never bear the responsibility of cleaning up this mess. I am a visitor—*a foreigna*—passing through. And I will leave as quickly as I came, just like the storm, without ever knowing what it truly means to rebuild a home after disaster. When I leave this island and go back to my comfy bed, they will still be here—*for years*—rebuilding their home.

And I will be gone.

And I will have forgotten.

A twinge of guilt passes through me as I realize everyone's hesitance to accept me. They feel like I will never bear the burden of what it means to call this place home.

And the truth is, they are right.

In their eyes, I am the hurricane that was passing through. I am the destruction that has uprooted their lives and left everything in pieces.

I am their hurricane summer.

And soon, I will be gone just as quickly as I came.

I walk back into the room as Mia talks rapidly on the phone.

"But I don't wanna leave yet," she says sulkily. She looks up at me as I walk in the door. "Yeah, she just walked in."

I make my way over to the bed and plop down.

"Okay," she says quietly. "Love you more." She snaps the flip phone shut.

"What?" I ask.

"Daddy said to start packing," Mia says. "He's coming to get us tomorrow morning."

My heartbeat quickens. I didn't think it would actually happen so soon. I didn't think he would actually keep his word this time.

I nod, in a daze as Mia leaves the room to return the phone to Aunt Herma. Thoughts of Hessan immediately flood my mind.

"Go home," he told me.

The words still paralyze me.

My heart aches at the thought of never seeing him again.

But I am no longer what he wants.

Leaving the island will be what is best.

All of a sudden, the door swings open, and Aunt Herma stands in the doorway. She looks at me with a palpable disinterest as she makes her way to the dresser to grab something. She pauses before turning around.

"Did you hear from your father?"

She already knows the answer. But it's the first thing she's said to me since our fight.

"Yeah," I whisper.

"He told you that you two are going home tomorrow?"

"Yes," I respond, looking down at the bedsheets.

"Good. Pack your things from now. You don't want to have him waiting."

Her eyes search the room. It's so clean that I silently dare her to say a word.

She does.

"Things will be returning to their rightful order when you're finally gone. I expect this room to be spotless when you leave."

She marches past me toward the door, nearly brushing me as she goes. A burst of energy races through me. I stop her in her tracks.

"Herma." It comes out forcefully, but I don't care.

I have something to say, and it is her turn to listen.

She turns around, shocked at my informal call. Her eyes dare me to speak. The words leave my mouth without second thought.

"I'm going to tell my father. About how you treated me. This summer."

My pulse races.

I don't care.

I want her to know.

"I'm going to tell him everything. Everything you did to me." For a moment, I think I might choke on my own courage. But there is no turning back now. "I'm going to tell him everything. Because it wasn't right. And I want you to know that."

This time my voice does not quiver.

It roars.

Just like it did on top of the hill.

Herma takes a step closer to me, a tight grin on her face. She has been waiting for this moment.

She has been waiting to finish me.

"You stupid bitch." Her eyes glare into me like laser beams. "You think I haven't told him *everything*? The way you've been gallivanting around the country like some *whore*? Dancin' on a promised man at a *church gathering*? Havin' sex with grown men at nighttime round ah Diana yawd?" Her words spit at me with the sharpest venom.

I am leaving tomorrow, and this is her final opportunity to show her truest colors. To paint me with her ugliest brush.

But I refuse to be her canvas.

"That's not true." I stand up, adrenaline scorching through my veins. "And you know it. So I don't care what lies you told my father. You were wrong. It doesn't matter what you say or how you try to spin it."

"Fuckin' eediat gyal." She lets out a laugh before stepping in my face. "You make me sick. Foreign gyal like you weh not even know how fi wash yuh own *panty*. Yuh come ah country and tink say yuh better den all ah we. Yuh tink say yuh special just because yuh come from foreign when all you are is a nasty *slut*. It doesn't matter how much fancy new clothes yuh put on. That's all you'll ever be. You don't think I haven't already told yuh fada that you'll spread yuh legs fi any man who want fi get inside?"

My body goes to stone.

"Please." She kisses her teeth. "You'll never be better than me. Den *any* ah we. You're nasty and used up. *Daddy's likkle dutty gyal*. That's all you'll ever be—"

"SHUT THE FUCK UP!" I scream. It bursts from my mouth, echoing throughout the room and pierces through the walls. "How dare you?! You're so worried about me you're not even paying attention to what's going on in your own home! Uncle Junior! Diana! YOU! YOU'RE ALL FUCKING MONSTERS!"

She raises her hand to strike me.

WHAM!

I catch her wrist in my hand, stopping her blow before her palm can brand my skin. I throw her arm back down. This time, I am not sad. I am not angry.

I am *done*.

I step closer to her. She stares at me, full of rage, the lines on her face deep as she looks at me in disgust. I will not let her have me. I will not let her take all of me before I go. I am no longer Tilla the foreigner.

I am Tilla the *warrior*.

I soften my face, allowing the shock of her attempted blow to pass through me. Her eyes are like daggers, but I will not look away.

I will take every strike.

I will feel every blow.

I will fight.

"You can't hurt me anymore, Herma," I whisper, staring her straight in her empty brown eyes. I see right through her, and I am not afraid. Not anymore. "You can't hurt me, because you have *nothing* that I want." It guts her like a knife. "This whole summer, you've tried to taint me. To *take me* from myself. You thought if you could turn my sexuality into shame, then you could smear me with it. But the truth is, you didn't want to fight me. You wanted me to fight *myself.* Because if you could make me believe my body was a weapon, I would eventually destroy myself with it. I would eventually drink the lies you tried to force down my throat."

She tries to get by me, but I block her.

"I'm sorry you had to give up your dreams. The man you loved. And I'm sorry that every time you see my face, you're reminded of it all." My voice grows stronger. "But you don't really hate me. You hate yourself because you will never leave this place. This is all you will ever be, and it *kills* you. It eats you alive."

I step even closer.

"Look at your home. Everyone in it. It's *disgusting.* You should be so ashamed. You were so worried about *my* dirty habits that you didn't even realize the real filth was living in your own fucking home. Well, I have news for you. It doesn't matter how much bleach you use, or how many times a day you clean. Your house is infested from the inside out. Not even God could clean it up."

I turn around and head toward the door.

Just before I go, the words fall from my lips.

"The only *dutty gyal* is you. Clean your *bloodclot* house."

27

Mia and I pack our bags early the next morning.

We've given away so much clothing that there's barely anything to pack. I roll our suitcases to the door after speaking to my mom. She's frantic to get us off the island and makes me promise to call her as soon as we get to town. Mia heads out to the yard to play with the country kids one last time, and I start saying my goodbyes. I find Richie collecting branches out front.

"Kyan-ah-da," he says when he sees me. "Me hear say you ah leave today. Ah true?"

"Yeah."

"Ah lie. Mass Tyson ah come fi uno?!" he asks in disbelief.

"Yeah. We go back to Canada tomorrow morning."

"Cockfoot! Me tink ah joke Kenny did ah tell."

I look around at the mess that litters the patio. The yard is completely uprooted and destroyed. Countrymen are out and about, walking past the yard with tools in hand as everyone works to put the island back together.

"I wanted to say bye to Dane before I left. Do you know where I can find him?"

"Him and Andre gone ah river dis mawnin'. Dem soon

come." With that, he takes off into the yard and around the side of the house to finish his duties.

I head back inside to say my goodbyes.

I have a heartfelt goodbye with Mama and Papa, and I skip right past Uncle Junior. I give hugs to some of the country kids and a longer hug to Kenny. I'm careful to avoid Aunt Herma and Aunt Adele, and I avoid going out back so that I don't run into Diana.

Around 9:00 a.m., there's still no sign of Andre or Dane, and I feel myself growing nervous. I pace the house as I wait for their return, scared that Andre won't be back in time. There's no way I can leave here without saying goodbye.

At 9:43 a.m., my father pulls up out back.

The yard is still flooded, and I can hear the engine struggle as the car tries to make its way through. I head out the back door just as my father slams the driver's door shut. He does not smile.

"Til," he says, assessing the destruction.

"Hi, Dad."

He gives me a half hug, patting me formally on the back. He doesn't make eye contact with me. "I need to speak to you. But not now. We'll talk in the car."

My stomach turns.

"Where's Mia?" he asks.

"In the front."

"All right. Well, let's get going. The roads are really bad."

He heads inside, and I'm filled with dread at how much he knows. I want to stop him in his tracks and tell him that whatever Aunt Herma told him was a lie. But I know this is not the time.

Right now, I need to find Andre.

My heart can't handle the idea of not being able to say

goodbye. Not after everything he's done for me this summer.
I can't have him think that I just left. I head inside to the bedroom and dig through my bag for a pen and find a scrap piece
of paper. Andre won't be able to read what I write, but I know
he will find someone to read it for him. I scribble onto it in a
last-ditch attempt, just in case.

> Andre,
> I will love you forever. Thank you for my summer. Thank
> you for showing me what it means to truly live.
> I will carry our memories with me everywhere that I go.
> I'll see you in "foreign."
> Love always & likkle more,
> Tilla

I run into Andre's room and pull his box of drawings from
under his bed. I shove the note inside the box before putting it
back where I found it, and then, I make my way to the veranda
where everyone gathers. Dad speaks with Uncle Wayne and
Aunt Shirley as Aunt Herma and Aunt Adele tend to Mama
and Papa. I breathe a sigh of relief when I see no sign of Diana.

"You ready, Til?" Dad asks when he sees me.

I look around the patio for Andre.

He's still not back.

"Yeah," I whisper.

Aunt Shirley walks over to me, pulling me into an aggressive hug. "It waz so nice havin' you girls. We're going to miss
you at church."

I nod, realizing Aunt Shirley was the only aunt who was
indifferent to me this summer.

"Thanks for everything, Aunt Shirley," I say as she releases
me from her grip.

"You say bye to everyone?" Dad calls over to me.

"Yeah," I lie. Aunt Herma avoids me at all costs as she feeds Mama and Papa their morning meal. I couldn't care less.

We have already said our goodbye.

Mia makes her rounds, giving hugs to everyone as Dad gathers the last of our things. I look out into the yard, doing one more scan for Andre.

He doesn't show.

Richie emerges from the house. "Kyan-ah-da," he says dryly. "Safe flight back." He gives me a quick and formal hug. It is much different from the embrace the first day he saw me.

But I guess we are different now.

"Thanks, Richie." I look out at the yard. The reality that I won't get to say goodbye to Andre starts to sink in.

My palms grow sweaty.

"Let's go, Til," Dad says as he descends the stairs. Mia follows behind him.

"Can you tell Andre I said bye?" I ask Richie, my voice desperate.

He nods casually.

I take one final breath and make my way down the stairs. As tears fill my eyes, I realize that not all goodbyes look like what you want them to. Sometimes there's no happy ending.

Sometimes there's just a storm.

I step down onto the grass, trailing behind my father. Just as I hoist my bag onto my shoulder, the gate swings open.

It's Dane.

He runs into the yard, screaming something I cannot understand. He waves his arms in a frenzy, and it seems he is rushing over to say goodbye.

"Mass Tyson! Mass Tyson!" He gets closer, and he trips over himself. He is out of breath.

Hysterical.

Something is not right.

"Mass Tyson . . ." He struggles to catch his breath, choking on his own words.

His eyes are bloodshot.

His face is bruised.

"Calm down, Dane . . . Wha'ppen?!" My dad's face grows stoic, concern furrowing his brows. Dane continues to choke, desperate to catch his own breath.

Agony pours out of him and onto the ground.

"We did . . . we did go ah river . . ."

"Wha yuh ah talk bout? Who?"

"Andre . . . We . . . we did go ah river . . ." All at once, Dane breaks. His words become inaudible through his cries. Bile erupts from his body and onto the grass.

He cannot breathe.

"Come nuh, Dane!" My father grows concerned. "Wha yuh ah talk bout?!"

"Di tide . . . di tide was too high," Dane sobs. "He said he could manage . . ."

Dane falls to his knees, heart-wrenching sobs falling from his lips as tears pour from his eyes.

"Answer me nuh, mon!" my father demands.

Dane looks up at my father, helpless and hollow.

The birds ring out.

The clouds fall from the sky.

I feel the island swallow me whole.

"Andre . . . he drowned."

28

Everyone has that one summer.

The summer that changes your life. It passes through you like a hurricane, leaving as quickly as it came. But once it has torn through you, nothing can ever be the same.

You are changed.

Hurricane Gustav ripped through the island of Jamaica at record strength, destroying everything in its path. It pummeled cities and ravaged towns, wrecking homes, killing animals, and taking the lives of countless people. Some couldn't find shelter, some didn't get home in time, and some were just casualties of Mother Nature's destruction.

Of God's will.

I have learned that when a hurricane passes through, it knows no favor. It takes no precedence. When the time is right and it is ready, it will destroy you. It will destroy everything. Even the good things. Even the things you love.

One hundred fifty-three people died in the storm.

And in its aftermath, it took my cousin.

I cry for eight days straight, but it is still not enough. I am a ball of devastation. Mom changes our flights so that Mia and I can stay for the funeral, and we spend the next week in town, waiting to go back to the country. We buy church clothes black as night, and I stay curled up on the couch, longing for my mother's arms. I long for her warm voice and the tender bedtime stories that she would pacify me with as a child. I remember crying if she reached the end of a story and I was still awake. I couldn't stand to be conscious when our time together came to a close. I would beg her to start over so I wouldn't have to discover what monsters lurked in the corners of my room, just waiting for her to leave my side.

But I always knew one day I would have to face the darkness on my own.

I cannot fathom how quickly my summer went from basking in the rays of a tropical wonderland to having the core of my insides torn apart. Ravishing me from the inside out. There is a scream inside me, desperate to get out. But no matter how many tears I cry, it is stuck in the pit of my stomach, swallowing me whole with each breath.

Andre is dead.

I ache as I think of the life he will never know. The promises I made to him of foreign, of a new life. Of art. Of opportunity. Andre will never know the inside of a shopping mall or the rugged feel of an art canvas. He will never know the feeling of dried paint on his fingers or of hardened clay molded to his hands. His life will forever be an incomplete sketch. A drawing with missing colors.

A doodle on paper.

He deserved to experience a life away from these people. I think back in disgust at how they cried for him. They are sadder for his death than for the quality of his life. They taunted him. Terrorized him.

None of their hands are clean.

The thought fills me with rage. It's as though adults make it their personal mission to scar their children. To burden them with their own insecurities and shortcomings as if we are responsible for their raging hearts. We are forced to drink their turmoil until, slowly, their blood spills from our lips and onto our hands, and we are stained. Scarred. Ruined. We are poisoned from the inside out.

And we are forced to clean it up.

I am sick at the injustices that adults demand us to carry. The way they vomit the bile of their sins onto our skin. The way they steal our spirits like thieves in the night. I think of my own father and the way my heart runs from my own body at his doing of just that.

It hits me all at once.

He is responsible. He is the lump that sits at the back of my throat. The anger that stirs in my heart and the rage that churns in my gut. He is the blood of chaos that swims at my feet. The darkness that consumes me when I am alone.

He is the poison and the remedy for my wounds.

He is the reason I longed for Hessan's love and fell into Jahvan's embrace. It was the love of my father that I desperately craved all along. He is the root of my faults and the eye of my disaster. He is the storm that brews in the depths of my soul.

He is the hurricane that lives inside me.

"Tilla."

I stare at the empty green walls as my father enters the room. I lie curled up on the bed next to my carefully folded black clothes. We are headed back to the country today for the funeral tomorrow morning. Dad's locks are pulled back into one, revealing the redness behind his gray eyes.

"Yuh almost ready?" he asks.

"Yeah."

"I'm going to go start the car. You and Mia get your shoes on."

He makes his way to the door, but my heart is on fire.

I have nothing left to lose.

"Dad?"

He turns around. He locks eyes with mine, and I'm nervous he can read my sorrow. The silence between us is fragile and strained.

I break it.

"You believed it, didn't you?"

He stares at me, confused.

"Aunt Herma. The things she said."

"Tilla. This is not the time—"

"You believed it. Right? You believed everything she told you. About me."

His face grows stoic. His eyes look everywhere but at mine. "I'm not doing this with you right now."

"Just say it. Say you believed it. That I'm a slut. A *whore*. That I'm no good. Say you didn't question it for a second—"

"And what was I supposed to believe, Tilla?!" he yells, frustration bursting out of him. "How do you think it makes me feel as your *fada* to hear say yuh ah run up and down wit *grown mon*? I can't even leave you alone for two seconds and you go embarrassing me in front ah di whole goddamn country! In front of my *family*. What was I supposed to believe?!"

"ME, Dad! You were supposed to believe *ME*!" I scream. "You were supposed to believe the best in *me,* and you didn't. You were supposed to protect *me,* and you didn't. You believed *them,* and that's why you didn't come back."

"I'm not doing this." He shakes his head. "You have no idea wha yuh ah talk bout."

"Then help me understand, Dad! Just tell me *why*!"

"Why what?!"

The inevitable rips through me.

"Why did you leave us?"

It falls from my mouth so faintly that I wonder if it even came out. Agony churns in my belly, forcing itself out through my mouth like vomit. It is the child who needed her father that speaks.

"Did you forget?"

"What are you talking about?" He looks at me quizzically.

"That you loved us." The space between us is haunting. He stands frozen in the doorway as the words pour out of me like my deepest confession. "I don't understand. I just . . . I've been trying to make sense of it, and I just can't. Mia and I . . . we flew across the *world*. Just hoping that when you saw us, you might remember. For so long, I thought maybe you just forgot or something. I thought . . . I thought seeing us might help you remember."

"Tilla." He takes a step toward me. Bags crease under his eyes, aging him in a way that I hadn't noticed before. "Look, I know this is a tough day for you—"

"*Why did you leave us?*" I say through gritted teeth. "Not just this summer. Not just this year. I'm talking about our *lives*. Why did you leave *our lives*?" I am burning to the core. I won't let him change the subject.

Not this time.

"Why did you *leave us*, Dad?!"

He stays silent as he stares back at me.

I search his gray eyes, but I come up empty.

I always come up empty.

"We love you so much, and you just abandon us. *Every time*."

"That's not true. I love you and Mia more than—"

"*Stop saying that.* Just tell me why. Tell me why that love wasn't enough."

"You have no idea." He shakes his head, and his locks swing back and forth. "It's easier to see it that way, Tilla. It makes you feel better. But that's not the truth. That's not the full story." His eyes gloss over. "It's not about you guys. It has nothing to do with you and Mia. It . . ." He pauses, frustration taking over. "You have no idea what it's like. To leave your *home* to be an immigrant in someone else's. You have no idea what I have to go through."

"What *you* have to go through—"

"I'M NOT HAPPY!" He erupts like a volcano, his words splattering like lava onto the walls. "Don't you get it?!" His eyes water. "Can't you see?! I'm not *happy*, Tilla!"

"That's not my *fault*."

"You think I don't know that?!" His voice is desperate. "It hasn't been easy for me, Tilla! Foreign . . . it sucked the life out of me. It took everything I had left. I left my home here for a better life. A life that *wasn't better*. And I know I haven't been the best father, but it's *me* who haffi deal with di consequences. *I* made those decisions, and now *I* haffi live with them—"

"No." I say it so sharply that it cuts. "*We* have to live with them."

He shakes his head, turning to go.

"Stop," I say through gritted teeth. "Don't walk away from me. Not again." My voice trembles as he turns around. "When I was younger, I cried myself to sleep every night holding your picture. I would lie in bed and ask God to bring you back, Dad. *Every night.* I waited, and I prayed, and I *begged* for him to bring you home, but he never did. Until my faith in God turned to fury. I was so angry that he couldn't just make you *love me enough*." My voice grows strained. "Every time you walked out that door, you took a piece of me with you. You took a piece of me until there was *nothing left*. And I'll never get those pieces back."

I hold his gaze.

He will swallow every word.

"I've loved you so much that it's *killed me*. So it's not *you*. It's *us*. We are the ones who have had to deal with the consequences of your absence. *We* are the ones who have loved you, and *we* are the ones who have had to bear the burden of *your* broken heart."

His gray eyes grow dark like a storm, and tears threaten to fall like rain. He opens his mouth, and I brace myself for what he will say next. It is a thunder that rumbles me to my core.

A thunder that destroys me.

"I don't know what you want me to say, Tilla."

That's it. That's all he says. It leaves his mouth void of emotion, striking me down like a bolt of lightning. It is the silent whisper that has threatened to kill me. The inevitable truth that I have tried to outrun:

There is nothing he can say that will change what is done.

We stand in silence as I study the heavy lines that crease his face. And for the first time, as I stare at my father, I see a man whose body has gotten older and whose bones are beginning to betray him. I see that the gray hairs that line his locks and speckle through his beard match the regret that sits behind his stormy gray eyes. For the first time in my life, I am not seeing him through the eyes of a little girl. I am seeing him through the eyes of a young woman. And my vision has never been so clear:

My father is a boy, trapped in a body that is growing old.

He is a man whose spirit is broken because of the decisions he's made. A man with many regrets. A man who finds it easier to blame *foreign* than to face the truth that there will be no do-overs. He finds it easier to blame everyone else for his pain.

Just like I find it easier to blame him for mine.

My father and I are one and the same. He is holding on to paradise because he is afraid of the reality that the paradise in his spirit died a long time ago. I am holding on to a fantasy because I am afraid of the reality that my fantasy of my father died a long time ago. This whole time I've been jealous of Jamaica, when the truth is that this island will not be what fulfills him either. It's easier to blame Canada than to face that after all these years of searching, he has not found what he is looking for. It's easier for me to blame him than to face that after all these years of searching, I will never find the father I am looking for. He can offer me no healing because he does not have it for himself.

We are both searching for ourselves in empty places.

He will never know how his words destroyed me. How I died to myself over and over again. How I am still trying to wipe shame from the surface of my skin.

But it is not his job to pacify my bleeding heart.

My father is still searching for his happiness. I can't fill that void for him, just like he can't fill mine. It is neither of our responsibilities.

And now, I must release him from the task.

He is not my hero. And in this moment, I feel guilty for putting that pressure on his shoulders. What a heavy weight to carry for a person who is just as broken as I am. What a burden to bear for an empty man. My father is a human, flawed and imperfect, and the inevitable truth about the chaos that rages inside of me is that he cannot clean it up. Only I can do that. So my fantasy of my father must reach its final chapter. My fairy tale of him must come to an end.

Sometimes little girls must become their own heroes.

I take a deep breath as I collect myself. I have to forgive my father. There is no other way. He will never give me the answer I am looking for. He will never be the *father* I am looking for. He will never be what makes me whole. It is not his job. And I have to forgive him.

It is the only way for the storm to pass.

"Okay," I say as I take a breath.

And it all goes quiet. The wind that rages inside me begins to settle. The rain that drowns me begins to subside. My heart stops scraping against my chest, and my breath comes back to my body. I feel misery melt from my shoulders with just three little words.

"I forgive you," I say.

I grab my things, I pick myself up, and I head through the door.

29

We arrive in the country just as the evening sun sets.

The house is filled with unfamiliar faces when we arrive. It seems people have come from all over to mourn the death of a Manchester boy.

The country boy with the midnight skin.

Everyone moves about, getting organized for the funeral tomorrow morning. I can't bear to socialize, so I take my bags and head straight to Andre's room. When I walk in, I plop down on his small mattress, and after a few moments, I doze off.

I wake up a few hours later to the black of night and the sound of a heavy bass penetrating through the house. I've slept through the evening, and I feel groggy and lethargic. It takes me a moment to even remember where I am. But then it comes back to me.

And heartache takes over.

BOOM, BOOM, BOOM.

What's going on?

I feel the bass in my chest as the house rattles. Suddenly, there's a knock on the door. Before I have the chance to answer, Richie walks in and turns on the light.

"Oh. Sorry, Tilla. Me neva know yuh did in here."

"No, it's fine. I was just getting up." I rub my eyes, trying to hide the pain that lives behind them. There's no use. I can see the pain behind Richie's glossy eyes as well. "Do you know where Mia and my dad are?" I ask.

"Everyone deh out back," he slurs, and I can tell he's been drinking.

"What's going on outside?" I ask. "What's with the music?"

"Nine night, gyal! Yuh never know?"

"What's that?"

"Lawd, Canada. Iz di celebration of life. A party yuh keep di night before di funeral. Nine days after somebody dead."

"Oh," I say flatly. A tinge of bitterness runs through me. I can't imagine anyone wanting to party right now. To celebrate.

"I think I'm going to stay inside." I go to lie back down.

"Yuh mod?!" Richie yells. "Yuh cyan miss di nine night. Yuh always haffi celebrate di passing so him soul can pass through before we put him in di ground."

I look at him like he's crazy.

"Come nuh, gyal!" he yells. He's clearly drunk. "Andre would be upset if him know say yuh never send him off." He drags me out of the room and into the hall. As I step out, I can't believe my eyes:

The house is *packed*.

People bump shoulder to shoulder as hundreds litter the small house. We make our way through a sea of drunk people who laugh and recount stories of Andre. His name echoes throughout the walls as the room vibrates with an aliveness of his memory. Laughter fills the room, and everyone praises his name with joy and reverence.

I've never seen anything like it.

We make it through the crowd and into the kitchen, and everything from crawfish to curry goat to jerk chicken and ox-tail is spread out as people push through each other to get a plate. Richie guides me out the back door, where the party is amplified, in full swing. An upbeat Junior Reid song fills the night, with a bass so heavy it vibrates in my chest. Although the backyard is destroyed from the hurricane, beautiful lights string from tree to tree, lighting up the forest. The night is *alive* as everyone sings songs and dances throughout the yard.

Aunt Adele hovers over a giant firepit, where she stirs a large pot of corn soup, and the aroma of burning wood fills the air. Aunt Herma walks around with a tray of sorrel, handing out Styrofoam cups, and Mama and Papa eat fish and bammy under a white tent. At the other end of the yard is another makeshift table where a group of men sip on a pack of Red Stripe and play an intense game of Ludi. Everyone is drunk and merry.

"Welcome to di nine night!" Richie says, his words slurring with a drunken pride. "Tomorrow we can be sad. But tonight, we celebrate Andre!" He takes my hand, spinning me in a circle. "Wait here. Me ah go get yuh a drink." He takes off into the party, tripping over his own two feet as he heads for the cooler.

I stare at the festivities in awe.

There's nothing I want more than for Andre to be here to witness this. I imagine how fun it would be to get drunk with him and dance the night away to reggae music. I imagine he would show me some secret trick of the party, like where they keep the good drinks or how the best part of the corn soup is at the bottom of the pot. I imagine him whispering secrets in my ear, telling me stories about everyone here. The thoughts make me anxious as memories of Andre flood me like a summer of hurricane.

Breathe, Tilla.

But I can't. I am consumed by his voice. By the sound of his laughter. The glow of his dark black skin and the soft coil of his hair. I feel sick, and this time, I am certain I will choke.

And then I lock eyes with my father.

He sits at a table with a group of men who play a game of dominoes. He waves me over, and as if by no doing of my own, my feet move toward him.

"Yuh all right?" he asks as I get closer.

My chest is tight as I recall our conversation earlier. It is in the silence between us. But here and now, he is the only familiar face in a sea of strangers. He is my only home, miles from my own. He is my father.

"Yeah," I say timidly. "I was sleeping."

"Good ting yuh get some rest. Nine night ah gwan till mawnin'."

"Oh . . . where's Mia?"

"I think her and Kenny are handin' out juice."

I nod.

"Here." He passes me his cell phone. "Yuh mother called fi you earlier." I stare at the phone, not taking it from his hands. Hearing my mother's voice would break me. "Let her know yuh all right," he says.

I give in, taking the phone from his hands.

I make my way across the party and down into the bushes. I find a quiet spot away from the noise before sitting down on a battered milk crate.

I press down and dial my mother.

The phone rings, sending a nauseous feeling to the pit of my stomach.

I don't want to cry tonight.

"Hello?"

"Mom." My eyes flood with tears.

"Hey, baby," she says softly. "Your father said you were asleep. I was worried about you."

"Yeah . . . I was really tired." My voice comes off weak, threatening to collapse in the presence of my mother. I imagine her sitting on the couch at home, tiny seashells intricately wrapped in her hair. She knows my pain without me saying a word. She knows my heart without me uttering a breath. I cannot hide from her.

"The music woke me up. I didn't know all this was going on."

"That's right," she realizes. "I guess this would be your first nine night. It's a Jamaican tradition. It's when the spirit passes through the night so they can transition to the next realm."

"Well, I don't really feel like celebrating," I say dryly.

"That's okay. You don't have to do anything you're not ready to do . . ." Her voice trails off for a moment. "Your dad told me that you and Andre grew really close this summer. He said you loved his drawings."

I bite my tongue as tears begin to sting the backs of my eyes. "Yeah," I croak. "He was a really talented artist, Mom. He . . . he wanted to come to Canada next summer." I can't fight the tears that stream down my hot cheeks. I bury my head deeper into my own arms.

"It's going to be okay, baby."

"It's not."

"Tilla—"

"It's not okay, Mom!" I cry out. "He's *dead*. Andre is dead, and he's not coming back." I can't fight the tears that escape all over me. "I loved him so much. He . . . he was my best friend."

"Oh, Tilla," she says softly. Agony and heartbreak pour from my chest and into the phone. But she does not impose.

She just listens.

When I am finished, she speaks.

"Tilla. Tilla, my *warrior*," she says softly. "Breathe, baby. Just breathe."

So I do.

"This summer you have traveled a sea I will never have knowledge of. Your heart has fought battles that I will never, ever know. But if there is one thing I knew for sure when I sent you on the plane, I knew that you would be victorious, Tilla. Because you are *our child*. I know what you are made of, and you are *so* strong."

I feel her words fall onto my skin, covering me like the blanket

I've desperately needed. Her words are soft and melodic, and they pour from her lips like a lullaby. "It's going to hurt for a long time. But it will be okay . . . eventually. I promise."

"You can't promise that," I whisper.

"Yes, I can," she says. "It always gets better, baby."

Her words are comforting, and for a moment, they hold me, wrapping me in her grace even from so many miles away.

"Your father and I . . . we haven't made things easy for you, Tilla. And I'm so sorry you've had to feel so much pain. But we're going to work things out. We're going to make it a better home for you girls."

She believes her words, and it nearly kills me. She has no idea of the devastation. Of the events this summer that cannot be undone. A tear rolls down my cheek as it hits me: She can't fix this. None of it.

Not this time.

We hang up the phone, and I navigate through the nine night, bumping into strangers as I go. I only take a few steps when I spot Zory and Diana in my line of sight. A wave of dread rushes through me. Just as I turn to go the other way, I hear a voice call out to me.

"Tilla!"

I freeze.

The blood drains from my face, and all the breath leaves my body.

I know that gentle voice anywhere.

I whip my head around to find him standing a few feet in front of me. The heavy bass is muffled as the sounds of people begin to fade out. I can hear my heart beating out of my own chest.

There is nothing but me, Hessan, and the warm breeze of the nine night.

He makes his way over to me, and I am a ball of nerves under his gaze. I want to burst into a million tears.

"Tilla," he says softly, reaching for my hand. In a reflex, I pull it away.

He studies me for a moment, realizing that I am upset. I stand firm in my defensiveness. He must know that his words held weight. That I died on those steps.

"I just . . ." He searches for the words. "I'm sorry . . . for your loss."

I search his eyes, and I notice that they're red as well. He's been crying.

Andre was his friend.

"I'm sorry for yours, too," I say delicately. And I mean it.

"I hate di way tings ended between us." His voice is strained. "Can we go somewhere and talk?"

"I don't know if now is a good time—"

"Please. I need . . . I need to talk to you."

The desperation in his voice almost brings me to my knees. I take a deep breath into my heavy heart.

"Okay," I whisper.

He grabs two Red Stripes from the cooler before leading me off to the side of the house. We descend the hill into a small clearing that sits just outside the nine night at the edge of the forest. We take a seat on a fallen palm tree.

He cracks open the beer, handing it to me before doing his own. The night breeze is hot, and the bitter drink instantly cools me as it softly fizzes down my dry throat. I am anxious, unsure of what he will say next. After a minute, he speaks.

"Tilla . . ." My name sounds like poetry flowing off his tongue. "I'm so sorry . . . for everything I said to you. You neva deserve any ah dat. You . . . you're a good girl, Tilla. I was hurt . . . I . . . That neva give me di right fi hurt you." He stares into my eyes, the expression on his face strained. "I want you to know it *killed me* fi see you like dat. And I'm really sorry . . . for all of it, Tilla. I'm sorry for everyting. I wish I could tek it all back." His eyes search mine. "I was just scared. I've never met anyone like you. I . . . I've never loved anyone like you."

My heart races as he says the words I have needed him to say for weeks. The words I have longed for. Cried for. *Died for.* But as I sit here, my body stone and my chest on fire, an eerie truth rumbles beneath my skin:

I don't forgive him.

It is a scary revelation. The wounds he inflicted are too deep. He may have been willing to risk it all . . . but I actually did. I sacrificed everything for him this summer. And yet, he had no interest in whether I was wrong or right. In whether I was *okay.* He looked at me through the eyes of his experiences and saw his mother. He deemed me guilty without even trying to understand the pain of what had happened to me that day.

He abandoned me in the storm, just like my father.

There is an eerie similarity to how they both disposed of me. How they threw me away and assumed the worst in me when my heart was on the line. *When I was on fire.* When I *needed* them most. I am not ready to forgive him for that, and if I do before it's time, I will be sacrificing myself just to feel his love grace my skin. And that is not the love I want.

That is not the love I deserve.

"Please say something," Hessan says softly.

He searches my eyes, but it is clear that this time, he cannot find me. I am not the Tilla I was back then. The Tilla who accepted a broken love in whatever form it came. The Tilla who put other people before the call of her own heart. The Tilla who did not know the sound of her own voice and the call of her own spirit.

I am not the Tilla I was before the storm.

"I'm not ready to forgive you, Hessan." My words drop heavy like a bomb, exploding between the two of us. "You have no idea what I went through . . . no understanding of how you ripped me open with your words. Of how I *bled* for you."

"I know, Tilla. And I was wrong—"

"No. You *don't* know. You couldn't. What Jahvan did to me . . . what he did . . ." The memory sends a haunting shiver through my veins. "You didn't even *ask*. You didn't care, Hessan. You have no idea of how I suffered. Of how I needed you the most." My voice begins to quiver. "You can't just love me and throw me away. I won't let you do that to me. And I won't do that to myself. Not again." An eerie silence sits between us as my words hang in the air. A ripple of laughter pours out from the party in the distance. "This place . . . this land . . . it's been paradise." I meet his gaze. "But it has also been poison." I place my drink to the side as the gravity of my own words hit me. "For so long, I thought I could build a home in you. I thought your love would help me escape my own devastation. I thought Jamaica would be the answer." The words leave my heart as I stare out at the party. "But I was wrong. I can't make a home out of other people. Or places. Not you, not my father. Not this island. I have to build a home within myself."

Courage consumes me like my deepest tide.

This time, I will not drown.

"I don't forgive you, Hessan." I look him straight in his hazel eyes. "Maybe in time," I say softly. "But right now . . . right now, we're better off as friends."

"Tilla—"

"You should be with Diana."

The words roll off my tongue with such an ease that I surprise even myself. As I gaze out at the nine night, I feel the energy of Andre permeate my bones. The boy who followed the call of his own spirit. Who marched to the beat of his own drum. Who flowed with the crumbling of nature and stood strong in the face of adversity. I think back to the morning of the hurricane when we stood up on that hill. The beautiful disaster to which we bore witness. I realize that Andre is now one with that sacred dance. And in this moment, I feel his spirit move through me, wrapping me in his rhythm and infusing me with the courage to stand on my own two feet. He is alive through the most important lesson that he taught me:

To surrender to the storm.

I stare off at the festivities that twinkle in the dark. The sweet smell of smoke fills the air as laughter and music rumble throughout the night sky. It is magic. It is palpable. It is *paradise*.

But it is not my home.

And neither is Hessan.

I cannot hide from the hurricane under his temporary shelter. I cannot hope his loving words will keep me dry. I must face the devastation that awaits at my door.

I must weather the storm alone.

Hessan looks away from me, disappointment bathing his face. I know I have hurt him for the second time, but I have to do what is right. I can't hold on to our broken pieces. I must surrender to nature's destruction.

To God's will.

I heard once that a girl's heart is an ocean of secrets. But as I feel my heart rage against my chest, I think it is an ocean of storms. As Hessan rises from beside me and makes his way back into the party, my theory becomes abundantly clear. I watch him walk away from me for the second time, but this time, I do not cry. I have no tears left. This time, I revel in the beauty of my own sorrow and the weight of my own broken heart. It has been cracked by my father, violated by Jahvan, broken by Hessan, and shattered by the death of Andre.

But it is time to put the pieces back together.

It is time to find my way back home.

30

Mom says you get two birthdays.

The first one is the day you are born.

The second is the day you leave home and give birth to yourself.

Standing in the middle of this bustling airport, I now know exactly what she meant. My father stands in front of me, his brown locks hanging down his back as I search his gray eyes for one last celebration. I don't find it. He avoids my gaze, quickly pulling me in for a hug. The tears that well in my eyes don't feel like anything to celebrate, but I know now that sometimes birthdays make you cry. Sometimes birthdays grow heavy lumps in the back of your throat that threaten to choke you on your words if you dare open your mouth.

Sometimes birthdays break your heart.

Be brave. Be brave.

I repeat it over and over again in my head as I squeeze my father a little tighter. My stomach drops, and I dread the moment he'll inevitably let go. In the air, I can taste the sweet melancholy of joyous hellos and painful goodbyes that only the airport can bring. There is a buzzing to this place that feels like the center of heartbreak and joy.

In the arms of my father,

I am the center of heartbreak and joy.

His hug is brief, and he lets me go, taking my heart with him as he pulls away. He smiles widely at Mia and me, oblivious to the pain that aches in my chest. The blood that spills out of me and onto the floor. But I know now that there will always be a hole in my heart the size of my father. And that is okay.

In time, I will learn to fill it with my own magic.

My own resilience.

My own love.

Just like what Andre did.

Mia runs into his arms, and he squeezes her tightly.

"You girls be good for your mother," he says as he puts her back down.

"Do you know when you're coming home?" Mia asks.

"I'm thinking in a few weeks. I'll let you know when I book my ticket."

I look away, not holding my breath. I pull the tickets from my bag and hand Mia her passport. She grabs her backpack from off the floor, and we situate ourselves to leave.

"Mi, head over to the line. I'll meet you there."

Mia squeezes in one last hug before dragging her feet over to the check-in line.

I turn to my father.

That familiar lump rises in the back of my throat, but this time, it begs me to speak. This time, it begs me not to fall victim to the love of my father.

It begs me to rise to the love of myself.

"I want you to know . . . Dad, I want you to know that . . ." My voice shakes, but I continue. I continue because this time I know what my own voice sounds like. "I'm not keeping your secret. Not anymore."

His face drops, confusion taking over.

"Tilla. What are you talking—"

"I'm not doing it, Dad. Either you tell Mom or I will. I know . . . I know that you might hate me for this, but I am willing to live with that possibility." I feel myself grow brave. "I am not keeping your secret. It is too great a burden to bear. And it is not mine to carry."

"Tilla—"

"I'm giving it back to you. Your secret. It's your choice what you do with it, but I won't keep it for you. Not anymore."

He stares at me, his gray eyes turning to stone. Disappointment covers his face.

But I am no longer my father's keeper.

I wrap my arms around him. "I love you, Dad," I whisper before letting him go. And the truth is, I always will. Because it if weren't for my father, I would have never faced the storm.

If it weren't for my father, I would never have faced myself.

Just then, a voice comes over the speakers, pulling me out of our goodbye.

"*Last call for all passengers boarding flight 614. Please make your way to the gate.*"

I grab my things, and this time, it is I who walks away from him. This time, I take my heart with me as I go. I love my father, but I must love myself more. Even if it *destroys* me. With one final wave, Mia and I take off through the airport toward the security gates.

We wait a few hours before we board the plane. I look over to Mia, who stares at the ceiling, bored and dazed. "Where's your DS?" I ask her.

"I left it."

"You forgot it?"

"I gave it away to Kenny."

"Wow," I say. "That's so nice of you, Mi."

"Yeah." She shrugs. "He'll use it more than I would."

"Aw, Mia." I pull her in for a hug. There's no way Mom can afford to buy her another one anytime soon. "I'm really proud of you," I say.

"Thanks." She smiles, her eyes sad.

It hits me that I'm not the only one who has grown this summer. She pulls out a bag of chips and begins to watch the people who pass by. I stir in my own thoughts, reflecting on the summer that I leave behind and the lessons that I am taking with me back home. I think of the memories that now live in my heart, and the secrets that will stay buried behind my lips.

How could I possibly begin to describe the summer of the storm?

The laughter. The adventures. The heartbreak.

The funeral.

Devastation passes through me as I reflect on Andre being laid to rest. The haunting sound of tears pouring through the church. Tears so heavy they resembled the rains that drowned the island. Images of Aunt Adele doubled over the casket flood my mind, her wails echoing the winds that tore through the country as we mourned together for the final time.

We were all grief.

I shake the memory from my skin as they finally call us to board. Mia and I slowly make our way onto the packed plane as people fill the aisles, eager to leave the wreckage of the island behind. When we reach our seats, I wiggle our bags into the overhead bin and pull out my pink hoodie. I slip it on before sliding into our row and grabbing the window seat. Mia slides in beside me as the plane settles, and a thick accent comes over the speakers.

"Ladies and gentle-mon, welcome aboard Air Jamaica flight 614 departing from Kingston to Toronto on this beautiful Friday afternoon. We invite you to sit back, relax, and leave your worries behind you. It is our pleasure to have you on board."

I turn my head to look out the window, desperate to take in

paradise one last time. It amazes me how in one summer, this island has engulfed me in ways I will never be able to describe. It is a song I'll never know how to sing, even though the melody is desperate to leave my lips. A story I wouldn't be able to tell, even if I had all the words.

A world that now lives inside me for the rest of my life.

I pull my seat belt a little tighter as I prepare for takeoff, when all of a sudden, I feel something poke me in my side. I look down to find a folded piece of paper sticking out of my hoodie pocket. I take it out and open it, unsure of what it is.

I almost fall out of my seat.

Staring back at me is an intricate drawing bursting with rich colored pencil. Brown hues fly across the page as rich blues, greens, oranges, and pinks spring to life. It is exploding with vibrant colors and vivid detail. My eyes well with tears as I realize what is staring back at me:

It is a drawing of me.

From Andre.

My heart nearly flies out of my chest as I study the immaculate craftsmanship. It is a picture of me standing in the hurricane, my eyes closed as I breathe in the land. I am completely breathless as my hands trace the paper. Tears spill from my eyes and onto the paper as I rack my brain for some sort of explanation.

When did Andre do this?

I stare down at the picture in shock as I realize I am wearing the same hoodie as when I arrived in the country. He knew I would put it back on. My mind races a mile a minute as the sound of the plane's engine takes over. I clutch my armrest to calm my beating heart as we speed down the tarmac.

We are finally going home.

As we continue down the runway, Andre's artistry leaves me in awe. My Afro runs wild in the wind as the presence of peace covers my face. My butterfly necklace rests on my neck, and a hibiscus flower sits gently in my hair. But as I stare down at his work, something rings abundantly clear: The lines that sketch my face paint a different picture from the Tilla I was before.

I have changed.

I found courage on this island. Strength among these people. The magic of Jamaica now runs through my veins, feeding me from the inside out. Its bold energy is the rhythmic melody that now pacifies my beating heart. Its hot sun is the igniting fire that now roars in my gut. I have been made of the land, the breeze, and the trees. I have been refined by its rugged terrain and soothed by its calming waters. I have been re-created here—woven like a sacred dance orchestrated by God himself. He ripped me apart like a thousand storms and brought me to my knees so that I could finally feel the beating of my own heart. So I could finally surrender to the summer of my own hurricane.

The plane rips down the runway, and nerves prickle through my body.

Faster, faster, faster.

I fold the picture back up, clutching it tightly in my hands. I take one last glimpse of paradise, and squeeze my eyes shut. As we lift from the tarmac, Andre's words echo in my mind:

What we go through . . . it meant fi serve us . . . and if it cyan serve us, it can at least change us. Mek us betta people. Stronger people. Yuh cyan 'fraid of a likkle rain and breeze.

And then it hits me.

When they ask how I weathered the storm, I will tell them I did not. I was uprooted like the palm trees and shot down like the birds from the stormy skies. I was ravished like the zinc houses and devoured like the soil as it swallowed itself whole. I was ruined. I was disaster. I was dancing in the eye of God's will.

"Thank you," I whisper as we ascend into the sky.

How beautiful it was to be destroyed.

ACKNOWLEDGMENTS

Thank you, God. You are my greatest love.

When I ran through the hurricane, I knew it would not be in vain. You had a plan to use my pain for purpose. You are always speaking to me. Even when I'm so frustrated that I can't hear. Thank you for your tender, sweet rhythm. The melody you have sung over my life. I get it now. And I can finally sing along.

Thank you, Mom and Father. This is for all the stories in your heart that I may never get the chance to read. The lives you lived before me. The pain, love, and joy your hearts must know. Thank you for loving me. For doing your best. It was more than enough. Thank you for giving me life and naming me Life —with a name like that, of course I would have a story to tell.

Mom, thank you for all of your sacrifices. Words are not enough. Your love has given me wings. You are my reason. Thank you for never limiting my idea of who I am. For letting me be my own person. Thank you for being the first person to tell me I could be anything. That I am everything. You never put a ceiling on my dreams and you led by example. You drove me to every audition. You encouraged every leap of faith. I am the light because you were first. Because you gave me permission to be. You are my favorite part of this life. You are my home. My heart. Your love is a miracle and you are the catalyst that made this all possible. I love you so much.

Father, thank you for giving me Jamaica. My culture. For teaching me my roots. For insisting on all those two-month trips to Jamaica when all I wanted to do was have a regular summer with my friends. Thank you for insisting that I love my hair. For never letting me get a perm (even though I did anyway). Thank you for raising pure-hearted Island girls. Those memories will stay with me forever. The smell of Uncle Winston's house in Kingston. The smell of your suitcase every time you would come back home. The mangoes. The hurricane. The sweet, the sour. The biggest lesson life can teach you is forgiveness, and I found it through my love for you. Thank you for holding me in Jamaica under the orange tree. Christening me among the ancestors. My story was written before I even knew.

Thank you, Ingrid Hart. You are my greatest coach. There is no book without your love, time, guidance, and magic. You shape a story like no other. You have a divine talent for understanding stories and people, and I have watched you wield your magic all my life, all over my life. Thank you for all the days and nights you helped me break this story down and put it back together again. You are a true sage, a master at your craft, and my divine shepherd. Canada's best acting coach. A gift to the world. A grand alchemist. A walking miracle. You are an expert at story structure and character development, and when I win my Oscar, it will be because of you. I believed I could succeed in this industry because I saw you do it first. You are a trailblazer and your impact in the arts will inspire many generations to come. Thank you for being my example. For leading the way so gracefully. For showing me the window into my own soul. We will travel many more lifetimes together.

Thank you, Lori Mohamed. You are a visionary and a true friend. My best friend. The CEO of this story. You lead fearlessly and have given me the courage, time and time again, to trust myself. I am bold because you were first. You gave me the strength I needed to be brave. It never sounded crazy to you. Thank you for teaching me what it looks like to believe in my own vision. To trust the sound of my own intuition and go fearlessly toward my dreams. Thank you for all the sauna sessions and Starbucks runs where you helped me find this story. All those aimless strolls in Chapters just trying to figure it out. You always did. Thank you for all the Caribanas, Fetes, and Celebrations of life. Thank you for your magical mind and your never-ending confidence in all that I am. Thank you for teaching me that it's okay to be fierce. That there is no wrong answer. You will lead many more empires, Trini Queen.

Thank you, Sanjana Seelam. You are the definition of a boss and I learn so much from you every time we speak. Thank you for fighting for me, protecting me, and always uplifting me. Thank you for advocating for me and helping me learn to advocate for myself.

Thank you to the amazing team at WME. I'm eternally grateful that you believed in the power of this story.

Thank you, Emily van Beek. My amazing agent. I'm so grateful for your passion and enthusiasm for this story, and I'm humbled by the love and hard work you've put into making this book a success. I'm so lucky you came along this journey with me. I'm delighted that our lives crossed paths, and I look forward to all that magic that's to come!

To the incredible team at Wednesday Books:

Thank you, Sara Goodman. My amazing editor. Thank you for being so fearless in picking this book. Thank you for being bold in your choosing. I'm so grateful for your love, guidance, and care. Thank you for championing this book. Thank you for pushing me beyond myself. For believing in me enough to know that there was more story waiting to be written. You are such a rock star, and I'm so thankful for your love and enthusiasm for this story. Thank you for always hearing me—truly *hearing* me—and always valuing my perspective. I'm eternally grateful to you for giving me a chance to be heard. My life is forever changed because you believed Tilla's story was worth it.

A special thank-you to Kerri Resnick. I am so grateful for the endless love and passion you put into getting this book cover right. You made it perfect. You are a brilliant and phenomenal art director. I'm so thankful for all the love and time you poured into this cover.

Felice Trinidad—you captured the cover photo of my dreams. Thank you for your heart, your passion, and your incredible artistry.

And to the wonderful Wednesday Books team—Mary Moates, DJ DeSmyter, Beatrice Jason, Sarah Bonamino, Brant Janeway, Angelica Chong, Devan Norman, and Jessica Katz. My endless gratitude goes out to all of you for your tireless work and passion for this story. I appreciate you all so much. Thank you with all my heart.

Erica Tucker, you are a rock star publicist and I'm so grateful to work with you!

El'Cesart, thank you for your brilliant artistry on the endpapers. Thank you for capturing the spirit of the river!

A very special thank-you to my powerhouse team at Untitled—Naisha Arnold, Stephanie Simon, Rebecca Wyzan, Alex Platis, and Emma Lewis—you are what dream teams are made of! Thank you for your love, care, and support. I'm so grateful for all of you, and I'm excited to go on this journey together.

To my extraordinary family:

Thank you to my uncle, Kuya Gwaan. Thank you for all the Kwanzaa celebrations where you taught us how to dream. That was my foundation and where it all began. You created a safe haven where the children's voices mattered. Where our stories were important. Thank you for hearing us, and for making everyone else listen, too. You gave us a pen, and you gave us an audience. Every Kwanzaa. And now we will all change the world because of your love. You believed the children were the future, and you were right. You fostered my Kuumba, and because of that I discovered my Nia. I love you.

Makeda Bromfield—I'm so grateful to have a sister as cool and as beautiful as you, inside and out. You are so smart, and I'm so grateful to have had you as an advisor for this story. You inspire me every day and I love you so much. You always keep me laughing. Thank you for keeping my Patois sharp every day in the kitchen. I wouldn't have been able to write this book without you keeping me on my toes. We're pretty much fluent at this point. Dem tink say we ah fraud but we ah di real ting! See it deh! To rawtid!

Amani Thomas—my very first best friend. My very first co-star. Remember playing "Lakeisha and Laquisha" when we were five years old? The elaborate story lines of raising our babies (Makeda and Xavier) as we balanced our work life and our fleeting boyfriends? I'm laughing as I write this. Thank you for playing with me all those years. I am shaped by our childhood innocence. Our games and playtime. May those stories live forever. I love you just as long.

Xavier Thomas—my water sign soul mate. Your love and belief in me extend far beyond anything I know. You are my younger cousin but I look up to you so much. Thank you for your positivity and your radiant spirit. You make life brighter, and you inspire me so much. But don't get it twisted, I'm still racing you to a million.

Rosalee and Donovan Thomas—my favorite duo. You have brought so much sunshine and laughter to my life. Your love and support bring me so much joy. My life has been shaped by the security of knowing that you are always a few blocks away. Your presence in my life has brought me so much peace. I love you both, eternally.

Siya Gwaan—you are a star, constantly inspiring me through your mere existence. Your words. Your crown. Your melanin. Your magic. Please keep writing and singing and don't ever stop. I can't wait to buy your bestseller. Your creativity will change the world. I love you big big!

Rosemarie Hibbert—you taught me how to shine. How to take up space. How the fun of life is always there, waiting for me to pick it up. You bring the party, every single time. And you taught me how to bring the party to my own life. You are strength, personified. The definition of resilience and power. The original diva. The first superstar I ever knew. You set the tone, baby! The rest of us are just trying to keep up. I love you, always.

My Queen Grandmother, Daphne Hart—thank you for all that you are. You are a manifestation of God's love. I am only here because you were first. I know I get my love of writing from you and the incredible story of resilience that you lived first. Thank you for writing the story of your life, so that I could write mine. I can't wait to adorn you in purple diamonds.

Daddy Burge—the original Don Dada. May your soul rest in the sweetest peace. You were the first to see my light. To believe in my shine. The first to tell me I was a star. The confidence you had in me is etched into the fabric of my bones. Do you see what you did?! I am your vision come to life. I can't wait until we celebrate again. Until then, I will continue to live out the promise we made of paradise here on earth.

Ashley Iris Gill—you will change the world with your art. Thank you for believing in my creativity and fostering me at such a tender age when the world was against me. You protected me when I needed it most. You saw me when they didn't. Thank you for believing in my teenage art. #PockzForever

Trisha Bromfield and Clayton Collins—I am so fortunate to have you as older siblings. Thank you for helping shape me into the woman that I am. You are both full of deep wisdom that I value greatly and our talks have always inspired me to expand. I love you both so much. I'm so grateful to be able to not only call you my siblings, but my friends.

Aaliyah Hibbert—you gave me the confidence to finish writing. You made me feel like someone was excited to hear my story, and that made me excited to keep going. I kept writing because of you. Thank you.

Mila, Kendell, Triniti, Tafari, Naveah, Zayden—knowing that you look up to me has given my life deep purpose. My very first fans. I can't wait to return the favor. I love you.

Auntie Shernette and Uncle Tony—you always keep me laughing. Thank you for the joy that you have brought to my life.

My sweet Zulu, I will love you forever. Thank you for being my foundation.

And a blessed thank-you to the Goddess Oshun, who I called upon many times, sometimes without knowing. Thank you for your divine love. I am honored to be a portal for your sacred spirit.

Thank you, Tomi Adeyemi, for the magic you inspired inside of me. Watching your story unfold gave me courage and most important, hope. I am so thankful for all of your guidance and support along the way.

Thank you, Adam Silvera, for your courageous heart. You have been an incredible mentor to me, and I'm so thankful to you for your time and wisdom. Thank you for championing me and always pushing me to champion myself.

Thank you, Jemma Hendricks. You were one of my first readers, and one of the first people to fall in love with Tilla. Thank you for being a part of this journey and believing in me when I needed it most. Your heart is made of gold.

To my incredible therapist, Shawna—I've had the most beautiful breakthroughs for this book because of you. You are a true goddess. A light worker. A guide. Thank you for leading me back to myself. For helping me connect the dots. For helping me honor the pain of the little girl who still lives inside me. You taught me how to hold her hand. How to give her all the love she always deserved. Thank you for showing me how to burst wide open, in spite of it all. Thank you for giving me the tools to heal myself, so that I could help others heal as well.

To all the lost boys and girls of Jamaica who I roamed the countryside with—you are the true magic of the island. Dane, your spirit shines so bright. The adventures. The games. Court. The treks to the river. The imprint you left on me will live forever. Wherever you are in the world, I hope this book is proof of how your magic shaped my summer and changed my life.

And last, but definitely not least—thank you, Andre. You are the heart of this story. Without the love you showed me, there would be no book. The friendship you extended to me as a young girl gave me a home in a foreign place. I saw God inside of you, and it inspired me to write. You are my childhood soul mate. My island angel. I am forever changed by our Hurricane Summer.

And for the ancestors,
Who are always with me.
Guiding me.
Holding me.
Whispering to me.
Thank you for leading me to the page.

Ashe